REST IN PEACE

Kiran Nagarkar is one of India's most highly regarded writers. His critically acclaimed novel *Cuckold* was given the Sahitya Akademi Award in 2000. Nagarkar's other works include *God's Little Soldier* which was a best-seller in Germany and the *Ravan & Eddie* trilogy. One of the sharpest critics of India's socio-political scenario, he is also the author of the play *Bedtime Story*, which had been banned for seventeen years, and the screenplay *Black Tulip*, published as a single volume in February 2015. Nagarkar received the Order of Merit of the Federal Republic of Germany in 2012. Tata Literature Live! and the Chandigarh Literary Fest gave him lifetime achievement awards in 2015 and 2016 respectively. His novels have been translated into German, French, Italian, Spanish, Portuguese as well as Marathi. Nagarkar also writes in his mother-tongue, Marathi, and has penned plays and, in fact, began his career in the language in 1974 with his first novel *Saat Sakkam Trechalis.*

Praise for *Rest in Peace*

'That Bollywood still beckons people to itself can be understood by the works of novelists like Kiran Nagarkar who could not resist the temptation and come out of its aura. But Nagarkar has something more than just leading the readers to a land of fantasy. Nagarkar's characters are never sentimental and the novelist loses no opportunity to be satirical.'

– Shams Afif Siddiqui, *The Telegraph*

'A consummate storyteller, Nagarkar's style does not come in the way of a superbly structured plot. Words and sentences are fused with the destiny of the story and although you are not expected to be struck by a dazzling vocabulary or mind-boggling imagery, there are times when the reader just gets caught in places and hovers there awhile savouring the sheer beauty of imaginative eloquence.'

– Janaky Sreedharan, *Deccan Herald*

'If you haven't read his books you have been deprived of an exquisite reading experience. Each of Nagarkar's books is brilliant.'

– Saudamini Jain, *Hindustan Times*

'*Rest in Peace* is a post-script to a post-srcipt. However, if you like a rollicking romp through the lives of Ravan and Eddie, pick it up ... It has everything – drama, action, suspense, disbelief...'

– Krish Warrier, *Views on News*

REST IN PEACE

Ravan and Eddie

KIRAN NAGARKAR

4th

First published in India in 2015 by Fourth Estate
An imprint of HarperCollins *Publishers*

Building 10, Tower A, 4th Floor, DLF Cyber City, Phase II,
Gurugram Haryana – 122002, India
www.harpercollins.co.in

This edition published in India in 2017 by Fourth Estate
An imprint of HarperCollins *Publishers*

P-ISBN: 978-93-5177-580-5
E-ISBN: 978-93-5177-043-5

2 4 6 8 10 9 7 5 3

Typeset 11/13.5 Adobe Garamond
Jojy Philip, New Delhi 110 015

Printed and bound at
MicroPrints India, New Delhi

Part One

Falling ... falling ... falling...

Sometimes Ravan talked such crap, absolute and utter drivel. 'Do it, Eddie, just do it.' Here he was, Eddie Coutinho, s/o Violet and the late – it had been a lifetime of 'late' as far as Eddie was concerned – Victor Coutinho, suffering from such a bad panic attack, he couldn't breathe, he couldn't swallow his own spittle, he couldn't move. He was paralysed but that didn't prevent Ravan from dishing out dollops of Eastern, or maybe it was just Hindu, wisdom.

'Leap into the unknown. It's like nothing you've experienced before. It's exhilarating, it's totally liberating.'

Would someone please shut him up? Better still, just strangle him.

Falling ... falling ... falling...

What the hell had Ravan been talking about before they went over the edge? 'It's like nothing you've experienced before.' Big philosophical stuff about letting go. 'It's the purest form of freedom. It's the closest you'll ever get to Nirvana.' How would he know what that is, you have to be dead to experience it. Besides, wasn't it meant only for Hindus? As far as he knew, Catholics were stranded on an island called 'purgatory' till Judgement Day. Besides, who could predict when the day of reckoning would turn up? Tomorrow? A trillion years from now? Oh Lord God, help me. What should I do?

Falling ... falling ... falling...

Was it possible that that stupid Ravan was right? That if you forgot about the bottomless pit in your stomach, the experience would be the most deliriously thrilling one of your life? Dare he say it, this was heaven. Close your eyes and you could float forever. Frankly, he had no idea whether he was ascending or descending, maybe they were the same.

Something strange was happening. His whole life was being screened. Not in any linear order. The past, present and future kept shifting tracks. The editing was a bit of a rollercoaster. At times it was brisk, jerky and fragmented and at others coherent and fluid like a majestic river in full flow. But always comprehensible, the good and the bad, things he would rather forget and things he would have wanted to go on forever ... like a new unforgettable melody wafting into his mind, almost full-blown and ready to be recorded; like Ravan and Eddie's first music LP being released and shooting straight to the top of the charts; like being with Belle, breathing in the scent of her, making love to her.

If you were to ask him or Ravan what was the happiest moment of their lives, they would both have the same answer. Wasn't that curious, you couldn't have found two more dissimilar people than the two of them. But there was one thing they shared beyond all their differences and which wiped out the whole debit account.

You could never accuse them of having been lucky by birth or upbringing. No sugar daddy, no fairy godmother and certainly no godfather to direct them or encourage them and cushion the journey called life. There was no silver spoon sticking out of their mouths. And yet they had what both the supremely rich and the super-poor rarely had. Most people botched their lives or blundered through them. Oh, make no mistake, Ravan and Eddie had had more than their quota of failures, bumbling through everything they did. But since childhood they had known exactly what they wanted to be. They wanted to be actors, superstars really. And nothing else. But it just so happened that everything they did, every thought, every word they said or didn't say, every action of theirs had at its core, music. Music was like breathing. Not like, but exactly the same as breathing. They took it for granted that everything they did was a preparation to making it as actors. It had been a long preparation. There was no end to the diversions, wrong turns, bickerings, falling-outs. All these years, success had eluded them. Now they had made it, made it really big; alas, not as actors but in an altogether different field. Music. Like the song said, 'Jaate thé Japan, pahunch gaye Cheen'. Yes, they had set out for Japan but landed up in China.

1

So this is what the big time meant, Eddie thought. You had dinner and stood on the balcony of the fifth floor of CWD Chawl Number 17. It was stifling in the house even though you had three medium-sized ceiling fans, all of them running at top speed. You got into your tight-fitting short shorts (short as in eleven inches short), took off your shirt and came out in the hope that there might be a wisp of a breeze. Nothing. Just dead air. Was this what the phrase 'time stood still' meant? He had had a long day at the workshop but at least he had finally found, after eight days of trawling through second-hand shops, the automobile engine part he had been looking for.

It was not cats who had nine lives in India but cars. Actually every Indian car was worth two cats at least. Now if you were one of the lucky souls who owned a car and had not yet managed to mangle yourself; and if some truck driver hadn't yet slammed into it and turned it into tin plate; or your grandson hadn't driven it over one of the hairpin bends in the deadly ghats on the way back from a drunken weekend in Khandala, very likely a smart mechanic could give it at least another five or six lives. Eddie had been working on a 1967 Ford Mustang for the past ten days and had finally managed to locate an undamaged gearbox from Chor Bazaar, that purgatory of all inanimate objects and, who knows, maybe of living lost souls too.

He had better get back in and go to bed. Tomorrow was a double whammy of a day. Shooting in Borivali National Park till four in the afternoon and then an evening shift at the workshop. He must be very tired, for he had begun to see visions. Imagine a Chevrolet Impala driving across the open ground next to the Sangh gymnasium where he still worked out every day. No doubt he would be seeing a Lincoln Continental or a Mercedes next. The driver of the Impala got out and spoke briefly to one of the passers-by. It got even weirder now. The Impala pulled up in front of his chawl. The chauffeur got out, opened the rear door on the right and a man in white, the size of three polar bears, struggled to come out. It took the driver and another helper to ease the triple-bear from the car. The light above the stoop had been missing for over a decade now and Eddie couldn't see the man's face but he was shuffling laboriously up the few steps leading to the staircase. Why was he bothering to climb, Eddie wondered, he was so fully inflated, all he had to do was let go of his assistants and just balloon his way up. This is when things got completely bizarre. A Mercedes rolled in from the other end of the open ground and came to a halt behind the winged Impala.

It was close to 11 p.m. but despite the late hour a crowd had begun to gather around the two cars. Who the hell had the people in the two cars come to see? Well, he would know soon enough. This was CWD Chawl No. 17, the best grapevine in the entire universe. Nothing, but nothing, ever stayed private here. In the next minute or so the news would be flashed across the five continents and the Antarctic. He went back inside and turned in for the night. Five minutes later, maybe seven, there was a knock on the door. Eddie cursed under his breath and opened it. It was Ravan.

'Raj-ji wants to see you and me.'

'Who?'

'Raj-ji as in *Barsaat, Awaara, Shree 420, Bobby* and so on and on, not to mention, RK Studios, where you and I spent hours and days and weeks hoping to get a break in the films.'

'Very funny, Ravan, but I am tired and we have a shoot in Borivali tomorrow at eight a.m. So good night.'

'He says he's seen *Hulla Gulla*, thrice, and heard the songs a million and nine times and can't get over them. He wants us to do the music for his next film.'

'You're kidding.'

'Look out over the balcony. His Chevrolet Impala is down there and next to it is Prakash Mehra-ji's Benz. He wants to see us after Raj-ji is through.'

The next day, Ramesh Sippy, Shakti Samanta, Yash Chopra, were already queueing up or on their way to meet Ravan and Eddie. And that was just for starters. Directors, producers, financiers, distributors, stars and superstars were all waiting to see them. The last came inconspicuously in cars large enough to fit in a couple of ocean-liners, and with an escort of two pilot cars, four security guards and five retainers, not to mention a hairdresser just in case a photo opportunity presented itself, and always incognito in dark glasses the size of elephant feet, any time between 11 and 1 at night, sometimes even 2. Their drivers parked the Impalas, Volvos, Lincolns, Porsches, the rare Alpha Romeos, Jaguars, Buicks, and even vintage Ferraris bought second-hand from embassy and consular staff returning home to their own countries, opened the doors for their masters who held their noses, asked for elevators to take them to the fourth and fifth floors and then heroically trudged up, albeit with great difficulty and serious episodes of breathlessness.

Imagine their surprise on discovering that their arch rivals were ahead of them, not to mention behind them. But you had to hand it to them, they were not just professionals, they were from Bollywood, the biggest film industry in the world. They were marvellous actors, they greeted each other like the proverbial long-separated twins, they hugged and embraced, enquired about wives and sons and daughters, condoled deaths in the family and swore to have dinner with their colleagues that very week.

It's so long since we got together. Do you remember the good old days when we came to this city the very first time, what greenhorns we were, had never seen a Western-style toilet before in our lives. I'll let you in on a secret. Even after I got my first break and bought a place of my own and got married, I still sat on my haunches on the ceramic rim of the toilet bowl as I had done in my home in that small town outside Agra, for at least three, maybe four years. (Big fake ha, ha, ha, here.) It was nothing short of a revolution, a traumatic one, when I finally put the seat down and sat as I would at the dining table, the only difference being that I was sitting down to take a crap and not a meal. Now I can't manage squatting down on an Indian toilet for the love of all the money the mafia pours into our films. If I did, I would need someone to give me a hand or never get up again. Those were the days, what? I'll get my secretary to call you. No, I'll call you myself. Pukka. Say hello to Bhabhi-ji.

Shoot, bloody panwati, of all the people in the world I had to run into this twit today, this jackass of a producer without a shred of talent, and that too in this place. I thought I would be the first to get here, just my infernal bad luck. He might have beaten me to it but I'll outbid the bugger many times over and rope in those two music directors and, take my word for it, the biggest hit of next year will be mine and mine alone. It will do a silver jubilee. Make it golden. Want to bet on it? We'll do a diamond jubilee or my name is not...

By the evening of the second day, hordes of people from Mazgaon, Byculla, Parel, Mahalaxmi, Masjid Bunder and even as far as Mahim and Kurla started streaming into the open grounds where the shamiana for the annual Ganapati festival was put up and the image of the elephant god installed for ten days, and where the Sabha held its daily sessions. Indeed, they would have clogged up the staircases and corridors of Chawl Number 17 and there would have been a stampede had not the elders formed a vigilance committee, issued identity cards to the residents of the building, and even posted wardens at the entrance to prevent any outsiders from gate-crashing.

But that did not exactly resolve the problem. Forty families per floor, six floors in all. That worked out to one thousand six hundred and eighty residents, give or take a few, in that one chawl alone, at a conservative estimate of seven members per family. All of them, including palsied great-grandparents, grandparents, babes-in-arms, close and distant cousins were jammed in the narrow staircase, stuck to the walls or plastered to the steep ceiling above. How could they absent themselves to have a meal, take a leak, or go to bed? What if they lost their spot and at that very moment, perish the thought, an ethereal presence wafted past?

Oh, to feel the breath of incandescent stars; to be within touching distance of directors and producers who were privy to the lives of these divine creatures; to be able to tell your unborn children that you'd had the privilege and the honour of being in the company of these goddesses whose every move, action, affair, utterance and screen appearance you followed as if your life depended on it. No, not 'as if', you dummy, for truly, your life drew sustenance and assumed meaning from the mere fact that they lived on the same planet as you. On the third morning, three photographers from *Stardust*, *Filmfare* and *Screen* took up positions on the fourth and fifth floors and the tremulous equilibrium between the film world and that of mere mortals was violated. When one of the luminaries from the celluloid universe started the arduous climb to the Himalayan heights of the fourth and fifth floors, one thousand six hundred and eighty residents wanted their photographs taken with him. They pressed forward, engulfed the man, fell upon him and tore him to shreds. Well, almost.

But that was only the beginning of the director/star/producer's travails. For when he finally made it to Ravan's place (Eddie had to be called down since Violet did not fancy Ravan sitting in her house sipping coffee with her guests), the same one thousand six hundred and eighty folks who had mauled, stripped and dismembered the visitor tried to squeeze into Parvatibai's home.

Where, you may well ask, where were all these princes of the Hindi film industry who were elbowing, jostling and knocking each other down in their haste to sign up the new sensations during the six weeks that poor Eddie and Ravan had waited for a mere word of recognition while *Hulla Gulla* ran in the cinema halls? What had taken them so long? Many things, they said, though not for lack of trying. Like what, Eddie asked. Well, for one thing, the director of the film, ClickClick Kapil, had gone AWOL. He got married and was out of town on his honeymoon. Not even his first assistant director knew his whereabouts. He had not left behind a forwarding postal address nor a telephone number. What about his family? They were business people from Kanpur but the story was that since ClickClick

Kapil had been pig-headed about going into films instead of joining the family business, his father had severed all ties with him.

That, however, was not such an insurmountable obstacle. After all, the one standard and reliable way to obtain information under the circumstances was to get in touch with the music director whom the new pair, Eddie and Ravan, had assisted all these years. They contacted every small and big-time composer in the business but not one of them had any idea who Ravan and Eddie were. Actually, they too were mystified by this pair of composers nobody had ever heard of and yet who had made such a sensational debut. For a while it appeared that the universal ignorance about them could only be attributed to professional jealousies and was the result of a conspiracy of silence. Strangely enough, nobody had heard of the writer of the lyrics, someone called Asmaan, either.

The film folk soon realized that they were barking up the wrong tree and creating a problem that did not exist. The solution was ridiculously simple. Look up the telephone directory and you would get the numbers and addresses of both. It should have been as easy as one, two, three but there was a 'but'. Admittedly, there was a tradition in the Hindi film industry for a great many music directors to be known only by their first names, several of them superb talents like Roshan, Ravi, Naushad, Shankar–Jaikishen, Jaidev, Khayyam. But try looking up two first names from among a million or two surnames even if one of them was called Ravan. When ClickClick's first assistant director revealed that neither E nor R had a telephone, it was clear that this was the end of the road. Either there was nobody called Ravan or Eddie or they were so reclusive, even Greta Garbo or Suchitra Sen seemed publicity hungry in comparison.

There was one other reason, one that none of them cared to mention. Come on, be honest, was it even remotely conceivable that anybody who lived in that ghetto known as the CWD Chawls would have the sophistication, not to mention the genius, to transform a dead-on-arrival movie called *Hulla Gulla* into a blockbuster and that too with ground-breaking music, choreography and fight sequences?

* * *

All these years, the CWD Chawl dwellers had had a different take on R&E. Look at those two boys, well grown-up men now. They were nobodies, good for nothing, they were just trash, Hindu and Roman Catholic trash. (No point digging up old dirt but it was public knowledge that that Ravan was a murderer.) Sure, they had big dreams and they talked big, that Eddie had even spoken of going to America and storming Hollywood but where had it got them? Do you know what they were? Failures, the biggest failures in town. They had failed their secondary school exams. Hell, they didn't even make it past the tenth grade. They had tried everything, they flitted from job to job; you name it, they had failed at it. Between the two of them they had been bandwallas, driven a taxi, run a bootlegging joint, gone to prison, yes, both of them, tried their hand at moving to the Middle East to make a quick buck, been auto mechanics, and, believe it or not, they had even fancied themselves as actors. Nothing worked. How can a born failure be a success?

And yet it was coming to light of late that there were numerous prophets, sibyls and soothsayers in the vicinity who had foretold that despite the fact that the two boys would suffer innumerable setbacks, they would have glorious futures, their names would be on every marquee. You wait and watch, they claimed they had prophesied a long time ago, it was merely a matter of time before Bollywood came knocking on the doors of those two young men.

It was clear from day one to Mrs Godbole from Chawl Number 33 that Ravan Pawar was meant for greater things. She had seen an eagle descend and come to rest on the window of the Pawar home the day Ravan was born. The venerable Patrick Rodrigues who had run away from home when he was fourteen, boarded a derelict tub as a stowaway, worked as a deckhand on the *Ephesus*, a Greek ship that carried manganese ore between Goa and the major European ports, fought in WWII with the British troops under Montgomery and lost a leg and an eye, recalled that he had cast Eddie Coutinho's horoscope when he joined the Sabha to see how the little boy was going to shape up. What he had seen instantly was that the boy would do all the wrong things and yet come up trumps. Imagine a Catholic boy making a name in the Hindi film industry. It was inconceivable. Catholic men became extras and Catholic girls were cast as vamps and nightclub singers. Eddie would take the same path but in time he would reinvent the Hindi film industry and recast the Catholic community's relationship with Indian films.

But the one whose clairvoyance had reached farthest, it would appear, was the court clerk, Mr Tamhane. He had known on the very day Ravan was conceived that this boy would alter the face of Hindi film music and become a beacon of hope for his generation and those that would follow. Don't you remember, he asked, how I had encouraged Ravan at every step and juncture of his life, how I had chosen his band Cum September to play at my son's wedding, how I had guided the boy and then the young man through the tricky undercurrents and shoals of life?

It was hard to tell what the two people at the centre of all the frenzied goings-on made of the last two weeks. A happy tornado had blown Eddie and Ravan sky-high, maybe off the globe itself. All their lives they had struggled and striven and been rebuffed at every stage. Now they'd made good. Cloud nine, better still nineteen or ninety, is their new address but that hyperbole cannot even begin to describe the change that had occurred in their status, the way they were perceived and the manner in which people were vying with each other to get their attention. Occasionally, you could catch a beatific smile bordering on the vacuous on their faces but it was a smile of incomprehension. Were they having an out-of-body experience? They weren't sure whether it was for real or it was a hoax they were perpetuating on themselves. Something larger than life had taken place and they couldn't get their heads around it.

Eddie and Ravan had been signing contracts as if they were practising handing out their autographs. It had crossed their minds that they should get some professional advice before committing themselves. But they had no idea whom to consult in legal matters. Besides how could they say no? There was no dearth of music directors in the city. Refusing these stalwarts of the film industry, some people called it the film mafia, would have only one consequence: before they knew it they would be blacklisted and no one would ever offer them any work again. No, come what may, they did not want to face the drought again. Besides, why would all these famous film people wait for hours to meet them if all they had in mind was to take them for a ride? True, very true. But wasn't it also true that there was more than an element of sophistry in that impeccable logic? Ravan and Eddie would have to be the Buddha and Jesus Christ rolled into one not to savour every moment of this happy reversal of fortune.

* * *

Eddie's mother, Violet, was not impressed by all these film folk who had chauffeur-driven, foreign cars and seemed to think the world went round because of them. Her father had had three cars, all of them first-hand. It wouldn't have occurred to her to be discourteous but she was happy that barring the occasional foolhardy producer or director who walked up an extra floor, they all terminated their visits at the fourth storey where her son's musical partner, the one whose name she would rather not utter, lived. She had no desire to exchange a greeting or word with these people whose exaggerated politeness and 'haan-jis' and 'nahi-jis' were at times so patently false that she wondered how her son did not see through them. The problem was, she trusted her son Eddie even less.

In truth, Violet was perplexed. Had her son finally turned over a new leaf? Should she be proud of him? Or was this another of his scams? She couldn't figure out why all these people from the film world were suddenly clamouring for Eddie. And for that man who was supposed to be his partner. Did they really think that her son was so gifted? She was his mother, she should have been the first to spot his talent. How come she had been completely blind to it? Had she been wrong about him all these years? Or had he enlisted all these fancy people in an elaborate charade to fool her as he had done so often in the past?

She had heard the music her son and that man from the fourth floor had composed; was there any option, it was being played on the radio in every household in the CWD Chawls all the time. It was not her kind of music but should she be proud of him nevertheless? After all, other people seemed to think it good enough to pursue Eddie all the way to his home. She might not have cared for these filmy types but still, it was a disgrace that Eddie had to entertain them in these environs. If only her late husband, Victor, had had some gumption and got them a nice two-bedroom apartment with a well-appointed living room where Eddie could talk to his visitors one to one on an equal footing.

The mother–son relationship had been rocky for a long time now and yet when she saw Eddie sitting at the dining table to sign another contract, she could not help remarking to Pieta, 'Tell your brother to go through every word in the papers he's signing lest he discover later that he has just signed away his life.' This was the first communication, albeit indirect, that Violet had had with her son since the filmy hordes had begun to land up at all hours of the day and night. Eddie's ears pricked up. Violet Coutinho had written her son off a long time ago. He had nearly ceased to exist as far as she was concerned when she had discovered that Eddie had contracted an unmentionable disease from some woman in Hindi films. But it was evident now that she did care about what happened to him. She had been watching over him all this time. How could he possibly ignore her words? She knew him as nobody else did. Reading a contract was beyond him. He could perhaps understand each word individually, though that too was doubtful, but try as he might, he couldn't bring himself to read a single sentence through, let alone a full paragraph.

Unlike Eddie, Ravan was more persevering. He had tried, on three different occasions, to get to the bottom of '… herein after called the MUSIC DIRECTORS, which expression shall, when the context admits, include the Music Directors' executors, administrators, or assignees…' and so on and so forth. He had discovered at the end of the exercise that he had suffered irreversible brain damage and yet was absolutely no wiser than he had been before starting out.

They were already composing for two films, *Haar-Jeet* and *Meri Biwi ka Pati.* But no more signing contracts till they had got sound legal advice.

2

All his grown-up years, Ravan had eaten his heart, liver and every other vital organ out hankering and yearning for Ms Pieta Coutinho, but had remained persona non grata in the Coutinho household. Now the prize had dropped into his lap of its own accord and he had no idea what to do with it. For instance, how, when and where was he supposed to meet her? Granted that ninety-nine per cent of Bombay's teenagers and younger generation had the same problem but that didn't make life any easier for him. Besides, ninety-nine per cent of Bombay did not have to contend with one Edward Coutinho, a.k.a. Eddie, brother of the aforesaid Pieta nor with the mother of the two siblings.

The garden on the hill in Mazgaon was not a place worth considering since half the tenants of the CWD Chawls congregated there. The only time the place was empty was during the monsoons when all it took to be soaked to the marrow was fifteen seconds, and another five and three-quarters of a minute to be afloat. That narrowed the possibilities for Ravan and Pieta to mostly the coastline of the city and a few gardens in south Bombay. If you could take the day off work, there was the stretch from Nariman Point to the Mafatlal Swimming Pool where you could sit on the parapet next to the sea from 11 a.m. to 4.59 p.m. or, if you were venturesome, step out on to the concrete tetrapods and let the sun turn you to toast and then char you to black carbon. After 5 p.m., the geriatrics and exercise freaks took over the broad walkway and the parapet was packed with a penguin-density of couples: college-going teenagers; young graduates, postgraduates and other hopefuls looking for jobs and setting out to conquer the world; clerks, professionals and executives in their early and mid-thirties. It did not matter whether they were unmarried, married or divorced, almost all of them faced the sinking sun and waited for darkness to start groping and necking. It was the same at Chowpatty beach, the two gardens on Malabar Hill, Worli Seaface, the sands at Shivaji Park and Bandra Seaface, and Naaz Café where Pieta had dropped a bombshell and told Ravan he was no longer going to be single.

'This must be the ninetieth time in two months that we're sitting in this cafe? All the waiters know us and make snide comments about us. It's as if we've made Naaz our second home. Maybe our first home. Can't we ever be on our own without being surrounded by others?' There was a note of desperation in Pieta's voice that Ravan hadn't heard before. This was when Ravan was still an extra and driving a taxi and the two of them had been together for just over two months.

Ravan would have parted with his non-existent kingdom, run a numbers racket or sold his soul to the devil just so long as he was given possession of a room; one room, no more, never mind how narrow or dark, but furnished with two chairs, that's all. Why was he lying to himself? A room, two chairs, a bed and a mattress with a clean pillow-case and a clean sheet, please. But that too would not do. If they got access to a place, he did not want it to be a furtive assignation.

'How about going to a movie? A morning show on Sunday or a matinée?'

'Haven't we seen enough reruns and butchered morning shows? All the couples in the theatre know that nobody's interested in the film and are there to do what you and I want to, except that that too leaves us so dissatisfied.'

Ravan's vocation, circumstances and future had changed dramatically since the 'extra' days and yet that hadn't made any difference to his and Pieta's predicament. As a matter of fact, he felt he had been much better off when he'd been a taxi driver. The taxi was their refuge, their safe haven, their private chamber. Pieta and he could drive anywhere they wanted so long as it was within the city and the owner of the fleet didn't suspect that he had been playing hookey. But one had to be careful for other reasons as well. Whatever transpired in the backseat of a moving taxi was nobody's business, but if the taxi was idling and the driver attempting to have silent converse with his lady friend, a crowd would gather within seconds and the police would be locking you up for indecent behaviour, unless of course some monetary compensation was made for outraging the policeman's modesty.

Ravan had moved up in life and the taxi had gone and so had the fleeting moments of intimacy. In spite of the Bollywood bigwigs thronging to meet Eddie and him, Ravan was still not making money but the good news was that Pieta too had risen in life. She was now the second-in-command of the computer department in her organization. They could once in a while afford to go to Matheran for a weekend. For his birthday, Pieta had hired a car and the two of them had driven down the Konkan coast and spent a night and a day at Ganapati Pule, the tiny seaside resort that not too many people had heard of.

Ravan knew damn well that the crux of the problem was the other half of the partnership which was responsible for the music, choreography and fight direction in their first film, *Hulla Gulla*: Eddie Coutinho. They were the closest of friends now but how could Ravan forget that they had started out as mortal enemies. He had been responsible at the ripe old age of one, never mind how inadvertently, for the death of Eddie's father. Some memories, it would seem, never fade. From his reading of the Bible some years ago when he was on the verge of converting to Roman Catholicism with the express purpose of wooing Pieta, Ravan was well aware that the apocalypse was round the corner, sooner rather than at some hypothetical date in the future. If he was certain about anything in life, it was that Eddie would go ballistic if he so much as suspected that there was something going on between Ravan and his sister.

No, he wouldn't go ballistic. He would do what the Spanish peasant had done in a movie Eddie and he had seen recently at the international film festival. He couldn't remember the name of the film but the English translation went something like *The Inheritance*. The story centred around two families for both of whom the inheritance was not wealth, family heirlooms or industrial empires. Quite the contrary, the protagonists were dirt poor. Their only wealth, the only two things they treasured, was the honour of the family and vengeance. It was the only purpose for which they lived. And just as surely, it would be the reason they would die, prematurely. No one remembered what exactly the bone of contention had been. In truth, they couldn't even say for sure whether there had indeed been a cause or a grievance to begin with.

Ravan re-ran the last sequence of the film in front of his eyes now. Three generations of day labourers – grandfather, son and grandson – bent over saffron plants in fields that stretch all the way to the horizon. It is laborious back-breaking work, just three strands of saffron per flower. Behind them the grandson's wife is walking with a slow heavy tread, a wicker basket that holds lunch for the three men in her hand. The grandfather looks up. There's a man wearing a straw hat with a huge brim shading his face, whistling tunelessly as he heads for a dip in the rivulet that runs alongside the field. The man waves out to the grandfather and the patriarch waves back as he bends down again to collect the saffron. The grandson's wife calls out as a shadow falls across the old man and he looks up. The man with the straw hat has raised his scythe. The old man closes his eyes as the blade lops off his head. It's the turn of the son now. And then of the grandson who is none other than Ravan. Ravan keels over, crushing the basket of saffron flowers under him. He sees the pregnant Pieta running as fast as she can but the gentle curve of the steel is at her throat and out the other end.

Ravan doesn't mind dying at Eddie's hands. He has known since he was a child that Eddie must kill him but he can't bear the thought of Eddie murdering his sister because she's taken up with his friend.

* * *

Eddie and Ravan were beginning to understand how skewed their view of film folks was. It was entirely because they had run into all the wrong people in the past. No, you don't torch an entire orchard because a few mangoes have gone bad. The directors, producers, stars and the others from the industry who were coming to meet them were without exception kind and thoughtful, the soul of courtesy. They were warm and effusive and unstinting of praise. What breeding and what impeccable manners. Not once since Ravan and Eddie's star had risen had any of them referred even obliquely to the squalor, the overcrowding, or the cramped, airless single rooms in which the two friends lived with their families. The visitors behaved as if they themselves did not reside in palatial bungalows in the Juhu Reclamation Scheme or in Pali Hill but had spent all their lives in chawls like CWD Number 17. Some of them sat on the floor and chatted with Parvatibai. They drank the thick brew that passed for tea in the Pawar household in the cheapest crockery though Ravan and Eddie had seen what tantrums they threw on the sets if the Makaibari Darjeeling or Premium Orange Pekoe (they wouldn't stoop to drink anything else) was not made just so and served in the finest paper-thin porcelain tea-service; oops, and don't forget to warm the teapot. If it got late and Parvatibai served them dinner, the same food which she cooked and supplied to the mill and factory workers, they ate it not merely without complaint but with relish.

They invariably had stories about how terribly poor they themselves had been. Often, Ravan got the feeling that it was a spur-of-the-moment kind of poverty. There was something competitive about their former impecunious state as if it had been invented to make Eddie and Ravan and their families feel at ease. Of course it was not all fantasy. Some of them had certainly been down and out or had left their cosy homes where their mothers had looked after their every need and their future had been secure because Papa had a successful hardware or readymade clothes business which they would inherit in due time. But they had turned their backs on all this and landed up in Bombay because like Eddie and Ravan they too had dreamt the Bollywood dream. But that was all a long time ago and their recollections were laced with so many romantic filters and so much yearning, one might begin to believe that to be a pauper in a broken-down chawl, fighting for survival, somehow ennobled you instead of making you petty, envious and insecure, and was a precondition for the creation of art. Ravan was grateful to them for making the effort, but for some reason he couldn't explain why their well-meant journey down memory lane only seemed to make him feel more self-conscious about his own single-room home and the common toilets he and his family shared with thirty-nine other families.

The only sour note was struck by one of the last of the visitors. However perfunctorily and reluctantly, Eddie and Ravan had at last sat down together to go over the first of the signed contracts when there was a knock on the door.

'Yes?' Ravan was relieved to get a break from reading the unreadable legal verbiage.

'My name is Prajapati Sehgal.' The man was so nondescript, Ravan wondered why the name sounded vaguely familiar. 'A rather pompous name, king or emperor of the people. You know what parents are like. They are ambitious for their children, especially if they have not been able to achieve what they wanted for themselves in life. You would rather I did not come inside?'

The switch of subjects was so abrupt Ravan was thrown off. 'I beg your pardon. Please come in.'

'If it's not too much trouble would you call your partner, Eddie Coutinho? That way I won't have to repeat myself.'

'He's here with me.'

'What a good omen to find you both together. Congratulations. That was outstanding work you did for *Hulla Gulla*. Something very different, a breath of fresh air.' Mr Sehgal handed his visiting cards to the two of them as he sat in one of the three new folding chairs with cushioned seats that Parvatibai had bought for the new class of visitors to their home. Ravan glanced at the card. It mentioned some vague film production company called Swaraj Films. So he was from the film business. The operative word was 'was'. Neither Eddie nor Ravan had heard of him. As very recent extras who had spent years doing the rounds of every back alley connected with the film world, they knew that if they had not heard of someone, he was either a hoax, passé or as good as dead.

'I rejoice in your good fortune. Enjoy it to the hilt … while it lasts. It generally comes with an expiry date.'

'For your information, we've already got forty-seven contracts,' Eddie said testily, wanting to nip this kind of talk in the bud.

'Give it a few more days or weeks. It will go up to sixty, even seventy. It's a sure-fire way of killing the talent or genius you may possess though it's too early to know which it is. Right now you smell of the box office. It's an acrid sexy scent and everybody wants to get into bed with the two of you. The moment the magic stops working, they'll drop you and get a new lover before you can close your eyelids. Let's see how long the love affair with you lasts.'

Who was this know-all dishing out gratis advice? The film people who had come earlier were gracious, falling over each other to please the new musical sensations. Mr Sehgal was just the opposite, not uncouth but a little too conscious of giving it straight from the shoulder. He obviously fancied himself and had an opinion on every subject.

'In that case what are you doing here?' Eddie didn't want to hear anything more from this intruder who was trying his utmost to put a hex on them. 'At number seventy-one, according to your own theory, all you can get is graveyard music.'

'It's unlikely that you would know who I am but I used to make films with social themes that were super-hits. Then fashions changed, social themes went out of the window and I had a string of flops, four in all. Everybody has been telling me that my career passed its expiry date long ago. I realize now that my later films had a message overload and not enough fun and entertainment. I want one last hurrah. I've found a good story, an unusual love triangle, tense as a thriller and this time around, the moral of the story is not hammered home. All it needs is great music to make it a hit. That's why I'm here.'

'Why would we want to be associated with a flop master?' Eddie thought it was about time to nail the guy and shut him up once and for all.

'You're right, no reason at all. But there's something special I can offer you. I will give you only half of what the others have promised.'

Ravan couldn't help laughing. 'However tempting it might be, I think we'll try to manage without your special offer.'

'Let me finish. Nobody, not even you, knows whether you are a one-shot wonder or you've got staying power. It might be only half the money the others promise you on paper. But I will give you the full amount by cheque, not some time in the vague future but the day you sign up. And if the music sales cross an agreed-upon sum, you'll receive twenty per cent of the profits.'

'The chances of that "if" materializing are, I guess, close to zero,' Ravan countered. 'Otherwise, you wouldn't be making us the offer.'

'I can't deny that it's an iffy proposition. But you're going to find out the hard way that most of the time you won't even get half the promised money. And what you get will almost never come on time.'

'You're bad-mouthing the whole industry just to scare us so that we will take up your assignment.'

'I don't need to malign the industry, it does that pretty well on its own. And yes, I would like you to do the music for my film before taking on anything else. I'm sixty-six and I don't have much time. You're hot property just now and I will try to parlay your names into getting the remaining finance for my film.'

You had to hand it to the man, he had some gall revealing all this and yet think he could make suckers of them.

'Would you care to hear the story of my film?'

'Maybe some other time.' Ravan thought that was done with finesse.

'Good. Give me a call and we'll have a story session.'

Was the man stupid? Couldn't he see that they were just not interested? Well, there was nothing either Ravan or Eddie could do about it. If Prajapati Sehgal couldn't take an unsubtle hint, he would just have to wait till kingdom come for his story session. The elderly film-maker, however, wasn't through with them.

'If you need any help, don't hesitate to call me. Even experienced old hands like me can get taken for a ride. Oh, one last thing. When you come for the story session, would you please bring along Asmaan-ji. Half the credit for your success goes to her. She's a real original. Completely off the wall as the Americans say. I doubt it if your music would have been anywhere as good without her lyrics. Her unique way of looking at the world demanded that the music too should break with the past and seek a new idiom.'

* * *

Prajapati Sehgal was obviously one of a kind. His only specialty, it seemed, was that he had the kind of evil eye that could poison ambrosia. It was not the most felicitous of moves for him to be spreading his largesse of home truths at their very first meeting especially when he wanted them to do the music for his film. The only sensible response was to ignore the man. One of his comments, however, irked Ravan no end. It stuck like lint to his brain and try as he might, he couldn't seem to get rid of it. Who the hell was Prajapati Sehgal to suggest that R&E's success was at least partly, fifty per cent to be exact, due to Asmaan? For days Ravan refused to think about it, knowing all the while that at some point in time he would have to confront his shabby reluctance to admit her role in their hitting the jackpot. The lyrics she wrote and the stories she narrated felt so mainstream that few people noticed how different her take on life was and how subversive she was under the glossy finish of the surface.

Sudden success was one of those lifts in the Air India building in the reclaimed land at Nariman Point. It shot up from the ground floor and went straight all the way to the top in one crazy breath, leaving you dizzy and disoriented. It was amazing how quickly even a temporary bout of celebrity had induced amnesia in Eddie and him. But their ingratitude was a shade more glaring. Asmaan was their friend and they had ignored her. The curious thing was that instead of the guilt galvanizing them, it left them paralysed with shame.

Obviously, Eddie too must have been mulling over their selective forgetfulness about Asmaan for he came over late one night and said, 'Let's go see Asmaan. I checked with the Junior Artists' Union. She's shooting at R.K. Studios tomorrow.'

Asmaan was a blue-green mermaid that day, sitting awkwardly on a bench, unaware of her surroundings, scribbling away as she always did, her concentration a ray of intense laser light that should have set her notebook on fire. She looked up, didn't see R&E standing in front of her, bent down to jot something, looked up again, threw her notebook aside and rose on her soft mermaid tail to hug them. Fortunately, Ravan caught her before she keeled over. It was worth circumnavigating the earth a dozen times merely to see the sheer joy on her face. No recriminations, no anger, no sullen withdrawal symptoms.

'Wow!' She was like a child who could not contain her delight. 'You did it. You deserve every bit of your success.'

'*We* did it. The three of us,' Eddie told her as he drew her away from Ravan's arms and hugged her.

'We intend to do it again. And again. Together,' Ravan said when Eddie set her down on the bench and gave her the gift they had bought for her. She tore open the envelope.

'A cheque for seven thousand rupees? What for?'

'Oh, nothing special.' Eddie tried to sound casual. 'Spend it on whatever you fancy. For instance, you could finally do something that's been on your mind for so long.'

'You mean get my boobs enhanced till all of Hugh Hefner will disappear between them?'

This was the delicate part. Actually, there was no way of coming clean without getting into tricky waters.

'Nah. Your boobs are the most shapely pair on either side of the Suez. You could fix that lovely nose of yours which your brother Yaqub knocked out of shape.'

'You don't like my nose?' She sounded hurt.

Ravan tried to smooth things over. 'We love you and love everything about you, including your lovely nose.'

She laughed. 'What liars you both are. Thank you, thank you.'

* * *

The first month-and-a-half after the cars started rolling into the grounds in front of CWD Chawl No. 17 had whizzed past in an intoxicated blur. There was never a free moment for Eddie and his friend to fully comprehend or appreciate the seismic changes that had occurred in their lives. The pair might be listening to the bubbly Nasir Hussain as he outlined the plans for his next three films on the fourth-floor balcony, or closing the door of Shakti Samanta's car as he got into it and waved goodbye but they rarely ever seemed to walk the earth. They were floating on some cloud, an inane grin pasted on their faces. Who could fault them for looking a trifle dazed?

The number of producers, directors, actors and financiers who had come to court the new musical duo had tapered off at around fifty-nine and then at least for a while there were no more. The reporters and the cameramen had also disappeared, leaving the two feeling a little empty. Eddie and Ravan were aware that the euphoria of being discovered was bound to fade away one day. Yet it caught them off-guard. There was no transitional gradient which would lead them gently back to normal life. Even if they took the cut-off point as fifty films and not fifty-nine, since some of the parties involved had yet to send them the contracts, they were faced with the prospect of composing about three hundred songs at an average of six per film. That's without counting the fifty soundtracks.

Hollywood, British, French and Japanese films cheat their audiences of a full hour of entertainment. That would never do in India. The typical Hindi film had to cater to the paisa vasool expectations of the audience. They would feel they hadn't got their money's worth if the running time of a film was less than a hundred and fifty minutes. More but never less than that. *Mother India* and *Mughal-e-Azam*, for instance, went on for more than three hours. In the good old days each film had at least ten songs. Many others had fourteen or thereabouts. Now the numbers had gone down a bit. Six to eight. But every now and then the producers wanted ten or twelve. *Hulla Gulla* had twelve. E&R had signed up thirty films for fight direction and another twenty-four for choreography. Had they lost their marbles when they signed the contracts? How come they did not even bother to do some basic arithmetic and compute just how much work was involved? Did they have the vaguest idea of what they were committing themselves to?

3

Ravan knew how to deal with sudden bonanzas of luck and that phenomenon called *Denewala jab bhi deta, poora chhappar faad ke deta*. When the good Lord gives, He tears open the roof and showers you with favours. But Ravan had learnt that if you had any sense, you would not fall for that old song. Instead, you would get the ceiling repaired quickly, ask your mother to neutralize the nazar someone had cast on you and get rid of the evil eye. Most important of all, ignore the magician's cheap trick. And wait patiently for the bad days which are bound to come.

Of the two boons that had befallen him (at least that's how he saw it), Ravan had less difficulty dealing with the movie moguls who had converged on his home than with his ladylove. He marvelled at how smoothly Eddie had made the transition from extra to showman with the sudden influx of the film folks into their homes. There hadn't been a hint of self-consciousness in his friend (it was as if he was on a first-name basis with these people) while he himself had no idea how to respond to all the hyper-praise showered on them. He was well aware of his shortcomings, he could never be comfortable as a celebrity but somewhere in the depths of his self-knowledge he was also conscious that it didn't really matter how these visitors rated him. Many of these people who had come in their fancy cars were just as illiterate as he was. E&R's fate would be decided not in the dingy, dreary one-room tenements called the CWD Chawls but in the recording studios and by the box office. And just as relevant, the fates of all these people who had knocked on their doors would also be riding on them.

With Pieta, however, he was out of his depth. He had convinced himself that Pieta and he would be a mismatch like no other. They had been going around, needless to say clandestinely, for several months now when he finally worked up enough courage to blurt out, 'It's not going to work.'

'What's not going to work?' Pieta asked.

'Us. This relationship. Everything.'

Pieta didn't hit the roof or get hysterical as he had expected. She looked concerned and sympathetic. 'Oh dear, we seem to have a situation here: a Catch-22 situation.'

'What's that?'

'It's a double bind. A no-go situation.'

'Why's that?

'You see I can't give you a divorce because we're not yet married. And when we are, it will be impossible because the Catholic faith doesn't allow it.'

'Why would I want to ask for a divorce?'

'Precisely. Why would you? So that's settled then.'

Ravan had the feeling he was doing a vertical climb on a smooth granite wall with paraffin oil dripping down it. He looked closely at Pieta, scrutinized her face for clues. She looked back at him, even more concerned and sympathetic.

'What seems to be the problem, Ravan?'

What seems to be the problem was one of Pieta's favourite lines from their favourite Laurel and Hardy film. As with L&H, the solicitude implied in the query was often a prelude to sheer mayhem. There were many variations but this was the one that Pieta liked most: the two comedians are speeding away from a bunch of vicious villains. Suddenly the getaway car stalls on the shoulder of a mountain. Stan opens the hood, fiddles around, gets back in and tries to re-start the engine. It's dead. He gets out again and throws a tantrum on the road from where both Oliver and he can see that the goons are catching up with them fast. His partner gets out of the vehicle, strolls over and asks in a solicitous voice, 'What seems to be the problem?'

The question makes Stan hopping mad. Literally. He does a miniature stampede on the ground all by himself. 'What do you think is the problem? This automobile's going to die on us just when we are in a spot of trouble.'

Stan immediately proceeds to rip off the left mudguard. Oliver watches with intense interest and then bends down and dislodges the right mudguard. It's Stan's turn now. He yanks out the radiator cap and lobs it far away. Laurel watches in amazement as the cap flies up and falls somewhere in the distance. Straining his every nerve, Ollie hauls the whole radiator out and throws it on the ground. Stan takes over, pulls the battery out and flings it down. They will watch each other patiently till one by one they dismember the engine, the wipers and bumpers, the doors, the seats. In the meantime, the crooks have caught up with them. They park their car and stroll over to watch Stan and Laurel hard at work. 'What seems to be the problem?' the chief hood asks. The vehicle is by now fully dismantled.

'What seems to be the problem? I'll tell you what the problem is.' Stan is still in a murderous temper. He walks over to the hoodlums' car and takes the driver's seat while Oliver gets in on the other side. The goons are watching with keen interest, waiting to see what comes next. Stan and Oliver take off waving goodbye to the thugs. 'Take care now. You don't want the police on your heels. Follow us.'

'Are you taking the mickey out of me, Pieta?'

She looked hurt. 'How could you possibly think such a thing?'

He was even more confused now. He was about to tell her that this was nothing new; she had made an ass of him before, not once but many times over but the trouble was he could never tell whether she was taking him for a ride or was in earnest.

'What is it, Ravan? What ails you?'

Why did her phrasing sound so theatrical? He should have been on his guard but she was the soul of sympathy.

'How can I do this to you? We belong to different worlds. You've got class. Me? I'm in "the extras" class. You go to art exhibitions, lectures, plays. You work in a fancy air-conditioned office as VP, software development. I don't even know what that means. I've never seen you without a book. What do I read? The trade magazines. Or Asmaan's lyrics. And she has to explain the meaning of the Urdu words half the time. Even the days when I used to read the Bible religiously to win you over are gone. What will we talk about?'

'Oh no, I hadn't realized we had nothing in common.' Pieta looked shocked. Was she putting him on? One thing was certain, she was a far superior actor than he was. 'Then we've wasted the last six months deluding ourselves that we were madly in love and having a terrific time together while you showed me what you called the taxi driver's Bombay. Nooks and crannies and corners and unknown places I would never have known on my own. Or sitting together on Chowpatty beach holding on tightly to each other while the rains turned us into purée. You're right, no point deluding ourselves. It's best we break off now. Once and for all. We're grown-ups; however difficult it might be, we can handle it. Please don't say hello to me when we run into each other on the staircase. Or anywhere else. Bye, Ravan.' Pieta turned on her heels and left before he had time to respond.

Ravan looked at her receding back in alarm. How could she leave him? He had thought they would talk things over, consider the pluses and minuses of their relationship from every angle and whether they had a future together. Maybe they could take a break from each other for six months to see if this was just a temporary infatuation or there was something more to it. What was the matter with him, why would it take six months to find out if they were really serious about each other? One month would do the trick. Frankly, even a week would be more than enough. Maybe he had overstated the case. He didn't think he could last a day without her. What had he gone and done, the fool that he was? He ran after her. She was nowhere in sight. Damn. Damn. Damn. He had lost her for good, he was sure of that.

She was waiting for him at the corner behind a sugarcane juice stand.

'Who were you chasing, Ravan? It's not even a few minutes since we broke up and you are already running after some other woman?'

Ravan should have known Pieta better by now. She was a mistress of diversions and subversion. It was a verbal game of false starts and intricate twists and turns. By the time she was done with you, you could no longer tell east from south and north from west.

'Now, if you are through trying to impress me with your abject humility and modesty routine, may I be permitted to get in a word edgeways? We've been living it up since we got together as if there were no tomorrow. It's been marvellous renting a car and driving up to a hill resort like Matheran for the weekend or going down the Konkan coast and stopping at a lovely sea resort. But no more extravagant spending. This month onwards I'm starting a recurring deposit account in the bank and so will you. We are going to buy a little flat when we collect enough. Every month I am going to put by two thousand from my salary. If I get a raise, I'll save more. You too are going to commit a fixed sum every month once you know approximately how much you can set aside.'

Ravan's face fell. 'No more going out? I don't want to give up today for tomorrow.'

'Don't get mad, Ravan. I enjoy the trips and the lovemaking as much as you do. But if we have a place of our own we can make love as often as we want. Besides, I'm not suggesting we won't go out any more. We'll still have lots of fun but if we don't start saving now, we will always have to go to hotels for just a few hours of privacy.'

How come everything boils down to just two things, Ravan wondered. It was always about a place and privacy. Actually the two were the same.

Pieta had stuck to her word for six months. And then her grandmother had to be hospitalized because of a heart attack. Even Eddie who liked to pretend that he had no attachments was beside himself with worry. The recurring deposit was gone in no time and Eddie too put in whatever little he had saved and warned Ravan that he might have to touch him for cash. Within a week, Granna seemed to recover but on the tenth day she lost consciousness and Pieta was forced to take a loan from her firm.

'Granna was the only one who didn't blame you for my father's death,' Pieta told Ravan when she was keeping watch over her grandmother in the hospital. 'I wonder if my mother saw that as a betrayal. She is past sixty-five and yet she's far more lively than the rest of us put together. She is the only person who's sane in the family.' Pieta was lost in her thoughts for a while. 'You better root for her, Ravan. Pray to all your gods to bring her back safely with her heart and her sense of humour intact. You won't find a better ally than her.'

'Was it Jesus or the Hindu gods who did the trick?' Ravan teased Pieta after Granna came home.

'Maybe they got together.'

* * *

On the first of October a nuclear device went off in Eddie and Ravan's face and reduced them to silence and bewilderment. Hard as it was for them to believe, they had planted it themselves. Alakh Niranjan Films sent them a notice informing them that 'Whereas you are under contractual obligation to supply the musical score for our film *Aaj Nahi Toh Kal* within thirty days, and as it was now over seven weeks past the due date, you are liable to a penalty of the sum of Rs 300,000. Furthermore, the penalty would rise at the rate of Rs 50,000 for every week you default.'

Three hundred thousand rupees, what the hell were the Alakh Niranjan people talking about? There was obviously some mistake. They had already recorded three of the eight songs for their film. But Alakh Niranjan was not their only client. They had to keep everybody happy and so they were recording songs for five other films simultaneously. They knew Prakash Shetty, he had been amongst the very first to visit them in the CWD Chawls. He had come over thrice, every time with gifts for the two of them and for their mothers and even for Granna and Pieta. Not just that, he had refused to leave unless they said yes and signed the contract. He hadn't said a word about a penalty for not delivering the score before the deadline. Indeed, they had gone over the contract; well, at least skimmed through it. They didn't recall seeing anything even remotely suggesting a punitive clause.

They went over to the Alakh Niranjan offices to sort out the misunderstanding with their friend, Prakash Shetty, but they were told he had prior engagements that day and then he was going out of town for three weeks. The secretary advised them to see his finance manager. Where was there room for a misunderstanding? the chief accountant had asked. It was all in black and white, he said, and pointed to section 3, clause 7F. Even a blind man wouldn't have missed it. Could they not renegotiate the contract, Ravan enquired. They would give their word to have the entire music track ready within a couple of months. They were really good friends of Mr Shetty. He had been to their homes and had dinner with them. What's friendship got to do with it? the finance man asked. This was business. Had they forgotten that that was precisely the reason why a contract was drawn up, so that there was no scope for what they called a 'misunderstanding' and precisely why they had been sent the notice? If they knew what was good for them, they would hand over the full musical soundtrack, songs and background music immediately. Otherwise, the three hundred thousand would become five hundred thousand and keep climbing.

Three hundred thousand rupees. Where was that kind of money to come from? What had they got themselves into? Or rather how were they going to avoid this catastrophe? Within the next four days they received seven more notices. Suddenly, Pratap Saxena of Mega Entertainment Films, Rajesh Trivedi of Triveni Movies and all those wonderful people who had been so effusive when they were courting R&E had disappeared behind a pitiless and inexorable entity called the production company or studio. You needed to learn a different language to talk to a company and Ravan and Eddie didn't have it. How does one throw oneself at the feet of a company and plead for mercy and latitude? The honeymoon with Bollywood, Ravan and Eddie had to admit reluctantly, was turning sour.

It began to filter slowly into their consciousness that while the contracts they signed were written, not in ink but in inflexible iron-clad clauses, sub-clauses and sub, sub-clauses that bound them hand and foot, body, mind and soul, and gave them no breathing room, the same conditions did not apply to the producers. A couple of producers had made the initial payments but most of the others routinely skipped their own obligations. Many of the very folks who had sent the notices to Eddie and Ravan had not bothered to pay even the very first instalment. Three of the parties had sent cheques which had bounced right back. When this was brought to the notice of the producers or the chief accountants in the production company, they were incredulous. How could that be, there must surely be some error; there was enough money in the account to bankroll not one but three multi-star productions. They would take it up with the bank and make sure that this kind of thing never happened again. They apologized profusely and reissued the cheques. And the cheques bounced again.

Pride be damned, they would have to eat crow and go see Prajapati Sehgal. He had said that if there was ever a problem, he would try and help them out. They would score the music for his new film. It was true they had not taken a shine to the man but what choice did they have now? He was the only one who had spoken of giving them the full amount before they started work, though they had not bothered to find out how much he would pay. They had ignored him for months. It was doubtful if he would even agree to meet them. And if he did, he would most likely cut them down to size by telling them he would only cough up half the amount he had in mind earlier.

They took Asmaan with them.

'Delighted to make your acquaintance, Asmaan-ji,' Mr Sehgal greeted Asmaan warmly. 'You've brought poetry back to Hindi film lyrics, a new kind of sly poetry full of irony and sharp teeth.' He turned to Ravan and Eddie. 'I knew you wouldn't ditch me. But I must confess you had me worried. You took your own time and I had begun to fear that I had misread your character. I was betting that it was not the money you were interested in but the challenge of making entertainment meaningful once again that would bring us together.'

Ah Prajapati Sehgal, how mistaken can you be. We need to disabuse you immediately. It's money and nothing but. How about three hundred thousand rupees to start off with?

For the next two-and-a-half hours Prajapati Sehgal told them the storyline over lunch and went on to describe the situations where the songs would come in and what they would be about and yet there was no mention of payment. It was Asmaan who took the bull by the horns.

'Eleven songs? That's a hell of a lot. Isn't it rather old-fashioned to have so many?'

'Just to set the record straight, there were twelve in *Hulla Gulla*. I'm an old-fashioned film director and I intend to give my audience their money's worth.'

'And how much do you estimate,' Asmaan smiled archly at him, 'we are worth?'

'One-and-a-half lakhs between the two music directors and seventy-five thousand for you.'

One-and-a-half lakhs? Was the man kidding or what? That was just half of what they owed Alakh Niranjan.

'Let's go,' Eddie said.

Eddie, Asmaan and Ravan had decided on a strategy before they saw Mr Sehgal. Whatever happened, they must appear to deal from a position of strength and not let on that they, or rather the two men, were in dire straits. If the film director apprehended that they needed him far more than he them, the game would be up and he could beat them down even lower than the 'half' he had promised. Unfortunately, things did not go according to plan.

'Mr Sehgal,' Ravan blurted out at the door, 'we're here because we are in trouble and very likely going to prison.'

'Let's go,' Eddie said sharply to Ravan and stamped on his foot.

'We need three lakhs. Just for Eddie and me. We'll compose music for two of your films.'

Prajapati Sehgal laughed.

'Are you stupid?' Eddie turned viciously upon Ravan. 'I told you let's get out.' And added with an extra-bitter emphasis on the film director's name, 'Can't you see, you fool, Sehgal Sahab's laughing at us?'

'Yes, I'm laughing. I'm laughing because Ravan thinks I'm still good for two more movies at my age. I will be grateful if God, whoever and wherever he is, permits me to make this one. All right, Eddie, let's hear what the problem is.' And then he smirked. 'Has one of the producers invoked a penalty clause and threatened you with legal action?'

Eddie looked incredulously at Prajapati Sehgal. 'How do you know this?'

'No clairvoyance there. It's an old trick to scare newcomers in the business. I suspect you will be getting many such notices.'

'We already have. Are we in serious trouble?' Eddie seemed to have forgotten all talk of leaving.

'Trouble, yes. Serious? Perhaps. That's if you adhere strictly to the letter of the law. But as long as I am here and I can help it, we'll scotch the notices before things get out of hand.'

'Scotch how?' Ravan asked. 'By bribing the judges?'

'You are already beginning to sound like Bambaiyya film people, Ravan. They think anyone can be bought, including judges.'

'So how do we get Alakh Niranjan off our backs?'

'Let's take it one step at a time. When you signed the contracts, did you stagger the delivery dates for the different films?'

'Not for the first six films,' Ravan informed Prajapati. 'We were on a high with our new-found success and the producers were so friendly, we didn't bother to check the dates for delivery in the contracts.'

'We'll show all the contracts to my lawyers. The most important thing to remember is don't sign any more contracts till you have a realistic idea about how many songs you can deliver in a month without compromising quality. Don't cut it too fine. You will need some slack. Don't panic. No one's taking you to court at the moment. What you've received is a legal notice. Our lawyers will answer it.'

'So what do we do?' Eddie asked.

'You prove your good intentions by keeping your part of the deal. That's by recording the songs and the background music as soon as possible. But not, make a note of that, before you record the music for my film. Because if you don't,' Prajapati Sehgal leered wickedly at Eddie and Ravan, 'I'll take you to court. Jokes apart, don't concentrate on one film alone just now because then you really might land up in court by the time you get down to the fifth.'

'And what happens if we're dragged to court?'

'I'm coming to that. The judicial system in India and perhaps all over the world,' Prajapati Sehgal explained, 'has one and only one purpose: procrastination. In a sense it's geared to give the guilty party a very long rope to hang itself by. On the other hand, if you are the victim, you would be lucky if your children, more likely your grandchildren, live to see justice being done. However, sometimes the same judicial process can help the innocent. That's what we are going to do. Use the law to put right what is wrong.

'Fortunately, there's an instrument in the law books called an injunction. It can stop legal proceedings in their tracks. If anyone does take you to court, and as I said, I doubt anyone will, our lawyer will pile up injunction after injunction till the production company is stonewalled and is left no room to manoeuvre. Don't get me wrong, if we were to go by the letter of the law, you don't have a leg to stand on. They didn't drug you or thrust a knife at your throat when you signed up. You did it voluntarily. It's just that you happen to be complete greenhorns and they are taking advantage of that. Frankly, there's only one ace up your sleeves. Money. Like everybody else, producers, financiers, distributors hate to lose money; only more so. All we want to do is to make them realize that they might win the case seven or seventeen years down the road, but if they want to cut their losses and get their film released, they better come round and compromise with you. Not just Alakh Niranjan but all those who have signed you up.'

* * *

'I can't ever trust you, can I?' There was such rancour in Eddie's voice, Asmaan thought he was going to assault Ravan physically. 'What happened? Did we not have a deal?'

Ravan stared at his feet.

'When I ask you a question,' Eddie stepped up and confronted his friend, his truculent chin thrust barely three inches from Ravan's cast-down eyes, 'I expect an answer.'

'I'm sorry.' Ravan still would not look up. How could he possibly tell Eddie that it was his sister, Pieta, who'd had a good feeling about Prajapati Sehgal? She had seen him only once and that too fleetingly while she was climbing up and he was going down the stairs of CWD Chawl No. 17, holding on to the banister after his meeting with the music directors. He had looked at her and said spontaneously, 'You must be Eddie Coutinho's sister.'

Pieta had to turn around since she was already past the man. 'I beg your pardon?'

'My name's Sehgal. Prajapati Sehgal. I just met your brother and Ravan. Your parents must be very special to have such good-looking children.'

Pieta had blushed. She had no idea that there was such an obvious resemblance between her brother and her.

'Thank you for the compliment. What about Ravan?' Pieta was shocked by her own question and the fact that she had actually asked it.

'Ah, Ravan. He and your brother have the looks of film stars. But Ravan's different. There's something mysterious about him. I can't quite put my finger on it since today is the first time I met the new music sensations. He has a sort of brooding presence as if there were a lot going on behind that quiet façade. Why do you ask? You obviously know him better than I do.'

'Just curious. You seem to be a quick reader of people.'

'You'll be surprised how often I get things wrong.' He shrugged his shoulders. 'Good night, Ms Coutinho. 'Insha Allah, we'll meet again.'

* * *

Weeks after the first meeting with Prajapati Sehgal, Ravan and Pieta had been sitting on Chowpatty Beach, eating bhel, when she remembered her chance meeting with Mr Sehgal. Ravan made a face and told her how the man had talked about an expiry date on E&R's

talents and how he was not sure whether they were just a one-off musical sensation or they were marathoners.

Pieta had laughed. 'That's not such a terrible thing to say. I would rather he was honest with you unlike the other film people who flatter you shamelessly because they want something from you and think you are too dumb to see through their lies.'

'You are saying that only because he flattered you.'

'Probably. But you tell me that I'm lovely at least ten times a day. Are you flattering me or just being truthful?'

Ravan cracked up. 'Just being my normal toadying self and currying favour with you.'

'Sure, I believe you. All you want to do is get under the sheets with me.'

Ravan's ears went a bright red and Pieta teased him about it all the way back home.

'Well, at least I hope you do.' Then as she was getting out of the cab, she said, 'I think he's okay, Ravan.'

'Who?'

'Your Mr Sehgal. Don't you wish to find out whether Eddie and you really are long-distance runners?'

* * *

Ravan was about to tell Eddie that he was right, he had behaved like a heel, but Eddie was in no mood to listen. 'I'm through with you, Ravan. I can't work with someone so unreliable. I wanted to punch you in the face right there.' Eddie scrunched up his face. 'The trouble is, you might have got us out of one hell of a bind because you panicked. With any luck, Sehgal Sahab might just save our arses for us. But in the future if we agree on something, we stick with it even if you start getting cold feet. We can always talk about it later on and change our stance. So what's it going to be? Are you with me or aren't you?'

Ravan put the palm of his hand on his heart and said in a charged emotional voice, 'Till death do us part, I will be with you.'

'Heaven help you, Ravan, you're such a dreadful actor.'

4

The effect of that meeting with Prajapati Sehgal was like castor oil. In one stroke it flushed out all the clogged debris and the fears of a long spell in Arthur Road Jail. But far more importantly it broke the back of their agonizing suspicion that R&E were a one-musical-score wonder and their careers were already over and done with. Neither Ravan nor Eddie had dared to speak to each other about the insidious terror of that presentiment. They had not even allowed themselves to admit that the thought had cast a shadow over their lives and that everything they touched might be still-born.

They had recorded eight more songs since the time they received the notice from Alakh Niranjan Films. They were serviceable tunes, the producers and directors for whom they had recorded them were happy and they might even have made it to the top twenty at Rhythm House but that was when R&E took a decision to which they would remain true in all the years ahead. They would set their own standards. Almost anybody with a bit of musical talent could write tolerable scores and songs. But there would have to be a better reason for someone to approach Eddie and Ravan; indeed a far better reason. They didn't actually discuss it, they couldn't even remember who had mooted the thought, but they dumped all eight songs. They would never speak or brag about it. Some things, they wouldn't call them principles, were just too private even for the prodigiously extroverted Eddie to talk about but they would always be the harshest judges of their own work. They might come from vastly different cultural backgrounds, their musical pasts couldn't have been more disparate but what they shared was a highly evolved musical sense, and an unerring instinct for what constituted the passable, the competent, the good and what set the bar.

By now they were no longer playing catch-up. They had taken the jocular threat made by Prajapati Sehgal to heart and recorded all but two songs for his film *Trikon*. The full soundtrack for *Aaj Nahin Toh Kal* had been delivered but the film wasn't released because one of the superstars from the film had filed a suit against the company. Needless to say, Alakh Niranjan had used that as the excuse for delaying payment to Asmaan and E&R.

There had been no overt plan about how they would share the workload, what each one's contribution would be, how they would critique the music they composed, and how they would refine it. But it did not take them long to work out a system that was limber and flexible and yet anchored them to a routine. The division of work was simple. In the initial stages of composition, Eddie took over half the songs and Ravan the other half. That's when they were dealing with even numbers. If there was an odd one remaining, they would both try to attack it. And who was to decide the better composition? They would, who else? One thing they were clear about, it was never about Ravan or Eddie; the songs, the soundtrack for a specific sequence and what was best for the particular situation and the overall mood of the film were the only considerations. Leave the choice to the director, producer or one of the superstars of the movie and you could wager that nine times out of ten, they would choose the most mediocre.

They soon settled down to a daily rhythm of working. Composing music was never a nine-to-five job. When a few bars or a tune occurred to you in the loo, at the gym or as you were waiting in the queue to get milk at 5 in the morning, you memorized the bits and pieces, or if you knew how to score music as Eddie did, you pulled out a small pad and jotted down the notes. Ravan had begun to learn the Western system of notation from Eddie when they were working on the score for *Hulla Gulla* and now that they were seriously into music, he was getting adept at B flats and E minors, but he was more comfortable memorizing the tunes. The duo worked with whoever had been chosen to write the lyrics but most producers realized that the words and the music seemed to fit far better when Asmaan was the lyricist. The journalists would always ask the same question:

what comes first, the lyrics or the tune, and all three of them had the same answer: both. Eddie would sit with a small, second-hand Moog synthesizer for hours, going over the same phrases or riff, looking for something which was still unknown to him, and yet he was sure that he would know precisely what it was when he hit the right combination of notes which would become a full-fledged melody.

Ravan would wake up at all hours of the night and go to the terrace and walk back and forth or sit down on the parapet and gaze at the two-day-old crescent of the moon and then start humming a sliver of a tune. Sometimes he would get into a 1 Ltd bus at the Colaba bus station and ride all the way to Andheri and on the way back get out at a stop or red light and walk into the nearest Irani shop, order tea after tea while jotting down an incipient melody. Most of the time, however, he plonked himself on the floor, pulled out the multi-stringed bulbul tarang, plucked out a haphazard series of notes with a plectrum and played with them, changing the order, weaving in and out, trying to inch closer to the core of the melody.

Eddie came to his friend's house to compare notes, choose which of the various versions of a song they would record, discuss which singer should sing it, which instruments would be needed and who would play them. They wrote down the complete score, they noted exactly when and where each instrument came in, which players had solos, where the different tracks melded into one and how they wanted to pace the music and the singer. Their songs had the kind of simplicity and compelling melody that no amateur singer could resist. It was only when a professional playback singer came for a recording that he or she realized that the compositions were sly and full of guile.

Often, Asmaan joined them and once in a while adjusted the lyrics to make the music and the words inseparable. She was a fast worker but she preferred to sleep over whatever she had scribbled and not make do with an impromptu verse merely because the producer or director was happy with it. She was now in demand as a songwriter though not everybody was enamoured of her unorthodox way of looking at life and the sting in the tail that her seemingly innocuous lyrics often concealed. She had turned one of her stories into a screenplay that had just been bought and, to quote her version of just how much it was appreciated, it had been buggered, butchered and f...ed right royally till it was totally unrecognizable and made absolutely no sense, but she was willing to bet it would go on to become a hit.

E&R were, however, still novices not only at the legal stuff but at the technical aspects and tricks of recording. Unlike others in the business who had done their apprenticeship with well-established music directors, learnt the ropes and only then graduated to becoming composers in their own right, Eddie and Ravan had come in from the cold and all their learning was on the job and experiential. When they made mistakes, and they made plenty of them, they had only themselves to blame. Every blunder came with a heavy price tag in terms of money and time and they had no option but to learn fast.

The 'general' in general knowledge in India is rather different from what the rest of the world understands by that term. In the subcontinent, it refers almost exclusively to the world of films and film songs. Indians might not know the name of the Father of the Nation, the only male river in the country or the last Indian to have won the Nobel but wake them up at 3 in the morning; no, ask them while they're submerged in a deep anaesthetic coma, the names and 'bios' of film stars, producers, directors and even music directors, and they will tell you their birthdates, the colour and size of their birthmarks, names of their children and grandchildren, the first movie they made, the names of the characters they played, who their heroine in each film was, how much they made in white the previous year and how much in black, what were their lucky colours and lucky numbers, who they were sleeping with on what date and who was two-timing his mistress and wife simultaneously while location-shooting in Shimla.

Of course, nobody knew the names of behind-the-scenes professionals like cameramen, lighting crews, or the continuity person who made sure that the actress didn't change her clothes seven times for the same scene unless, of course, it was for a song sequence when it was mandatory to have costume changes at least fifty-eight times. The most invisible of the lot were the recording technicians. They were the faceless ones, the ones whose names moved so fast at the end of the movie credits, and were in a font size so tiny, no one got a chance to read them. Not that you would want to, either.

The technicians were delighted to see the overnight sensations called Ravan and Eddie (can you imagine more ridiculous names?), who in their eyes were nothing but dubious upstarts, flounder at every step. Call it luck, chance, fluke, the conjunctions of stars in the heavens, happy accident or what have you, the pair had had a freak hit. But the technical folks were willing to bet that they were one-film wonders and would be forgotten and buried when their second film was released. The jokers didn't know the most elementary facts about recording, sound levels, how to lay multiple tracks and layer the sound. The sound guys were delighted with every goof-up, error, misjudgement and mistake the pair made. It was proof, if any were needed, that their next film would be their last. No one would touch the duo ever again.

It didn't take long for the stories about Ravan and Eddie's technological ineptness to be embroidered and blown out of proportion. For the first time, news about the recording of songs spilled over not only into trade journals but even film gossip magazines. It was a lesson Eddie took to heart. As ClickClick Kapil had told them at the very beginning of their careers, their biggest asset was their sensitive ear. They had dog ears, they picked up fractional quarter-tone modulations that almost nobody could. Their learning and insights into what worked for them and how they wanted to approach each film came from a process of slow accretion rather than a study of theory or passed-down wisdom.

It was Eddie who grasped the potential for publicity in the stories about their gaffes and clangers that were doing the rounds. If the public loved news about Eddie and Ravan's blunders and boo-boos, who was Eddie to stint on them. He deliberately committed outlandish faux pas when he was in the company of the sound technicians and went overboard exaggerating his ignorance. He was a godsend to the film mags. They spiced up the stories with their own concoctions and the public lapped it up. The duo were now always in the news. They had broken another barrier. Thanks to Eddie, music directors and playback singers too had begun to get star billing.

5

'What should I do, Ravan?' Eddie asked Ravan as they sat on the low parapet on Marine Drive which kept the Arabian Sea at bay. 'I've finally found just the right lyrics for Belle to record her very first song. It's Asmaan's poem, 'The Crystal Ball'. But try as I might I can't compose the music for it.'

Eddie had never spoken about his break-up with Belle or what he planned to do now that she had been back for months. He had told her when she had returned from London with her new super-rich boyfriend Veerendra in tow that when the right lyrics came along, he would compose a song for her and that would be her debut in Hindi film music. The days had turned to weeks and the weeks to months and then suddenly Eddie had gone into a frenzy of activity and spent a week working on that one song but he didn't have much to show for it. He was trying too hard and the harder he tried, the more stilted and stale the music sounded. Believe it or not, the man had composed fifteen tunes, close to twenty-five was more like it, for just that song. He was restless, short-tempered and unhappy; he had the heebie-jeebies, he couldn't sleep, he was having a crisis of confidence and Ravan was worried that the man was on the brink of a nervous breakdown.

The musicians in the orchestra had nicknamed the second half of the musical duo R&E, 'Bindaas, koi-problem-nahi, Eddie'. They were right, Eddie didn't have a care in the world when Ravan and he turned up at the studio to record a song they had composed. He would bring a box of mithai and distribute it to every member of the orchestra or he would breeze in singing the song they were about to record at the top of his voice and everybody would be yelling '*Aur ek baar*, Eddie Sahab, *aur ek baar*; encore *ho jaye*,' and he would be only too happy to oblige. He was a hard taskmaster but he made work exciting and fun. The atmosphere in the studio where sometimes there were thirty-five to fifty musicians (for one operatic number there were a hundred and seven of them) was like a carnival. Eddie could put everybody at ease, crack a joke at his own expense, sit down with them and play the drums, the horn or the piano. He knew everybody by name, how many children they had and what they were doing. Baptisms, thread ceremonies, engagements, weddings, he attended them all. If anybody was in a spot of trouble, Eddie would quietly slip a fifty- or hundred-rupee note into his pocket.

'I was a fool to have told Belle that I wanted her to do a song for us. I'm sure I was trying to impress her, maybe make her realize what a hell of a guy I was. It was all about me and what she was missing out on.' It was Eddie's day for self-flagellation and there was no stopping him. 'Take my word for it, she's going to be one of the best singers in this country and in America. She deserves someone much better than me. I'll just call her and cancel the whole thing.' The next moment he had changed his tack. 'No. We can't let her down. You compose it, Ravan. You are the inspired one, I'm just a musical hack. I've been deluding myself all these years.'

Ravan had had enough of Eddie's tirade against himself.

'Sure I'll do it. I'll compose the music for Belle's song.'

'Oh God, I don't know how to thank you. You are the only friend I have. You're the best, Ravan, the very best.' Eddie's face brightened but Ravan interrupted him midway.

'Yeah, sure. I'm the best and the greatest. And I can do that song. That's not the problem. But you're forgetting what we offer. It's not Eddie or Ravan. It's Eddie and Ravan. That's the way we work, remember?'

'Why are you bringing that up? I'm having difficulty with this one song, that's all. And that's why I'm asking you to compose it. Is that so difficult?'

'No. But you've turned this song into some kind of do-or-die matter. And you're ensuring in advance that you will fail.'

'I don't want to hear all this bhashan from you. I want a solution, not a bloody lecture. Will you compose the song or not? Yes or no?'

'No ultimatums, Eddie. Let me finish what I started to say. If you fail with this song, you're going to psych yourself into believing that you're going to fail every song.'

'I thought you were my friend.'

'I am. And that's why I won't take the easy way out and I won't allow you to do it either.'

'What's that supposed to mean?' Eddie was screaming at Ravan now.

'Do you know what you've set your mind on? You want to write the greatest song ever written for Belle. Not just in film history. The greatest song in history, full stop. But you and I know better than that. There's no such thing. We compose songs for a particular character in a particular movie. At times it might be for a duet or maybe a choral song. But there is always a context. Do you remember what Sehgal Sahab told us? Never compose a song in a vacuum. He insisted we hear the full story, get intimate with all the main characters, get inside their heads. We must know what the character is thinking about and going through at that moment. Is there a crisis in her life, a dilemma? Is she standing at a fork in the road, agonizing over which one she will take? Has she fallen in love? Has she got out of a bad relationship and is she feeling free and exuberant? It's never about us, Eddie; it's about that man or woman on the screen and what his or her emotional state is at that time.'

'I know all that,' Eddie hissed but soon there was a change in his mood. All his hostility had drained out of him and he looked lost. 'What do you want me to do?'

'We're going to the Sabha Vyayamshala tomorrow early morning and we are going to work out till we are so exhausted, we won't be able to walk home, let alone think any more. The day after, we'll sit down and you will have a song for Suhanaa, the heroine for Sehgal Sahab's film.'

* * *

Ravan was right. Eddie was at his place two days later at 6 in the morning. Ravan pulled out the harmonium from under the bed and turned it towards his friend. Eddie's fingers ran over the octave quietly and he closed his eyes. For some reason, he decided not to use the harmonium on this first run.

When Eddie and Ravan were working on a song, Parvatibai hardly ever left the kitchen. But she came out today and stood silently leaning on the inner doorframe. It was such a haunting melody, it was like a prayer. Parvatibai sat down on the floor next to Eddie. Ravan shook his head and smiled. He knew that sometimes the finest compliment you can pay is to honour the work with silence. Eddie's voice and song seemed to linger in the air till finally Ravan stood up and got his long Indian transverse flute from the cupboard, placed it just a fraction away from his lower lip and softly, very softly improvised the opening bars that would waft in the main melody, and now Eddie paced the song differently as he accompanied Ravan on the harmonium and sang once again. The song would come in at various points in the film. Sometimes it would be a joyous number full of hope and light and self-assurance. At other times it could evoke an elegiac mood of muted yearning for the times that had gone by and could not be brought back. And then again it would recur throughout the film as Suhaana's theme song.

Parvatibai went into the kitchen, put a few smouldering coals in a stainless steel thali and dropped a few chillies and salt on it and exorcized the evil eye from both the young men.

Ravan spent the day composing the musical accompaniment while refining the melody and suggesting slight changes. Sehgal Sahab had dropped in on his way back from the day's shooting and they had played the taped song to him and he had said, 'Well, even if the movie fails, we'll recover the costs because of your music. Just record it and I'll shoot right away. We're running over budget.'

When Eddie and Ravan had finalized the full version, it was time to call Belle. Both the Coutinhos and the Pawars had phones now thanks to their mentor, Sehgal Sahab. Eddie called her from Ravan's house.

'I have a question for you, Belle?'

'Go ahead, shoot.'

'Just wanted to ask you whether you would care to record a song for us?'

There was silence at the other end and then she sounded miffed.

'You're pulling my leg.'

'Why would I? I'm talking about work. Would you like Ravan to confirm the news?'

'You and Ravan really want me to record a song for you? For a Hindi movie?'

'I thought I'd told you that when we had chai and bun-maska at the Light of Asia many moons ago.'

'I didn't believe you. I thought you were just being nice. And you know I hate "nice".'

'When do you want to hear it?'

'You tell me.'

'How about tonight?'

'I'm meeting Veerendra for dinner tonight. When are you planning to record it?'

'We don't have that much time.'

'When?'

'The day after tomorrow.'

Eddie didn't tell her that the deadline for the recording was long past and Prajapati Sehgal was getting anxious.

'I'll be there in half an hour.'

* * *

Ravan had spread a durrie on the terrace and placed four cushions on it and brought a chair for Belle just in case she came in a skirt and found it hard to sit on the floor. But Belle was in a salwar-kameez and made herself comfortable on the durrie. She noticed the fourth cushion and asked, 'Who is this for?'

'For Asmaan,' Eddie told her. 'This is her song; most of the lyrics for which we compose music are by her. She wanted to hear how we'd messed up her words and when we told her that we wanted you to sing it, she said she had to check out who this Belle is.'

'I've got enough food for more than six people. I know just how hungry you get, Eddie, and I didn't want you dipping into my plate since I am already starving. But where's Asmaan?'

'On her way from Bandra. Should be here any minute. She insisted we start.'

The moon was on the wane but it was a clear night and the breeze from across the Arabian Sea brought intimations of the approaching monsoons and the balmy scent of the rains. The lights in the CWD chawls were being switched off one by one and barring the noise of the thinning traffic and the occasional car horn, a restful quiet had begun to descend upon the place. Belle listened to Ravan as he explained Suhaana's state of mind and the mood of the song. When he had finished, Belle looked expectantly at Eddie. But there was not a sound out of him. The pain and bafflement of the years since Belle had stopped writing to him from London rushed past him like a speeding train whose brakes had stopped working. She had been his anchor and solace in all the years they had been together in Bombay. She had written to him again and again telling him how bored and depressed she was and how she would be back the moment he had saved enough to buy a tiny apartment in the suburbs. And then one day as if in the middle of a sentence, she'd disappeared. It was exactly like day and night, no twilight zone in between. What had gone wrong?

There was so much riding on the song for Eddie, but he could not unlock his tongue and it began to look as if Belle had made a mistake cancelling her dinner with Veerendra. She went over and sat next to Eddie and put her hand on his back. 'So much pain, Eddie, so much pain. If we want to survive we must dump it or we will go under.' Was she talking about Eddie or about herself, Ravan wasn't sure. His flute hit a deep, sombre note so full and meditative, it set Eddie free and now his voice was clear and limpid and it carried all the way to the horizon. He sang the fourth segment of the song.

It was Eddie's turn to look at Belle for a reaction but she appeared preoccupied and wouldn't meet his eyes. Her face had clouded over and she had withdrawn into herself. He knew then that Ravan and even Prajapati-ji had lied to him; Ravan because he didn't wish to discourage Eddie and Sehgal Sahab because he couldn't afford to wait any longer. Belle, he knew, wouldn't lie. Perhaps she couldn't because she didn't know how to fake it.

'Do you think,' Belle asked finally, 'I could hear another segment, something very different in mood?'

Eddie realized that Belle had changed. She could, as a matter of fact, fake it. It was clear she was merely stalling for time, trying to figure out how to tell him she didn't want to sing for him. Ravan could read Eddie's mind as if he was wired to it. Before his friend could react, Ravan piped up, 'May I sing "*Meray saath chal aye suraj, aye humsafar*" part, Eddie? I know you sing it so much better, but may I try my hand at it?' He laughed, a self-deprecating pure Ravan laugh. 'I want to impress Belle.'

Eddie shrugged his shoulders. Poor Ravan, trying so hard to shield his friend from the truth and heartache. Eddie could have told him not to waste his time or his voice. Asmaan waved to Belle from behind the open door of the terrace but put her index finger on her lips to signal that she wanted to listen quietly from behind the door.

Ravan's voice rang clear and crystal. And now finally Belle broke the ice.

'Some matches are made in heaven, at least that's what we're told. I've no idea where yours was made but the three of you,' she laughed, 'are a real pair. Maybe you're just one like the Trinity. All I can say is you were made for each other.'

It was while they were having dinner that Belle hesitantly said what had obviously been on her mind for some time.

'I think what you need is a real pro. Someone who understands the amazing nuances in the music and the weight of the words and the almost magical bonding of the lyrics with the music.'

'Why don't you just tell the truth,' Eddie blurted out, 'that you don't care for the song and that's why you don't want to sing it?'

Belle looked at him uncomprehendingly. 'Don't like which song?'

'Actually I think Belle is right,' Ravan butted in and caught her attention before Eddie could answer. 'That song really does demand a real pro. What was it that you said? You described it so well, the kind of singer who would have to understand all those qualities that make the song so special.' Eddie was about to interrupt Ravan but he didn't get a chance. 'That's the only reason why we came to you. We wanted someone new but every bit as professional and as steeped in music as you are.'

'I don't understand you. I thought you agreed with me.'

'You're right. I do agree with you.'

Asmaan came to Belle's rescue. 'What Ravan is trying to tell you is that the song was composed for you. Yes, with just you in mind. Because you can do things that the other singers who've been around can't. Or won't. If you recall, most of our composers have pushed the female voice to a stratospheric pitch till it borders on what can only be called dog-whistle shrill. If I have understood them right, our two friends wish to restore the full range of a woman's voice as it used to be with so many of our finest classical singers. From the kharj, that's the lower octave, to the topmost reaches. The Suhaana character, as you've seen, has a song that requires the full breadth of a woman's voice. It must have the power to hit the listener with gale-wind force but also to whisper intimacies; be soft, gentle, ebullient and happy, introspective and ironic. That's a tall order but they think you've got what it takes. What you want is a good night's rest. Because you have just one single day to rehearse a nine-and-a-half-minute song. You record the day after. I wish you luck. Make the most of it.'

* * *

'No, no compromises.' Belle reacted as if Eddie had made an indecent proposal. She had been practising the whole day and had come over to see Eddie and Ravan in the evening. 'All I'm asking for is a little more time. I know that the meter at the recording studio will start running at nine and the whole orchestra will be waiting for me.'

'Belle, stop, stop, stop. Will you listen to me for a minute? It took Ravan and me a full seven days to keep getting it wrong. And then by the morning of the eighth day, we'd got it right. And now you're told that you've got exactly twenty-four hours to get it right. That's totally unfair, I agree. But since the deadline for the recording cannot be shifted, I was trying to make life a little easier for you by simplifying a couple of the tricky bits.'

'I don't want it *easy*, Eddie. I want to get it *right* and to get it perfect. I don't know how you guys did it, it's seven different songs and yet it's the same song. But do you know what I'm beginning to understand about your work? It seems so deceptively simple but the more I try to get my teeth into it, I see how complex it is and how intricately interwoven and layered.'

Eddie pointed to Ravan. 'There's the culprit, the master of deception.'

Ravan looked shocked and made a face.

'He keeps working at it,' Eddie told her. 'Chipping away, peeling layer after layer till we are down to the absolute essentials, making it sound simple and easy while tying each loose end so that you can't make out where the thread begins and where it ends. It's all one piece, organically held together.'

'There's not a note in the whole composition I want to change. But do you know why I need a little more time? Because I don't want to merely reproduce the song like a parrot. I have to internalize it so that it's a Belle song, a song that is as much yours as it is mine.'

'How much time?' Ravan asked.

'Can we start tomorrow after lunch at two instead of nine?'

'Let me check with Prajapati-ji first and then with the studio.'

'Tell Sehgal Sahab, we'll keep our deadline. He'll have the tape in his hands the day after tomorrow morning.'

* * *

It was past 9 at night and they were only halfway through the recording. This was Belle's first time with these musicians and theirs with her and it took a while to understand each other's ways and to knit them into a tight, coherent unit and elicit the sound, timbre and tone that were unique to the group. In between the tea breaks, you could hear Belle talking to Veerendra on the public phone in the corridor even if you had no desire to eavesdrop. He must have been peeved at having to spend the third evening on his own for she was soothing, solicitous, motherly and patient.

You could almost hear him ask over and over again what time she would be back and her guarded answer, 'I can't say for sure what time I'll get home, sweetheart, but I will rush back the moment I'm through with the recording. I think you are going to love this song. I'm really so lucky to get such a terrific chance for my Hindi film debut.'

It was close to one and they had been making good progress. Everybody was exhausted but Ravan had ordered another round of masala chai and south Indian coffee. The liquid refreshments, the chocolate cake Eddie had ordered and the fact that only the last track was left, seemed to revive everyone's spirits and put them in good humour.

The musicians were sitting down for the final session and Eddie and Ravan were going over the final track with Belle when Veerendra walked in. 'Let's go.'

'Hey honey, what're you doing here?'

'Taking you home. You said you would be home by midnight and we'd go out dancing. It's one thirty now.'

'I miscalculated. These things take more time than one estimates. And then everybody was tired and so we took a break and our batteries are recharged and raring to go. One more hour, baby, just one more and I'll be with you. You go on ahead.'

'I'm taking you home.' He had got hold of her arm.

'This is the last song. We'll sail through it. Look, the orchestra's waiting for me.'

'They can wait till kingdom come. We're going straight to the Taj.'

'Veer, please let go of my arm.' She disengaged her arm. 'Listen to me. You go home. I'll finish the last bit and before you know it I'll be with you.'

'What're you doing here, Belle? This is just a Hindi film song like thousands of others. Bollywood produces nothing but trash. Everyone in the West laughs at the crap they dish out.' He pointed to Eddie and Ravan and shrugged his shoulders. 'And you certainly don't want to be with these ... these nobodies. You're going to cut a disc in LA. You're going to be an international star. You're going to be top of the pops.'

'They're my friends, Veer, good friends.'

'Do you have any idea where these guys come from? I checked, they are from the CWD Chawls.'

'What's that supposed to mean? We're both tired and will say things we'll regret later. Go home.'

'I am going home. And you are coming with me.' He had got hold of her arm again and was dragging her out.

'Stop it.'

Ravan stepped forward but Belle shook her head. Veerendra was nearly at the door when Belle whisked her arm away. 'Don't. Don't you ever do that again.'

Veerendra slammed the door of the studio and walked out.

Belle ran her hand over her dishevelled hair. Her throat had flushed scarlet and she glanced around, not registering her surroundings. She looked at Eddie and Ravan but she was not seeing them.

'What am I doing with this man? Sometimes one gives in to avoid a scene. But the more you give in the more the other person keeps demanding.' She smiled a wry smile way beyond her years.

Who was she was talking to, Eddie wondered.

6

Ravan looked at the envelope with a growing sense of panic. It was as if he was caught underwater and was trying desperately to come up for air but someone was holding him down. His chest was being steadily squeezed and he couldn't breathe. He had the feeling that he was caught in a time warp. He had regressed at least fifteen years if not more. Fortunately, he was certain it was a false alarm though he had to admit the handwriting was uncannily similar to that of a person who had plagued every moment of his adult life. A few years ago, his luck had turned and he had got the news that this man had met his just deserts and was no more. For once the gods had come to his rescue, never mind how belatedly, and like Eliza Doolittle from *My Fair Lady* he could have danced all night.

He read the first word and then the first sentence. That was enough to tell him that the incubus had perched comfortably on his neck and he could look forward once again to a lifetime of dread, terror and torment. But why was he pretending to be surprised when he had so clearly foreseen, almost from the very beginning, that Three Point One, that was the name of the letter writer, was his fate, destiny, nemesis or whatever you chose to call him.

> Talisman,
> This isn't a posthumous letter sent from my grave. Despite all my ill-wishers, enemies and so-called friends, I am very much alive. I don't have to make a mistake twice to learn a lesson. Once is enough. I learnt through the grapevine that the people who betrayed me in Bombay were unnerved to hear that I had got away. It took them time to locate me. Since then, they have been

gunning for me, knowing that I was bound to come after them some time or the other. They also knew what to expect once I got my hands on them. I will not merely subject them to the most prolonged torture and a very slow death but will destroy their entire extended families, however distant the relationship. So they recruited the seniormost personnel in the Bombay Police to hunt me down. But as I had told you in an earlier letter, if someone can be bought, rest assured, he can be re-bought. Clearly, if a person is for sale, his loyalty will always go to the highest bidder. I took care not only to buy all the top police officials but I recorded the monetary transactions on a hidden camera just in case one or all of them put themselves up for sale again or decided to play both sides. I had, I must admit, one particular advantage. I was the man on the spot.

In due time I located a suitable corpse and that hallowed institution which, I suspect, the Indian police invented, a fake encounter, was staged and I was declared dead. But here I am, writing to you in chaste Urdu. I am in good health and working overtime not merely to expand business but to get into new areas. I think I'd told you in my earlier letters that I took refuge with someone whose methods are, to say the least, primitive in the extreme, but who came to my rescue when I needed to become invisible. The most sensible decision he had made in his life was to link up with a father-and-son team of politicians who are members of Parliament and have a spotless reputation. If someone has the temerity to oppose the two leaders, they go out of their way to be attentive and fall in line but somehow or other, the obstreperous party tends to disappear.

In the good old days, my host here would have been called a dacoit and that would not have been a misnomer. But I can say without too much modesty that thanks to me he has gained enough polish now to have aspirations to being a politico himself. It has taken a long time but I have convinced him that the days of the brigand are numbered. I have impressed upon him the importance of moving away from his barbaric, uncouth ways and crossing over into legitimate areas of business. What is remarkable and even more valuable than the money to which he has given me free access, is the trust he has placed in me. I have been absolutely above board in all my dealings with him. When the two of us were in Delhi some months ago, I got him to shave his beard which had made him look like an ogre and then took him to a Raymond shop and bought him his first three-piece suit. You can't imagine how proud he was. He couldn't take his eyes off himself nor thank me enough. He has still to get rid of his ingrained village ways but I am sure given time, he will gain enough polish to pass off as the genuine article.

Mine has not been an altogether altruistic endeavour. I am the frontman in all his business dealings but I am also the brains and the prime mover behind them. The result is that I am seen as the face of the enterprise. This is not an unhappy outcome. My host treats me as his junior partner who has to report to him but the market sees things in a different light. When I return to my first mistress, Bombay, I will not come empty-handed. I will already have my finger in several pies. By that time he will realize who the boss is and who the junior partner.

I believe you had stopped making payments when you heard the news of my demise. I suggest you immediately make sure that you catch up with the backlog and just as important, don't forget to pay the interest.

May you never cross Allah. Or me.
Khuda Hafeez.

* * *

Ravan had never spoken about the writer of the letter, the mafia boss Bashir Akhtar, a.k.a. Three Point One, to anyone, not even to Pieta. One mistake, he had made just one mistake and had paid for it not once but more than a thousand times over. Frankly, he was no longer even sure if it was a mistake. Fairly early in his career as a taxi driver, he had picked up a passenger who it turned out was being chased by the police. Ravan had no idea when the man slipped out of the cab at a red traffic light. The next morning, Ravan had found a leather case stowed away in a corner under the front seat. There was a fat wad of thousand-rupee notes and a leather pouch with gold bricks in it.

The police had stopped his cab and even looked inside. Imagine what would have happened if they had found the briefcase. He would have been in jail instead of the passenger. A week passed and Ravan decided it was too late to hand the bag either to the police or the taxi union. What Ravan had needed as an aspiring actor was a brand-new wardrobe which would catapult him to the attention of the producers and directors. He borrowed a small sum, three thousand odd, from the briefcase to have two three-piece suits tailored. In the meantime, Pieta had hired his taxi to take her, of all the places, to Falkland Road, the red-light district. This was in the days when the Coutinhos, including Pieta, would not even acknowledge his presence on the planet. Ravan discovered way too late that Pieta had gone there to have an abortion. When she didn't come back and he went in search of her, she had been so badly mangled, she was barely breathing. But for the money the passenger had left behind, Ravan would not have been able to save her.

The day after the tailor delivered the suits, the passenger called at Ravan's place. He insisted that Ravan had abused his trust and as punishment, forced him to transport and deliver smuggled goods.

The underworld wars in the city were hotting up and Bashir Akhtar's own men had betrayed him. Ironically enough, it was Ravan who one morning inadvertently warned the Mafioso that the police had surrounded his building and were waiting to grab him. There was a bizarre fallout from all this. Three Point One began to think of Ravan as his lucky talisman. That was the beginning of his one-way unsigned correspondence with his delivery man. He used the 'talisman' as a confessor, a sounding board and most of all to philosophize about his profession and distil the wisdom of his experiences. Needless to say, the handwriting on the letter paper disappeared within minutes after it was exposed to air.

* * *

Five years would pass by, even ten, and yet Asmaan, Eddie and Ravan would not be able to grasp what transpired that day. It was a day like any other in Bombay, hot and humid and the flesh melting like chocolate in a child's sticky fingers. All the songs for *Trikon* had been recorded and filmed but Prajapati Sehgal's secretary called at seven one morning and asked them to come to Sehgal Sahab's residence in Bandra.

Sehgal Sahab and Asmaan were waiting for them at the wrought-iron gate of his bungalow.

'Where are we going?' Eddie asked Asmaan in a whisper as she sat sandwiched between him and Ravan at the back of Sehgal Sahab's Ambassador.

She shrugged her shoulders. 'You tell me.'

'Gulmohar Lane,' Sehgal Sahab instructed the driver.

They were climbing up Pali Hill now. At the junction of Gulmohar and Champakali, the car turned left, climbed two hundred metres and came to a halt at a large oblong, empty lot with a newly painted hoarding: 'Shivkripa Developers, *Dharti, Akaash, Avakash*'. A priest was lighting a fire and chanting Sanskrit shlokas. Prajapati raised his hand in greeting to the group of people standing around the smouldering embers and joined them. When the puja was over, a tall, middle-aged man in a paijama-kurta handed him an axe.

'Prajapati-ji,' he said, 'please do us the honour of breaking the earth for the new development. You were the first person to sign a contract with me when I was a nobody. You brought me luck and I have never looked back.'

Sehgal Sahab was not exactly a midget but he looked on the verge of keeling over as he raised the hefty wooden shaft with both hands. The sharp beak of solid steel went up and came down but barely made a dent in the earth. The developer gestured to one of the labourers to take over but Prajapati-ji was not about to give up that easily. The tool swooped down again and again till it had clawed and dislodged a few clods of dry dirt and then you heard the sharp sound of iron hitting rock.

Was Sehgal Sahab building a new house? But he already had one. And if he was building a second bungalow, why was his family not here? Besides, the plot was large enough to house a maharaja's palace, and if the elderly director had that kind of money, why was he unable to finance his new film all on his own?

'I keep forgetting that we are on a hill,' he said as he handed the axe to the host. 'I brought some friends of mine with me to witness my prowess as a pehelwan.' Prajapati laughed self-deprecatingly. 'The two gentlemen here may look like any average Bombayites but they work out daily and would have your most seasoned workers pinned to the ground in thirty seconds flat. They would have been the right choice for the ceremony today. But let me introduce them first. This is Asmaan Adamji. She doesn't pump iron but she can kill you with words. And that is Eddie Coutinho and to his right is Ravan Pawar. They are music composers who choreograph fights and dances on the side. And this here is my old friend, Harkishan Chaddha, of Shivkripa Developers.'

The builder welcomed the newcomers and opened a box of mithai and distributed it amongst the guests and workers. The whole ceremony had taken barely fifteen minutes but by then Prajapati Sehgal was already impatient to leave.

'Harkishan-ji, I'm sure you and your team want to get down to work. We will bid you alvida and wish you all the best.'

'Where are we going?' Eddie asked as they got into the car.

'To my office. I want to talk some business with you.'

* * *

'So, what do you think of the place?'

'Which place?' Ravan asked, bemused.

'What do you mean which place? The one we went to this morning.'

'We didn't think a thing except to wonder why you made us come all the way to Bandra to see you dig a two-and-a-half-centimetre hole,' Eddie countered.

'What about the view? After all, you were not at sea level, but on Pali Hill.'

'Yeah, sure. It felt like being on top of the Himalayas, freezing cold, except that we got roasted.'

'What if you were on the eleventh floor with a magnificent view of the Arabian sea?'

'We were on the ground floor, which is how high the building was.'

'Yes, but you are going to stay on the eleventh.'

The film director was beginning to look more and more smug as he saw Eddie and his companions get progressively more exasperated.

'Okay Sehgal-ji. Enough cloak and dagger stuff,' Asmaan said. 'Can we cut to the chase now? You didn't ask all three of us to troop down to Bandra and on to Pali Hill for the sheer joy of seeing us.'

'About time, I think, that the three of you moved out of your premises and got your own apartments.'

'What about the bungalow in Shimla, the yacht off Monte Carlo and the stash in the Swiss banks?' Asmaan asked.

'I'm in earnest. *Trikon* will be released in three more months, six at the most. I have no idea if the film will fly but you are on your way. And you're not likely to get such a good deal ever again. Let me lay it out for you. The three-bedroom flats will cost you seven lakhs each.' Prajapati unrolled a blueprint of the plans for the apartment. 'Here's the drawing-cum-dining room. As you can see it's pretty spacious. But the bedrooms are not mingy, either. The master bedroom can easily fit in one more bed, apart from the fact that there's enough cupboard space for a family of nine. One bedroom for the children and the guestroom could serve as your music room. All three bedrooms have attached bathrooms. But it's the light that will flood into all the rooms that is so marvellous. And the view of the sea will be nothing short of stunning. And lest I forget, take a look at the huge balcony.'

The three listeners were silent for some time.

'God knows you have been more than kind to all three of us,' Asmaan spoke softly. 'You saved Eddie and Ravan when they were in trouble. So the last thing I want to do is to sound ungrateful or rude. I don't wish to speak for Ravan and Eddie, but I fear all three of us face the same quandary. Forget seven lakhs, right now we won't be able to raise a lakh even if we pool our resources. So I'll take leave of you. Ravan and Eddie will have to speak for…' Eddie and Ravan were already standing up. 'I think they've already spoken.'

'Don't you think you owe it to me, and who knows, maybe even to yourselves, to hear me out if only because I'm twice your age and the elderly in our part of the world have managed to pull off the hoax that even though they are senile, they are sitting on a treasure trove of wisdom?'

They sat down unwillingly.

'Let me give you the full lowdown on the contract. You get the flats at a very special rate because, for some mysterious reason, Harkishan thinks that I bring him good luck. I have not bothered to ask him if I am auspicious for him, why can't I do myself a good turn and bring some good luck to my own ventures?

'Seven lakhs to be paid in ten instalments of seventy thousand rupees every three months. You make a down payment of twenty thousand within a week. The remaining fifty thousand you pay at the end of the first three months. You fail to pay on time, you lose your apartment. You will get your money back of course but only when the building is ready and all the apartments are sold. Remember, you will not get any interest on the money you have paid.'

'And how do we get hold of seventy thousand every three months for two-and-a-half years?'

'I will not sugar-coat the facts, Ravan. Two of your films will be released in the next three months. If they are super hits, especially the songs and the lyrics, you get to raise your fees. But if they're not, you head southwards. It's human to have ups and downs. I am afraid you are not allowed that luxury. I don't know how you will do it but you will have to make sure that whatever you touch turns to gold. I have one other suggestion. You've got seven films in the pipeline at the moment. Whoever pays you in advance, even if it's only half your normal fees, gets priority. That way you can make your quarterly payments.'

'If at all we buy an apartment, why would we want a three-bedroom place? A one-bedroom place would be more than enough for us.'

'No, it won't. You live with your parents. And Eddie with his mother, grandmother and sister. Asmaan has an even bigger family.

You will want them with you. Plus, you will soon have your own families. Now is the time to think right and make a one-time investment. I give you my word you will never regret it.'

'We've been gazing at the stars in the firmament. It's time to come down to earth,' Asmaan spoke for all of them. 'It's just too much of a pipedream and I can do without it. I have five sisters, a brother and a pair of parents, all of them jobless. The money disappears even before I get to check whether it's real or fake. Sometimes I think I was better off when I was an extra. It certainly paid better and more regularly than writing songs. Besides, don't forget the hidden costs. The registration fees will be substantial. Then the new home will have to be furnished and the kitchen will have to be set up. No, thank you.'

Eddie followed suit. 'There are still all those legal notices against us, and though three of the parties have agreed to a compromise, the rest are still hanging fire. And we keep bleeding every time the lawyers open their mouths or write a letter. All my life I've been told I spend what I don't have. Now I've lost my nerve and want to play it safe. The chawl is all I know. A few more years won't make a difference.'

'I want to say just one thing to all three of you. You've done your time. Now when it's time to break out, you are like those prisoners who are about to be released but prefer to stay in the safety of the jail for fear of the open world. Whatever decision you take, it's okay with me.'

There was nothing more to be said and slowly Asmaan, Eddie and Sehgal heaved themselves up.

'I think I will take a chance,' Ravan said. 'I'll buy the place.'

'You rat,' Eddie swore at his partner. 'I should have known better than to trust you. You did the same thing last time, you did exactly the opposite of what we had agreed to.'

Ravan didn't see the point of telling Eddie that he had not agreed to anything.

'Have you got a stash hidden some place?' Asmaan confronted Ravan. 'Have you thought the matter through or are you merely getting carried away? We all want to move to a better place but it's not such a bad idea to save first and then aspire to bigger things.'

'No, I can't say that I've looked at all the pros and cons but if we don't take a risk now, we never will.' Ravan could see that Asmaan knew that he was winging it. It had been a split-second decision taken at the very last minute. And he had only a vague idea why he might have been so rash and foolhardy. If there was one lesson being an extra had taught him, it was that tomorrow may come the day after, two years later or after you were dead. That's what being poor meant, you grabbed what you could while it was still there.

'That sounds highly laudable but what if you're being unrealistic and we end up failing?'

'There's a good chance of that.' Ravan smiled ruefully. 'But if the three of us are together, we might just pull it off. Besides as Sehgal-ji said we'll lose the interest but we'll get back whatever we've put in some time later.'

'You didn't even bother to ask us,' Eddie fumed.

'I thought my saying yes would make you rethink things.'

'You are getting bloody cocky, aren't you? You kept quiet right through the discussion and now you spring this bull on us. But we have no intention of changing our minds. So what are you going to do?'

'Keep trying to persuade you, I guess.'

7

Ravan looked down. Night was settling in and the pit was a dark cavernous hollow scooped out by a meteor or a glacier from the Ice Age. The building in which he had reserved the flat seemed to be going fourteen stories down instead of up. He climbed down the makeshift steps and stumbled against a dead mound and nearly fell to the jagged, rocky bottom.

'Watch out, you stupid fool. Can't you see where you're going?'

The voice was oddly familiar. 'No. I can't. It's a solid cube of darkness.'

'What are you doing here?' the man asked Ravan.

'I think that's a question I should be asking you, Eddie.'

'Oh, I was just visiting a cousin and wanted to take a break.'

'So you climbed down all the way to the bottom of the pit where the three buildings are supposed to come up.'

'Yes, it's too noisy up there.'

'You want to tell me what's going on?'

Eddie took a long time to answer. 'You think it's too late for Asmaan and me to change our minds and buy the flats?'

* * *

Eddie and Asmaan would have to pay a late fee of ten thousand rupees each but by the next three days they too had booked their apartments. Eddie had wanted all three of them to live in the same building. All Ravan's subtle manoeuvring and machinations to live separately and have a clandestine life with Pieta, it was obvious, were doomed. But he was lucky, Asmaan put her foot down.

'No, no, and no. No way.' Asmaan was, as was her wont, brutally down-to-earth. 'The two of you are in each other's hair constantly, sometimes eight to twelve hours a day. Live in the same building and you'll have found the ideal recipe for hating the sight of each other. As for me, I've had to live with five sisters, a brother and my parents all my life in one room. I'll do my duty by my family though I am not sure why it's my duty and not my brother Yaqub's. If we ever move into our own apartments, I'll send them cheques every month but I don't mind if I don't see them for the rest of my life. And while I love you both, I would like some privacy and I would like a life.'

'Oh, I thought we could all live in the same building,' Eddie said despondently, 'and none of us would ever be lonely for company.'

'You've got it wrong, Coutinho. I want to be left alone; I want to breathe my own air and not inhale the fetid farts and sweat and halitosis of the five hundred and sixty-seven residents in my chawl. If you're afraid of being lonely, Eddie, you better remain in your CWD Chawls where everything is public; sex, bonding and unbonding, murderous fights, happiness, sulking, exuberance, defecation, first love and the nineteen others that are bound to follow. I want to find out what it's like to be lonely. I want to taste this chimera, this fabulous creature called aloneness. I want to nuzzle up to it and make love to it seven times a day. Maybe I will tire of it someday but I would rather leap from the terrace of my new flat than go back to my chawl.'

'And what if I can't handle being alone in the new place?'

'Oh sweetheart, I will be there for you. All you have to do is call and I will take the next ride down in the lift and be with you. But let's not jump the gun. I'm going to be smart this time. I don't know how the two of you are going to play it but I'm not going to breathe a word about buying the apartment to my family. Do you know why? Because they'll jump down my throat and want the little money I save in their own pockets and I will never hear the end of how selfish I am. Besides, the place will be mine only if and when I pay the last instalment, which as we all know is a very iffy proposition.'

'Oh, I was already scheming about how to break the news to Belle and impress her. I can't keep a damn thing to myself and nearly always end up regretting it. What about you, Ravan? You planning to tell your mother?'

'I don't know, I'm having second thoughts. What if, as Asmaan says, we don't make the last instalment, or the second one for that matter? Maybe it's a good idea to wait and see how things work out.'

* * *

A long time ago when Ravan was starting out and had a brass band of his own, his very last client had predicted the limits of how far Ravan's talent and ambition would take him. The tip of your nose, he had said, that's how far you will go. Ravan hated the man but couldn't help admiring him for having got the measure of his missing self-confidence. Even after the songs from *Hulla Gulla* began to break records, a private space, a place of their own (two rooms plus kitchen and a bathroom and toilet attached, please) where Pieta and he could be by themselves was the outermost limit of his expectations. He would smile wryly and wonder what would happen if they ever realized their fantasy of moving into their own living quarters. Would the shock be too much for them? Would they just lie down and breathe their last, a beatific smile on their faces?

Ravan was a dog ceaselessly gnawing at a wound. Should he or shouldn't he tell Pieta about the reckless gamble he had taken? He had no idea how she would react. She came from a family that had once been landed gentry in Goa, very, very rich, but that was a long time ago and she herself was born in a chawl and, like Parvatibai, her mother too had had to work all hours to keep the family fed and clothed. More to the point, Pieta was by nature a circumspect person, especially since their first attempt to collect money towards buying a flat had failed. Would she be furious with him for not knowing his limits? The other possibility was worse. What if Pieta took off on a euphoric high only to discover that Ravan could not meet the payment schedule and the Pali Hill flat was nothing but a bad fantasy? One thing he was certain of: if that happened, she would sink into a terrible depression. Not only would that be the end of his relationship with her but it was unlikely that she would ever trust him again.

All Ravan's vacillation, however, had to take a back-seat because the most pressing concern at the moment was money. The financiers, distributors, the market and the media had been fairly cool before the release of Prajapati Sehgal's *Trikon.* They couldn't forget that his last four films with their heavy-handed social messages had bombed. But *Trikon* was a new kind of hybrid for Bollywood; the love triangle had been cast as a thriller and worked despite its strong feminist slant and social theme. By the third day after its release, it had taken off and word-of-mouth had done the rest. The music had done even better than *Hulla Gulla* and as always the repeat audiences came for the songs. At age sixty-seven, Prajapati Sehgal was once again hot property and Asmaan was already writing the screenplay for his next venture. Needless to say, Ravan and Eddie would get to score the music after the story and screenplay had been approved. But while it was universally acknowledged that they were amongst the top musical teams in the country at the time, only two production houses had given them an advance, and that too after cutting their fees to half the promised amount.

But, interestingly enough, they got offers from three younger directors who had the same thought: Who better to choreograph the dances than the very people who composed the songs and the music score? And since a few directors wanted their film to have a tight, coherent feel, they decided that the action sequences too would be designed by E&R. And of course they wanted all this finished in two months. Who were Ravan and Eddie to look a gift horse in the mouth? Eddie was still a member of the Sabha gym, the Vyayamshala. He practised there any time he was free while Ravan kept in shape and honed his skills in Mr Billimoria's tae kwon do academy. Eddie and Ravan rented the Sabha Vyayamshala from five to six in the mornings to choreograph the fight sequences and got down to the dance numbers after eight at night. The rest of the day was reserved for composing music.

What Ravan was discovering was that not letting Pieta in on his secret investment was having exactly the effect he was trying so desperately to avoid. He was losing her. She was getting more and more depressed since she was convinced that they were never going to have a place of their own. There was one query from her that made him cringe.

'Are you really working that hard,' Pieta asked him, 'or is it an excuse to avoid seeing me?'

What could Ravan say? That it was both? The worst part was that Pieta did not sound peeved or neglected. It certainly was not an accusation. In truth, it was nothing more than an observation and an admission of her culpability in being so low and unresponsive over the months. It was not that they didn't meet. Ravan made it a point to put aside time at least once or twice a week to be with her but however loath he might be to admit it, it was easier not to be with her than be with her.

'Just a few more months till we carve out a name and niche for ourselves and prove that we are not a one-shot musical miracle, I promise you, Pieta.'

By the end of the second year, the first eight instalments for the flat had been fully paid. That's when Ravan's troubles got totally out of control. You could draw a line right down the middle of Ravan and partition him and you would see the two diametrically opposed factions battling within. Curiously enough, the line fell exactly between day and night. He spent nights vowing to himself, come the next day he would spill the beans and let Pieta in on the secret about a building on Pali Hill called Akaash where he had booked an apartment for them. Maybe, just maybe it would work like a magic potion and the earlier effervescent and ebullient Pieta would be restored. The thought worked like the old Aspro ad films. First shot: Man winces theatrically with pain as he holds his forehead in his hand and groans. Second shot: man swallows a pill that's handed to him. Last shot: lo and behold; headache, cold, fever, all gone instantly. Man smiling ear to ear.

Daylight undid all the nocturnal optimism and resolve. Had he gone out of his mind, he wondered. There were still two more instalments to go. And anything but anything could happen in those six months. He had become the tennis ball between two unforgiving players who whipped him from one end of the court to the other and it seemed the volleying would never cease. As long as Pieta was not aware of it, it would not be calamitous if he did not make it to the finishing line. The money would be secure and, infinitely more important, he might still win her back.

When he deposited the second-last cheque in the Akaash account, the conflict escalated to breaking point. The schism within him got so vicious, there were times when he would rather have pulled the curtain down on the apartment. What was the point of it all? Why was he working so hard? Pieta was slipping right out of his hands and he had no idea how to hold on to her. All he thought about these days was money; he thought about it even when he was working on a song and he had little doubt you could hear the hankering and metallic sound of greed loud and clear when you played one of the R&E melodies. Somewhere along the way, everything he had fought for and prized seemed to have become meaningless.

* * *

Talisman,
I had said to you that I would complete the story of my teenage mistress some other time. The truth is, like most on-going stories, this one too will be finished only when one of us is no more.

One foolish man, the fabled 'other' woman or sautan and, as if that was not complication enough, she bore me a son. Did I know what a chain of calamities I was unleashing upon myself? Perhaps the question I should be asking is, would foreknowledge have changed anything? I doubt it. A man in the throes of a mad passion can see the consequences of his actions but will not forsake his madness. Barely three years after my marriage, I had two sons, the eldest who would be crowned heir apparent and head my empire after my death, and the second son by a woman who refused to be my wife.

It was not for want of asking her that she remained the 'other' woman. God knows I had asked her more often than I care to admit. In the beginning, she'd said she wanted a civil marriage, knowing full well that I would never agree to one. How would

I when the only legitimate form of sanctifying betrothal is by Islamic nikah? Besides, I knew what she would do were I to give in. She would seek a divorce the day after marriage and her lawyer would ask for a stupendous alimony. But she deliberately changed her tune more often than the days in the calendar. She said she did not care to be wife number two. At other times she insisted she did not wish to be unfair to my first wife and make her feel insecure. I had argued that there was no reason for my first wife to feel apprehensive since the Prophet himself had four wives. Besides, I would make sure that she was well looked after.

On other occasions she insisted that her independence was more important than her son's bastard legal status. She would not, no, she absolutely refused to change her religion; and come what may she would never permit her son to embrace Islam. In truth, there was only one religion for her. Hate. She hated me because I had made her pregnant. Because I would not allow her to abort my child waiting to be born. Most of all because I had ruined her ambition to become not merely an actress, but the first amongst stars. If she could have started life anew, she would have disowned her own son, left him on the steps of an orphanage and pretended she was a virgin. For that is what Indian cinema demands. If you want to be a heroine and stay a heroine, it did not matter how many abortions you had had, so long as you were not a mother.

She had various other ways of getting back at me for ruining her career prospects. She would not allow me to name my own son after the Prophet or by any other Muslim name. She chose the Hindu name with great care: Jagannath or Lord of the World. It was meant to be a slap in my face since for me there is only one God and his name is Allah. I insisted on calling him Mohammed but as the boy grew up under the tutelage of his mother, he responded only to Jagannath.

If I had had any sense of self-preservation, I would have poisoned her or ripped out her heart and fed it to the wild dogs who roam around Cuffe Parade at night and make it impossible to get any sleep even at 3 or 4 a.m. But in her defence, I have to say that she had a code of honour. She fought her own battles and would not stoop to going to a lawyer. She had one other remarkable quality: she had the patience of rocks, mountains and nature. Give it time, she believed, and everything would fall in place. Her most potent weapon against me was the son she had given me. He had come between her and her dreams and ambition. She couldn't bear the sight of the child. But here's the mystery, the more she detested him, the more he clung to her.

He was fixated on her. He still is, even though he's a grown-up young man now. He would do anything she asked of him. By anything, I mean absolutely anything. Does that surprise you? I hold my head in shame for I am no different. She would sleep with me once in three months, sometimes twice in a day and then refuse to share my bed for weeks. She invariably proved her point. Eden, yes paradise itself, would be a wilderness without her. It's curious how I end up talking about her when what is most on my mind is my son, the second one. Time and again I would ask myself what my relationship with the young man was. The truth is I still don't know.

When he was a child, he was shy and withdrawn. He looked so serious as he read the storybooks his mother bought him. When he was not reading, he was busy doing homework. I worried that he would turn out to be a bookworm and wanted him to play sports and be outdoors. He would acquiesce to my wishes but I could tell that his heart was not in it. I made it a point never to discriminate between him and my elder son. As a matter of fact, I might have erred on the side of indulgence, trying to compensate for the fact that he was not my legal heir. He was always respectful but respect is no substitute for affection. The little boy doted on his elder brother but since my wife disapproved of the 'bastard', as she made it a point to call him, it didn't help matters. Besides, my first son was older and at that age a younger brother is nothing but a drag. I tried to draw my little son out of his cocoon even though I was busy expanding and consolidating my business. I would take him to the beach or to a hill station for a holiday. I even remember seeing two or three Disney films with him. But it was not the same as staying in his mother's house which I rarely did since there was not much joy there.

You can imagine how happy I was when he chose to study law for I had hoped against hope that he would become a famous lawyer. Who should know better than I the value of a fine lawyer? I bought him a car and I prayed that, Insha Allah, he would become the Chief Justice of the Supreme Court.

Even before I left Bombay, the dynamic between my younger son and me, his older brother and his mother, was changing rapidly. I think what he must have instinctively sensed all along (I'm sure it has sunk deep into his consciousness by now) was that he was not part of the family the way my older boy was. I wanted to explain to him that the blame for this lay with his mother and not me since she refused to get married or let me adopt him. In the early years he was too young for me to talk to him about such matters. And now it's too late.

Some weeks ago my informants in Bombay told me that he'd given up the study of law and joined my rivals, the very people who betrayed me and took over the formidable business I had built. I have tried to phone him several times but he refuses to take my calls. I have talked to his mother and warned her about the dire consequences that must surely follow if he didn't forsake his new friends. She laughed and told me the fruit of the tree does not fall far from it.

I can't quite make up my mind about what hurts me more: do I grieve because he did not get his law degree, especially since he was but a month away from his final exams? Or is it because he has betrayed me? Fathers want their sons to be like them. The one ambition I've nursed, the one sleepless dream I have had every night, is that my sons will not follow in my footsteps. And what does my younger son do? He becomes my mirror image. He opts for the one line of business I would do anything to prevent him from joining. The young will do what they want and not heed wiser counsel. All that a father can do is to watch helplessly.

Why would he do this? Did his mother egg him on to take this path to avenge my having cheated her of her career? Or was the boy getting back at me for not being my first-born? It's human nature not only to seek answers to whys and wherefores but not to rest till we've assigned blame to someone or the other.

I don't know why but I keep thinking I have failed, Talisman. What hurts most, I ask myself, is it the loss of a son or the birth of a new and far more dangerous enemy? I can take care of the enemy without. Time, and time alone will decide whether the enemy within can defeat me. Don't underestimate the young man. He's my son in a way that the older boy can never be. He's smart, he's a fast learner and here's his great strength, he does not make the mistake of underestimating his enemy, either.

Khuda Hafeez

PS: I'm told you have started making payments again. That's sensible of you.

8

Had Ravan been fooling himself all these years thinking that he knew Eddie? What was he to make of Eddie's relationship with Belle? He could think of only two alternatives: Eddie was so much in love with Belle that her being in the same town and getting to see her once in a while was all the joy than he could bear. Or his friend was so devious, he hadn't once let on what devilish game plan he had in mind to win her back.

It wasn't that Eddie lacked for company. He was a natural; he could charm the skirts off any woman; no, there was no dearth of women … except none of them was Belle. But what if Eddie had got it all wrong and Belle was not interested in him? What if all she wanted was to be friends and nothing more? What if she was never going to be his? What then?

Actually, if the last encounter the musical duo had had that day with her friend Veer was anything to go by, Eddie was seriously delusional. Eddie and Ravan were discussing a choreographic assignment in Ravan's home when one of the neighbours' children knocked on the door. 'Someone down there wants to talk to you.'

It was Veer, standing by his vintage Bugatti.

'Come down both of you.' It was classic Veerendra Malaviya in alpha male mode. 'I want to talk to you.'

'You want to talk to us?' Eddie threw the question back at him with fake innocence.

'Yes.'

'In that case you should be the one coming up.'

'Don't act smart. I have never been to a slum before.'

'All the more reason to come up and complete your education. And it's called a chawl. It's a shade above a slum but not much.'

'I can't bear the stink here. Come down this minute, both of you.'

'I don't think it's a good idea.'

'You better. It's about Solange.'

Solange – that was the name Veer had chosen for Belle's international recordings.

Eddie and Ravan walked down. 'We're listening.'

'You are messing up Solange's career plans. I told you the first time we met at Volga's, I planned to launch her internationally; not be an invisible player in a small local pond.'

'Not that small a pond, more like the ocean. Indian record sales are often higher than the combined sales of American and British pop artists.'

'We leave this weekend for the States. We are in the last stages of negotiating with Virgin Records for a major contract. We'll sign the contract with whoever offers the best terms and settle down in the States. What you pay is not even small change. We don't need it. Besides, one of the stipulations of the contract, I'm sure, will be that she can't sing for anybody else.'

'Who's we, Belle or you?'

'What difference does it make? She and I are not only together but I'm her business manager and I take all decisions for her.'

'I don't know why I keep thinking that Belle's no longer a minor and can take good care of herself.'

'Okay, smartarse, either you play ball or I give you my word, I'll make sure neither of you gets any work anywhere in this country.'

'Is that a threat?'

'Just a statement of fact. Do you know who I am?'

'Now, why do I get the feeling that you are about to tell me whether we want to know or not.'

'My name's Veerendra Malaviya. Virat Malaviya's son. Just in case you don't know, we are the second-biggest name in industry in the country. You name it, we are in it. Cement, polyester, petroleum refineries, liquor, telephone cables, steel. We are also the biggest builders in the country. All this we've achieved in the last thirty years. We can make or break this economy. We've got every politician and police officer in our pocket.'

'Why don't you just say you are the mafia?'

'Wrong, the mafia too fits into our pocket.'

Veerendra was already sitting in the car and revving up the engine.

'There are two songs lined up for Belle,' Eddie told him, 'and I am certain there are more in the pipeline.'

'That's your problem, not hers.' He seemed to have second thoughts then. 'Look, I'll be fair to you both. Name your price. I'll not haggle and we'll be quits. Think about it and let me know.'

Veer, as Belle called him, revved the engine and the car did some macho sputtering and roared off, leaving the two friends disoriented and marooned in their own thoughts. Did Veer know that Eddie was not only Belle's former boyfriend but that she had been about to marry him a few years ago? What was clear was that Eddie and Ravan were for sale as far as Veer was concerned, but did he realize that he was also putting a price on his girlfriend? Ravan watched Eddie from the corner of his eye, worrying about what effect Belle's sudden departure would have on his friend's state of mind. Now that he thought back, he remembered that there had been talk of Belle signing a contract with one of the major record labels some time ago but she hadn't mentioned the subject again. And since she seemed to have settled down to a life in the city and was enjoying working with them and her new celebrity status as a playback singer in Bollywood, it had slipped Ravan's mind, and much more likely Eddie's too, that she might still want to go abroad and make a name for herself like Freddie Mercury.

* * *

Eddie and Ravan had finished recording with the eccentric but remarkably talented Rajan Kumar and were wrapping up for the day when Belle walked in.

'I'm sorry that Veer came over to tell you about the record companies wanting to meet us to sign a contract. I was supposed to break the news to you but he's like a child, he gets so excited he wants to share the good news with everybody.'

Didn't quite sound like wanting to share good news, Ravan thought, more like crowing about it and rubbing Eddie's nose in the dirt.

'I should have given you notice when you wanted me to record a couple of songs for you, but the foreign labels called to say they would like to finalize the contract next week.'

'Congratulations,' Eddie told her. 'This is fantastic; really very exciting news. Your voice is pure gold. They are going to love you. And you're going to love it there.'

'Oh Eddie, that coming from you means so much to me. Then you're not angry with me for leaving at such short notice?' Eddie shook his head. 'Thank you, thank you so much.'

* * *

'What do you mean she has left?' Asmaan asked when she found out that Belle was no longer in the country. 'You know damn well we chose her to be the voice for the heroine in *Sapno ka Raja*.'

'She's about to sign a contract with a major foreign record company. Her friend Veer seems to be in charge of her affairs.'

'And what about your affair with the lady? Where's that going?'

Perhaps the directness of the question threw Eddie off. He seemed to think it over for a while. 'Nowhere, I guess.'

'What did you have in mind, Coutinho, that you were all honey and roses when you saw her after she returned from England? You must have had some kind of powerful mojo to think you would get her back from the Malaviya scion.'

'I thought I had not one but three mojos going for me.'

'And what were they?'

Eddie switched on a killer bashful look and smiled. 'Me. Can you see anybody resisting my charms?'

'No contest.' Ravan nodded vigorously. 'No woman, whether nine or ninety, could keep her hands off you.'

'Number two?' Asmaan prodded Eddie.

'Belle's a born singer. I reckoned she would realize that no other music directors could use her voice and exploit her talent as we did.'

'Three?'

'I reckoned my biggest ally would be young and obnoxiously arrogant Veerendra Malaviya. I was willing to play the suitor in the wings till she saw the light and ran to me.'

'Big mistake. If you offered me the Malaviya millions, I would disown you this minute, never mind how obnoxious he may be. Besides he is rather sweet on her.'

'That's all there is to it. My mojos didn't stand a chance against his.'

'Who are you going to replace her with for the song? I can't see anybody at the moment who has the range she has.'

'Let's keep that song on hold as long as we can. Ravan and I will start looking around.'

* * *

'Where are we going?' Pieta asked as they got into the taxi. It had taken Ravan a quarter of an hour of cajoling to get her to come out with him.

'Oh, no place in particular.'

'I thought that's where we've been going ever since we got together.'

Careful, careful, Ravan warned himself. Change the subject and change tack before it's too late. He remembered the advice the mafia boss, Bashir Akhtar, a.k.a. Three Point One had given him on his very first day as a taxi driver in a previous incarnation. Cars have four or five gears, he had said. Life on the other hand has hundreds. Even the most complex and intractable situation can be retrieved from the brink if you change to the right gear. The trick was to know the precise gear for each situation. If only Ravan had the master key to all the gears needed to negotiate life. The whole of last year he had watched helplessly as Pieta withdrew into some opaque corner of her mind. It wasn't that she didn't put up a fight. She fought valiantly. Every now and then she would call him on the phone from her office and tease him that there was no escaping now; she had notified the office of the Registrar of Marriages and he was coming over in exactly six weeks to CWD Chawl Number 17. She would slip the ring on his finger and the noose around his neck. And then add after a minute, 'It's a life sentence, Ravan. No parole for good behaviour. And since you are a Hindu, you are stuck with me for seven lifetimes.'

At other times she would tell him he had lost his chance and wish him goodbye. She had found a sugar daddy who, unlike Ravan Pawar, genuinely appreciated her. He was going to buy her a Boeing 747, an island in Greece and build a seventy-two-storey mansion with a helipad on the terrace for her in Monte Carlo. She bought Ravan presents when it was not his birthday, tried every gimmick she knew to snap out of her black moods but over the months she had been steadily sinking into a state of hopelessness and had become uncommunicative. On both the good and bad days he feared that there was no getting her out of the dumps.

'What colour would you want for the curtains in our home?'

'Good try, Ravan, but I no longer want to live in dreamland. You have no idea how often I've played the game of house-house with myself. I know the colour of every wall in our apartment. I know the colours and designs of the hand-printed kalamkari bedcovers for our bed and the super-soft Egyptian cotton bed sheets over our mattress. I can tell you with my eyes blindfolded what crockery we will have for everyday use and the porcelain on our table when we entertain. But I no longer care to lie to myself. All it does is to give me grief. Our life's not going anywhere, Ravan. We belong to that no man's land called the middle class and, that too, the bottom rung. We're condemned to aspire to what we cannot have. Why did you tell the driver to take us to Bandra?'

'Come again.'

'Why did you tell the driver to take us to Bandra?'

'Because we hardly ever venture beyond the dargah at Haji Ali. We downtowners forget that the south of the city also has a north. Everybody's talking about a new restaurant in Bandra which is supposed to serve fine seafood. I've been so busy in the past few months, I thought let me take a break and we could check this place out.'

'Travel fifteen kilometres for a meal? That's a criminal waste.' Pieta saw Ravan's face and looked stricken. 'I'm so sorry, Ravan. I've lost the knack of enjoying myself. I no longer know how to take pleasure in simple things but what's worse, I've turned into a blight. The logic seems to be if I can't have fun, I won't let anybody else have it, either. I can't bear the kind of person I've become. But I'm going to try, try really hard to change and bring back joy in our lives.'

'Why don't you go easy on yourself? Who knows, the feisty Pieta of old times might just be round the corner.'

The taxi had come to a halt.

'Where's that fancy restaurant?'

'I think it's on the top floor.'

'That's an odd place to have a restaurant unless it's a revolving one like the one at the Ambassador Hotel in Churchgate.'

Ravan rang the bell at the door for a long time but there was no response. 'Maybe the bell doesn't work,' he said and pushed the door.

'How come there's no signage? What's the name of the place?'

'Oops, must be the wrong floor.' Ravan switched on the light. 'Maybe we should take a look at the view.'

'What are you doing, Ravan?' Pieta pulled him up sharply. 'This is somebody else's apartment and they'll catch us trespassing and hand us over to the police.'

Ravan was relieved that he had managed to dodge the question about the name of the place.

'I don't think this is a good idea.' Pieta kept shaking her head but Ravan pulled her in as he switched on the lights.

He opened the window of a large bedroom. The wind whooshed in like a feral animal and took a swipe at them with its grizzly paw.

'I'm leaving, Ravan. I don't want to be caught.'

'One more minute, that's all. Just look at the sunset. Then we'll call the lift and look for the restaurant.'

Pieta walked back reluctantly from the door. 'One minute, that's all.'

Ravan looked out of the window, clenching his fist to push back the memory of nearly losing the Pali Hill apartment. Not just him, but Asmaan and Eddie too couldn't make the last instalment. How he loathed the kernel of truth in clichés. All the acid in his stomach welled up at the thought of the slip between the cup and the lip. A fortnight before Eddie, Asmaan and he were to take possession of their apartments, one of the biggest production houses in the country, Prithvi Films, declared insolvency. Ravan was still twenty thousand short, Eddie twenty-five and Asmaan could only manage thirty-five out of the seventy. The three of them had gone trooping down to the accounts office of Prithvi Films for a week and every day they had been told they would be paid the next day. Now there was a big old-fashioned lock on the door with a tape and a red shellac High Court seal imprinted on it. A badly typed notice on cheap yellowing High Court-issue paper stuck to the door declared that the Prithvi offices were shut down under Section something-or-the-other. Whenever Asmaan or Ravan called the owner, Prakash Deewan's residential number, they were told that Deewan Sahab was in a meeting with bankers. The next day they landed up at the Deewan bungalow.

'You'll have to go to London to meet them,' the security guard told them. 'Sahab and his family left a week ago.'

'What nonsense. We were told Deewan Sahab was in a meeting as late as eleven last night.'

The Gurkha security guard laughed. 'If you call him again at the office now that's what you will be told all over again.'

'When will they come back?'

The man looked amused. 'Maybe next year. Maybe never.'

'What are you keeping guard here for then?'

'Where will I go till I find another job? At least I have a place to sleep here.'

They were running out of time. They had no option but to approach a bank for a temporary loan. They tried four different banks and assured the officers in charge that there was no problem with collateral. Their almost finished three-bedroom apartments in Pali Hill would be more than enough security against the loan. After all, they had paid all but one instalment and the loan would be just temporary, at the most for a couple of months. The officers listened patiently but as there was no fast track in the banks it would take a month-and-a-half to process their application papers and another month at least before they got the money in hand. They struck gold with their fifth attempt.

'E&R or R&E and Asmaan-ji in person and that too visiting my office. This is a red letter day for me. Imagine asking my family when I get home this evening to guess who came to see me today in my office? Never would it occur to them that it was the three of you.' The bank manager, Mr Samant, couldn't stop shaking their hands. 'I'm an ardent fan of yours. I know every song you have written, Asmaan-ji, very daring you are. And I can sing your songs blindfolded even if I am woken up in the middle of the night.'

Eddie started to tell him that you did not need eyes to remember a song, a good memory was enough but Asmaan stepped in hurriedly while slapping her friend on the shoulder, 'Isn't that fantastic, Eddie? He can remember our songs blindfolded.'

'Wow, that's amazing.' Eddie went overboard feigning astonishment. 'You must have X-ray vision like Superman.'

Asmaan was not quite sure what Eddie meant by that statement but she knew the symptoms and could see that Eddie was itching to get a rise out of the bank manager.

'Go ahead, test me.' The bank manager was on a roll. 'I mean it, test me. Don't be embarrassed. Ask. I'm waiting.'

'Manager Sahab, we came for some work. Actually to ask for a short-term loan.'

'Arré, I can give you a loan today, tomorrow or a month later, any time you ask. But first you test me. I am a breathing, living encyclopaedia on E&R and A. See what an apt acronym I have coined. ERA. You represent the beginning of a totally new era. Just ask me. Quote any line, first, sixth, last, I will recite the whole song with every note of the instrumental score.'

'How about *Big Fish Eat Small Fish*?' Ravan asked. All three of them were willing to listen to the man all day just so long as he gave them the money.

'Yes, I will. Just listen. Note how I pick up every nuance and improve your song. There's a lot you can learn from me.'

Just then the phone rang. Several 'Yes sirs' were followed by 'I'll be there right away'. He turned around deflated. 'My boss. Got to go. But I promise you we'll do this next time. I'll astound you. Now about your request for a loan. Fill in these forms. If you get all the papers and contracts of your agreements with the builders and if that is really enough collateral, I will pass the papers in four days flat. And you will have your loan.'

'Four days, not a day more, you are willing to give your word about that?'

'My word is worth its weight in gold. Make sure the agreements are on my desk tomorrow morning.'

They didn't wait for the next day. They brought the forms and the papers back that same day just to be on the safe side. Four days later, they were at the bank an hour before it opened.

The bank manager greeted them heartily.

'The early bird catches the worm. Your papers are ready.'

'And the cheques for the loan?' Ravan asked

'Everything in good time. Your papers have gone to the head office. Within a month-and-a-half, maybe even a month because of my special recommendation, you'll have your money and your apartment.'

One-and-a-half months. Maybe one. There was just one consolation for Ravan. It seemed more like a vindication. He understood then that if the loan had come through or if Prithvi Films had paid them their dues on time, he would have kept thinking what an ass he had been not to take Pieta into confidence. He looked at Asmaan and Eddie. He was sure there would be hell to pay; after all, it was he who had been instrumental in getting them to invest in the apartments despite their conviction that the risk factor was far too high. But they were still digesting the news.

'Let's call Prajapati-ji,' Asmaan said as they got out of the bank, 'and get it over with. Let's tell him the deal's off. All three apartments will have to revert to the builder.'

Prajapati-ji wasn't in the office and so they left a message with the secretary that since they could not make the last instalment, the apartments would be reverting to the builder.

'Amen,' Eddie intoned. 'Now I have a suggestion. Let's go to the Rendezvous at the Taj tonight and splurge.'

'What a good idea,' Asmaan seconded the proposal instantly. 'About time we celebrated something, never mind if it's a failure.'

They got back at two in the morning. Violet woke up and said to Eddie, 'Mr Sehgal was here after ten. He had gone to your friend's place downstairs and then he came up. He was surprised neither of you was at home. He left this envelope for you.'

The handwritten message on the note inside the envelope said: '12 per cent interest. Same as any bank loan.' Eddie met Ravan as he was coming up to see him. He had the same envelope.

* * *

However unwilling Pieta might have been to enter the apartment, she was mesmerized by the 70 mm view from the windows. The sun was like an exhausted child who refused to go to bed. It glowered as it resisted slithering down the abyss at the end of the ocean. Poised at the edge of the horizon, its huge orb rested like a lit balloon on the glittering waters. The large bedrooms looked out over the sea, and now, as they entered the L-shaped drawing-cum-dining room which had French windows the length of the exterior wall with a two-and-a half-foot-high transparent glass barrier and a wrought-iron grill on the outside, the flaming red rage had coloured the Arabian Sea like a bloodletting. Pieta stood transfixed, unable to move. The rapid transformation in the demeanour of the sun was astounding. It had become a nimbus, a numinous glow.

Ravan dipped into his pocket and slipped something into Pieta's hand.

'What's that?' she asked.

'The key to our apartment.'

* * *

'I don't get it. You hated this place all your life.' Eddie had a difficult time keeping his voice down. 'All the years we've been in CWD Chawl Number 17 you've wanted to move to an apartment which was airy, had lots of light, a lovely view, a room of your own with a toilet and bath attached. The new apartment has everything you want. A room of your own with a stunning view of the sea. Granna and Pieta will share a large bedroom. Why, Mom, why won't you come with me to your new home?'

'Your home. I'm so happy for you, Eddie. But my home is here.'

'You don't understand, you don't have to work any more. No more sewing to support the family. No more cooking. The servants will take care of everything. I will make enough for all of us.'

'Nothing to do all day, I'll go out of my mind with boredom.'

Eddie was nonplussed. He had no idea what other mothers did when their husbands or sons were out working.

'You'll have Granna for company. Soon we'll have a car and a driver. Once the car drops me at the recording studio, the driver can take you anywhere you want. How about that, Granna?'

'Just what I've been waiting for all these years.' Granna's eyes sparkled and she leered theatrically as she flipped the pork chops in the pan. 'Mother and daughter will cruise around town. What do you say, Violet?'

Violet made a face. 'You'll have to go on your own, Mother.'

'All right then, we'll buy you the latest electric sewing machine and you can set up your own tailoring business in Pali Hill. Lots of rich people there. Stars and producers and businessmen. Old and new money. Who knows, if the business takes off, you might start your own line of clothing and employ a dozen seamstresses.'

'I've spent all my life in this room. I would be lost anywhere else.'

Eddie had run out of arguments. It hadn't occurred to him that his mother would refuse to move. Was she still carrying on with her old vendetta? He looked around desperately for help.

'Granna, will you talk to her? Can you … can you make her see sense? How can I go to our new home without all of you?'

'Don't do this, Violet,' Granna spoke with some asperity. 'All these years you have berated Eddie for being a wastrel and a good-for-nothing. And yet silently you've always nursed the hope that he would do something worthwhile with his life, make a name for himself. He's done better than any of us or he himself had hoped. Now he's bought a flat, don't you want to share in his joy?'

'You go with him, Mamma. The two of you have always got along better. Pieta and I will stay here.'

* * *

It had to happen. It was a matter of time, that's all. The only question was how come Ravan and Pieta had got away for so long without being caught. 'You've redone your house?' Eddie's tone was accusatory.

'No, it was not done before,' Ravan corrected him, 'and there's still a lot to do.'

'Who bought these furnishings, bedcovers and curtains for you?'

'Please don't tell them but I stole them from the neighbours. Do you mind?'

'Okay, wise guy, you might have paid for them but I know your taste, Ravan. It's a shade worse than mine.'

'No, it's not.'

'Yes, it is. Do I have to remind you of the golden age of your Cum September Brass Band and its fantastic costumes designed by none other than the king of Sri Lanka. The spectrum has seven colours but you had managed to come up with twenty more and bunged them all in till you had begun to look like a V. Shantaram film set.'

'As if yours were any better.' Ravan tried to divert Eddie with a counterattack.

'I will be generous and not even mention how superior we were musically but fair's fair. My Bandra Bombshells were leagues ahead of your Cum September, Go September bandbaja in our dress sense.'

'Why do I keep remembering the gem of a sentence with which your one-time paramour, the B-grade star, the divine Ms Sapna-ji had greeted you? What was it she said? If I recall correctly she told you on your very first visit to her house, not studio, mind you, for a screen test at nine at night that you looked like a cheap birthday cake with horrid artificial colours from an Irani café.'

'Why, Ravan?' Eddie asked Ravan with a fake choked voice. 'Why would you remind me of that woman who took me for such an inglorious ride and then gifted me with the clap? Oh Ravan, I thought you were my friend.' Eddie sank to the floor. 'I guess we're even now.'

He was running his fingers through the fabric of the curtains. 'This has a woman's sureness of touch. It's not showy, it's real good taste. Who chose it for you? Out with it.'

Ravan knew he was caught and however much he tried to twist and turn and wriggle his way out, he was not going to succeed. But there was still much to be grateful for. He couldn't stop blessing all the gods whose names he could remember offhand for the simple fact that Pieta, who had chosen every single item starting from bath-mats, napkins and towels, to bed sheets, bed and cushion covers and who had got the kitchen running, was not at home just now.

Ravan tried to sound casual. 'Oh, nothing special. I went to the furnishing shop and there was someone like an interior decorator there who came over and took measurements and asked me a few questions and showed me samples of colours and fabrics and that was it.'

'You've seen the curtains I have on my windows. They are so boring, I can only bear to look at them with my eyes closed. But I can't work up the enthusiasm to go through hundreds of rolls of cloth and compare them and finally choose a couple.'

How come, Ravan thought, it did not occur to Eddie to turn to Pieta to guide him and help him furnish his place? Perhaps this was how a sister–brother relationship worked. You wouldn't dream of consulting a sister however smart she was.

'Actually, I was hoping to take Belle along with me. If only she was here. She has such fine taste, she would know exactly what would look good in which room.'

Belle. Now that was a minefield Ravan took great pains to skirt around.

* * *

Ravan was never one for tempting fate, especially when it came to treacherous matters like good fortune but even he was willing to grant, under duress of course, that he and his two friends had made good, and yet often it felt as if nothing had changed. Asmaan was getting to be a name not merely as a funny, ironic and cynical poet but as a writer of intense, romantic lyrics with a disturbing philosophical slant. And now she was also being recognized as a screenplay writer. Eddie and he were not doing badly on three fronts, music, dance and *de danadan fightum fighta* stunts. But there seemed to be some law of nature which did not permit one's personal life to run harmoniously with one's professional life.

Ravan had got his girl, he had got the apartment, and then everything had come to a standstill. Sooner or later, Eddie was bound to find out about him and Pieta and that would be the end of their friendship and musical partnership. He dared not think about 'What then?' As for Asmaan, she was unhappier than ever before. Ravan remembered how she had reacted when Eddie had suggested that all three of them live in the same building and on the same floor. She had instantly vetoed the idea. Eddie was still hankering for company, the company of one particular person, but Asmaan's own words had come to haunt her. 'I want to find out what it's like to be on my own. I want to taste this chimera, this fabulous creature called loneliness. I want to nuzzle up to it and make love to it seven times a day. Maybe I will tire of it someday but I would rather jump from the terrace of my new flat than go back to the chawls.' Well, she had better get ready to do just that, jump.

'It took all of three days for my youngest sister, Reshma, to knock on my door,' Asmaan told Ravan. 'She'd bought a small cardboard suitcase with her. Will you believe it, I'm still not familiar with that thing called the peephole. All I know is open doors till late in the night. And if you have as many people as we had in our place in the chawl, you left the doors open often at night too. If only I had looked through the peephole, I would have let my sister ring the bell for ever. "I can't, I just can't stay in that place," Reshma told me. "It's so noisy and crowded. I have to appear for my finals next month and

I need to study; study very hard if I am to get the best grades and become a pilot."

'"How did you find out where I was?" I asked and instantly realized what a foolish question that was. We both live in Bandra except that they are in the east and I in the west. Sooner or later someone or the other was bound to spot me in the bazaar or the railway station. Just my bad luck that in my case the house-warming party took place almost before I got the flat. "Oh, never mind." I attempted to put the best face on it. "Just tell me you haven't told anybody else."

'"Of course not." Reshma looked shocked that I should even suggest such a thing. And then added, "Except Zeenat, naturally." That's the fourth sister from the bottom. My sisters are better gossips than any extra but Zeenat, or Jeenat as mother calls her, is in a class of her own. "I had to," Reshma added virtuously, "otherwise, everybody would have landed up at the police chowki looking for me."

'How thoughtful of you, my dear, I wanted to tell her but that would have been pointless sarcasm. Besides, she would have taken it as a compliment. I didn't need to look into the tea leaves at the bottom of the cup to know that the deluge was about to commence. Zeenat and Jabeen are the ones that my parents had got married with a lot of fanfare just three years ago despite my virulent objections.'

'Oh, how come you didn't invite us for their marriages?' Ravan asked.

'Because they were getting married to much-married and divorced brothers. And because that was in a past life when we were junior artists and I thought my dear brother Yaqub, whom you had thrown for a spin in the air before he made a crash-landing inside Mehboob Studios, and his mother, who incidentally happens to be mine too, would not have taken too kindly to your presence.'

Ravan couldn't help smiling.

'No joking matter, Ravan, none at all. Zeenat and Jabeen were married to two brothers who talaqed them within a month of each other. They came home deflowered and disgraced. Since then my parents have been after them to go back to these dear men who cannot stop asking for further proofs of devotion in the form of more dowries. So then my two darling sisters, who claimed I was jealous of them when they got married before me, came over without so much as a by-your-leave to be given asylum in Avakash.'

How come, Ravan marvelled, Asmaan could speak off the cuff with such speed and articulation and make perfect sense without getting out of breath? How did she know so many words and how come they were always at her beck and call? At such times, she was like one of those slot machines from a Las Vegas casino in a film when some Hollywood heroine struck gold and the coins poured out dudhdhuddhuddhuddhuddhud.

There were times when Ravan was not sure whether the line between real life and soap was drawn in water. Just a fortnight ago, Asmaan, Eddie and he were off to meet a new producer when they spotted a taxi bursting with luggage turning into the driveway. There was a faint smile on Asmaan's face and she mimicked a child's lisp. 'Welcome, welcome. What a shame I won't be there to greet Mummy, and Pappy, and my beloved brother, Yaqub.'

Eddie and Ravan watched as Yaqub helped his mother to alight and then the two of them manoeuvred the paralytic father out of the cab.

'Did you know they were coming?' Eddie asked her.

'What an idea. Why would they tell me?'

'Do you want us to wait till you take them up to your place?'

'What for? My dear parents and Yaqub, not to mention my sisters and I, will be spending a lifetime together now.'

The next minute she was her old sparkling, chirpy self. 'Who should I move in with now? How about my two favourite bachelors? Shall I park my fabulous trousseau and butt in your flat in Dharti, Eddie? I hope your mother won't mind your living in sin with a not-so-devout Muslim, but Muslim nevertheless, or should I go hang out with Ravan? Else I could always go back to my room in the chawl. It must be lonely for company.'

Ravan wanted to scream and tell her to shut up, shut up, shut up. Both Eddie and he knew how hard she had had to work to get this place and what it meant to her. They couldn't meet her eyes but knew that a brittle caricature of a smile made of thin glass was still fixed on her face.

'Don't tell me that you are going to come to fisticuffs over who should marry me. I promise to stay fifteen days with Ravan and the next two weeks with you, Eddie.'

Ravan couldn't get over the stark contrast between Eddie's and his own family and that of Asmaan's. Parents lived with their sons, that was a given. And not just in the good old days. Even today, many orthodox parents would not so much as drink a glass of water at their daughter's home. This was all the more so amongst Muslim families. Violet and Parvatibai were freaks. They had been cussed, refusing to come and live with their sons. Asmaan's parents and brother, however, seemed to view things rather differently.

'Let's go,' Asmaan said and walked towards the taxi stand at the corner.

* * *

The bell, the accursed bell rang. Ravan knew who it was and knew it would keep ringing till he had said goodbye to this world. Unless he got up and opened the door. And he was damned if he was going to do that. He kept trying to persuade himself that sooner rather than later, Eddie was bound to realize he was not at home and leave. Or at the very least, it would finally register in his thick head that there were times when he was not wanted and would graciously depart. Ravan shook his head, he was deluding himself. Eddie was not going to take his hand off the bell till he opened the door. Then the bell stopped, oh the relief of it. But Eddie was yelling dementedly now. 'I know you are at home. I saw you drawing the curtains as I was coming over. And I checked with the security guard and he had not seen you leave.' The bell was ringing again. 'Are you okay, Ravan? You've been looking out of sorts of late. Have you passed out? Why don't you answer? I am going to knock the door down and come in. Just relax, Ravan.' He tried to sound calm. 'I'll be in in a minute and I can give you CPR. Lele Guruji taught that to us when I was a member of the Sabha and I haven't forgotten...'

The door opened a chink.

Eddie had retreated to the back of the corridor to get a flying start and kick the door open. He stopped mid-air.

'You are in there?' Eddie looked bemused. 'And alive?'

'Would you rather I was not?'

'Smartarse. Are you going to open the door and let me in?'

'I can't.'

'Why not?'

'It's complicated.'

'Why are you whispering? And what's complicated about my coming in?'

Ravan smiled sheepishly. 'There's someone here.'

'Good. I would be happy to meet the person.' Ravan would not budge from the door. 'Oh.' Eddie's eyes jumped out of their sockets. 'You mean you have company? Why, you rat, you chhupa Rustum, carrying on behind my back. Not bad, Ravan, not bad at all. When do I get to meet the lady?'

'She's shy. Very shy.'

'Not with you though, I can see that. Well, I guess you don't want me around. Have a good time.' Eddie walked to the lift, and suddenly turned around. 'I know who it is. It's the interior decorator.'

Ravan smiled mysteriously and closed the door. Pieta was waiting for him in the bedroom. 'No more, Ravan. I've been telling you since you moved into Akaash that we can't play this game of hide-and-seek forever. Besides, don't you want to get married?'

Ravan smiled bitterly. 'You want to get married. I want to get married. My mother asks me every day when you and I are getting married. But you know perfectly well what your mother's going to say – over my dead body. What are we going to do then?'

'May I remind you that you're getting married to me, Ravan, not to my mother. I'll try my best to persuade her.'

'And what if she says no?'

'Let *her* say it, not her proxy, Ravan Pawar. We'll take it from there.'

Ravan wanted to ask whether she had any idea about how her brother would take the news but thought the better of it. There had been drama and tension enough for the day.

'Promise me you will give me just a few weeks more.'

'Why? What will change within a few weeks?'

'Nothing. Maybe everything.'

'That sounds intriguingly cryptic but I know you, Ravan, you are just playing for time. I'll give you three months. That's the cut-off date. You got that? Not a week more; no, not a day more.'

9

The only reason Ravan wondered whether Mrs Meenakshi Venkatraman was snooty or suffered from acute shyness was because she lived on the fourteenth floor which was where both the Carnatic and north Indian classical music came from. It seemed impossible for her to make eye contact with anyone. Ravan would say 'good morning' or 'evening' to her if they happened to be together in the lift or lobby and she would either stare at the floor or at the vacant space on the right or left of his face and barely nod her head in acknowledgement. Her husband was the MD of some multinational company and seemed to spend half his time abroad. They had the whole top floor to themselves. He was always in a suit and tie and if you caught him in the morning, his forehead had the horizontal stripes of ash of a Shaivite. His vocabulary did not extend beyond ten words. 'What's up, Mr Pawar? How's the music business?' What would his response have been if Ravan had said 'Terrible'? Or 'Couldn't be worse'? But he too emulated the laconic speech of his neighbour and made do with 'No complaints'.

Mrs Meenakshi Venkatraman was always dressed in the most exquisite Kanjeevaram silks. She was fair and tall and had a dancer's easy, upright posture. She hardly ever wore make-up and did her best to be invisible but something about her made you turn around to look at her again. Maybe it was her intrusive silence which drew your attention to her; maybe it was the way her striking saris were draped that imbued the lady with a quality halfway between a dignified reserve and haughtiness; or perhaps it was her aristocratic bearing that did the trick.

Ravan had heard that she had three children. The older two were in the States while the daughter Sukanya was about to join Jai Hind College. On her good days, Sukanya Venkatraman would flash a smile but more often than not she behaved as if she didn't know him and seemed to wonder how he had the gall to be on the same planet as her.

Ravan had recently learnt on good authority, who else but Pieta, that the teens were a difficult time.

'Did you have a rough time?' he had asked. And she had countered with 'Did you?'

He had laughed and said, 'I don't think chawl dwellers are permitted the teens.'

'I did try to be sullen a few times,' Pieta told him, 'but realized quickly that if no one paid any attention, it's pointless to sulk.'

Mrs Venkatraman would wake Ravan up at 5.45 in the morning with a Surya stotra. Her voice would ascend magisterially to greet the arrival of the sun god in the purest enunciation of the ancient Sanskrit chant and she would follow it up with at least two-and-a-half hours of riyaaz. But he soon realized that she was not a reliable wake-up alarm clock, which was a little strange. Classical singers, especially those from the south, were creatures of habit and with good reason. A strict adherence to routine was an essential element of training. Mrs Venkatraman seemed to be highly disciplined and that made it difficult to understand why after seven or ten days she would alter her timings and start her practice sessions at 9.30 or 10 in the morning. Then suddenly she was back to her early-morning musical exercises.

Her voice had a haunting quality. You could not pin it down. It could be raw as an exposed nerve and the next moment intimate and playful. It had the deep, resonant timbre and rich texture which Ravan associated mostly with the Muslim tradition of classical singing. But what made Meenakshi Venkatraman stand out was the passion and rebellion behind that bitter-sweet voice. Ravan was loath to interpret the back story of a person by merely listening to her or him. But try as he might to ignore the depths of disappointment, despair, and the unsettling tragic undercurrents, all of them vehemently tamped down, he kept coming back to them.

She was obviously trained in Carnatic classical music and her taiyyari was so solid, she could whip in and out of the three octaves in one breath. After two or three hours of pure classical music, she sometimes turned to the canonical Urdu poets from the eighteenth and nineteenth centuries. She handled Ghalib and the other older ghazal writers with the same ease, feeling and understanding with which she essayed a complex raga composed by Tansen or one of the other great ancients. There was a level of comfort with Urdu which made Ravan think that she was from Hyderabad. That would explain why he thought that even though she was a Hindu, perhaps she had an ustad as a teacher and belonged to one of the Muslim gharanas.

* * *

'May I come up?' Asmaan called from the lobby phone. 'I won't stay long.'

'What if I want you to?'

She laughed, not very convincingly. 'See you.'

'You want to talk?' he asked her a few minutes after she had walked in.

'No.'

'You want to be left alone?'

'No.'

She paced up and down the drawing room.

'Hold me, Ravan, just hold me. I'm not trying to come on to you.'

He was about to say something smart-arsed but sensed this was not the time for it. Ravan held her tight in his arms. Asmaan was shaking. They stood there maybe five minutes; maybe less, maybe more. When she disengaged from his clasp, she sat down and started talking. It was as if she was in a trance. She was staring at Ravan but he was sure she was not aware of him. It was as if she could no longer hold back everything she had been suppressing.

'"What's going on?" I asked my mother when I returned from a script meeting. "Who moved my things?"

'"Beti, your older brother needs privacy. Soon he'll be getting married, you understand that, don't you? So I helped him take all your belongings out and put them carefully into the drawing room. It's a bigger room and you will have much more space and also you'll be with your dear sisters instead of being all alone."

'"My room was locked. Where did you get the key?" I asked.

'"That was no trouble," she told me. "Yaqub got a locksmith from the market."

'"Sit down, Ammi." I offered her a chair. "Are you comfortable?" My other sisters were pretending to be busy but I can assure you they were all ears. "Good. Now I have something to tell you. If you and your son or anybody else so much as opens my door even a centimetre, I will call the police and have the lot of you thrown out, bag and baggage. Don't for a moment think that I am making an idle threat. If Yaqub's clothes, shoes and all his other things which are in my room are not removed in the next ten minutes, I assure you I will fling them down from my window. And you and your other daughters will put every single thing that is mine back in my room. I didn't invite you or the rest of the family here. This flat is mine and in my name. I pay for it every single month. I've taken a lot of shit from you, your son, your husband and my sisters. Don't ever, ever take me for granted again."

'"How dare you talk like that to me?" She rushed towards me as if to slap me. "I am your mother," she screamed.

'"Shut up, you are no mother to me. You and everyone else is welcome to move out right now." She was still seething but something in the equation had changed.

'"What shall I tell Yaqub?"

'"How about trying the truth? He wants a room to himself and a wife, he could get a job and buy his own place. And lest I forget, let me have the duplicate key."

'She cursed the heavens for this ungrateful daughter who was no daughter of hers but a chudail. I had no problem with that so long as I got the key back.

'"I don't ever want to see your face. I'll just pack up and go back to my own home."

'"Good idea. But not before you give me that extra key."

'She slapped it into the palm of my hand. I opened the door to my room. "Get moving and do what I told you or move out."'

'Come into the kitchen,' Ravan told Asmaan. 'I'm going to make a "market" for you. It's a blend of tea and coffee that has a kick that no hooch can give you.'

Asmaan sat silently while Ravan prepared the concoction he had seen his mother make for him after he had driven a taxi all night and had shot the whole of the next day. He poured about a half litre of milk and ten teaspoons of sugar, make it a dozen, added two heaped teaspoons of tea leaves, cardamom, nutmeg and cloves while separately preparing south Indian filter coffee. When the coffee was ready, he added it to the tea and let it boil some more and then laced it with just a touch of chilli powder, poured it into a mug and placed it in front of Asmaan.

'What's it like?' Ravan enquired.

'What?'

'The drink?'

'Oh ... Vile,' she said. 'And utterly unforgiving. It's a satanic drink. Just the right thing for me.'

The nose which Asmaan's brother had broken some years ago had been straightened out but the pent-up rage kept boiling over and distorting her face.

'Do you know what I have dreamt of all my life since I was a child?'

Ravan shook his head.

'I'll tell you only if you promise not to laugh.'

Ravan pinched the skin over his Adam's apple. 'God promise.'

'You are already laughing at me.'

'I'm sorry. Tell me.'

'Of a bathtub. I had seen *Come September* or some other Rock Hudson and Gina Lollobrigida film in which she's buried under mountains of foam with just her head and feet showing. That's the kind of tub I aimed to get when I was flush with money. Maybe I would never really have been able to waste water that way after all those years of standing for hours at the communal tap. But just imagine having that bathtub and maybe once a year on my birthday soaking in the sheer, obscene luxury of it. I have longed for so much banal stuff, I could give Julie Andrews a run for her favourite things. Shall I tell you some of them?'

Ravan thought she was asking for his permission. She had no time for that.

'I have yearned, and how, for a single toilet all to myself so that I could take a crap without ten or fifteen people knocking on the door telling me to hurry up even before I had squatted and often the knocking got so urgent, I had to close shop, barely managing to wash my arse. Don't blush, you too have been through the same. I wanted to pee to my heart's content instead of always reminding myself not to drink too much water because then you can't control the faucet. I wanted to shave my armpits and legs without nicking myself in a dozen places and having to hide behind a makeshift, dirty curtain knowing all the time that one of my family was waiting impatiently for me to finish. I wanted to buy a full-length mirror with two side panels because all these years I had not seen my own body. I wanted to look at my boobs once in a while and find out whether they were sagging and needed propping up. I wanted to see the shape of my nipples in a mirror in broad daylight. I wanted to treat myself to a bikini wax and see myself in a thong. I wanted to wear a sari not by guesswork but taking my own time draping it the way I like to. I wanted to wear an expensive perfume like Paloma or Chanel Five without my sisters and Yaqub emptying the bottle before I could lay my hands on it. I wanted to lie down on a mattress without my sisters' legs thrown across me. I knew I would never own an apartment but that didn't stop me from indulging my third-rate imagination.

'Do you remember telling me that you keep touching every wall in your flat because you still can't believe that all that space is real? I'd promised myself that if I ever got myself a place in a high-rise with no other apartment looking into mine, I would wander naked with all the windows open just to prove to myself that the place was mine and mine alone. And now all I want is to go back to that room in the chawl and lock the door from inside and not answer even if there's a fire and the firemen are yelling at me to come out. Anything, absolutely anything to be away from my beloved family.'

Ravan looked at her a long time. 'May I ask you a question?'

'Ask two.'

'Why don't you throw them out?'

'The thought has crossed my mind; not once but many times. The problem is they will be back the next day.' She seemed to be lost in thought. 'I'm not being entirely honest, am I? There's another bigger problem. Actually, I'm beginning to think that it's an insurmountable problem. I believe there's some phrase to the effect that blood is thicker than water.'

'I would be happy if you moved into one of the rooms here.'

'That's generous of you, and I believe you mean it. But I'm not entirely blind, Ravan.'

'How do you mean?'

Asmaan laughed. 'Oh nothing. We might get on each other's nerves and that might just be the end of our friendship. I can't take that risk.'

It struck Ravan that Asmaan knew far more than she let on. She knew, he was sure now, about him and Pieta. How could he have been so naïve as to persuade himself that Asmaan hadn't figured things out? She was not only wise to the ways of the world, she saw through Eddie and him and she saw through her own stratagems and delusions. For all her rage and fury and her intense desire to be alone, she knew she would not be able to throw her family out, not even that brother of hers. They were parasites and they might suck her dry but foreknowledge did not always mean you were able to act in your own interest.

Ravan took the lift down with her.

'Where are you going?'

'Oh nowhere special. Just thought I would accompany you home.'

'That's thoughtful of you but I will have to learn to take care of myself.'

'And how will you do that if Yaqub assaults you?'

'Do you remember the Taser you bought to protect me … and my way of showing gratitude was to instantly knock you down with it?'

'You nearly killed me.'

Asmaan opened her handbag and showed him a similar gadget. 'I've bought a new compact model. If you like I can use you as target practice again.'

'That's generous of you but I'll pass.'

'Thanks, Ravan. Good night.'

When they got out of the lift, Ravan kept walking with her.

'I told you I'll handle this on my own.'

'I'm sure you can but I would rather sit on the stairs for a few minutes outside your place.'

Asmaan shrugged her shoulders. 'No drama please, Ravan. I have had my fill for the day.'

'I'm coming up for my peace of mind, not yours.'

'You can be so pig-headed, Ravan.'

* * *

Ravan had decided to sit for half an hour but he didn't have to wait that long.

He heard Yaqub's voice rising. 'How dare you throw my things out and ask Ammi-jaan to go home?'

There was a further altercation and then the door opened and Yaqub peered out.

'Hi.' Ravan greeted him jauntily. 'How's life?'

Yaqub slammed the door but Ravan's foot stopped it before it shut.

Asmaan sighed and shrugged her shoulders. 'I told him you were sitting here but he didn't believe me.'

'I'll still get you.' Yaqub turned to Asmaan. 'He won't be sitting here all his life.'

'He's right, Asmaan. Do you think I should work on him right now?'

'Nah. He's a reasonable man. He knows if he so much as lifts a finger against me, you and Eddie will want a private session with him.'

'You don't really want to upset me, Yaqub, do you? I suffer from high blood pressure and then I become unreasonable. Always a pleasure to meet you. Just holler and I'll be right over, Asmaan. Good night.'

* * *

Ravan's barely acknowledged acquaintance with Meenakshi Venkatraman would have continued at a tepid temperature for the rest of their lives but for the freak bout of rain that lasted for three days and flooded the city. He had finally bought a third-hand, maybe it was a seventh-hand, Fiat Padmini some weeks back and when the skies finally cleared, Ravan went to see his parents since all telephone lines were down and he had no idea how they had fared. He took Parvatibai shopping for groceries to the Byculla market and dropped her home when it started to pour again.

Ravan was past the petrol pump at the Turner Road traffic junction when he braked and reversed. A completely drenched woman was trying to flag a taxi desperately. When he rolled down the windowpane, his guess was confirmed. It was Mrs Venkatraman. Her car had obviously broken down and she looked exhausted. How long had she been waiting? Ravan got out, held the door open and said, 'Please get in.' He had thought she would refuse but she got in meekly. Her teeth were yammering away and Ravan reached for the blanket that he kept on the back seat in case the temperature in the recording studio turned icy cold.

Torrents of water were rushing down the hill and the traffic had snarled up. Hands clenched, Meenakshi Venkatraman stared straight ahead blindly. Ravan would have liked to ask her if she was okay, if he could do anything to make her comfortable, but her obdurate silence stonewalled him and would not allow any trespassers through. How could such quiet, Ravan asked himself, wear him down till, like her, he couldn't wait to drive into the Akaash compound and let her out? And yet there were at least a dozen-and-a-half questions he wanted to ask her. Did she give concerts? How come he hadn't heard her name before? Who was her guru? Why did she switch from riyaaz at dawn to a time later in the day? Was it because she believed in the classical theory that the full richness of a raga could only come through when it was sung at a particular time of day or night and only in the right season? He wanted to tell her that he had not heard anyone sing classical music with such passion, that there were times when he feared not just for her sanity but even his. The car hadn't yet come to a halt when she stepped out, leaving a trail of water on the seat and on the marble foyer, and, without waiting for him, took the lift up. It occurred to him that throughout the ride she had not said a word but had walked away with his blanket. Would she rather that he had not given her a lift?

10

Neither Jesus H. nor the devil himself could help poor Ravan as he jabbed at the button to summon the lift up but it was already on its way and he was hurtling down eleven storeys, skipping five or seven steps at a time, and all the while Eddie was hard on his heels just two floors behind him, a butcher's knife in hand, screaming like a pack of hyenas giving chase. Eddie had called just a couple of minutes before on the intercom from the lobby of Akaash. 'I've seen you, I've seen you with Pieta at Bandra station. You bastard, I'm coming up right now. You shit-face, to think I forgave you and trusted you. Let me get my hands on you. You've been carrying on with her God knows how long behind my back. You killed my father, you swine, and now you want to destroy my family. Mamma warned me but I didn't listen to her. I should have killed you, I should have killed you a long time ago and spared my mother. You are finished, Ravan, no more reprieves, no more pardons, no sir, no more amnesties. This is payback time. This is when you get your innards slung on the clothesline, your eyes gouged out, your balls chopped off, your thingumajig made into a Barbie doll's purse. This is the end, my friend, the very end.'

Ravan tried to put his scrambled brains back so he could come up with a quick escape plan but it was no use. How could he possibly face Eddie after what he had done? Stupid fool that he was, he should have jumped out from the eleventh floor. Too late now, he was on the second floor. Besides even if he had leapt out from his own balcony, knowing his luck, all he would have managed was to break his pinky or get his head stuck in a geranium pot. Decision time, he was on the ground floor. What should he do, oh God, what should he do?

Get into the car in the basement or…? Somebody had just paid off a taxi. It was swerving out of the gate when Ravan ran out and swung the rear door open and hung on to it, his feet dragging fifty, maybe a hundred metres. He couldn't hold on any longer, the skin on his knees and the flesh below had been scraped and shredded completely. He was about to let go when the traffic lights changed, and he was able to clamber in, his trousers torn and his shoes looking like plucked chickens.

Oh how could he have been so naive and hope to deceive Eddie. His erstwhile friend might have looked dreamy-eyed as if he were sleepwalking through everything he did but Ravan should have known the man didn't miss a damn trick. He was watching, always watching. He had eyes in the front, at the back, right down his flanks, his chest, maybe even on his butt and, like Shiva, one in his forehead. And like the great Destroyer, all he had to do was open the third eye to incinerate Ravan as they did every year at the Chowpatty beach at the end of the Dusshera festivities when the effigy of the ten-headed king of Lanka was set on fire symbolically to celebrate the victory of Ram over Ravan; of good over evil, of light over darkness. No symbolism here though, just the real thing.

* * *

Eddie had been searching for that viper-in-the-breast-of-the-Coutinho family for the past two days but the swine had vanished without a trace. Where could he have gone? How long could Ravan hide anyway? The weekend was almost over and they had a meeting on Monday morning with Asmaan to chalk out the music and dance numbers for the Filmfare Awards Night a month from now. Of the five films nominated for the best music score that year, two had music by them.

Whether they won or not, Eddie had decided he would grab the mike and tell the select audience of a thousand and five hundred people in the auditorium and the millions who would watch the programme on TV in their own homes, the whole contemptible history of his former partner, everything, yes everything, starting from the murders of his father and the Father of the Nation and how he had seduced his poor innocent sister and was still bent on destroying the Coutinho family. He hadn't made up his mind yet but he might just decide on the spur of the moment to slash and carve up Ravan in front of the TV cameras.

Sunday evening was when Eddie paid his weekly visit to his mother. No point getting there in daylight and being mobbed by all the would-be singers in Mazgaon and the rest of south Bombay. He had asked his mother and Granna to come to the awards night but not Pieta. He was going to have a talk with her, a very, very serious talk indeed. After all, he was the only man in the family. It was his duty to uphold the family honour and to make sure that the Coutinho name was not tarnished. He had read that in some parts of Pakistan and even India, they practised honour killings, bumped off the daughter, niece or sister who had brought shame on the family. Ravan might have done black magic on the Coutinhos but there was no getting away from the fact that Pieta had been at least a willing victim, if not an accomplice. She would have to pay for this unforgivable transgression, perhaps with her own life.

Violet, as her son had expected, had opted out by pleading that she would not be able to stand the tension of not knowing till the last minute whether her son would win the Filmfare Award or not, and anyway Hindi film music was not her cup of tea. Granna, on the other hand, had been more than game. She had even asked Eddie to buy her a flowing, ankle-length midnight-blue silk gown. 'My time has come,' she had told Eddie.

'Ma, I will not have talk of death in this house.' Violet had jumped down her mother's throat.

'Who's talking about death, Violet? Just getting ready to be spotted by those high-flying directors at the Filmfare function. Can't wait to land on the casting couch and ravish all those men.'

Violet had snorted, 'You are impossible, Mother.'

'You are just envious, Violet, that my name will be up in the marquee lights while you sit here gathering cobwebs in your hair, pedalling that sewing machine. You should have seen Sehgal Sahab making eyes at me when I was at Eddie's place last time. He told me he had spent his whole life looking for me. He wants to cast me as the first sixty-eight-year-old femme fatale in Hindi movies who will do a striptease and seduce the hero away from the anaemic, droopy heroine. They keep talking about anti-heroes. I am going to set a new trend. I am going to be the world's very first anti-heroine. Who knows I might even decide to get married again.'

Eddie had guffawed and hugged his grandmother. 'You are a scream, a real rock 'n' roll Granna.'

'Don't encourage her, Eddie,' Violet snapped at her son. 'She's disgusting.'

* * *

Pieta was not at home, she rarely was these days. It was over three months since Eddie had last seen her. As the VP of software development in her company, she travelled all over the country and occasionally even abroad. It had been something of a mystery, however, where she disappeared when she was in town but now he knew what exactly she was up to. Granna was making her legendary and patented ham sandwiches for Eddie. She made the most delicious ham sandwiches in the world. Come to think of it, her ham sandwiches were the closest that mankind had come to tasting manna. He must get Granna to make them for Ravan. It would teach him how superior Goan cuisine was to Maharashtrian food. Over a generously buttered slice of freshly baked pao, the light porous white bread which Goan Catholics had inherited from the Portuguese, Granna set adrift juicy honeyed ham shavings transparent as the warp and weft of a Chanderi sari, garnished them with a touch of mustard and a sprig or two of coriander plus mint and then, almost as an afterthought, laced the sandwich with a drop of ancient port. As you placed this mirage-morsel on your tongue, you were convinced you were having an orgasm but it was happening in your mouth. Before you knew it, it was gone and you could never say for sure if you had made it all up or it was for real until you had the next ham sandwich and the whole cycle repeated itself.

What was going on? Had he lost his marbles? How could he think of asking Granna to make sandwiches for Ravan when he was responsible for destroying the Coutinho family? Eddie was aghast that he could think of Granna's ham sandwiches when the honour of the Coutinho family was at stake. There was no question about it. Ravan had been doing black magic on the whole family.

* * *

Parvatibai had dispatched the evening meals to her clients and was washing the dishes. The sun was packing up for the day, lighting up her son's silhouette in the window. Ravan had got a maid to help his mother with the cooking and the cleaning but she had thrown her out within a month, saying she was more work than help. He didn't get to see Parvatibai often these days though she would have been the first to admit that that was her doing and not his. Ravan had wanted his mother to move in with him to his new apartment in Pali Hill but Parvatibai had been adamant. What would she do there apart from cooking for her son? Imagine her talking to his new neighbours in that fourteen-storeyed building. 'Na re, baba, I will die of boredom there.' Besides he had a girlfriend now though it was a big secret and Ravan had forbidden her from even mentioning the lady's name. Every now and then, Parvatibai would arch her right eyebrow as if pointing to the young woman living upstairs and ask pointedly, 'When? I can't wait forever. I would like to have a grandson soon.'

In her own undemonstrative fashion, she was proud that her son had made good. She remembered him as a child. He would clap his hands to his ears as she started singing '*Dil deke dekho*' or '*Khoya khoya chand*', and then a minute later beg her to stop singing altogether because she was tone-deaf. Imagine, he composed his own songs now and the whole country sang them. She had to be careful though not to break into one of their songs when Ravan or Eddie were around. Eddie was more polite and suffered silently. 'Have a heart, Mai. Spare us your singing,' Ravan would tell his mother. But Parvati would be in full flow and often ignored him just to see his reaction. 'Here, Mai. I'll pay you handsomely to refrain from entertaining us with your lovely voice. Do you want to be paid by the line for your silence or by the word?'

'By each letter of a word. Otherwise I will continue.'

'You are a mercenary blackmailing your own son.'

But there was no banter between mother and son today. Parvati had tried to draw him out, she had even attempted to sing, but he had been lost in his own thoughts. 'What's on your mind, son?'

'Nothing really, just thinking about work.'

'Have you had a tiff with your lady-friend?'

'No, nothing like that.'

Parvati knew there was no point probing further. When Ravan wished to be uncommunicative, a fire under his feet would not draw him out. Was this where he was born and spent the better part of his life, Ravan wondered as he looked out of his mother's window. It was uncanny, the first time he had returned home after moving to his new apartment in Akaash, he had nearly asked the taxi driver to turn around and drive back. Had he suffered from partial blindness since childhood? How else could he explain that he hadn't noticed in all the years he had lived here how shabby the CWD Chawls were? There was no paint on the walls and whole chunks of plaster had fallen off. The iron beams inside the buildings had corroded and were staining the ceilings the colour of Coca-Cola. The original buildings built by the British were rock-solid but the Bombay monsoons and the total absence of any but any upkeep or repairs had taken their toll. Half the CWD Chawls were propped up with thin wooden struts and one had to navigate around them to enter anyone's home.

For the past two days he had had to use the toilets at the end of the corridors. Of the four on their side, two were unusable since the cisterns did not work but when the queues were long in the mornings, people used them anyway. Ravan would have liked to drive back to his apartment on Pali Hill unwashed and unshat except that that was out of bounds for him. The gutters were overflowing and burbling, the lines for water at the public taps were much longer than they'd been just a couple of years ago, and the water supply was down by thirty per cent though the municipality refused to admit it.

Had he ever noticed that there was only one window in each home and it was in the kitchen, so it was always dark in the front room where his father's curled-up body would be lying on the sole bed facing the wall or he might be turning the pages of his compulsory daily reading, the trashy afternoon rag called *Bittambatmi*, as noisily as possible and then proceeding to mouth each letter like a child in pre-primary triumphantly forming a word. The word *Bittambatmi* meant every little bit of news but Parvatibai preferred to refer to it as 'everything, absolutely everything but the news'. There was almost no converse between father and son; not that it was any different between Parvatibai and her husband, either. Shankar-rao was always there in the room and yet he was really a father-in-absentia. He seemed to exist just beyond the margins of Ravan's consciousness. If his mother was not living here, he suspected he might have disowned the chawls and his past and claimed that he was from the Andaman Islands, Mexico or Melbourne. He knew he was deluding himself. If you stood directly under the light, you could escape your own shadow but there was no breaking free of your past.

He noticed he had become much more sensitive to the spiritual dimensions of decay, degeneration and disintegration since he had moved away. The chawls had begun to sag and droop in the last couple of years. It was as if they were demoralized and in the throes of despair. They had lost the will to make it to the next day and were merely waiting to breathe their last, but death kept playing hookey. The people who lived here seemed beyond hope and there was an air of abject resignation about them as if they did not think they deserved any better. They made babies just as compulsively as Asmaan's father and yet they were destiny's eunuchs. All anger, rebellion, and the cussed desire to break out had been scotched out of them at birth. It gave Ravan the creeps to think that he had been one of them just a few years ago. But what was even more scary was how deeply and quickly his soul had been corrupted by a little success, a pinch of fame, a car and a three-bedroom apartment on Pali Hill. Poverty was no longer a simple fact of life, a mere matter of the way you had been dealt your cards. It was the fall of man, the original sin. You held your head down and covered your genitalia the way Adam and Eve had after their eviction from paradise. He had wanted to disown his home today, who knows tomorrow it might be his friends and the day after his mother.

The only reason he kept coming back was because his mother and Pieta still lived here. But even if they left, he knew that at some point in time he would have to make his peace with the chawls. Otherwise, he must get lobotomized and erase all trace of memory, and with memory his music too would abandon him. What then would be left of him?

Ravan couldn't fathom how the CWD Chawls and the Sabha Gymnasium had shrunk as he had grown older. Was it merely a matter of perception? After all, concrete and stone and brick couldn't possibly contract. Had his mother too begun to grow smaller by the day? He must look at her carefully when she was not aware of it. Would she believe him if he told her that she was being steadily miniaturized? Would Pieta's Granna also turn into Thumbelina if she lived to be a hundred? And what about him? Would he too shrink like them? He would have liked to stand in front of a mirror and check his height. But his mother had still not got a full-length mirror at home. Maybe she was wise and understood that if there was no mirror, a person could never shrink. And what about Eddie? Did he look at the mirror every day and measure the minutest changes in himself? Ravan would never find out now. He had lost the only friend he had.

* * *

Granna was trying out the new dress in front of the full-length mirror while Eddie looked out of the kitchen window. He should have brought his portable tape recorder with him and played the new Led Zeppelin and Steely Dan. He was restless and couldn't sit still. He went over and asked Granna for the fourth time when she wanted the driver to pick her up for the Filmfare Awards function. When was his mother coming home? Damn it, didn't she know he was waiting for her? He had been so lonely, lost and bored these past couple of days he was willing to jump out of the window. He looked down and his heart leapt. Ravan. There was no mistaking it, that head peeping out under his own window was Ravan's. Oh, what a relief it was.

'Where the hell have you been, Ravan? I've been looking all over for you.'

Ravan tried to rotate his neck a full 180 degrees to get a glimpse of his friend but he had already pulled his head back. 'Arsehole, arsehole, arsehole,' Eddie kept swearing at himself as he smashed his head against the kitchen wall. How could he miss someone he hated so much?

'I'm coming down to kill you, Ravan,' he leaned over again and yelled but Ravan was no longer there.

'Where are you going, Eddie?' Granna asked as she saw him flash past in the full-length mirror but he was gone.

Eddie tore out of the house and skip-jumped down three floors. He skidded to a halt as he recalled there had been a man crouched on the landing right next to the Coutinho home. Smart trick, Ravan, very smart to park yourself where I would never expect you to be. You thought I would run out into the street after you and I almost did but I am not as stupid as you think. I will get you yet. Eddie retraced his steps, walking up softly on the balls of his feet. He couldn't believe his eyes. Ravan was still on his knees, his head bent forward as if waiting for the blade of the axe to come down. What jiggery-pokery was his devious little mind up to now? But Eddie was wise to him and none of his hokum was going to work any more.

'Get up.'

Ravan didn't move.

'I said get up.'

Ravan had either gone deaf or he was pretending that he had turned to stone. 'You dirty, lying bastard, to think I trusted you. I'm going to kill you, Ravan.'

'Do what you will. I deserve the very worst.'

'I'll tell you what I'm going to do.' That's when the first blow nearly knocked Ravan down. 'Do you really believe I am going to be impressed with this pathetic bit of acting? That I am going to buy this patently false act of contrition and let you go?' After that there was no stopping Eddie. He was hitting out wildly, knocking Ravan's head against the wall, missing his quarry half the time, slugging him in the chest, pulling his hair, slapping his face.

'Why don't you fight back, you wimp? Don't you have any self-respect? Be a man.' And all the while he was laying into Ravan, he knew that the sin of Cain would be upon him and he could never forgive himself. He was out of breath and swaying unsteadily as he chanted, 'I'm going to kill you, Ravan. You hear me, I'm going to kill you.'

'You do that,' Violet interrupted her son, 'and your sister's going to be a widow even before she gets married.'

Eddie stared uncomprehendingly at his mother while Ravan began to shake his head slowly as if disowning himself.

'What? What are you talking about?' Eddie's mouth had fallen open.

'Pieta's going to marry this man. You may not like it and I can't say I do either but she's made up her mind and neither you nor I can change it. Why are you shaking your head, Pawar? Are you now denying the woman who loves you?'

'She promised me she wouldn't tell you for at least another few weeks.'

'You better sort that out with her. Listen carefully, young man. All I know is that she's a good Catholic girl and doesn't care to live in sin with you. You take good care of my girl. Because if you don't, you will have to deal with me. I think you're aware that I don't forget and I don't forgive.'

Who was this woman, Eddie wondered. She couldn't possibly be his mother. It had been an article of faith since his childhood that Ravan was Satan, the devil incarnate. It was the founding myth of his family. And here was his mother telling him that his sister was going to marry the devil. Had she gone out of her mind? How could she have forgotten that this man had killed his father the day before their son Eddie was born, made her a widow and orphaned him and his sister? And if that was not unforgiveable, the man was a Hindu. What was wrong with his mother? How come she had not carved up her daughter's innards and hired the local mafia man to kill Ravan?

11

It was around a fortnight after their mute journey in the rains but the blanket had still not been returned. It was an old shawl, one Ravan had had since childhood and not very warm but he felt snug and cosy when he was wrapped in it. Ravan swore daily that he would go up to the top floor, stand outside the Venkatraman home and sing an ode to his shawl. No more postponing, he told himself. It's now or never. He suspected it was going to be the latter but he would not allow himself to admit it.

The bell rang. Since he knew there was only one person who would land up without calling first, he took his time to open the door. Mrs Venkatraman stretched out her hand to give him a brand-new shawl still in its pristine transparent plastic cover with '100% Pashmina' stamped on it. And an envelope with his name written in long hand.

'What's this?'

She smiled and pushed the shawl into his hands.

'No, Mrs Venkatraman. I couldn't possibly take this beautiful pashmina shawl.' Oh, what a fraud he was. Not bad, he thought, a pashmina in exchange for an old, ratty shawl. There were lots of battered old pots and pans in the kitchen. He wouldn't mind being gracious and obliging if she wanted to borrow them and replace them with new ones.

'Won't you come in?'

She shook her head and turned to go up the stairs. He followed her.

'In that case I'll have no option but to come up and return this lovely gift.'

She looked hurt. Again he couldn't avoid thinking she was expecting some kind of rejection.

'I, I beg your pardon. I didn't mean to be so rude. Please have a cup of tea with me. After all, we are neighbours. I'll make the tea in a jiffy and then you can go back home.'

What was the matter with him? He had really put his foot into it now. She looked stricken and seemed to be fighting some inner battle.

'Please.'

Her lips moved back and forth frantically, the hands curled into a mad pugilist's fists while her throat emitted an occasional choked sound but not a syllable came forth. She shut her eyes in a superhuman effort to swallow her rage and frustration while she kept trying to extrude some sound or word from her mouth.

He caught a glimpse of her climbing up the stairs as he entered his own home in a dudgeon, went to the kitchen and switched the kettle on. How could he have been so dumb? Not such a felicitous word that, in the context of what had transpired today. How come he hadn't cottoned on, despite all the pointers that had come his way that she was mute? How the hell was she going to talk if she had no voice box? How insensitive of him. He had meant to be friendly. Instead, he had merely ended up hurting her and alienating her for good. There was a problem though. If she was mute, who the hell had been singing all these months? He would not have been interested in her but for the music. Was it her daughter Sukanya who had that astounding voice? Even if she was a child prodigy, that kind of timbre, maturity and wide-ranging repertoire were impossible while you were still in your teens. There was only one other possibility: she was playing recorded music. A bit difficult, he thought, to believe that he couldn't tell the difference between a live performance and a tape. But how else was he to explain the music?

The electric kettle was whistling madly. Who was he making the tea for, she wasn't there and he didn't want any. He switched it off and went into the drawing room. Mrs Venkatraman was sitting on the sofa. What was he going to do? He had made such a fuss about asking her for tea and now that he knew that she wasn't going to say a word, or rather couldn't, he found that he had nothing to say to her either. Whatever stormy weather she had run into earlier, there was no longer any sign of it. She sat there serene as the Buddha. The pleats and pallu of the bottle-green Kanjeevaram glinted softly.

'I'll bring the tea in a minute. We have hand-me-down crockery till we save some money and buy something halfway decent.'

Why was he telling her all this? There was a faint smile on her face but nothing critical, just amused. He was going overboard trying to conceal how nervous he was and achieving the exact opposite result by revealing all. When he had finally served tea, he was about to dip a glucose biscuit in his cup but stopped himself just in time. This was absurd, why was he behaving like a teenager?

'I'm sure you'll find the tea thick enough to float on but I don't know how to make your kind of watery Western tea.'

Not bad, Ravan, not bad at all, he thought. Go right ahead, put all your seventeen hundred feet into your mouth. How the hell did he jump to the conclusion that they drank watery Western tea in their home? Maybe they didn't drink tea at all. And that marvellous choice of words. Not 'light' but 'watery Western tea'. What was the name of that Dale Carnegie book which Pieta detested and was in every Wheeler Book Shop at the railway stations? *How to Win Friends and Influence People.* He would write the antidote to it. *How to Lose Friends and Make Enemies Instantly.*

She was making faces again. Or rather her jaw and lips were twisting and contorting while her eyes squinted and hiccupping sounds escaped her mouth. Had something got stuck in her throat? Was she suffocating? He was about to ask if she wanted a glass of water but she was emitting a stream of broken nnnnnnnnnnnnnnns.

'Now you know,' she said.

The ceiling was swinging wildly. Ravan had to hold on to his chair to prevent himself from falling over. No, he didn't know, he wanted to scream out loud, he didn't know a damn thing any more. What was she doing to him? What kind of tricks was she up to? Why was she messing with his mind? He was sure she was indulging in some kind of voodoo. What a bloody fool he was, he couldn't see what was staring him in the face all these days, weeks really. She was not mute and her voice box was fine. She just had a very serious stammer.

That was it. He clammed up. There was nothing, absolutely nothing he could think of saying after having made such a royal ass of himself. The silence between them sagged like those cables that stretched from electric tower to tower on the way to Pune. She didn't seem to mind it but he was getting more and more agitated. Within minutes, maybe it was even less than that, he had worked himself into such a tizzy, he felt thc quiet was choking him.

He went into his music room and fetched his tanpura. It took a minute to tune it. He closed his eyes, strummed the fretless strings and struck a sombre basso profundo note. And suddenly the past was with him. His first guru, Navare, was a trumpet player in a brass wedding band. It was as tuneless and dismal an ensemble as any other wedding band in the city but Navare, who smoked bidis and whose lungs whistled and wheezed with asthma continually, knew his north Indian classical music. Hansadhwani was the fourth raga he had taught Ravan. Even more than the average traditional guru, Navare was a cantankerous old man with a nasty tongue and would have made certain that Ravan did not progress beyond the first raga till he was dead and gone ('he' as in Ravan and not Navare) but for the fact that weddings demanded a variety of film songs in those days, many of them based on ragas. That was how Ravan learnt at least a dozen ragas.

There was a reason why Ravan chose '*Laagi lagan pati sakhi sang*'. He knew he couldn't attempt any of the major ragas which could take around an hour to do justice to them. More to the point, while he might know the fundamentals, he wouldn't be able to sustain a raga for more than fifteen minutes. If he had understood his first guru correctly, Hansadhwani would always be a short but sweet raga. He was in no hurry and he certainly did know his Hansadhwani. '*Laagi lagan pati sakhi sang*' lasted just a few seconds beyond ten minutes, but Ravan dovetailed into '*Vatapi Ganapatim*', the Hansadhwani from the Carnatic classical musical stream, without taking a break.

So far, Mrs Venkatraman had listened to his recital quietly. From the corner of his eyes he could see her mouth fall open in surprise. A smile broke on her face and seemed to linger there. She joined in and slipped into his '*Vatapi Ganapatim*'. He let go. She was the lead singer now and he was merely following her. Gradually, all his confusion seemed to disperse and he felt at peace with himself. He would follow her wherever her voice took him. There was something comforting about being with her. He had the oddest feeling that she would protect him from all musical blunders and that seemed to set him free.

And then suddenly it hit him. Where did the stammer go when she was singing? She was utterly at ease and there was nothing diffident or tentative about the way she handled a raga or its elaboration. She was in her element when she was up there flying solo, especially when she was improvising within the framework of the north Indian classical spectrum. No inhibitions, no boundaries, the whole of the sky was hers to explore. She was as much at home with Carnatic and north Indian classical music as she was with the lighter forms like the tappa, hori, thumri, dadra, jhoola and the ghazal.

'I had no idea you could sing so well. Wh-wh-wh-wh-where did you learn "*Vatapi Ganapatim*"?'

Ravan smiled guiltily like a schoolboy caught copying. 'I'm a parrot, Mrs Venkatraman.'

'P-p-p-p-p-p-p-parrots too learn from someone else.' She laughed. 'No, seriously. Y-y-y-y-y-y-y-y-y-y-y-you must have had a good teacher – your p-p-p-p-pronunciation is almost like that of a cultured native speaker. You mispronounced only two words and got the stress wrong on one.'

'I have a very good teacher. She lives upstairs.'

Mrs Venkatraman was about to brush off his answer when something about his tone made her change her mind.

'You recorded me?'

Ravan shook his head.

'Th-th-th-th-th-then how?'

'We couldn't even afford a radio at home. The only music I heard was when someone in my chawl or the paanwala outside the compound was playing Radio Ceylon or later on, Vividh Bharati. I had no option but to develop my musical memory and absorb every word, every harkat in one go since there was no knowing when I would get to hear the song again.'

She looked at Ravan in wonderment. 'Th-th-th-that's an amazing story. You have nearly total recall in music.'

Ravan laughed. 'Nothing special, just force of circumstances.'

'A l-l-little more than that, I would think. R&E is one of the most p-p-p-popular musical teams in the country. My d-d-d-d-daughter Sukanya plays your music all the time in her room.'

'You'll be surprised how often I feel I fall short. Whatever kind of songs we compose, they would be the better if I had mastered at least one sort of music. I used to be in a brass wedding band. My bandmaster was a good but erratic teacher for a little over a year-and-a-half. I even had a brass band of my own later.'

'I-i-i-i-i-i-i can't help wondering h-h-h-h-h-how far you would have gone if you had trained systematically under a real teacher.'

'I could still do that, couldn't I?'

* * *

Talisman,

There have been major developments and I have to confess that I am a divided soul. It is the proudest moment of my life and it simultaneously poses the greatest threat to me and everything that I have been working towards all these years in the wilderness. Should I rejoice or arm myself and wage a battle to the death? Or should I be wise, abandon all thought of returning to my city and migrate to Abu Dhabi or Dubai?

The underworld, as it's called by the media, has been in a turmoil for the past nine months. It is my younger son, the one who carries not my surname but that of his Hindu mother, who is responsible for changing the power equation in the city. It is ironic that I don't detect an iota of myself in my older son but can see the bloodline so clearly in the younger one. With what finesse he has taken over as the second-in-command of my arch-rival. There is no mistaking whose son he is.

One of his first moves was to ruthlessly eliminate all those who had betrayed me. He convinced his boss that once a traitor, always a traitor. He was, he said, making sure that the hierarchy in his new home would be safer with the elimination of these blackguards. That may be so but I know that he was avenging the terrible betrayal that his father had suffered at their hands. And in the bargain also safeguarding his own future.

If I were the boss of my enemy's forces, I would beware of this young man. He's ambitious, he's wily and he does not take any chances. He does his homework, calculates the risks and strikes only when he is sure of vanquishing the enemy. He will bide his time but it will not be long before he takes over as the supremo.

Has the phrase 'caught on the horns of a dilemma' ever been more meaningful than as it applies to me at the moment? All I can say is that I wish my son the very best and yet hope that when the time comes, as it surely will, I will not be found wanting as the final authority to whom all owe allegiance.

Do the right thing by me, Talisman, or you will live only to regret it.

Khuda Hafeez.

* * *

It took a couple of months for Mrs Venkatraman to capitulate but Ravan was persistent and finally his upstairs neighbour agreed to give him lessons through cassettes which she recorded at home. Ravan thought he was making good progress when close to ten weeks after the tape-recorded tuitions started, his teacher turned up at his door. She did not have to speak for Ravan to know that this was the end of his music classes.

She was reluctant to come in but Ravan guessed that she would rather be inside his home as she prefaced everything she said with prolonged bouts of stuttering and stammering. He showed her into the drawing room and quickly disappeared into the kitchen to make sure that she would not refuse a cup of coffee. Truth to tell, he hoped to delay hearing the bad news. But obviously she preferred to come clean as fast as possible.

'Tea or coffee? Or would you prefer—'

'This is not working,' she cut in. Wow, Ravan almost said that word aloud. She's got rid of her stammer.

'What's not working? The tea or coffee?'

'The-the-the-the-the-the, the lessons.'

'Why? Have I been making too many mistakes? I assure you I try to do my best. But I will work harder.'

'The fault is mine.'

Where was this coming from? Was she merely being diplomatic to make the medicine more palatable?

'Wh-wh-wh-wh-wh-what is happening is that you feel constrained to get it just right. Which means you are concentrating all your energies on being a copycat. You're afraid to try out anything that strikes you on the spur of the moment for fear that I will be displeased if you get something wrong. I-I-I-I-I-I've heard you when you're c-c-c-c-c-c-composing at home. You take all kinds of risks, you even deliberately go borderline off-key to get the emotion right. But all you are concerned with when you are recording for me is getting the syntax and grammar perfect. That won't just kill the raga, it will end up k-k-k-k-killing your love of music.'

Might as well bell the cat, Ravan thought. 'Am I to understand you won't teach me any longer?'

'I don't recall saying that. I will be coming over whenever both of us are free if that's okay with you and your wife Pieta.'

When his teacher left, he did a silent, jubilant dance, maybe it was a harvest-cum-monsoons-cum-praise-every-Hindu god, African-cum-Maori-cum-Amerindian-cum-Russian gratitude dance and when Pieta came back home that evening he made love to her over and over again.

* * *

The pressure to meet the deadline was intense and the singer, Urvashi, was a bundle of nerves while singing the femme fatale's song, '*Suraj ko chhupa do/ Mera saajan ghar aaya/ Raat kabhi na beetey/ Piya ka saath kabhi na chhute*'. She insisted that the music for the antara came in a note too late when the problem lay with her. The song suddenly took a steep and abrupt dip and shot back just as fast but so far she hadn't managed to change gears quickly enough. Eddie knew she could do it but it would require time and that was definitely in short supply today.

'Let's make it a duet and sing it together,' Eddie whispered to Urvashi. 'You hate me, remember? The mafia boss has sent you to make sure that you seduce me so that one of his men can bump me off. But then something strange happens. Fate reverses the order of things and you fall in love with me. Madly, irresistibly and uncontrollably in love. So much so that you are willing to disobey your boss and risk dying to be with me. But there's a problem. I can only spend one night with you. As the sky lights up, I must leave you because that's when the boss's hit-men will come to kill me. The sun then is the villain. When it comes up, I will have no option but to make my escape. One night is all that we have and we must make the most of it. Which is why, as the song says, you want someone to hide the sun and extend the night forever.'

They were already in the midst of the third rehearsal when there was a call for Eddie in the studio office.

'What had I told you? Don't interrupt the rehearsal, did I not?' Eddie yelled at the peon. 'So what's your problem? You wish to record the playback instead of Urvashi here?'

'The party on the line said it was important,' the peon muttered apologetically.

'Yeah, sure. If I don't take the call, the sun will never rise again, right?'

The poor man had no idea what Eddie was talking about.

'Oh, never mind.' Eddie turned to Ravan, 'Take the call, Ravan. Please. Tell whoever it is that I've finally found the love of my life. Her name's Urvashi and I'm busy making out with her.'

* * *

'Is that you, Eddie?' the voice at the other end asked. 'Can you hear me, Eddie?'

Yes, Ravan could hear her all right but he didn't want to acknowledge it.

'Oh no. Don't tell me I've got a bad line.'

Why was he being so pig-headed? It was not Belle's fault that Eddie was still hung up on her. Asmaan had often maintained that he was in love with Belle even after so many years only because he had been jilted and she was with another man. She had sound instincts but she was not absolutely certain. Ravan was. His friend and partner was irrevocably in love with the lady. And that's what made life so difficult for him.

'It's me, Ravan, Belle. I can hear you clearly now.'

'Ah, Ravan, so good to hear you. You pulled one hell of surprise on all of us. You walked off with Pieta and will soon tie the knot. Congratulations. A long-distance hug from me.'

'Thank you. Eddie is rehearsing a song that's about to be recorded with the orchestra. He didn't know it was you calling. Should I get him?'

'No. I called Eddie's home and Granna gave me the good news. All four of you, Eddie, Pieta, you and Asmaan have moved to Pali Hill into your own apartments. God knows you deserve the very best.'

The trouble with Belle was that you could resolve to give her the cold shoulder, declare her off limits or even, enemy number one, but she always disarmed you and turned you into a drippy, tail-wagging puppy begging her to pet you.

'Granna said both of you would be at Premier Sound today. I know it's presumptuous to ask after so long but do you remember that haunting song you wanted me to sing before I left without any notice? I know I shamelessly let you down. I was a fool, Ravan.' She paused as if unsure of herself. 'It's already been recorded, right?'

If only it had already been recorded, Ravan thought. He felt such conflicting emotions that he daren't answer. Belle was saying hello, hello and then the line got cut off. He wanted desperately to lie and prevent her from coming back so that Eddie wouldn't suffer any more. His friend was just beginning to accept that Belle was not returning. Now if she did, he would once again be caught in the deadly vice of hope, entirely false hope, because Belle and Veer were an item and nothing Eddie did or didn't do could change that.

The past was long past for Belle. She had moved on, while it would always be the present for Eddie. Couldn't Belle see the obvious and spare Eddie further hurt? It seemed to Ravan that Eddie and his first meeting with Belle and her new friend Veerendra in Volga (nothing Russian about the restaurant except the name) had occurred in a past life. To be fair to her she had made it plain to Eddie that there was never any question of their getting back together. Eddie had told Ravan that she had specifically used the word 'never' and he had laughed it off saying he didn't know how to count till never. That should have told Belle something. Either she didn't wish to decipher Eddie's remark or she took him at his word. There was something else. She didn't seem to notice that Veer went out of his way to be as offensive as possible to Eddie. And yet there was no denying that Ravan liked her and that was not entirely owing to her amazing voice. She just had this knack of spreading good cheer. She could work right through the day and follow it up with another shift at night without a murmur. Three-quarters of the orchestra, if not the whole lot of them, were half in love with her and did not once mention the rulebook or timeframes and shifts.

Now if he had got it right she was coming back unless … unless he told her the song was already recorded.

The phone rang again for a while. Ravan finally picked it up.

'The line got cut off,' Belle said in exasperation. 'That song's been recorded, right?'

'Yes,' Ravan whispered.

'The line's bad, Ravan. I'm afraid you will have to shout into the receiver.'

'No, the producer ran into financial problems. Now he's raised the money and he wants it done as usual the week before this one. The release dates for the movie are already fixed.'

'I love that song so much I would pay you both if you allowed me to sing it. I've finished recording ten tracks for my debut album and only the last one's left. That should be in the bag by tomorrow and I could leave the same night for Bombay. Will you and Eddie forgive me for ditching you?'

'Veer told us that your American contract will not permit you to do any work with anyone else.'

'That's because he doesn't know me. There's no way I am going to give up my work in India. Besides, how can the Hindi music market be in competition with the English? The people here are clueless about how huge the Indian music market is. Anyway, the long and the short of it is that my contract does not prevent me from recording Hindi or any regional songs. Will you and Eddie be able to make the producer hang in there for just one more week?'

'We can ask the producer but can't guarantee it.'

'Try, do please try. I like, no, I love singing for you and Eddie.'

Damn. Did she have to say that? What was worse, she actually meant it. Now he too would have no choice but to try his best to persuade the producer.

'Who was that?' Eddie asked when Ravan returned to the recording room. 'You were gone for some time?'

'There was a break in the call.'

'A likely story. Bet it was one of your girlfriends.'

'Yours too.'

'Oh yeah, sure.' Eddie jerked awake suddenly. 'Belle?'

'Yes.'

'Why didn't you call me?'

'I told her you said you were not to be disturbed because you were making out with Urvashi.'

'I could kill you in cold blood, Ravan.'

'I know. That's why I told Belle to come right back.'

'All right, smartarse, what's the deal?'

'The lady will be back within a week. She still wants to sing the song.'

Poor Eddie, Ravan thought. It was going to be the same story all over again. His friend wouldn't have learnt a damn lesson and would have set himself up for another disastrous heartbreak. Disastrous heartbreak, is there any other kind? How about a joyous, life-affirming, heart-warming heartbreak?

* * *

Eddie cottoned on to the new trend before it became the fashion. In the past, music directors like Anil Biswas, Burman-da, Naushad Sahab dressed casually in kurta-paijamas. Jaikishan-ji wore drainpipes and a jacket while his partner, Shankar-ji, favoured a suit just like the perfectly groomed and debonair Madan Mohan-ji. But the business of crafting a reputation, Eddie sensed early on, was beginning to go in a very different direction. It would not do for new composers to be almost invisible or anonymous. You had to stand out. What you wore helped set you apart and became your identity, something extras could never have. Bappi Lahiri, for instance, was swimming in chains, bracelets and baubles. Some others wore brocade achkans that reached below the knee and long strings of pearls. It looked as if style was at least as important as substance. Sometimes, Eddie thought, style was all that counted these days. But that would never do for Ravan and him. Style would always take second place but a very important second if he had anything to do with it. It was odd that Ravan, who was on the ball when it came to music, was infuriatingly dheela and casual about clothes. It was a wonder he didn't come for recordings in his former taxi driver's khaki.

Eddie chose PerfectoFit, one of the most exclusive and expensive tailoring establishments in the city, located behind the Taj Mahal Hotel, and spent hours with Angelo who had trained in the Mecca of tailoring, Italy. The two of them were going to invent a radically different style for Eddie and he in turn would convert Ravan by the sheer force of his new persona. Eddie had no idea how Italians spoke English but if it was anything like Angelo's high-pitched avalanches of words with an 'o' attached to all nouns and verbs and sometimes everything in-between including full stops, then both Italian and English were in dire trouble.

Angelo spoke of something called 'concepto couture' which, it appeared, comprised the totality of a man's personality. He claimed it was like talking to a homeopath; every little thing that a customer told Angelo counted. Not just your physical features and measurements but your aspirations, your mental landscape, your spiritual topology and how you wished to bridge the gap between what you were and how you aspired to be perceived in the public arena.

Eddie told him of the forthcoming Filmfare Awards Night and how he and his partner were likely to receive the awards for the best music and the best music directors of the year, and how they would be conducting an orchestra while Belle and other playback singers sang their songs.

'What about your partner?' Angelo asked. 'If you are a team, you must have a ditto inseparable-twins look, no?'

'You're right. That's why I came here first. I will select the look and I am sure he will follow.'

The two of them pored over catalogue after designer catalogue and together they formulated the 'concepto', or to be precise, Angelo did most of the talking and Eddie did the nodding and added a word or a suggestion here or there.

Angelo insisted on three trials. 'Your skin is perfecto fit, no?' he queried. 'So must your suit. Any slack, anything sagging or extra is a criminal offence in my book. That's why I call my studio PerfectoFit.'

Eddie was to pick up the suit on Monday morning. Since Pieta was going to work, he gave her a ride to the office in his new car. At the last minute he asked her, 'Are you in a hurry?'

'No. Office starts at nine thirty. I am twenty minutes early thanks to you.'

He was not in the habit of consulting Pieta on any matter, least of all in the highly sensitive business of designer clothes now that R&E were becoming so important in the music industry. But she was travelling with him and, anyway, how would it hurt if she happened to come to PerfectoFit?

'Good. Come with me. I'll drop you at the office after we finish an errand. It will take me just ten minutes and you'll be very much on time.'

'Where're we going?'

'You're about to find out.'

'Like dat?' Pieta regressed to an eleven-year-old's voice and her eyes bulged out. 'Secret, secret? Dutty secret?'

'Yes, like dat only.'

Eddie introduced his sister to Angelo who did his heavy Italian gallant number, ogled excessively at the lady and said, 'Mamma mia. You have a very beautiful sister. Molto bella. If I was only thirty years younger, I would sweep her off her feet and marry her in Capri.'

'She's rather weird. She might say no to your proposal,' Eddie yelled from behind the trial room door.

'Not thirty years ago. Nobody could resist me, not the women nor the men.'

'What do you think?' Eddie asked his sister when he came out of the dressing room. 'How do I look?'

He was in white tails with a white bow tie, a white waistcoat and a white cummerbund. The suit had a classic cut. And yet something was different. It took Pieta a minute to zero in on the variation. The lapels of the jacket, the waistcoat and the cummerbund had delicately embroidered vines in green chain stitch and tiny red and pink buds done in satin stitch.

'Well, what's the verdict?'

Pieta thought a bit and then said emphatically, 'It's an amazing fit, almost as if it was tailored directly on the body.'

Angelo swelled with pride. 'It's pure art, not craft, signora. That's why people come to me. That's why they pay what I demand.'

'Sure, but how does it look? On me?'

Pieta hesitated for a moment. 'Nice, very nice.'

Was it the split-second vacillation? Or was it the unseemly hurry with which she tried to cover up uncharitable thoughts about the PerfectoFit suit that made Eddie suspicious? 'What's wrong?'

'Nothing. It looks terrific. Nice, very nice.'

Eddie paid Angelo, picked up the suit now hung on a hefty wooden hanger and cocooned in a zipped plastic bag, and drove off. Pieta knew she was in for a grilling, more like an inquisition.

'Out with it? What's wrong? It's important that you tell me. I got it specially tailored for the Filmfare Awards Night.'

'Nothing's wrong. It looks good on you. But I'm not an authority on men's clothes. As a matter of fact I don't know the first thing about them.'

'Cut the bull, Pieta. You can't fool me. A straight question deserves a straight answer. How do I look in the new suit?'

Pieta knew she was caught and wished she could open the door of the speeding car and fling herself out.

'I don't know.'

'You do. The truth and nothing but.'

Pieta sighed. 'I am not good at this. You really should ask someone who's into fashion.'

'I am asking you, not someone else.'

Pieta gave up. 'You're not going to like this. Shades of a gigolo or an up-market pimp.'

* * *

Pieta was right, Eddie thought. It was his mistake, no question about that, to take her along and consult her. She didn't know the first thing about men's clothes. Didn't she say as much? There was a moment in the taxi when he could have boxed her ears. But really he should have had more sense than to ask for her opinion. Belle was the only person he knew who had an unerring eye for style, whether women's or men's. He should have taken her instead of his sister to Angelo's to see him in his brand-new incarnation.

12

Who would have imagined that Eddie would be happy to see Veerendra Malaviya? But he was. It meant that Belle was back in Bombay. Eddie could see Veer from the corner of his eye through the glass window of the studio but not hear him since Ravan and he were recording a 1950s kind of song with an elaborate orchestral arrangement. He had thought he would greet Veer after the song was canned but the Playboy Prince was in a hurry and the door was thrown open despite the red signal. The recordist was screaming from behind Veer, 'I tried, I tried to hold him back but he pushed me aside, switched off the red light and stormed in.'

Suddenly Veer was standing behind Eddie, locking his right forearm around his throat tightly and jerking it back hard. Eddie blanked out and slid to the ground as Ravan wrestled Veer away.

'You shit-face, I happened to glance through *Star World* magazine on the flight here and learnt that you've been making out with Belle.'

The violin player closest to the door rushed out and fetched a glass of water. It took Eddie a while to get his bearings while he drank the water slowly.

'I take it you believe every word written there.' Eddie managed to get the words out finally.

'Why would they lie?'

'Because…' Eddie took Ravan's hand and helped himself up. 'Because gullible folk like you want so hard to believe their lies.'

'I'm nobody's fool, Eddie Coutinho. I assure you that piece was well researched. It even dug up the fact that you used to have a band called Bandra Bombshells which was so lousy, nobody gave you any work and you had to close it down.'

'Yes, the Bombshells bombed out. But we couldn't have been that bad. After all, Belle was the lead singer and look where she is today.'

'That's because of me. No credit to you. And her name is Solange now, not Belle. I'm here to give you a message from her. She doesn't care to see your face again. And she certainly doesn't want to sing for you people or any Bollywood music directors. She can't afford to damage her reputation abroad now that her album *I'm Done with You* is being released for the Christmas season. Besides, that's part of her new contract. So leave her alone. Because if you don't, you'll find yourselves behind bars.'

'On what charge?'

'Stalking, harassment, obscene phone calls, does it matter? The police know which side their bread is buttered. Stay away from Bel … Solange. Or who knows, you might meet with an accident.'

'Thanks for warning me. I trust you know that everything you said just now has been recorded. Now go and play with little boys your own age.'

The back of Veer Malaviya's hand flashed across and slammed into Eddie's face. It was such an unexpected blow, Eddie lost his balance and fell backward again. Some members of the orchestra were up and walking menacingly towards the intruder.

'I think you should leave now.' Ravan steered Belle's friend out of the door towards the lift.

* * *

It must have been 10 in the morning the day after Veer had muscled into the studio. E&R were busy mixing tracks when the door opened and Belle peeped in. The volume was pumped up on the speakers and it was hard to hear her. Ravan switched the music off.

'Don't I get a hug from my two favourite music directors?' She didn't wait for an answer but ran in and gave Eddie a hug and then Ravan. 'Hard at work as always. Don't you guys ever take time off?' She looked at them quizzically for a long minute. 'You don't look very happy to see me today?'

Eddie smiled. 'Just surprised.'

Ravan marvelled at Eddie's self-control. He had made it a point of honour never to mention Veer to her, never mind how obnoxiously he behaved. If Belle was to return to him, it would have to be on her own steam and not because Eddie told tales about Veer, regardless of how true they were.

'I'm here and raring to go.'

'We didn't know when you would show up.'

'Now you know I'm here. But don't we need to rehearse?'

'Of course. How does tomorrow sound?'

'Anytime you say. I am all yours. One question. What's wrong? Why are you fielding all the questions, Ravan?'

'Just happy to see you back with us,' Eddie whispered and she hugged him again.

'Not half as happy as I am to be with you both.'

'We'll rehearse in the morning and record in the afternoon. How about that?'

'I can't wait for it to be morning. Even when I was in the midst of recording in the States, I kept practising your song just in case you still wanted me.'

'We want you. And how.' Ravan sang the words.

She turned to leave, then stopped. 'You won't tell me, but I know something's not quite right.'

'How about having dinner with Granna and me tonight,' Eddie asked. 'Since you happen to be her favourite, you will be served food fit for the gods.'

'Her favourite but not yours.'

Eddie blushed but dodged the question. 'I'll have to come clean. I was not being altogether honest. I wanted you to see our new place.'

Actually, Eddie did have an ulterior motive. The Filmfare Awards Night was round the corner and Belle alone would be able to grasp the fine art of the 'concepto couture' suit.

* * *

'What's this fancy dress for?' Granna asked Eddie who was keeping a lookout for Belle from the balcony that evening. 'Have you made me work me to the bone, cooking for you two, only to discover that you are going out for dinner?'

'Nope. Just waiting to get a response to the new suit from the lady.'

He was at the lift even as he saw Belle's taxi enter the driveway. It seemed to take hours for her to come up to the eleventh floor. The steel doors finally opened.

'Wow. What's going on here?'

He knew it, he just knew it. Belle would instantly grasp what he was trying to do and respond positively to it.

'How do I look?' Eddie beamed.

'Like Libera-che.'

'I didn't catch that. Like who?'

'Oh, that stuffed toy, the one whom the old ladies adored. We used to call him Liberace, like an ace in the card pack, remember? But the Americans corrected me and said the Italian pronunciation was Libera-che.'

Eddie was not sure which was worse: gigolo/high-class pimp or Libera che-che-che-che. You had to hand it to Belle. Unlike his sister, she didn't put a gloss on the subject but shot point blank. It hurt. And how. But one thing was certain: the Perfecto suit would not see the light of day ever again.

* * *

Eddie rushed to Chor Bazaar before going to the rehearsal that afternoon. He knew exactly what he wanted. It took him some time to find the right place and even more time to find the right size. He was ready for the Filmfare Awards Night function. *Trikon* picked up eight awards in all. As expected, Prajapati Sehgal got the award for best direction, Asmaan for the best lyrics. *Trikon* won four other awards, including the one for the best actress. And it was no surprise that R&E walked off with the best music award for the same film.

Eddie would have liked to claim that he was conscious of turning what passed for couture in film circles on its head but was chastened by now and had begun to understand that his ideas of high fashion did not always find favour with others. What he couldn't deny though was that he had succeeded far beyond his most extravagant expectations as Ravan and he launched into '*Big fish eat small fish*', the song from *Hulla Gulla* that had broken all previous records, that night. The two music directors were a study in contrast, Ravan was in a kurta-paijama and Eddie in battle fatigues.

The press corps and the TV reporters mobbed Eddie and wanted to know what this new avatar of his signified. Eddie didn't have a clue and for once he was laconic and created an air of mystery.

'Isn't it obvious?' The media people looked confused and lost. 'I am at war.'

'War? Against whom?' they asked.

'It's an all-encompassing concept; one that keeps evolving.'

'Awesome,' one of the younger members of the press gasped. Ravan too stared at his friend incredulously. How come he could never talk such horse shit and, that too, with such supreme confidence and aplomb?

'Forgive me but what is that supposed to mean?' one of the press corps asked.

Eddie was not a particularly articulate guy, the sort who could instinctively devise the whole architecture of a carefully reasoned argument: one with a set of sentences with clauses and sub-clauses in a state of perfect balance like an intricate Calder mobile suspended in the air. But something happened to him when he was in the public eye. He was able to tap into words he didn't know he knew. He had the facility of an innocent liar or an actor. He actually believed the words he spoke.

'We're are at war with poverty: poverty of imagination, poverty of creativity in film and art, but most of all the poverty of life in our country. We stand for all the unfortunates, the wretched of the earth [this was a phrase he had heard Pieta use once], the have-nots who are never on the radar, the extras and the marginalized [that last was courtesy Asmaan when they were extras in a former life].

'We have an agenda. The haves are always afraid that the poor will steal their wealth, start a revolution, ransack their homes and leave them penurious. It does not occur to them that there is a very simple but effective remedy. Why would the poor want to steal or grab their property if they too were to become well-off? Which is what our music and message is about. We intend to make everybody into haves.'

'Are you talking about our films?' the reporter asked.

'I leave it to you to decide. All I can say is, look at *Trikon* and you know where the majority of films stand in comparison.'

That shut the wise guy up. The curious thing was that even Ravan wasn't sure whether he should take Eddie seriously or if it was just hot air.

13

And now the deed was done. Father Agnello D'Souza of Saint Sebastian's Church and the Registrar of Civil Marriages had both pronounced, albeit not on the same day, Pieta and Ravan man and wife. The wedding had gone off without a hitch but there had been considerable horse-trading prior to it. Pieta had initially put her foot down and refused to have a church wedding unless the Pawars got a Hindu marriage ceremony but that was unthinkable as far as Violet was concerned. Imagine the barbaric practice of lighting a fire as the couple walked around it seven times while a Brahmin priest muttered various kinds of mumbo-jumbo asking the whole pantheon of Hindu idols to witness and bless the marriage. Parvatibai would have liked to see Pieta wear a green nine-yard sari and the bride and groom perform the saptapadi in the Mahadeo temple she visited every evening but she was willing to give in and make any concessions just so long as her son got married to the woman he had loved for so long believing that that was never going to happen.

Apart from the Catholic nuptials, Violet Coutinho had one other precondition: Ravan and Pieta's children had to be brought up as Catholics. But Pieta would not hear of it. After all, religion was an accident of birth. You didn't choose it, you inherited it from your parents, and very likely you were stuck with it for life. The chances of you being able to do a rethink were close to nil. And even if you were that rare bird who consciously wished to disown your parents' religion, there was not much of a chance of that happening since inertia was the easier option. Pieta wanted her children to decide whether they wanted to be Hindu, Catholic, Buddhists, Muslims, agnostics or just plain atheists.

The banns had been announced and the date of the wedding was fast approaching but mother and daughter seemed to have reached a point of no return when Violet changed her strategy. She cornered Ravan when he came to visit his mother and dropped by at the Coutinho residence. 'Ravan, I have a question to ask you.' Violet's tone was unusually friendly but there was no missing the subterranean intimidatory note and Pieta was immediately alert. 'Would you have any objections to your and Pieta's children being raised as Catholics?'

'Children?' Ravan looked flummoxed.

'Before you answer, please remember that if you say no, my grandchildren will go straight to hell. And you will be responsible for that.'

'But we are not even married yet.'

'Now is the time when you should be taking these decisions and not after you are already a father. God forbid that something should happen to your new-born child and the baby be writhing in hell forever because you failed to baptize it.' Ravan knew his Bible but he didn't quite grasp why his putative new-born child would be writhing in hell.

Catholic or Hindu, what difference did it make, it was an academic discussion as far as Ravan was concerned. They were never going to have children. 'I certainly don't want our children to go to hell. At least not because of me.'

Violet looked triumphantly at Pieta. 'See, Ravan is far more reasonable than you are. He doesn't wish to jeopardize the fate of your children. I take it the matter is settled once and for all.'

'Not at all, Mummy. My position hasn't changed. Not one bit.'

'What's your problem?' Violet asked her daughter. 'Why are you being perverse and denying your children their right to worship our Lord and seek the kingdom of heaven?'

'Don't you know that Ravan will do anything to please you? His first memory, one that we sowed in his mind, was that he was responsible for Papa's death. Since then he has made guilt his vocation. If that was not bad enough, he has had the gall to woo your daughter and he now believes that he can only make it up to you and the rest of the family by agreeing to whatever you ask. Not that that would ever suffice in his eyes. Frankly, not even his going to the Catholic version of hell would be reparation enough. It's up to us to do the right thing by him and not allow him to make foolish promises.'

Ravan tried to tell Pieta that since the children were merely a speculative proposition with no basis in ground realities, it shouldn't make a difference to either of them whether these hypothetical progeny of theirs were brought up as Moonies or Scientologists like Tom Cruise. He should have known better than to propose such a cavalier solution.

'You stay out of this. Someone has to stand up to my mother. Since you won't, I will.'

But Violet was adamant and it looked as if the marriage was on the rocks before it was sanctified. That was when Pieta played her trump card. She offered her mother a choice. Yes, she was willing to compromise and have a church wedding. If that, however, was not enough, she would say no to both, the Catholic nuptials as well as bringing up the children in the Catholic faith. And who knows, have a temple wedding.

Violet knew Pieta. After all, she was not only her daughter, she was as wilful as her mother. She did not make idle threats. Violet fumed but she decided to make the most of what was on offer. She could always take up the subject of the children's faith later on. The civil ceremony had been another bone of contention. 'Why would you want to have the marriage validated by a secular authority? Isn't a church wedding, witnessed by God and his Son, sacrosanct?'

'It is, Mummy, but what if Ravan discovers he can't bear the sight of me and wishes to be set free?'

'I keep telling you don't marry him but you won't listen. Hindu men are not like their Catholic counterparts. Their philosophy of life is easy come, easy go. I'm warning you, once he has you, he'll walk out on you.'

'Haven't you forgotten something?' Pieta asked archly. 'What about me? What if I find him intolerable and begin to loathe him? The Church doesn't allow a divorce without a dispensation from Rome and that is hardly ever given. The civil registration allows for a divorce. How about that?'

Violet was a staunch Catholic. She would never have given her husband a divorce even if she had wanted it more than him. Unfortunately, he had abandoned his family by dying even before Eddie was born. She should have ticked Pieta off then and there for her duplicity but her daughter had got her cornered. After all, Pieta was marrying a Hindu. Under the circumstances, an exit strategy was not to be dismissed.

* * *

As far as Ravan knew there wasn't a centimetre of free space in Bombay proper and yet there was not a week, more likely a day, when a new building was not shooting up in the city. There was a new breed of termites called builders who were hand-in-glove with the politicos and the mafia. They devoured hundreds of hectares of land and spat out or maybe they shat high-rise slums the next day. There was no room for playgrounds, thoroughfares, light or air. The new buildings pressed in on each other and squeezed the roads into narrow mediaeval lanes.

But here were Ravan and Eddie at a complex of dozens of skyscrapers that were coming up behind what Ravan had always thought of as the farthest corner of Wadala East. Obviously, he had got his geography wrong for the new development seemed to extend way past the horizon.

Ravan had had second thoughts, third and fourth too, about what Eddie was planning to do. He had cautioned him several times but he couldn't possibly object any more. It was a minor miracle that Eddie was still talking to him after he had married Pieta and Ravan didn't wish to try his luck any further.

'How do you know he's here?' Ravan was convinced Eddie was going round and round the network of newly built twisting roads and getting nowhere.

'Because I've been tracking him. The manager of the project told me Veer's father has ordered him to be at the site every day by eight thirty a.m. His eight thirty a.m. starts around four in the afternoon.'

'You sure you want to risk this? You think what you're planning to do will be seen as nothing but a juvenile prank, but it will earn you a very adult punishment.'

'Veer thinks he's invulnerable because Papa will take care of everything. Fortunately, Veer too has an Achilles' heel. And that's where I want to hit him.'

They found the yellow Bugatti parked in front of the one-storeyed office building. The security guard informed them that the Malaviya heir apparent was inspecting the progress in Block 'C' today. Eddie drove further, turned right and parked the car in an inconspicuous lane. He opened the dickey, picked up the epoxy resin gum, several thick sheets of foam rubber and jute gunnysacks and they walked back to the Bugatti. Ravan remembered a conversation he had had with Eddie when his friend had first broached the subject.

'How are you going to get inside the car?'

Eddie had marvelled at his friend's ignorance. 'Have you forgotten that I worked for years in an automobile workshop? I can hotwire any car.'

'That's a theft, Eddie. They could slap a criminal suit against us.'

'I've no intention of stealing the car; just going for a swinging ride, that's all. Besides, he has threatened to put me behind bars anyway.'

Eddie eased the Bugatti on to the road and drove to 'G' Block. He had scouted the place well. This was where three heavy-duty cranes were parked.

'I'll steer the boom and lower the magnetized lifting gear directly above the Bugatti. You and I have practised the sequence over and over again. Make sure that the big steel disc of the crane lands softly on top of the Bugatti. Leave the rest to me. Once I switch on the electrical button, the disc will get magnetized and we will be in business. Oh, lest I forget, mind your head.'

The boom was overhead now and the steel cables descended gently till they were positioned a metre above the Bugatti. The electromagnetic disc came to rest in extreme slow motion on the roof of the car. Ravan gave the thumbs up to Eddie and then it was up, up, and away. Veer Malaviya's Bugatti was afloat, steadily rising up in a perfect straight line. What would happen, Ravan wondered, if the electrical current failed and the vintage car went into free fall? It did not bear thinking of.

Time for Ravan to disappear into an unfinished structure where he could hide as well as have a clear view of the office building, the road and the boom of the crane, and wait for the young scion. The manager of the Malaviya Paradise project had told Eddie that however late Veerendra turned up for duty, he left on the dot of 6 p.m. Ravan could see Veer walking jauntily with three assistants in tow towards the office shed, twirling the car keys around his index finger. He waved to Eddie. The Lord and Master of the Universe must have suddenly applied the brakes for the earth stopped spinning and came to a dead halt. Veer skidded, his mouth fell open and he seemed to be swallowing all the air in the atmosphere. He was screaming but not a sound escaped his voice box and now he was hopping and leaping like water on a scorching hotplate. His companions watched him in alarm. Was he having an epileptic fit?

'My Bugatti.' The dam had broken and there was a deluge of swearwords and imprecations. 'Where the fuck's my Bugatti?' He turned upon his assistants. 'What did you do with it? I'll kill you, the whole lot of you. Behenchod, if anything happens to my Bugatti, if there's even a hint of a scratch, I'll tear your eyes out. I'll sack you if I don't get it back in mint condition this moment.'

Eddie's timing could not have been better. The sunflower-yellow Bugatti whooshed down and jerked to a stop in front of Veer. He sprang back in horror. His hand reached out to grab the car but the Bugatti retreated as rapidly as Veer chased it. Now it was to his right and the next instant it had swung to the left. It stared him in the face and then it was behind him. The young man was out of breath and panting. Fortunately, the Bugatti too had lost steam and stood still till he made a grab for it. His hand caught hold of the bumper even as it took off vertically. He couldn't make up his mind whether to hang in there or let go of the car. He dropped down. It was a dizzying sight, the boom of the crane was going round in wider and wider circles, making a terrible whipping sound, and the Bugatti was swinging wildly. Ravan dared not look up. There was no question about it. The Bugatti was going to slip and come crashing down. Veer sat down on the road and wept uncontrollably.

'Please, please stop. I will give you money, as much as you want. Just leave my car alone. My father will kill me if something happens to it. Please, I beg you.'

Malaviya Paradise had gone eerily silent. The three assistants watched their boss nervously from a safe distance. Veer looked up at the sky. There was no sign of the Bugatti. It was sitting in front of him. He dusted himself and opened the door. There was a note stuck to the windshield. 'Veer,' it said, 'the next time you strike me or threaten me, the Bugatti may have an accident and fall from the twenty-first floor.'

* * *

Falling ... falling ... falling...

Ravan would never get used to how tempestuous Pieta's emotions were when the two of them finally got together. He remembered their wedding night. He had called out to her just to make sure that she would be in the bathroom for at least a few more minutes so he could hide the ruby and emerald necklace and the gold anklets he had bought for her under the pillow and she had stormed out naked.

'Pawar, get this straight. If you call me Pieta ever again, we are through. I don't give a damn whether the Pope or Cardinal Gracias approves of it or not, I will divorce you.'

'You can't be serious. What am I supposed to call you? Agent X or Mrs Pawar?'

'I'll have you know that this is no joking matter. I loath my name and I expect you to do your duty like a good Hindu husband.'

'And what may that be?'

'You don't know?' she asked, exasperated. 'Give me a new name since I'm supposed to be starting a new life when I married you this evening.'

'What's wrong with Pieta?'

'Imagine being called pity or compassion, or piety and that too in a foreign language? I refuse to be that weepy, heart-rending Michelangelo sculpture of the Virgin holding the crucified Jesus. Do you realize that I must be the only person in the world to have that weird name?'

'Who gave you that name?'

'My great-grandmother.'

'That's your father's grandmother?'

'Granna's mother-in-law. She had a dream many years before I was born that if Mummy had a girl she should be called Pieta.'

'Did your mother like the name?'

'She detested it.'

'Then why didn't she call you by some other name?'

'There was a catch. My great-grandmother had prophesied that if I was not called Pieta, I would die. There was also some politics involved.'

'Politics?'

'The inter-familial variety. My father's family wanted me to be called after his grandmother, Phillipa. What gall, my mother thought. Socially and in every other way they were so much inferior to us, according to her. Who were they to tell her what she should name me? Suddenly, Pieta was okay since she could use her grandmother's soothsaying to snub my father's family.'

'Which brings us to the big question, so what do you want me to call you?'

'You should know, you're the 'indu husband, right?'

'Give me a break, Pieta.'

'You used that name again. That's the end.'

'I'm sorry, I honestly am. How about Piya? No compassion or pity in it. Just love. Plus your mother will think it's merely short for Pieta and it will keep the evil omens at bay.'

She was not convinced till he did what all Hindi film heroes do. He sang her a song, a very old one by Pankaj Mallick, 'Piya milan ko jaana'.

'Promise me, you will always sing for me.'

* * *

Friday morning, 10 a.m. The members of the orchestra had been rehearsing the song for Sehgal Sahab's next film with Ravan and Belle for the past four hours but there was still no sign of Eddie. He had not missed a rehearsal or recording before. The receptionist had called his home every quarter of an hour but there was no answer. Eddie or no Eddie, the rehearsal had to go on and then the recording.

Ravan had four parallel tracks running simultaneously. He had to be extra vigilant about the scoring of the music and the instrumentation. That was Eddie's forte and Ravan could feel a sense of unease amongst the musicians. Belle was bending over backwards to be supportive but he kept avoiding her eye because she would ask the same question he was asking of himself: Where the hell was Eddie?

Ravan had a fairly good idea of Eddie's whereabouts and was aware that he should have gone to the police the previous evening when they got back after the Bugatti ride and reported that Eddie was in mortal danger. He could have told you that if you have a sense of foreboding and know in advance what the future holds, you can't claim that you were taken by surprise. It's always wise to bear in mind the Scout's motto: 'Be prepared'. Prepared for what, you may well ask. Don't be naïve. It's never for a windfall or Madam Fortune showering you with favours. Never. Always be prepared for the very worst. Rest assured it will come to pass.

But Ravan was also aware that to be forewarned is to merely advance the calamitous blow. For there is nothing as potent as fear. It paralyses you. Suspicion is king and betrayal is everywhere. Mother, father, brother, spouse, progeny, friend, and alien, you can't trust anybody. The only one who will stand steadfast is your enemy. He will never let you down. He'll stab you front, back and sideways.

The rehearsal was over by 4.30 and the recording took another half an hour.

'Congratulations, Ravan. You did a damn good job single-handedly.' Belle spoke to Ravan after the members of the orchestra had left. 'Now, do you want to tell me what's going on? Where is Eddie? I knew something was amiss even when I got back from the

States. I could see that he no longer wants to work with me. He can't keep up the pretence of a close professional relationship and friendship any more. He hates me. He can't bear to see my face, that's it, isn't it?'

'Will you give me two minutes to answer you?'

Ravan ferreted through the collection of the recorded tapes and switched on the one in which Veer's voice had got recorded accidentally.

'Why didn't Eddie tell me about it? Why didn't you tell me?'

'I can't answer for him but I suspect he thinks it's not fair play because that would be stacking the deck against Veer and prejudicing you. That's why he hasn't once mentioned how loutishly Veer has behaved and abused him. At times me too.'

'Are you telling me that Veer has done this kind of thing before?'

'Yes. You were recording your first song with us late into the night when he barged in and dragged you out. You tried to cover up for him by saying wealth can also be a handicap.'

'Yes, I did. I'm sorry.'

'He's done it over and over again. But now I fear there's a real emergency. Will you ask Veer where Eddie is?'

'How would he know?'

'Because Eddie decided enough was enough.'

'High time too. What did he do?'

'He strung up the Bugatti on a crane and let it swing high up.'

'You're joking. Veer loves that car more than any of his other possessions, including me.'

'Let's just say Veer was upset. Very, very upset with Eddie. He was screaming murder. I think he meant it.'

'Oh my God. Let's go.'

'I don't think Veer will want to see me.'

'Don't waste time. Ravan. I might need help.'

* * *

'Hey sweetheart, I was going to pick you up for dinner,' Veer gushed when Belle rang the bell of his apartment on Napeansea Road. 'What's that man doing here?'

'He's with me.'

'He stays out.'

'Where's Eddie?'

'How would I know?'

'You're such a bad liar, Veer.'

He laughed, quite pleased with himself. 'Why the sudden interest in Eddie?'

'He's my friend. I knew him long before I came to know you.'

'Oh, so the rumour that the two of you are an item again is true. Poor you.'

'Where's Eddie?'

'I guess you could say he's resting.'

'Where's Eddie, Veer?' Belle's voice had taken on a menacing edge.

'You really want to see him?'

'Yes.'

'Where are your manners, dear? Yes, please.'

'Yes, please.'

'For some reason he seems to be seeing things upside down.'

Belle and Ravan were racing up the stairs of the duplex apartment.

'That man stays here.'

'He has a name and you know it. Ravan. That's his name,' Belle yelled back. 'And I want him with me.'

'Yes, he does look like a bouncer from the slums.'

They were upstairs now and running along a corridor with rooms on the left. Belle pushed open door after door. It was dark inside the corner room.

'He's getting the same treatment he gave my Bugatti, except I tried out a variation.' Veer had followed them.

Belle could see better now. A rope was tied around Eddie's ankles and he was hanging upside down from a pulley.

She lifted Eddie's head up and whispered, 'Eddie, can you hear me?' There was no response. Even in the darkness, his face looked abnormally red and swollen. 'What did you do to him?' She took Eddie's pulse. 'How long has he been like this?'

'I can't quite recall.' Veer was trying hard to appear nonchalant.

'Do you realize he's unconscious? God forbid, if anything should happen to him…' She didn't bother to compete the sentence.

Ravan lowered Eddie and untied the knot.

'Where were you when I nearly passed out seeing my vintage car swinging on a rope fourteen floors above the ground?'

'Eddie should've dropped the Bugatti on your head after you punched him in the studio. Let's rush him to hospital, Ravan.'

Ravan was already headed for the stairs with Eddie in his arms.

'Where are you going?' Veer tried to stop Belle. 'You leave now and you need never come back.'

'I don't intend to.'

* * *

Weeks and months went by and Asmaan and Ravan were still waiting. They couldn't figure out what was going on.

'It's six months since Belle broke off with Veer.' Asmaan finally cornered Eddie. 'So what are you waiting for?'

Eddie knew that he was under twenty-four-hour surveillance. Not just him but Belle too. He was surprised that Asmaan had taken so long to confront him. She and Ravan went pointedly out of their way to avoid the subject of Veer or even Belle and yet it was obvious that they were watching every move the two of them made. Sometimes he thought they wanted a closure, a happy closure to the Belle–Eddie saga more than he did.

'Why don't you mind your own business, Asmaan?' Eddie tried to wiggle out of the tight spot by taking the offensive, knowing fully well it was not going to work.

'Make no mistake. You are my business. The three of us have always looked out for each other. Isn't that so, Ravan? And don't give me one of your lousy diplomatic answers, Pawar.' That put paid to poor Ravan. 'A straight answer, Eddie. It might put you out of your misery.'

'Well, I figured I've been patient for so long, what does it matter if I have to wait a little longer? I want her to know that she doesn't owe me anything out of pity or because her boyfriend was such a lout. I thought I would wait for her to make the first move.'

'In that case you might have to wait till you are six feet under. Why are you playing coy, Coutinho? Life, my friend, is not short. It's over before it starts.'

But this was one time Eddie would not follow Asmaan's diktat. Belle would have to make the first move. If only it was as simple as that. Since the time Belle had first returned from London on Veer's arm, Eddie had taken the long-term view and hoped that his former girlfriend would discover at some point that the new man in her life was a nouveau-riche boor and drop him. He had long since given up all hope of that happening when all of a sudden she had broken off with Veer. Unfortunately, that break had not translated into a fairy-tale ending. Yes, she had thrown her lover out. But Eddie was sure it was a lovers' quarrel and they would make up sooner than later.

Veer was still persona non grata. The problem was Eddie had not been asked to fill the vacancy.

14

Talisman,
Let me tell you about my elder son. I had taken it for granted that he would carry my name and bloodline to posterity, take over my business interests as I grew older, consolidate and transform our various assets into an industrial empire. I sent him to the most expensive schools, got the best teachers to give him tuitions at home. I enrolled him in a prestigious college, don't ask me how much of a donation I had to cough up to get him admission. After he graduated, I planned to send him to one of the top universities in England or America. It was at that critical juncture that I had to leave Bombay thanks to the machinations of my enemies and those who I had thought were closest to me. But my son was never interested in his studies. All he cared for was cars, gambling and girls. The moment I was out of sight, my wife mollycoddled him and let him do whatever he pleased. The fool would neither go abroad to study nor was he willing to attend to our various business interests and shore them up at the very least.

You must be wondering why I am going on about the past. Because this time around I do not know what I should do. Yes, one can look after one's enemies. If one survives the betrayal of one's friends, one can indeed teach them a lesson they are not likely to need again. But, Talisman, what does one do if the members of one's own family stab you? As you know, instead of drawing closer and being doubly supportive, my family blames me for abandoning them as if I had wilfully set out to do this. Things have been going from bad to worse but I must now reconcile myself to an even greater betrayal.

My wife tells me that my son is carrying on with my mistress. I don't know whether to believe this or not. It's not inconceivable that my wife may have encouraged the liaison as a way to get back at me. It's just as possible that she has fabricated this story since she has always hated the sautan and is counting on me to do something drastic.

I will of course check and recheck my wife's story. The question is, what am I to do with my son if my wife is telling the truth? Doubtless if my mistress is guilty, she will get her just deserts sooner rather than later. But that still leaves the question of my son. Should he not suffer the same fate that those who betrayed me did, or will? Truly there is no dilemma worse than that posed by one's own blood.

Pray for me, Talisman, bring me good luck. Pray that I become a man again and eliminate all my enemies, and that my friends and family will quake at the mere sight of me.

May Allah and the Prophet, peace be upon him, guide me.

Khuda Hafeez.

* * *

Falling ... falling ... falling...

Ravan was waiting, watching Pieta as he pretended to listen to the news with her. She must certainly have seen through him by now and realized that she was living with a man with nothing but vast empty spaces in his head. He was a cypher. He was almost illiterate, he didn't read, he knew nothing about art, business, science or culture; he was an ignoramus. He had missed out on all the higher things that made life worth living. Poor woman, since she was a Catholic she would not be able to leave him and she would have to live with nothing but regret all her life.

What foxed him though was that they had not yet had a single serious scrap. Weekends were when they were together two whole days and nights and yet they didn't seem to get enough of each other. It was hard to believe but she appeared to enjoy being with him, talking about inconsequential things like her colleagues at work, office politics, Asmaan's tongue-in-cheek stories about her family. Every now and then they would ask Belle, Eddie and Asmaan for an impromptu meal. The only other person from Bollywood whom she invited was Prajapati Sehgal. When she was out of town on work, even when she was in the States or Europe, she called every night and told Ravan how much she missed him. Was she lying? That was so unlikely he felt ashamed even thinking it.

The Sanskrit word 'maya' kept buzzing around Ravan's mind like a bee he couldn't get rid of. Odd isn't it, he would have to ask his Muslim friend Asmaan to explain the deeper philosophical implications of the Sanskrit word, but what he understood of it was that everything was maya or illusion. There was no purchase on life in that four-letter word. It was like the air around you. You could slice through it, punch your hand through it and there would be nothing to show for it, nothing clung to it. Even water left traces, not air. If there was something called maya in his own life, it was his life with Pieta. She was maya. And like all illusions, he was sure she too would disappear.

'Really, Ravan, what bizarre notions you have of companionship. I have such intense conversations with you when we make love. I have conversations with you when I am not with you. I am constantly talking to you. And sometimes the best conversations we have are when we are both lost in our own worlds.'

She taught him that a quiet, unobtrusive and easy silence too was a form of communing between two people who loved each other. He tried, he tried very hard to tell himself that she was being kind and he shouldn't believe her but despite all his efforts, Pieta had a calming effect on him. And gradually over the years he had relaxed and begun to enjoy the company of his wife without feeling guilty that he had conned her.

* * *

Overnight, perhaps even sooner than that, Eddie found that he was almost incapable of practising self-control any more. For some reason, the word sex seemed so half-hearted now. He was convinced that the biblical 'knowing' alone would show Belle how much he loved her. When he was learning to play the piano and the works of Bach with Belle's mother, she had told him that the great composer had had twenty-one children, eight from his first wife and thirteen from the second. Well, he was all set to better that record. All he had to do was to ask her to get hitched to him.

The problem was it would be almost tantamount to proposing marriage to a widow whose husband had just been interred. Besides, there might be an even greater complication. What if Belle didn't exactly fancy him any more? After all, they had not been lovers for a long time. Not that it would matter. He was so horny he was quite capable of not waiting for an answer from the lady. But he was in luck. He would not have to restrain himself. Belle's last album had struck gold and she was off to the States to record a new one.

She had said she would return in five months but was back in three. Now Eddie was confronted by a rather different set of quandaries. The raging randiness had forsaken him. He had been almost entirely immune to doubt his whole life but now he was plagued by inhibitions which acted like a series of speed-breakers that immobilized him. He was at a loss to understand how he could have changed so much that he felt he was living with an alien. Let alone making love to Belle, he daren't even let his hand brush against hers. Rather late in the day he became acutely conscious that Veer Malaviya was younger than him. Besides, he was far more sophisticated than Eddie could ever aspire to be. Maybe he was a superb lover; maybe his father had employed a teacher who had trained him for years in erogenous exercises that Eddie couldn't begin to imagine; maybe he had learnt things in high society and in the fancy colleges he had attended that took lovemaking to an altogether different plane and drove Belle insane with pleasure. And yet all these put together could not compare with the erotic appeal of being loaded to the gills.

How could he ever compete with Veer or satisfy Belle? The only way he could play safe was to never touch her so that she wouldn't discover that he had been neutered.

Perhaps Belle got tired of waiting for him and decided to confront him. 'I can see that it's payback time and I'm now getting my much-deserved comeuppance.'

'What's got into you?' Eddie thought it was he who owed her an apology.

'Maybe you don't care for damaged goods and we're going to settle for a platonic relationship.'

'Are you nuts? Who do you think I was waiting for all these years?'

'Oh Eddie. Do you have any idea how much you've begun to sound like a Bollywood film hero?'

'Not like,' he corrected her. 'I am. The one and only.'

'Sweep me off my feet,' Belle smiled archly as she closed in on him and put her hand inside his trousers, 'superhero.'

* * *

'Do you want to hear the idea for a new screenplay?'

'Do we have a choice?'

Asmaan gave Eddie an icy look. 'No, you don't. It's called *Goongi*, the dumb one. It's about a married woman who's been raped and left for dead by a man in a mask. Her husband walks out on her when he discovers that she's soiled goods. While her family feels for her, they would prefer it if she didn't go to the police to lodge a complaint but just disappeared instead. After all, she has two other sisters and their prospects of marriage would plummet to zero if it became public that she had been raped. As is often the case, the police refuse to file an FIR. By now, Goongi is so embittered and disillusioned, she refuses to speak any more.

'Goongi thinks her life's over and done with till she happens to see a hit-and-run driver kill four people on the pavement and jots down the number of the BMW. But what should she do with it? If the owner of the car is rich, the police will not even register a case against the culprits. She soon realizes that she is the only witness willing to stand up to all those who wish to either buy her silence for a substantial price or silence her permanently. The dead of course do not have a voice but she realizes that most of the time the living too pretend that they are voiceless. Now she has found a reason to live and speak up. But she also knows once is not enough, she must stand up time and again if she and others like her are to achieve anything worthwhile. Simultaneously, she decides she will get to the bottom of who raped her that night when she was working alone in the office.

'There's, however, another dilemma that she must confront. Two men who have stood by her, her childhood friend who had a crush on her and as a doctor helped her recover from the trauma of the rape, and the lawyer who fights in the courts on her behalf, are interested in her. How does she know that they too won't turn out like her husband who abandoned her at the time when she needed him most? Can she get past her horrible experience? Theoretically, she understands that all men are not monsters but can her body understand this? Now she must choose one of the two suitors. Or perhaps there's another possibility.'

'Who's it for?' Ravan asked.

'There will be lots of buyers for this one. After all, rape is a good enough excuse for our film people to show lots of skin. But it's for Prajapati-ji. He's the only one who will do it justice.'

'Why would you tell us about it before talking to him?'

'Because I wanted to give you the context for the song I'm about to read.'

As always, Asmaan's lyrics were a fluid mix of Hindi and Urdu and a smattering of Persian. However deep the poetry was, it always had a lightness of touch. The curious thing was Eddie and Ravan would flip for it because they loved the sound of it but that made her mad. 'Don't nod your heads like all those asses who come to mushairas and say "*wah-wah, kya baat hai*" whether the poems are excruciatingly banal or transport you to some other realm. I am going to translate the words for you in English. It will not sound lyrical or poetic but if you don't get the meaning, your music too will be meaningless.'

Zubaan hain, par hai bezubaan.
Asmaan hai, par pairon ke neeche
Nahin hain zameen.

I can speak, but am bereft of a voice.
The sky's overhead, but no earth
Underneath my feet.

Give me and my kin a stone heart, God.
Stone hearts can neither bleed nor cry.
Who knows, maybe they won't feel pain either.
Rub my flint heart against that of another victim

And another and another
Till it starts a fire that will burn every
False man or woman.
Incinerate every false promise.

Take the flowers brought to my grave
And crush them under your feet.
Take the glib sentiment,
The revolution, the protest movement
That lasts a day and a night,
And flush them down the toilet.
And you can shove
The overdue apology you know where.
Salve for whose conscience?
And whose conscience does it ease?

If the tongue that lies
Will not cease its lying;
If the eye refuses to see
The suffering of another;
If the stuffed ears prefer to be deaf
Then let my stone heart blind the eye,
Yank the tongue out, and pierce the eardrums.

I do not need crippling crutches.
Those who promise change will never usher change.
If change comes, it's because I will change.
Because the stone will learn to breathe and
Turn into a living being.
And feel, see, hear, and find a tongue

Bezubaan ko zubaan de,
Andhon ko ankhein,
Beheron ko sunai de.

Give voice to the voiceless,
Eyes to those who are blind,
Hearing to the deaf.

'It's for her, isn't it?' Eddie asked and Ravan and Asmaan both knew who the 'her' in the question was. Ravan had talked so often about Meenakshi Venkatraman, they had heard her on tape and had hidden in Ravan's bedroom occasionally when she was giving him lessons.

When Ravan finished class with Mrs Venkatraman that morning, he teetered on the edge of blurting out something but couldn't seem to take the plunge. Perhaps he thought his teacher would help him out or at least make encouraging noises. He should have known better. Meenakshi Venkatraman kept conversation to the minimum.

'People think my friend Eddie and I are a duo like Shankar–Jaikishen or Laxmikant–Pyarelal but that's not the case. Most of the time we are a trio. Where would we be without our third partner, Asmaan? She is the one who writes the lyrics and we try and put them to music. If you will allow me, may I read a poem that she wrote a few days ago?'

She nodded her head.

'It's called "*Bezubaan ko zubaan dé*".'

When he had finished, there was no reaction from her.

'I've made a hash of it. It's a different poem when Asmaan delivers it. She makes it come alive and the words grab you by the throat.'

'Wh-wh-wh-wh-why don't you sing it?'

Ravan didn't pause to clear his throat in case Mrs Venkatraman had second thoughts. The sheet of paper with the lyrics was resting on top of the harmonium but his eyes were closed. He knew the poem by heart. When he was through and opened his eyes, Meenakshi Venkatraman was quiet for a long time.

She was at the door when she turned around. 'A-A-A-A-A-A-Asmaan must have written scores of songs for you. You didn't read those to me. Wh-wh-wh-wh-why did you recite this one?'

'Because it left a scar on me. It made me uncomfortable and yet somehow I felt good, even triumphant.'

'You still haven't told me why.'

'Because Asmaan, Eddie and I believe nobody but you could sing it.'

'Wh-wh-wh-where would Asmaan and E-e-e-Eddie have heard me?'

'They used to come here and sit in the adjoining room to listen to you when you started giving me tuitions.'

'You're not serious.'

'It's the truth.'

'I'm not a playback singer.'

'You mean you're a classical singer and would never do a film song.'

'It's got nothing to do with that. There's either good music or shoddy, lazy or downright bad stuff. A three-minute song, if done well, can also be a perfect gem.'

'Then what's the problem?'

'I've never done it before.'

'Neither had you given lessons when we started.'

'I can't. You know I can't face the p-p-p-public.'

'It will be just Asmaan, Eddie and me. You won't even see the orchestra.'

She was losing her temper now. 'I-I-I-I-I-I told you I can't.'

'I thought you liked the song.'

The lobes of her ears were flushed red. She walked out.

Four days later, '*Bezooban ko zubaan* dé' was in the can. Meenakshi Venkatraman would record many songs for E&R but the singer's name would always remain Anamika, the nameless one.

15

'Ravan,' Pieta called out, 'Ravan, did you hear me? Mrs Venkatraman's daughter Sukanya's here to see us. She's got a first in her final BA exams.' Pieta waited for an answer. 'Please sit down, Sukanya. He can't hear me.' Pieta shook her head. 'They tell me Ravan is a music director but I only know him as a bathroom singer. I might be dying here but try to get him to stop singing and open the door. Out of the question.' She disappeared then and dragged Ravan out buttoning up his shirt.

'Congratulations. Piya tells me you've got a first class. Amazing. How do you do it? Do you know I failed my SSC board exams? Twice.'

'I would give an arm and a leg to be a singer and composer like you.'

'What's the problem then? Can't get a better teacher than your mother. I should know.'

'I can't stand her kind of music.' Her lips curled contemptuously. 'She's the past, I'm the future. It's as simple as that.'

Ravan laughed self-deprecatingly. 'And where do I figure then?'

'You're the bull's-eye, the dead centre of music.'

Ravan shrugged his shoulders. He wasn't sure why he wasn't too happy with the compliment.

* * *

Talisman,

I've exciting news and I can't tell you how happy I am. And yet I come with a troubled heart and the burden of a rebellious and devious son weighing down my every step, not to mention the prospect of an internecine and bloody war.

First, the good stuff. Finally, finally it's going to happen.

After being in the desert for so long, I am hoping to be back in the arms of my first mistress. But let me not talk about this any more for fear that I will cast an evil eye on myself from my overwrought craving and yearning for Bombay.

I'm not unaware that I will be an outsider and foreigner in my own city when I return. Nobody will recognize me except my enemies and they too will assume with good reason that I am a spent force. But they are going to discover how wrong they are. Talisman, I have changed beyond recognition. As you Hindus say, I have assumed a new avatar. A full sixty-five per cent of the new businesses I have commissioned, some of them with foreign capital investment and partners, are totally legitimate in the eyes of the law.

With the liberalization of the Indian economy well under way, and the mill lands openly or surreptitiously becoming available for development, I am investing my host's and my money in real estate. Two of our companies are already some of the biggest players in the field. We're also cornering the construction business in a big way. Naturally we couldn't do any of this without the covert backing of our politicians. I am happy to tell you that whichever party wins the elections and comes to power in our state will not make any difference to us. We've been astute and made all of them partners in our various real estate development projects. This is triply beneficial. We have an insider's track to all information long before it becomes public and they direct us to the loopholes in the labyrinthine bureaucratic mazes which means we are at the finishing line before the others. And secondly, anybody who suddenly discovers a conscience has to think not twice but many times over before doing anything stupid because he's part of the racket and can be exposed in the media. Thirdly, we do have something like the last resort with us. They can suddenly find themselves missing in action.

It's quite astonishing how symbiotic the relationship between the licit and the illicit is in our country. You want to change the colour of your money, the real estate development business is the ideal money exchange bureau. You want to convert right to wrong, no problem, the politicos on your payroll will do it for you. You want the illegal to switch sides, why sir, the judges with ambitions larger than their capabilities will be only too happy to oblige.

But what about Judas? How do I bring him back into the fold?

Well, see you soon. May the blessings of Allah be upon you. Looking forward to seeing you again.

Khuda Hafeez.

* * *

It was uncanny, all these months Sukanya's and Ravan's paths had rarely crossed but now he seemed to run into her almost every other day. Was that nothing but a mere coincidence, he wondered, or was there something more to it than that? She began to drop in without notice, usually when Pieta-Piya was in the office or travelling on work. If he was at home, the chances were he was in his 'padded cell' as Piya liked to call the room in the corner of the house which she had got sound-proofed so that he could work undisturbed and to make sure that the neighbours wouldn't complain. Luckily, when he was there, he couldn't hear the doorbell; not that he would have responded if he had. Padded-cell time was meant to be solitary confinement; it was the only way he could keep his deadlines.

'Are you avoiding me?' Sukanya collared him one day.

'What makes you think that?'

'Because I came over yesterday and rang the bell for five minutes. I know why you didn't answer. Because my mother doesn't want you to give me an audition.'

'That's preposterous. We never talk about you.'

'She can't stand competition, especially from her daughter. She's worried that I might be more talented than her.' Ravan thought it best to avoid the internal dynamics in the Venkatraman family.

'If I am working at home, I don't hear the bell because the music room is sound-proofed.'

Ravan was opening the door of the flat one night when she accosted him. If only he had been going out instead of coming home, he could have told her that he was late for an appointment and the matter would have ended there. He knew he was being paranoid, Pieta had said as much to him. Anyway it was too late to do anything about it. Besides, whatever the young woman's views about her mother, the fact was Sukanya was his guru's daughter.

'Why is your work room at home sound-proofed?'

'Pieta was worried that since I make so much noise, we'll be asked to leave the place.'

'I would love to watch you composing your fabulous music.'

Ravan wished she would skip the compliments. 'Some things are so private, they are best done alone.'

'May I at least see the room where you work?'

'It's just a room with a harmonium, a mouth organ, a bulbul tarang and a set of flutes, nothing more.'

'I think you are being secretive just to create an aura around you.'

For some reason he couldn't quite explain, Ravan was superstitious about the mysterious visitations and workings of the muse and he didn't care to talk about how he worked and reworked his songs. This room was strictly private but he was tired and he had had enough of the young lady. He opened the door of the padded cell.

'May I go in?

'Not with your shoes on.'

She removed her shoes, went in and sat down. The harmonium was on the floor and her fingers ran over the keyboard gingerly.

'I can see that you are very nervous about letting a stranger into your sanctum sanctorum.'

Ravan wondered why he had been so tense. Maybe she was merely curious. Was he the problem instead of her?

She was about to leave when she turned round. 'When am I going to audition for you?'

'I'd no idea you wanted to become a singer.'

'Now you know.'

Every week there were at least two or three people, mostly young but sometimes middle-aged too, who wanted to audition for Eddie and Ravan. They never said no for one reason and one reason alone.

For years nobody had given them a chance to prove their worth or lack of it. Now, when someone auditioned for them, their conscience was clear and they were able to state upfront whether they thought the person had talent or not. That would be a little difficult with Sukanya considering she was Meenakshi Venkatraman's daughter, but Ravan had to concede that she had as much of a right to an audition as anybody else.

'I will check with my better half, Eddie Coutinho, and let you know by next week.'

* * *

Eddie and he were nervous but not Sukanya when she turned up at the studio a fortnight later. 'You all set for the audition?' Ravan asked her.

'You bet. Try me.'

'I want to clarify a couple of things,' Eddie said. 'This is just a test run, right? But we like to make it clear at the outset that this audition is happening at your request. What we are about to do is a scratch recording. It does not entail a contract. There is no commitment on our side. Neither is there one on yours. Is that understood?'

'Sure.'

'What we do is to ask you to sign a form that spells this out clearly so that there is no room for any misunderstanding.'

'Whatever you say.'

Once they had got her signature, Ravan asked, 'What would you like to sing?'

'"*Tera kya hoga Bhagwan*".'

'I hope you understand that there is no obligation to sing our songs.'

'I want to. It's one of my all-time favourites.'

Ravan was sure that he had not prayed as hard when he was trying to impress his first music teacher or the current one, as he did for Sukanya. And now Eddie and he sat in the glassed-in cubicle unable to look at each other. Was it possible that Mrs Venkatraman, who was so pitch-perfect that you could tune any instrument under the sun with just the first note of the Hindustani octave that she sang, had a daughter who wobbled and tottered unsteadily across a three-minute song blithely unaware of her tone-deafness? Sukanya went on to murder two more of their songs.

Who would tell her that she didn't make the grade? Eddie was much better at this sort of thing and would have done the job with clinical finesse. But Sukanya had approached Ravan and he knew that it would be unfair to pass the buck to his partner. He was pondering how to phrase the bad news when he heard Eddie come clean.

'I am sure you will take this in the right spirit, Sukanya. You're a lively, confident singer, but you have some way to go technically.'

Ravan was expecting a stormy meltdown but he had miscalculated the young woman's response.

'Don't imagine for a moment that I'm likely to give up,' she said chirpily and left.

A month later, Ravan was coming home late at night and had stepped into the lift when Sukanya got in as the doors closed. Had she been waiting for him, Ravan wondered and was immediately contrite. He didn't like himself when he was full of suspicion and imagined the worst about people.

'Hi.'

'Hello.'

'You haven't forgotten me, have you?'

'Do I already look like an Alzheimer's case to you?'

Sukanya leaned over and pressed the emergency stop button.

Ravan's eyebrows rose. Don't sound alarmed or angry, he told himself. Play this sensibly and it will pass. 'Anything the problem? Are you okay?'

She pushed him against the rear wall and was pressing against him now. Her tongue was forcing itself into his mouth and her right hand was at his crotch unzipping his fly. Ravan was about to push her away but then thought the better of it. He disengaged himself slowly and drew back.

'You've made my day. Imagine an attractive young woman like you noticing me. Only the third time in my life that it's happened. I'm on cloud nine. Thank you.' He pressed the button for the eleventh floor. 'But I have a wife. This will perhaps sound old-fashioned but I love her very much. Good night.'

The lift doors opened and Ravan stepped out. She was right behind him.

'This isn't your floor.'

'Stop wasting time and open the door,' she snapped at him.

'My wife's at home.'

'No, she's not.'

'Please go home. It's getting very late.'

'You better let me in because if you don't, I'll tell your wife that you invited me over and raped me.'

'What do you want from me, Sukanya?'

'I want a singing contract and a recording within a fortnight.'

'No point lying to you. Your voice is not up to scratch.'

'I know you're saying no to me only because my mother told you to.'

'Your mother doesn't even know you've done a test with us. Please don't do this. You'll regret it.'

'Open the door.'

'No, I won't.'

'I'm warning you, open the door. Or you'll regret it.'

'I'll take my chances.'

Part Two

16

An eerie silence. The meridian sun was a tourniquet being tightened till it had squeezed out and choked off the remnants of air. The oppressive heat weighed down on the town of Ghazab. Leaves drooped lifelessly from a few ancient trees as if they had been sculpted on a frieze. A lone man in a police officer's uniform appeared like a long-forgotten, translucent ghost in the distance. As he came closer, he saw a dog lying motionless on the road. The assistant superintendent of police bent down and called out its name, 'Hoshiyaar. Talk to me, Hoshiyaar. What's happened?' The beast raised its head feebly, its eyes mournful, bleated and sank back. The policeman could see the wound in its neck now, a bullet hole.

The officer went to the district police head-office but there was nobody in the front room. The flame of the kerosene stove in the corner was burning but the brewed tea had long since evaporated and the brass pot had turned an angry grey-red. The policeman turned off the stove and looked up. The lock on the armoury had been ripped open and all seven rifles were missing. He went to the lock-up at the back. The five hawaldars and the sub-inspector who worked there were sprawled haphazardly on top of each other.

The townspeople watched from behind their windows as the officer ran towards a squat British-style bungalow at the end of the road. He flung the door open. There were bodies lying on the floor in congealed pools of blood, two children, a boy and a girl, and two women, one close to sixty and the other thirty or thirty-two at the most. From a distance one could vaguely see that the children's throats had been slashed. As the officer looked at the note pinned to the door leading to another room to the left, his eyes glancingly took in the exposed legs of the women and the deep gashes on their breasts, thighs and legs.

'Nothing personal, Superintendent Jwala Singh. Just settling accounts. The previous officer-in-charge and his men killed eight of our children and raped and murdered our wives and mothers. Please accept our condolences for your loss. The score's even now.'

Jwala Singh read the letter for the seventh time, leaned shakily against a shabby writing table and sank into a chair. He sat there, blindly running his hand again and again over the note as if to straighten it out. When he finally got up, he walked towards his children, gently closed his daughter's eyes, then the son's, mother's and wife's.

'Cut,' yelled the director, ClickClick Kapil.

* * *

'How does it feel to launch your own production company?' Harish Patel, the film correspondent and critic asked Eddie while waiting for ClickClick to join them. It was a trite question and deserved a trite answer but this was R&E's first venture and Eddie frowned in concentration as he tried to articulate his response.

'It feels good. No, it feels great, grand. But more than that it feels right, as if the logic of our careers demanded it. Of course it's a big step for us, a total departure from what we have been doing for the last ten or eleven years.'

'Is it true that your friends from the industry and even your close family warned you to stick to your profession. We all know that the industry is a living graveyard of unfinished films and failed producers. Far more seasoned and shrewd professionals have come to grief when they strayed from their field and decided to become producers.'

'Nothing ventured, nothing gained.' Eddie had obviously expected this question and had rehearsed his answer. 'I'm sure our families and friends mean well but all the great breakthroughs in the sciences and arts have come from people who did not listen to received wisdom. We've tried to learn from other people's errors and mistakes. The most common reason for failure is a lack of planning. Hitchcock spent months, sometimes even a year, planning his movies to the last detail. Every shot was framed in advance; he knew exactly where the camera would be and what lens he would use, whether a shot would be a long shot, a zoom, a dead close-up, a pan or a trolley. The shooting took only a month or forty-five days and the editing was finished in a couple of months. The reverse ratio is the norm in our industry. We've made absolutely certain we're not making that mistake. ClickClick is meticulous to a fault. Between him and us, we've got the whole movie mapped out.'

'But what about those spoilsports called "unforeseen circumstances"?'

'We've factored them in too.' ClickClick appeared from behind the camera and settled into a chair. 'By budgeting an extra ten per cent for such exigencies. As Eddie told you, we've taken Hitchcock to heart. You've been with us for the last week and you must have noticed we are not merely on schedule, we are a day-and-a-half ahead.'

'You certainly seem to have done your homework.' Harish Patel turned to Eddie again. 'But you've doubled the risks for your film by not just becoming producers but by introducing two utterly unknown actors.'

Eddie laughed. 'Yes, two total unknowns. But no one had heard of us when we composed the music for *Hulla Gulla*, and choreographed its dances and its stunts. It might come as a surprise to you but we are finally doing the one thing that we've aspired to since we were children.'

'Ravan-ji, I believe you've not been well.'

ClickClick and Eddie looked apprehensively at Ravan. They had warned Harish Patel to leave Ravan alone but you could depend on the journalist to ignore any humane consideration for a bit of prurient gossip.

'Besides, don't forget we're trained actors. Method actors.' Eddie spoke up even before ClickClick Kapil could deflect Patel's nosiness and drew the journalist's attention away from Ravan. 'Superintendent Jwala Singh is a tortured character. He can never forget that Maan Singh murdered his wife, mother and children. He has spent his entire life hunting Maan Singh and though he's now the commissioner of police, he cannot for a day forget the past. He lives for one thing and one thing alone. Vengeance. It is mere chance that his duty and his personal wishes coincide.'

'Who decided that Ravan-ji should play Jwala Singh and you the dacoit?'

'The director, naturally, but we wouldn't have had any problem if our roles were reversed. Isn't that what acting's supposed to be, getting into the mind, body and spirit of any given character?'

ClickClick was not going to allow Harish Patel to go back to probing Ravan's 'health' as he called it. 'You've missed one of the most important things going for us.'

'What's that, ClickClick-ji?'

ClickClick leaned back in his chair and held forth expansively. 'All the planning in the world won't help if the story doesn't fly. Our story and screenplay are written by Asmaan-ji. Of the nine movies which have been made from her screenplays, all have broken even. She's not only the first woman screenplay writer to make it big, she holds an all-time record for the highest number of super-hits. Seven so far. And we're hoping ours will be the biggest in the annals of the Hindi film. She has been following the Jwala Singh–Maan Singh story and researching it for the last seven or eight years. The only reason the screenplay was not finished was because there was no closure. Then seven months ago Jwala Singh got his revenge. He caught the bandit chief just seventeen miles from here.'

'The question is, what's so unique about your dacoit film? There are at least a dozen I can name offhand that have dealt with the same subject in the last decade.'

'Sure you can.' Eddie left it to ClickClick to answer that one. 'You could say the same thing about boy-meets-girl films. You'll agree that the numbers go up exponentially when you consider these love stories. So why is it that *Casablanca* is a perennial classic while hundreds of others are forgotten? It depends on how compelling the story is and how you tell it. Asmaan-ji is not telling a simple dacoit story. It is a story of an obsession, an obsession that verges on madness. On the one hand, it is the clash of two titans in the manner of the Peter O'Toole–Richard Burton film *Becket.* On the other, it is a thriller: who will get the better of whom, the policeman or the dacoit? But what is unique about our film is that it questions fundamental assumptions. When you see how both the police and the dacoits trade in the currency of violence and brutality, the ethical high ground which the police are supposed to occupy disappears completely. So who is the villain?'

'Since Asmaan's the scriptwriter as well as the lyricist, the songs are not interludes for the audience to go and take a leak but are integral to the story. We've already recorded all eight songs for the movie.' Eddie took over from his director as if on cue. 'We are the first in India to shoot a film on the very locations where most of the action actually took place. It's raised the cost considerably but the results are gratifying. The authenticity makes for a very different film experience. The audience will feel the terrible heat of the sun and the dust storms in the Chambal valley in the summer just as they did when they saw *Lawrence of Arabia* and even though they may be watching the film in an air-conditioned theatre, they will be scalded by the scorching sun.'

'Camera ready,' the continuity girl shouted on the megaphone. 'Take your positions.'

'One question. Have you ever thought of making a film about your own lives?'

'You must be joking. Nothing interesting or dramatic has ever happened to Ravan or me. As you know we were the lowliest of the lowly. We were extras. Who would be interested in our lives? Not even us.'

* * *

Falling ... falling ... falling...

'Today is the day. Or rather tonight's the night when my fate will be decided. I don't mean to sound dramatic but you will understand the import of what I am trying to get at in a little while.' Asmaan unfolded a note Prajapati Sehgal had left on his table for her to read from at

the condolence meeting. 'It's a week since my film Goongi *was released. Almost all the reviews were in and so were the box-office receipts and I decided to have a private dinner last evening for just the inner circle, Asmaan, Pieta and Ravan, Belle and Eddie, to celebrate the event. Asmaan was in fine form and laid the basic parameters for judging the quality of the reviews.*

'"Isn't it obvious," she asked, "that all the critics who like our films have superb taste, fine insights, and rare critical acumen. As to all those who think otherwise, well, what can one say? Those poor sods can't tell the difference between horse piss and ambrosia."

'"Here, here." Everybody at the table clapped in unison and she read out seven or eight of the flattering pieces while ensuring that no mention was made of the two rotten tomatoes. It was indeed a lovely evening and we decided to meet the next morning to chalk out the plans for our next film.

'All of you who had taken the trouble to come last night, bear with me for just a few minutes. The good news is that you won't have to listen to me ever again. I have often wondered how the leaders of doomsday cults fix upon a date for the end of the world. Is it a random choice or is it predicated upon some arcane calculations and prophecies? It is quite another matter how these gurus and their groups of perfervid believers adjust to the fact of survival after the apocalyptic date has passed and it's obvious that they've made perfect asses of themselves.

'But here's a conundrum that I haven't been able to resolve. About a month ago I had a vivid dream that I would die in my sleep on 15 October. Do I believe in such things? I am an agnostic inclining to atheism. But I will grant that there are phenomena which defy explanation. Even if there was any truth to my dream, I would still maintain my agnostic stance. The human mind is one hell of an instrument but let's not delude ourselves. We don't understand a millionth of the mystery of the world. And I am truly grateful for that.

'If you are reading this note, it's obvious that I kept my date with the appointed hour. If it was a false dream, naturally you will not hear about this weird prediction. I wanted to be awake for the momentous event when the guy with the scythe turned up. That way perhaps I would be

able to understand the mystery behind the phenomena of soothsaying and astral influences. But knowing me and my set habits, I will most likely fall asleep as soon as I hit the bed.

'It's my death and I trust I am allowed to dictate how this meeting should be conducted. I have attended dozens of condolence meetings where all those present had to sit through interminable speeches praising the dead. We in India like to hear our own voices and despite instructions not to speak for more than three or four minutes carry on for twenty or twenty-five. By the time the last speaker is done, almost everybody is about to collapse from boredom, and cannot forgive the dead man for dying.

'Well, no speeches today except mine. Don't forget, I am dead and should be allowed my last wish. We are going to have a party but before that I want to tell you very briefly about my five children. The first two, a son and a daughter, I had with my one and only wife who died two years ago. Both of them are in the States and are practising medicine. The other three I had rather late in life. Luckily they were grown up by the time I begat them. Two boys and a girl. Asmaan, Ravan and Eddie.

'How many people you know have had a chance at a second life? Four flops in a row. My career, as you all know, was over. Dead. These three were my second chance. And by God what a second chance at life it has been. We have made three films together. How can I thank them? Some debts one can never repay. I certainly have no desire or intention to do so. Talk about being lucky. That's me. I love my five children.

'Ravan and Eddie, you have already informed my children in the States and told them that it is my wish that they do not come to see a dead man even if he happens to be their father. Now will you do the honours? Will you sing Asmaan's songs at the condolence meeting? Not sad songs. I want to go to the other world happy to have known all of you. As my next of kin in the country, you two will light the pyre. Alvida. Goodbye.'

Neither Ravan nor Eddie were in any mood to sing that day, but how could they refuse when Prajapati-ji, their newly discovered father, had asked them to get the party swinging? Asmaan accompanied them after the first song, then Belle pitched in and then all the others who had sung in Sehgal Sahab's films and soon it was a fest to celebrate his death.

*What did Asmaan, Eddie and he make of Prajapati-ji's dream? Ravan wondered. What would anyone make of it? But he could not forgive the man who had been their mentor and had guided them through the shoals and deadly undercurrents of Bollywood politics, hypocrisy, overkill, double-dealing and chicanery. Now he too had betrayed them. Asmaan had always maintained that when a screenplay writer ran out of steam or was plain lazy, he resolved a crisis by bumping off the main character. That's what Sehgal-ji had done, taken the easy way out. They were supposed to have met the morning after the post-*Goongi *dinner to discuss their next film when he had ditched them. No notice, no goodbye, no nothing. He had just walked out on them never to return.*

17

Eddie was not exaggerating when he said that the three of them, ClickClick Kapil, Ravan and him, had given the location for the film a good deal of thought. They had reconnoitred the entire Chambal valley and chosen a section of the ravines which was only twenty kilometres from the city of Gwalior and yet almost isolated from the rest of the world. That made it a little difficult for anybody in the film team to play hookey. Since the intention was to keep the shooting schedule as tight as possible, they had rented an old haveli not far from the north-western edge of the ravines, which had seen much better days. There was no water in the taps and the sewage pipes were either broken or clogged. Which meant using the toilets in the haveli was forbidden. The production manager had arranged for half a dozen 'thunder boxes' in makeshift bamboo sheds. They were cleaned thrice a day with a strong germ-killing bleach. Whoever was unhappy with the arrangements was free to squat in the fields under the open skies so long as it was not in the off-the-limit ravines.

Most of the minor roles were filled by extras from the old days. They were more than happy to be elevated to the status of character actors. There was roll call at 5 in the morning and one at 10 at night. The call sheet was for 6 every day, sometimes even as early as 5.30.

The production manager had hired cooks from the town of Jhansi. Tea was in constant supply and so were snacks. Everybody got up at the same time, ate together and ate the same food. The effect of this on morale and camaraderie was a trifle short of extraordinary. Nobody got a weekend off and yet there was hardly any cribbing and complaining. A water tanker brought drinking water from Gwalior every alternate day. The cast and crew took a dip in the stream called Chhoti Ganga or bathed in one of three bamboo sheds fitted with raised stone platforms which had channels to drain the water.

On the eleventh day of shooting, a scrawny villager with tobacco-blackened teeth and baleful eyes limped in with a wooden staff, stood in front of the camera and demanded ten thousand rupees.

'What for?' the cameraman asked him.

'That man there,' he said, pointing to ClickClick, 'he's done black magic.'

'Yeah, sure. I not only did black but red, green and yellow magic too.' ClickClick leered exaggeratedly at the man. 'Now get out of the way.'

'I'm not moving till you pay me.'

'All right, wise guy. You've had your moment in front of the camera. We're working to a tight schedule and every minute's costing a bomb. Leave.'

The man didn't budge. He leaned heavily on his staff to emphasize his limp and stared defiantly at ClickClick.

'Come on, move. Or I'm going to have to throw you out.'

There was something malign about the cripple's doleful eyes. 'Touch me and I will have the entire village here.'

'What kind of black magic did he do?' Eddie asked.

'He took pictures of my children and stole their essence.'

'What nonsense. He takes pictures of me every day and nothing's happened to my soul.'

'My eldest son Surinder is dying because this man aimed his *kamarrah* at him. Now my other children too are falling sick one by one.'

'I'm sorry that your son is sick. But my friend ClickClick has got nothing to do with it. Take your son to a doctor and he'll be fine.'

'I took my son to the vaid and he told me this man had done black magic.'

'I don't even recall seeing you or your children. Everybody in the village wanted pictures of their children, so I took them.' ClickClick was getting impatient. The sun was going down and he would not be able to get the last shot of the day. 'How come none of the others are complaining?'

'My neighbour Randhwa's son got high fever four days ago and now Pawan's three have fallen sick.'

'And it's all my doing, right?'

ClickClick's sarcasm was lost on the man. 'Yes,' the lame man replied stone-facedly.

'Too bad. Now move out of the way or I am going to miss the shot.'

'I am talking about my son's life here.'

'Let's talk this over sensibly,' Eddie intervened lest things got out of hand. 'What's your name?'

'Ramchander.'

'Ramchander-ji, here's twenty rupees. Take your son to a good allopathic doctor, not to some local quack. He will poke your son with a needle and he will be fine in no time.'

Ramchander pocketed the money. 'He's already had seven needles but the doctor says he can't do anything more. There's no hope now. That's why I took him to the vaid.'

'Get him out.' ClickClick was frantic now. 'Or we've lost the shot.'

Eddie dipped into his wallet again.

'If you give him money,' Ravan spoke for the first time, 'he'll be back for more.'

'What do you want me to do?' Eddie asked Ravan. 'If we don't get that shot, it's going to cost us a few thousand at least.'

Eddie handed Ramchander a hundred-rupee note and told him to take his son to the municipal hospital in Gwalior. 'If you think we are an easy touch and you can blackmail us, you are much mistaken. Don't bother to come back. It's not going to work.'

Four days later, Ramchander was back, this time with a policeman. It was still very hot in the daytime but the policeman was wearing his thick, winter khaki woollen overcoat that rode up his enormous belly. He had a week's growth of grey stubble and hooded beady eyes that looked lugubriously at the bunch of people who surrounded him. He had seen mankind up close and there was nothing to recommend it. There were only two varieties of human beings. Those who were nothing but trouble and the rest who were even more trouble.

'I've just cremated my eldest son,' Ramchander told nobody in particular.

'I'm sorry to hear that,' Eddie said.

'He was the sole support of the family.'

'What about you? Don't you work?'

'How can I? I'm a cripple. My other son Dasrath is dying now.'

'So what do you want us to do?' ClickClick realized that he had played into the hands of the man as soon as the words were out of his mouth.

'I want compensation for my dead son.' Ramchander leveraged the staff to manoeuvre himself in front of the director and block his way.

'Get out.' ClickClick was a laid-back director who rarely lost his cool but the sight of the unctuous Ramchander and the combination of obsequious self-pity and the insolent belief that the world owed him big time for his misfortunes seemed to undo his self-control.

'You killed my son. I saw you do black magic on him.'

'Get the fuck out of here.' ClickClick shoved the man aside.

'You brutally assaulted a lame man. I'm going to arrest you.' The policeman was looking expectantly at Ramchander while fiddling with the handcuffs hanging from his belt. The cripple had missed his cue but he was willing to make up for lost time. He began to scream as if ClickClick had performed an unnatural act upon him and that too in public. Before anyone could grasp what was happening, the handcuffs were around the director's wrists and the constable was leading him out of the ravines with the lame man limping behind him.

Eddie sat brain-dead in his producer–actor's chair. It had been a productive day and the morning's shoot had gone off well. Now a policeman was walking off with his director in handcuffs and *Jaan Se Pyara Dushman* was as good as interred. He attempted to piece together the sequence of events from the moment the wretched villager Ramchander had dragged himself over, his morose eyes wishing the whole world ill, but it just didn't add up. There was no telling whether Ramchander really believed that the camera had stolen his son's soul and was responsible for his death or he was merely blackmailing them. But that was beside the point. All ClickClick had done was to nudge Ramchander out of his way to get on with the shooting and the next thing Eddie knew was that his director was probably up for a jail term. Eddie glanced surreptitiously at Ravan for support, advice, quick thinking, even an I-told-you-so look, but his friend was holed up somewhere deep inside himself where no one could reach him.

How the hell had things come to such a desperate pass? How had Ravan become so inaccessible?

* * *

Falling ... falling ... falling...

It had come as a shock to both Ravan and Eddie when not only the film magazines, the industry journals and AIR Vividh Bharati, but even the mainstream newspapers had dedicated their weekend editions to 'The New Music: Ten Years of E&R or R&E', 'Ravan and Eddie: What Next?', 'Ten Years of the R&E Music Revolution', 'Eddie and Ravan, The Second Decade'. Had it been that long since Hulla Gulla*?*

Surely, Eddie hoped, these journalists must have got their dates wrong. My God, no, the two of them were getting old. And then Pieta had announced that she was pregnant. Every cliché under the sun about what babies can do, the miracles they can perform, even the ones who were yet to be born, was on display in the Coutinho and Pawar households. You would be forgiven for thinking that this was the Second Coming. Eddie wondered if the two families were going a little soft in the head though he himself was not immune to the occasional spasm of avuncular emotions. Indeed, the great thaw had begun.

Violet and Parvatibai had been civil to each other and even exchanged boxes of sweets and savouries for Diwali since Pieta and Ravan had got married but Violet had preferred to keep the relationship, as she liked to say, thus far and no further. Now there was much toing and froing between the two families. Violet and Parvatibai visited Akaash at least once a week and, as the pregnancy advanced, refused to let Pieta come to

CWD Chawl Number 17 because they thought it was not a good idea for her to climb five storeys. The rate at which they were knitting and buying clothes for the baby, one would have thought Pieta was about to have octuplets.

For years now, Violet and Parvatibai had prayed daily for a grandchild and now that Pieta was finally pregnant, Father Agnello was asked to say special Mass for the safe arrival of the baby while the Pawars had the Hindu Bhat-ji come over to do a puja to propitiate the gods. There was, however, a good deal of subterranean competition at work. Both families were drawing up endless lists of names for boys and girls though it has to be admitted that Parvatibai was completely outclassed by Violet. The names of Catholic saints alone accounted for the full calendar year. Add to that, there were at least over two hundred hyphenated double-barrelled first names in Violet's family tree.

Then there was the question of the naming ceremony for the child: would he/she be baptized in a church or would there be a Hindu barsa*? Here, too, the lady from the fourth floor was not in the same league as the one from the top storey. Pieta's injunction to her mother that any child who was born to Ravan and her would choose his faith only when he was past eighteen and not before and that until then no religion was to be imposed was completely ignored. Violet took it for granted that nothing less than a papal decree would proclaim that any grandchild of hers would have to be a Catholic. Or else, the Vatican would go to war with the subcontinent with the entire weight of the Christian world behind the Coutinhos.*

Then, in late September, Eddie received a call from Ravan around 2.30 at night.

'I'm taking Piya to Nanavati Hospital.'

'What's wrong?' Eddie had asked groggily.

'The pains have started.'

'I thought she was due in December.'

'Will you inform your mother, Granna and my mother and bring them to Nanavati Hospital?'

By the time Eddie got to the hospital with Violet, Granna, Parvatibai and Belle, who had returned just that morning after recording another album in LA, Pieta was lying in a bed in a private room, covered from head to toe in a white sheet, while Ravan sat in a chair looking as if he had been beheaded. He was not impolite but his answers to all questions were curt and monosyllabic. The nurse on duty was putting away the few things Ravan had hastily packed in an overnight bag while the registrar of the maternity ward wrote down the details of Pieta Coutinho's history, the diagnosis, the line of treatment given and the cause of death in the patient's medical file. Eddie realized that the hospital staff witnessed this kind of thing daily and yet he couldn't help feeling that they were somehow responsible for his sister's death.

'Can't you wait at least till we take my sister's body away?' Eddie turned upon the registrar as if he wanted to assault the doctor.

'I'm sorry, sir,' the doctor replied, 'but there's another patient who needs the room.'

Belle touched Eddie's elbow and steered him away.

Over the next few months, Eddie watched Ravan with a sense of growing disquiet. It was becoming clear to him that this man, the one who was his best friend and whose grief he was so keen to assuage, was not a human being at all. If you took his cardiogram, he was sure it would come out blank. The reason was clear. There was no heart there. Not once had he shown an iota of grief or any other emotion. At the funeral he behaved as if he was a mere passer-by who had to kill half-an-hour before catching a flight. Eddie did not recall him shedding a tear at the hospital, at the funeral or at any other time after Pieta's death. He went to work the very day after Pieta died. As far as Eddie could make out, Ravan ate his three meals, he worked out in their private gym, he slept, he got up, he went to work. Nothing had changed for him except that he hardly spoke a word.

Things came to a head after Meenakshi Venkatraman, or Anamika, the nameless one, as she was known to the public, finished recording one of Asmaan's most memorable lyrics. It was called 'I'll never be first. Second-best is the best I can do'.

I'll never be first.
Second-best is the best I can do.
What matter though,

You will be always first for me.
Standbys can't be choosy,
Understudies can't be picky.

You may not be my first
And if you move on,
You'll not be my last either.
But I'm a virgin still
And will always be one.
For I'm the Ganga.
Many take a dip in my waters
And come up cleansed and pure.
But the sins of others
Can never pollute me.

Ah, my reluctant lover,
Before you call me a whore
Ask yourself this
When was the last time
You caught yourself being faithful?

Asmaan was at her best when she was writing for Mrs Venkatraman. Meenakshi–Anamika warmed to the power of the words and got inside the character singing the song and added something intangible which spoke directly to the heart without ever allowing the listener the luxury of shedding a tear. Both Eddie and Ravan were lost in their thoughts on the way back. The car was climbing up Pali Hill when Ravan mumbled, 'I did it.'

'Did what?' Eddie asked.

'I killed Piya.'

Eddie couldn't get over what he had heard even as he got into bed and told Belle what had happened that night. 'He said it, just like that. Made a clean breast of it. I did it. I killed Pieta. Sorry, he said Piya. That's what she insisted he call her.'

'I wouldn't read too much into it, Eddie. I think he loved Pieta so much he still can't comprehend how she could have left him. The only way he can come to terms with it is to blame himself for her death. Just

as he was made to believe that as a child he was responsible for your father's death.'

Belle hadn't got the story quite right, though. Violet had told Eddie what had happened the day before he was born. Parvatibai was standing at the common balcony on the fourth floor with her son, Ram, for that's what his original name was, in her arms. Just then the unborn Eddie's father, Victor Coutinho, who was returning from his office had innocently waved out to Ram from the road and lo and behold, the stupid one-year-old baby had taken off and leapt out. He was in free fall and that should have been the end of him but Eddie's father had had the presence of mind to catch him and promptly had a heart attack. Well, Ram had survived and been renamed Ravan to escape the evil eye but there was no getting away from the fact that he had killed the very man who had saved him.

It was a few weeks after Ravan had told his friend that he had killed Pieta that Eddie woke up with the doorbell drilling a hole in his brain. He cursed whoever it was ringing the bell convulsively. 'Damn it, do they think we are deaf? What time is it? It's not even twenty-five to seven.'

It was the maid Godavari. She was panting and sobbing hysterically. 'What is it?' Eddie asked again and again but the only answer he got was more howling, though this time she also kept pointing her finger to the right. 'Our neighbours? They said something to you?'

She shook her head but the finger was still pointing in the same direction. Belle had joined him. 'It's Ravan. She has the key to his flat,' she said.

'What about Ravan?'

Belle ran inside and flung a pair of trousers and a shirt at Eddie as she slipped an old dress over her head and the two of them rushed to Ravan's apartment.

The air-conditioning was on but the drawing room was smelling something ghastly. It was the putrid stench of vomit, a combination of regurgitated bile and whisky. There were at least six empty strips of Calmpose on the glass table, a half-empty bottle of Johnny Walker scotch lay on its side on the carpet and next to it a lifeless Ravan with his nose in his own muck. There was a note on the table. 'What's the point?' it asked. There were two more sentences, one in Marathi and the other in English. 'Amhi jato amuchya gava. Piya's waiting for me.'

'Fuck. Fuck. Fuck.' Eddie picked him up in his arms as Belle rushed to call the lift. 'I'll kill you if you die, Ravan, I'll kill you.'

Eddie knew the Marathi words Ravan had quoted. They were from the great saint-poet Tukaram. Eddie used to sing that abhang when he was in the Sabha with Lele Guruji. He had not been able to understand the words in those days and even now they didn't make too much sense. It came to him as Belle drove the car to the doctor's that the mystic saint was talking about 'going home' or as Indians liked to say 'going to their native village'. What the hell was the matter with Ravan? Didn't the idiot know that home was when and where the two of them were together? The two of them were inseparable. E&R / R&E, that's what all the papers and magazines called them. There was no break between the names and the letters.

Eddie had to admit that he himself had been of no use to Ravan. On the contrary, he had had serious doubts about him. He had watched Ravan's interminable silences with alarm over the past few weeks. Eddie had expressed his concerns to Asmaan but she had echoed Belle's view that when something traumatic happens, sometimes people behave strangely. She had gradually taken Ravan under her wing as she had done with Eddie when Belle had switched off all communication with him while she was in England. But she had not stopped at that.

'This screenplay's for the two of you,' she said one evening a few months after Ravan had pulled through.

Both Ravan and Eddie were tired and keen to have dinner and go to bed. 'Can we do this some other time?' Ravan had asked her querulously. Asmaan was normally the soul of courtesy and consideration. But her answer this time was an unambiguous, 'No, we do it now.' There was no preamble, no preface, no introduction, no nothing; she plunged straight into a hundred-and-four minute reading of a script. She had good reason to be cocky for it took barely two-and-a-half minutes for the two of them to be hooked. It turned out she had done an enormous amount of research and worked on the quiet for three months on the screenplay of Jaan Se Pyara Dushman. *It was an amazing script, it gripped you from the eerie opening shot. It did what the best storytellers do, catch you by the throat and egg you to ask, 'And then? And then? And then?'*

'What did you mean,' Eddie asked, 'when you said this one's for the two of you?'

'Just that.'

'I'm sorry for being so dumb but I don't get it.'

'All the years we've been together, I've had to listen to you saying that the one thing you were meant for was acting. It was the sole reason, you said, why you were born.'

'Every extra will tell you that.'

'But not every extra can tell you that he had a screenplay written just for him and his partner.'

'Just for Ravan and me? You can't be serious.'

'I'm afraid I am. Those two roles are meant for the two of you.'

'Who's going to cough up the money for a movie with two greenhorns?'

'That's up to us.' Eddie could barely hear Ravan. 'We're going to make it happen.'

That was then and this was now, a good nineteen months later. Asmaan's screenplay Jaan Se Pyara Dushman *had worked wonders on Ravan. They had tried hard to find a producer and financiers for the project. Actually, there had been no shortage of producers keen to do the film except that they wanted two established superstars. It was Ravan who had roped in ClickClick Kapil. He was a big name by now and together they had got backing for the film. Through all that time, Asmaan had shepherded Ravan and they seemed to have drawn closer. Unfortunately, she was not there on the shoot and Ravan had gone back to being as he had been after Pieta died, hidden somewhere behind the dead eyes. The only time he seemed to come out of the hole he had dug for himself was when the cameraman's assistant yelled 'camera ready' and the clapperboard displaying the number of the shot and the take was slapped shut tight.*

18

ClickClick was calling out to Eddie desperately. 'Do something, Eddie. We can't let these two clowns ruin our film.' But Eddie had no idea what he should or could do to get the policeman to release the director.

'Stop, listen to me, hawaldar. Ramchander-ji, please stop. That's the director of our film. We can't shoot the film without him.'

'That's your problem, not mine,' the constable looked back and said officiously. 'A crime has been committed and that too in the presence of a representative of the police. The law will take its own course.'

'I'm sure we can work something out.'

'Do you think you can bribe an agent of the law?'

Eddie had half a mind to tell him, 'Why, you dummy, that *is* the law, that you can't get a damn thing done unless you warm someone's hand', but thought the better of it.

'Hawaldar, we both know my friend ClickClick just tapped Ramchander-ji on the shoulder, nothing more.'

'Assault and battery, that's what it was, and that too committed on a poor, helpless man whom God saw fit to cripple for life. Did you not hear Ramchander screaming in pain? But now I'm going to have to take you in too.'

'Me? What did I do?'

'You should ask. You tried to bribe an officer of the law who has served the nation selflessly for over twenty-seven years.'

Eddie looked at the policeman as if he had lost his mind. 'You've got to be kidding.'

'You will find out soon enough. Five to seven years is the least you'll get. Move, I haven't got all the time in the world.'

This jerk was in earnest. Eddie put his arm around the hawaldar's shoulder in a show of camaraderie.

'Take your arm off.'

Eddie was beginning to panic. 'Could I have a word with you in private, Inspector?' Eddie hoped that promoting the constable would inveigle him into the policeman's good books. 'Please.'

'What for?' The constable was still surly but he had handed over the rope tied to the handcuffs to Ramchander.

'You are a reasonable man. You know that we work to a very tight schedule. We've already lost half a day today. If we lose any more time, we'll be in serious trouble.'

'What do you expect me to do?'

'I'm sure we can find a solution that will satisfy all parties.'

'Maybe. If you make it worth my while.'

'You mean worth my while,' the cripple corrected the constable.

'Mind your business, Ramchander. And mind the prisoner.' The policeman was walking back towards the camp.

Eddie thanked the Trinity of the Father, the Son and the Holy Spirit, said a Hail Mary, and blessed all the saints in heaven as he walked briskly alongside the policeman. For a while there it seemed that he had run into the only honest constable on the subcontinent, and was relieved to find that the hawaldar would not break rank with his comrades and was open to reason.

'What would make it worth your while, officer?'

'Why don't you suggest a figure and we can take it from there?'

Eddie wished Prajapati Sehgal was around to guide and advise him. Maybe even ClickClick might have some idea how to conduct the delicate negotiations but that was out of the question now. As to Ravan, well, might as well ask the stones and the birds and the bees. Eddie decided his best bet was to pretend to be a man of the world and, instead of making an offer, steer the conversation to the stars, not the ones in the heavens but the ones on the silver screen and how close he was to them and would you believe it, one of them would soon be with them in the ravines. After all, policemen were no different from millions of star-struck Indians.

'Do you know who will be here in a few days?'

'No, I don't. And I don't give a fucking fart. Quit stalling and get down to business.'

'I could introduce you to the great Sapna-ji when she comes.'

'Tell you what, I'm taking you and that director of yours to the lock-up and you can spend the next few years jacking off with your Sapna-ji there.'

This wasn't working, not at all. Come to think of it, he couldn't have done worse. If he didn't change course immediately, it would be too late. Eddie came clean. 'I've never had to do this before. Frankly, I wouldn't even know where to begin. Just tell me what you want.'

'What are you two whispering?' Eddie was surprised how quickly Ramchander had caught up with them.

'Where's the prisoner?' the constable queried.

'Where will he go with the cuffs on him?'

'Get back this minute, smartarse. I hope for your sake that the prisoner's still there.'

'I've every right to know what you two are up to.' The lame man looked pointedly at the constable. 'It's my son who's dead.'

'Another word from you and I'll knock out the remaining dirty teeth from your mouth.'

Ramchander stared at the constable with undisguised loathing and scratched looping snakes on the ground with his wooden staff, unsure of how to respond.

'You owe me, Shyamlal,' he said as he retreated reluctantly.

Well, at least now Eddie had a handle on the constable. He had his name.

'What did he mean, Shyamlal-ji?'

'Who cares? Fifty.' It sounded like who-cares-fifty to Eddie. The crew and cast were watching the two now as Ravan sat in his chair staring vacantly into the middle distance.

'Sorry?' Eddie tried to puzzle that one out. 'Oh, I get it. Why didn't you say so earlier? We needn't have wasted so much time.' He peeled out a fifty-rupee note.

'Is this your idea of a joke?' Shyamlal looked sourly at Eddie.

'You said fifty.'

'Fifty thousand, you arsehole.'

Eddie needed to sit down.

'You aren't serious.'

'What do you think?'

'Where would we get that kind of money from?'

The hawaldar chortled humourlessly. 'You said every day costs you thousands of rupees.'

'Yes, it does.'

'So what's fifty thousand rupees to you?'

'A hell of a lot since every rupee has to be accounted for. That's why we have an accountant even on location who has to report back to our financiers. Under what head could we justify such a huge expense?'

'I'm sure you will think of something.'

'We are on a tight budget. Every Monday we get a fixed sum of money from Bombay and it has to take care of thirty-three actors, crew members and cooks for the whole week. There's no provision for unforeseen circumstances.'

'You'll make lakhs on your film and you're giving me this shit about being on a budget.'

'*Aapke mooh mein shakkar*. A film can make money only after it's released and that too only if it's successful. Right now there's no movie.'

'Is this what you meant by making it worth my while?'

'I thought it would be something reasonable.'

'And what would be reasonable according to your lights?'

'Whatever we can afford, I guess.'

'You've wasted enough time. Thirty thousand.'

'Nine thousand eight hundred and fifty. That's all the accountant's got. It's what we owe to the crew for last week.'

'You can keep it. Let's go. Writing two FIRs will take the better part of the evening.'

'What do we do now?' the cameraman asked Eddie.

'Can you give me just five minutes to settle things here?'

'If anybody wants to see you, let him come to the police station.'

'Ravan, will you take charge, please?'

Ravan didn't bother to look up. There were times when Eddie wanted to grab his friend and shake him out of his stupor. It was odd, Ravan was totally undemanding and yet Eddie had to watch over him every waking moment and often even when he was asleep. If you didn't put a plate of food in front of him and insist that he eat, he would have had no problem starving himself to death.

Shyamlal must have gone fifty steps with Eddie when Ravan ran towards them. 'Give Shyamlal the money,' he told Eddie.

'It's not enough. He won't accept it.'

'It is now.' Ravan pulled out the gold chain which hung from his neck under his vest and handed it to the policeman. It had lain there against his chest since the time Pieta and he had started seeing each other years ago. It was her first gift to him. She had put it around his neck, telling him that she didn't trust him, not one bit, but now he was chained to her forever. Well, that's exactly what he had done, tied himself to a dead woman. He had become a full-time member of the cult of death. As an homage to her memory, he had mummified Pieta. As if that was not bad enough, he had attempted to join her by trying to commit suicide. His self-pity was bottomless. He had begun to believe that he was nothing less than the victim of a cosmic tragedy. He could see clearly that his monumental silences were really an insatiable need for attention. He wanted the whole world to see how bereft he was and grieve for him.

'We'll be back,' Shyamlal told Eddie. 'This gold chain is worth nine thousand at the most. You still owe us the rest.'

* * *

Falling ... falling ... falling...

Pieta and he had little reason to scrap or squabble. She was not confrontational and neither was he. He loved stories and when she was in an especially good humour she would tell tales that Granna had told her about their home in Goa and the huge estates they owned and about the Portuguese governor's ADC who had wanted to marry Violet and her own voyage to Portugal by ship. She told him stories of novels she had read, about painters and paintings, the stars in the sky and the double helix in our genes. But he was wary of one subject that Pieta seemed to want to go back to time and again.

They were having dinner one night when Pieta said, 'Now that we're married I don't want to keep any secrets from you, Ravan. I owe it to you to tell you about the unhappiest time in my life. After all, you were the one who saved me.'

'But now only you can save me.'

'Me? What are you talking about?'

'Let sleeping dogs lie, Pieta. The past is the past,' Ravan said quietly. 'We're both done with it.'

'You may be, you have a clear conscience. I don't and it weighs on my mind.'

'Then you must go and see Father Agnello D'Souza. He has been your father-confessor from the time you were a child.'

'I want to confess to you. Any other husband would be dying of curiosity by now.'

'Unfortunately, the only husband you've got is me. And I don't want to know because I don't want anything to come between you and me. Certainly not the past.'

'You're not normal, Ravan.' Pieta's eyes had narrowed. 'Maybe you don't want to know because then you would have to tell me all your secrets.'

Ravan got up, went over to Pieta and began to massage her neck.

'I know what you're up to. You don't want to reveal all your dirty secrets. And so you're trying to seduce me with a Thai massage. But let me tell you it's not going to work.'

But it did. And yet there was no telling when she would feel once again that she had to confide in him and unburden herself.

* * *

An aerial shot of the Chambal ravines. The camera zoomed in slowly to reveal the natural formation of the landscape. It was as if some ancient giant had run his comb through the earth and left behind shallow canyon-like furrows. It was a maze down there. The walls of the ravines here were anywhere between five and eight feet high. As the telephoto lens of the camera zeroed in, you saw the Deputy Commissioner of Police, Jwala Singh, running in the channel of a deep ravine. Unbeknownst to the policeman, Maan Singh and his men were crouching in the ravine ahead of him. The dacoit bent down and put his ear to the ground and listened. He smiled, climbed up the ravine wall and stood twisting and curling his thick moustache, quietly watching Jwala Singh sprint towards him. When the DCP was barely three metres from him, Maan Singh jumped down. Jwala Singh had to pull himself short at the very last moment but had the presence of mind to draw out his revolver and aim it at Maan Singh.

'Not bad. Not bad at all. I have to admit you are fast on the draw. But will you shoot an unarmed man?'

'I've been waiting God knows how many years for this moment. I would rather take you into custody and let the law decide what to do with you. But if I can't do that, I will use the gun to good effect.'

Ravan was no longer acting, he was the police officer who had lost his wife, children and mother to that monster Maan Singh, and sometimes Eddie worried that Ravan's Jwala Singh would end up killing him because he confused Eddie with the dacoit.

'What if you've walked into a trap?'

'I'll still have time to empty the cartridge clip.'

'You sure about that?' Maan Singh looked around. His men were standing atop the ravines with their guns aimed at Jwala.

'You forget that my men are behind me.'

'I don't think so.'

The police officer turned around slowly. There was no one behind him.

'The information you received was right but that's because we planted it. You were in such a hurry to get me, you ran ahead. One of my men was already dressed in a DCP's uniform and your team followed him instead of you into the wrong ravine.'

'Where are they?'

'Safely corralled away not far from here. So you see, my friend, sometimes Mohammad doesn't have to go to the mountain, the mountain comes to Mohammad.'

'I'll get you yet, Maan Singh, even if I have to traverse the whole planet looking for you. I would search every nook and crevice of the heavens. Indeed, of the nether world too. If need be, I'll snatch you from the clutches of death itself.'

'Well said, my friend. One minor question. Just how are you planning to get away from here?'

Jwala Singh shook his head as if it had finally registered in his mind that the game was up for him.

Maan Singh laughed. 'Time to bid goodbye to the world, Jwala Singh.'

The police officer looked up at the sky slowly. A soft whir got louder and suddenly a military helicopter was over their heads. 'Isn't that a little premature?'

'Stop. Nobody move.' Someone interrupted the shooting. A bearded and turbaned, rough-hewn man was pointing a gun with a long barrel at Ravan in his uniform and the rest of the cast and crew from atop a ravine wall. But Eddie's gun had already gone off and Ravan fell back and collapsed dramatically. There was a loud report from the intruder's gun now.

'Throw your gun down.' His voice boomed over the ravines. 'Or mine will mow down the lot of you.'

'Cut,' ClickClick spoke into an old-fashioned megaphone.

'What the hell's going on?' Eddie yelled at the man. 'Can't you see we're shooting a film here? If you want to make a racket, do it in your own home.'

The intruder jumped down, gun at the ready, and walked up to Eddie. The resemblance between the two bearded men was uncanny. Soon, other men were sliding or leaping down, all of them with guns.

'This is Maan Singh's home,' the stranger with the gun told Eddie. 'If there's any intruder here, it's you and all these other clowns.'

'A likely story.' Ravan thought it best to scotch the man's overheated imaginings before they got out of hand and he too started blackmailing them like Ramchander. 'Everybody knows Maan Singh's in prison and going to be hanged.'

A scatter of bullets hit the earth at Ravan's feet and ripped it open.

'Stop, please, stop. What's wrong with you?' Ravan was dancing a frantic jig.

'Just trying to convince you that your news is somewhat stale.'

'I believe you, I believe you.'

Ravan couldn't stop shaking even after the fireworks ceased. The real Maan Singh slung his gun obliquely across his shoulder, twirled his moustache and ran his hand pensively over the parting in his old-fashioned Rajput beard.

'Are you *that* Maan Singh? I mean the real one?' Eddie couldn't contain his wonderment.

'Is there any other?'

The man's followers found the idea risible.

'If there's an imposter or pretender, let him come forward,' one of them told Eddie, patting the barrel of his gun, 'and we'll take care of him.'

'Isn't that amazing? We are making a film about you.'

'About me?' Maan Singh asked incredulously.

'Yes, about you.' Eddie offered him a chair. 'This is a stroke of luck. We're making an epic film about your lifelong enmity with Jwala Singh.'

ClickClick joined in. 'It's an adventure film about your exploits. You could be our special consultant.'

'He's our director,' Eddie explained. 'We call him ClickClick but his real name is Kapil. I'm playing you. See, I grew a beard just like you. I didn't want a fake one. What do you think? Have I got the look right? Honestly, your advice would be invaluable to us.'

'What would I have to do?'

'Just tell us about your life, your childhood, how you got into the business, everything.' Eddie's excitement was infectious.

'Do you know why we didn't shoot the film on a set in Bombay? Because we wanted to get the location and the atmosphere just right.

The most important thing for us is veracity. We want to get every detail right,' ClickClick clarified.

'Would my name appear in the film along with yours?'

'But of course,' ClickClick assured him. 'You could be the chief guest at the premiere.'

'Tell us how you escaped from the prison. The new episode will make the film really exciting.'

'I can assure you it's one hell of a story,' Maan Singh said with undisguised pride. 'Maybe it could be the sequel to your film.'

'I'm Jwala Singh. How do you think I will respond to your escape?' Ravan had had enough of his friends falling all over the bandit. 'I'll kill you if that's the last thing I do, isn't that right?'

Maan Singh had got Ravan's head in the crook of his arm and was about to jerk it sharply but Ravan's foot had locked in behind the dacoit's ankle and yanked him off balance. The two were rolling on the ground now. Eddie and ClickClick fell upon Maan Singh and tried to loosen his grip.

'Stop, Maan Singh-ji, stop. He's acting as Jwala Singh. How can we shoot the movie without your jaani dushman?'

Maan Singh let go of Ravan. 'I'm sorry. I get unhinged when I think of Jwala Singh.'

'So does he when he thinks of you,' Ravan said brusquely.

'Strange that you should mention it. I've often wondered whether we are twins from opposite sides of the mirror,' Maan Singh said as he stroked his beard.

'Don't you think it foolhardy for you to be here?' Ravan kept baiting the dacoit. 'This is the first place Jwala Singh will come looking for you.'

'On the contrary. He's sure to think I'll avoid this place because I expect him to turn up here. Which makes it one of the safest places for me at least for today. Besides, I don't ever stay in the same place two nights running.'

'So will you be part of our team?' Eddie asked, wondering why Ravan was so hostile to one of the heroes of their film.

'This is going to make a sensational story for my paper. Imagine, the dacoit Maan Singh breaking out of prison and turning up at the shoot of *Jaan Se Pyara Dushman*. No fiction could match that,' Harish Patel exclaimed.

'Who's this man?' Maan Singh was immediately wary.

'He's a film journalist.' Eddie filled him in on the details. 'He's covering our film for his newspaper. He's always on the lookout for a hot scoop.'

'Two conditions. This man won't write a word about me.' Maan Singh eyed the journalist with undisguised distaste. 'And no outsider will enter this place nor will anyone leave it without my permission.'

'It's a deal as far we are concerned,' Eddie assured the dacoit. 'How about you, Harish? Are you game?'

'Sooner or later someone's bound to find out. Why not let me do the scoop? I give you my word I won't reveal your whereabouts.'

'Not a word about me. You cross me and the consequences will be deadly.'

'In that case there's no point my staying here. I may as well go back home to Bombay.'

'Really? Let me give you some advice, newspaperman.' Maan Singh drew Harish Patel aside and sat down with him on a stone hump with his back to the rest of the film crew. 'You think I'm that stupid that I can't see through your pathetic game? You're not going anywhere. My men will be watching every move of yours.'

Just then, Shyamlal and Ramchander walked in slowly from a little by-lane.

'Have you got the remaining money? Because if you haven't…' the constable asked in his usual lugubrious tone.

'My second son too died yesterday,' Ramchander interrupted the cop. 'Poor Dasrath, he didn't die, you killed him. How many more will you sacrifice? Are you planning to wipe out my whole family? My wife can't stop weeping. I demand compensation. Right now.'

'Shut up, Ramchander,' the constable butted in. 'Give us the money or I'm taking charge of the camera and taking the two of you into custody.'

Maan Singh had his head lowered but watched the two men who had interrupted his talk with the journalist at a crucial moment from the corner of his eye.

'Have you got my friend's gold necklace?' Eddie asked Ramchander. 'It's the only memento of his late wife that he possesses.'

'The money first.' The policeman was adamant.

'What about my second son's death? We need to negotiate that first.'

The dacoit got up quietly and kicked the stick on which the handicapped man was leaning. Ramchander screamed and fell on his face. 'Welcome, welcome, Ramchander-ji,' Maan Singh greeted the villager who stared at his tormentor in disbelief. But it was the policeman's face that was crumpling in dread.

'Bhosdike, I had no idea that you fathered two sons in the seven months I was away. Quick work. Super-quick, I would say. And when did you get remarried? All I know is that you beat and tortured your first two wives to extract money from your in-laws and when you had squeezed them dry, you bumped them off.'

The constable was backing out as fast and unobtrusively as possible. 'Shyamlal-ji, *itni bhi kya jaldi hai*?' the dacoit sang the Bollywood film song. 'What's the rush? You're leaving without even greeting us? I hope my presence hasn't upset you.'

Shyamlal blanched and froze. He tried to speak but couldn't seem to get his tongue to formulate the words. His winter overcoat had large patches of sweat in the armpits and his face was dripping fear. Maan Singh went over and slapped him on his back. 'Is this any way to treat your old friends? Or new ones like these gentlemen here? Abey maderchod, does that camera belong to your forefathers or to your father-in-law that you're going to take possession of it? Don't you have any shame, harassing people who have no way of defending themselves?' Maan Singh switched to the next question as if he was still continuing with the same train of thought. 'Where's the necklace?'

The constable smiled inanely. He had not cottoned on that this was a question which required an answer from him.

'Where is it?'

Shyamlal hesitated for a few seconds. 'It's at home.'

'You had no intention of returning it, did you?'

'Of course, I was going to.'

Maan Singh's hand flashed and the constable reeled back, his hands thrashing waywardly to keep his balance and then he was wiping the blood from his split lower lip.

'At least do me the courtesy of not lying to me. And how about the money?'

'Most of it is with Ramchander.'

'Is that right, Ramchander?'

'He took more than his share plus the chain.'

'I don't give a damn who has what so long as you return every single rupee and the chain. Surjeet and Mahinder,' Maan Singh called out to two of his men, 'escort these two to their homes and back. They are not to talk to anybody, I mean anybody. You are at liberty to take any action you see fit if they disobey.'

When ClickClick called it a day as the sun set over the ravines and the light turned a reddening yellow, Maan Singh said he wanted to be alone with his deputies to formulate a plan of action.

'What's with you?' Eddie asked Ravan. He and ClickClick had been treating him as 'extremely fragile, handle with care' but they had another case of the same on their hands and if they antagonized the dacoit, it would be the end of *Jaan Se Pyara Dushman*. 'Why are you going out of your way to alienate Maan Singh? Do you want him to make trouble for us?'

Ravan applied the make-up remover carefully over his face with a cotton disc. He looked at Eddie and then spoke softly. 'There's some confusion here. He's trouble, not me.'

'What would you have us do? Tell him to get out when we are the intruders on his turf? Antagonize him and we'll be in far more serious trouble than we had with Ramchander and Shyamlal.'

'We don't need to go overboard with our hospitality and enthusiasm. Why invite him to be a consultant on the project? We already have a screenplay. Even if he says we got it all wrong, it's too late to change anything. Besides, he can't be the most reliable of sources when telling his own story.'

'We aren't planning to show him the screenplay or the rushes. Out of the question,' Eddie clarified. 'All I'm looking for is a peep into his mind. Asmaan constructed him from the outside-in from available facts. Maybe we can work inside out now.'

'I don't have any problem reshooting a bit. But only if something really striking comes through in our conversations with him.' ClickClick didn't want to commit himself to any fixed plan of action. 'Just minor but telling things. Don't forget we have set aside a little for exactly such exigencies. It's curious but you elicited a comment that was really revealing. He's aware that both he and Jwala are unhinged in their obsession with each other. Not just that, surely we can incorporate that one sentence of his into the screenplay. "I've often wondered whether we are twins from opposite sides of the mirror."'

'What if Jwala Singh and his men come after him?'

'They are bound to come, no two ways about that. That's why he's set up a twenty-four-hour watch in all directions. Besides, as he told us he'll move out tomorrow. There's one other thing. Now that Ramchander and the constable are taken care of, we'll wind up the shooting here in ten or twelve days at the most.'

'I know Maan Singh's kind a little too well,' Ravan said softly. 'He and his men are trouble. Make no mistake.'

Eddie looked puzzled. 'You've known dacoits before?'

'They might go by another name today in cities but they are from the same blood group.'

'Normally I would agree with you.' Eddie was in no mood to argue with Ravan. 'But he got rid of those two bloodsucking bastards for us. Oops, I forgot to give you your chain. I didn't think you would ever see it again. But he made sure you got it back. Besides, he has a stake in this film. After all, it's about him. And don't forget, crooks too have a code of honour.'

* * *

Falling … falling … falling…

They were making love when Piya said, 'I won't hold it against you.'

'Hold what against me?'

'I think you know what I'm talking about.'

'I don't. This is getting more and more mysterious.'

'What happened between you and Sukanya?'

'Nothing happened.'

'It's okay. It really is. We all slip up, it's only human. I did too. You were the one who brought me back from the dead.'

'I'm not pretending to be a saint. But nothing happened between her and me.'

'How else would she have known about the padded cell?'

'Because many months ago she insisted on seeing the room where I composed our songs.'

'Don't get so worked up, Ravan. I told you it doesn't matter. I won't hold it against you.'

'She wanted a singing contract and thought she could get it if she got me to sleep with her. When I didn't give in, she…'

'Oh Ravan, you don't need to make up these stories.'

No, no, no, no, no, no, no, you are wrong, Pieta-Piya. I protest too much; protest enough and more to convince you that I'm guilty. But the question is: how can you forgive me when I'm not guilty? God knows how many times I've told you that. Sometimes I wonder if you were so fixated upon forgiving me because you couldn't forgive yourself even though I had begged you to down the shutters on the whole sordid episode in Falkland Road.

* * *

The weather had begun to turn. It was still hot during the day but the nights were getting colder and the previous two mornings there was frost on the ground. Most of the actors and crew were from Bombay and wondered whether it had snowed lightly during the night. They could not stop marvelling that their breath turned to vapour and kept blowing their white smoky puffs of air into the faces of their friends. They were already wearing double pullovers and sheathing themselves in shawls and drinking hot tea by the gallon. The dip in the Chhoti Ganga was relegated to noon and later, if not skipped altogether.

The twilight here was different from dusk in Bombay, at least as winter approached. It was sensational, but so condensed that if you were not alert, darkness was upon you, and foxes and hares scampered past in the beams of the lights running on the generator. Dogs bayed, wild boars grunted and the occasional barasingha and his entourage thundered through a neighbouring ravine like an army in chaotic retreat. There was constant talk of snakes and how one of them might slither into bed. It made no difference that there had been no tigers or leopards in the vicinity for the last fifty years, someone or the other invariably spoke of having seen a big cat's pugmarks and then nobody ventured into the darkness to go to the toilets except in groups of five or six.

It was impossible to sleep after 5.30 in the morning however reluctant you were to get up. The damned birds, all nineteen million of them, woke up simultaneously and chirped and chattered without let. Come eventide, they would be at it again. Nobody ever saw their nests nor were there too many trees to speak of, except occasional clusters of prickly stunted shrubs or the rare banyan or peepul that hadn't been hacked down for firewood. But it was the moon that convinced the denizens of Bombay that they were in some other country, more likely a different planet. It was huge and yolk-yellow. All you had to do to touch it and swirl it around on your index finger was to stretch out your hand. When the moon was waning or missing altogether and you got up to take a leak at 2 in the morning and accidentally looked up, you saw a quivering sequined sky ablaze with stars crammed tighter than a Bombay local at peak hour.

Today's twilight was wave after wave of a purple sea pulverizing a sulphurous green coastline into a bruised blue. The people from Bombay sat around a campfire, eating chicken tikkas and corn-on-the-cob, listening to Maan Singh. The dacoit would disappear for a day or two without notice and just as unpredictably return. Ravan surmised he was fascinated with the film shooting, or more likely, he was a narcissist and wanted to watch his own story unfold in front of his eyes. He quaffed from a glass of the local brew and sprinkled the chicken with crushed chilli powder. Nearby, one of his men was roasting two goats on newly dug spits to celebrate the chief's escape and the big-budget feature film that was being made about him. At the back where the horses were stabled, Shyamlal and Ramchander sat tethered to a pole, their hands tied behind their backs.

'Aren't you people going to join me for a drink?' Maan Singh asked. 'There's enough for all of us.'

'We'll join you the day we finish the shooting here. Till then our contracts stipulate that we must abstain,' ClickClick explained.

'How did you manage to keep ahead of the police,' Eddie asked, 'when they were always combing the territory looking for you?'

'We are on top of the game because we disappear at a minute's notice and we know the lay of the land better than anybody else.' Maan Singh pointed to the hills in the distance. 'There are over a thousand caves in that stretch alone. They are our natural guardians. Some of them are open-ended on either side but most are blind alleys. Twice, a police search party has entered one but sadly never found its way out.' The bandit sighed. 'Poor things. Landslides too can be a problem in this area.'

'How about the villagers? Someone or the other is bound to report your whereabouts.'

'I wouldn't worry about them. They know that if someone tattles, the whole village will pay for it. And now that you are under my protection, they wouldn't dare try anything on you either.'

'The police tried everything possible to catch you, including getting the military to strafe you from a helicopter.' Eddie was still trying to get the details of the bandit's biography right. 'But they couldn't succeed all these years. What went wrong last time?'

Maan Singh's expression soured and he stared hostilely at Eddie as if he didn't care to answer the question. 'Let's just say my luck ran out while lady luck smiled on Jwala Singh.'

Harish Patel had recovered from his altercation with the bandit and was back in his journalistic avatar. 'The commissioner claims his intelligence network revealed that you were going to be in Aminabai's kotha for a night of dance and debauchery.'

'Sure, if you can call some stooge squealing on me intelligence.'

'Who was it?'

'The rat will know when I find out.'

'Who, the commissioner?'

'He too.' Maan Singh smiled enigmatically as he ran his eyes over his men. 'But I was thinking more of the culprit.'

'You were in the highest security prison and yet you did the impossible,' the journalist wouldn't let go, 'you managed to escape. The question is how are you going to elude the police now?'

Ravan watched Harish trying to elicit a coherent story from the bandit but kept his own views to himself. They were making a film about a real-life bandit, a man who stole and plundered, kidnapped and demanded ransom; raped and killed and terrorized whole villages and towns. But such was the wonderful legerdemain of art, whatever form it took, whether fiction, theatre, or film, especially the Hindi variety, it turned the bad guys into victims and you rooted for them. A work of art like Francis Ford Coppola's *The Godfather* made murderers and villains more real than reality. It placed you right in the middle of the action and yet simultaneously shielded and cushioned you from it. It was devoid of teeth and bite and toxic poisons and you always made it back to your family and your boring little job and your secure routine. Indeed art ennobled you. It brought home to you with such vividness how sensitive you were, how all-encompassing your sympathy for your fellow-men was while making you forget what utterly, unscrupulous monsters the Godfather, his sons and their soldiers were, so that you were rooting for them.

Then the real Maan Singh had walked into the lives of the film folks from Bombay and the ground under their feet had shifted and rocked. They were making a biopic. As far as they knew, the scriptwriter had studied the subject and constructed an edifice that was purported to be true to the original. Now they were faced with a very different dilemma. They were standing between two ill-fitting tectonic plates not knowing when they would slip in between and be crushed. Where did that fiction called life end and that fantasy known as the Hindi film begin? And which was which?

They might have smirked and giggled silently as Ravan bounced and pranced to the tattoo of bullets hitting the ground or when they saw that runt of a Ramchander and his officious companion-in-blackmail, Shyamlal, tied like cattle, but what if … what if … what if the brigand did not fancy their faces or found that he needed more room to breathe after being locked in a prison cell and the carbines picked them off one by one?

Did you see what a scrape that fool Harish Patel had got himself into? Wanted a scoop, he said. Now wasn't that the funniest story this side of the Milky Way? The only thing that these film gossip-mag journalists ever did was to invent, cook up, fabricate, concoct and trump up the same old lies about the same old stars day in day out and year in and year out: who was sleeping with whom, whose marriage was going down the tubes, who was being catty and, if you could tell the difference, who bitchy.

Now, suddenly, Mr Patel was suffering from an acute case of fantasy deprivation and had to put his life on the line to get at the real story instead of merely conjuring up the scenario from his cornucopia of tall tales and pathetic fibs. And what was the consequence of this one rash act? The look in the dacoit's eyes would have sufficed to incinerate the man. But the mouth of the long-barrelled gun was at his Adam's apple and it was about to go off. It was the closest any of the Bombay lads had come to being snatched by the god of death. Not just Patel but the lot of them were about to be wiped out as the dacoit's eyes glazed over with pure malevolence and the carbine swivelled back and forth, itching to be emptied because of the stupidity of one man. They might be on location but this was no film clip. Something had gone terribly wrong. The projectionist up there in the sky had got the wires crossed and jumbled fiction with reality.

But the crisis had passed. 'This must be your lucky day, Patel-bhai.' Maan Singh's face had eased into a smile. 'You'll live another day. But as your mother must have warned you, never test your luck for you never know when you will run out of it.'

It soon became apparent that once Maan Singh realized that he was the hero of the film (Jwala Singh was merely incidental as far as he was concerned), the outsiders came under his protection and no one, but no one, dared touch them. And now that the threat of imminent death had disappeared, the cast and crew could relax and reconfigure the very recent past and see that there was no denying the thrill and excitement of having been so close to danger. It was flat out the most memorable event of their lives. Imagine going back home to Bombay and writing your autobiography one day and relating how you had been held hostage by none other than the dreaded Maan Singh and had actually broken bread and shared partridge pickles with him and listened to his life story.

Ravan watched the bandit with a curiosity bordering on the pathological. It didn't take any special insight to see that Maan Singh was not a little impressed that he was the subject of a full-length feature film and was recasting himself to accommodate his own rising self-esteem. His voice was a shade more solemn and he expected the cast and crew to take him as seriously as he himself did.

He resented it when someone referred to him as a bandit or dacoit; he was a businessman and the head of a fast-expanding industrial empire. The timing of his capture could not have been more unfortunate. For several years now, Maan Singh told them, he had been working closely with a consultant and been chalking out a new strategy for expansion by going legitimate. As a matter of fact, he had been steadily negotiating to build an all-India network starting with Bombay, the commercial capital of the country. Jwala Singh had sabotaged his plans of diversification into several other areas of business just at the time when he was finalizing his move to Bombay in partnership with one of the smartest operators in the country. But he was out of prison now and intent on making up for lost time. All he needed was just a few days to figure out who had betrayed him.

* * *

The whole film crew and cast had got up earlier than usual since ClickClick wanted to shoot the funeral scene at the ghats of the Chhoti Ganga as the first rays of the sun set the water on fire. The corpses of Jwala Singh's men from the district police station and the bodies of the four members of his family were lined up in a series of pyres on the banks of the Chhoti as she was called by the locals. A group of policemen and a few senior officers stood at the back while Ravan–Jwala Singh in a white kurta-paijama stepped forward with a lit wooden torch and stood silently one last time by the side of his wife and mother. Seconds passed and then nearly a minute, and it seemed he would never move but finally he raised his hand, lit the two pyres, walked over to where the children's bodies were and, with a stony face, set their pyres ablaze and threw the torch into the river. When he looked up, he knew he was being watched from across the opposite bank. Eddie–Maan Singh was observing him through his binoculars. Their eyes met, then the bandit was gone.

It was already evening when Eddie, Ravan and ClickClick went directly to the producers' tent for their evening meeting to plan the next week's shooting schedule, script and dialogue changes, and who was required for which shot when there was a commotion outside. As usual the floodlights were on in the failing light. A heavily made-up eunuch in a shimmering red nylon maxi skirt, his mega-knockers pushing the lurid green choli to stiletto points, clapped his hard stony hands while massacring the song from *Kunwara Baap*, '*Saj gayee meri gali amma, sunhere gothe mein*'.

'Where's this creature turned up from?' Eddie asked, bewildered. 'I thought Maan Singh had given orders to his people not to allow anyone into the camp without his permission.'

By now not merely the Bombaywallahs but the dacoit's men had gathered around to enjoy the freak show. The eunuch seemed to target Patel. He made eyes at him and pinched his cheek.

'Ugh, stop it. Don't touch me.' Patel tried to shoo away the leering hijra but that only seemed to encourage him. 'Get away from me.'

The crowd roared and clapped even louder. The eunuch was delighted with all the attention he was getting and began to pirouette and leap about, adlibbing his own lewd words to the song. Ravan watched the man with distaste, took out a two-rupee note and handed it to the eunuch.

'Thank you for entertaining us but we have work to do. Please leave.'

The hijra brought his hands together in a thunderclap in front of Ravan's face and swiftly picked up his skirt. Ravan winced and shut his eyes tightly and found the eunuch holding his face in his implacable hands.

'Open your eyes, Ravan Sahab. Do you think you can give me a role in your film now that you've seen my acting talent?' Maan Singh laughed. The thick wiry beard parted in the middle had gone and a patina of cheap foundation had been laid on the face. 'If you didn't recognize me, no one else will.'

'Not bad, Maan Singh-ji,' Eddie gasped. 'You had all of us fooled.'

'This is no film, Eddie Sahab. My life depends on it.'

'Where are you going?' Patel couldn't help asking.

'See you tomorrow morning.'

'You are going to trace the informer,' Patel exclaimed, delighted with his own ability to second-guess the bandit.

'Let me give you some advice, Patel.' Maan Singh impaled the journalist with a cold stare. 'Do you know why God gave man a mouth? To keep his tongue under lock and key. And do you know why he gave us thirty-two teeth? To bite the tongue off if it starts wagging in other people's affairs.'

'Car coming this way,' the dacoit's sentry yelled from his lookout perch.

Maan Singh's men immediately drew a protective circle around their chieftain, their rifles cocked while the dacoit stuck his gun at the back of Ravan's head. The car came to a halt and as the driver opened the rear door, a cloudburst of perfume wafted out. Sapna stepped out in a froth of spangled aquamarine. You had to hand it to her. She was at least ten years older than the time she had seduced Eddie but she had maintained her figure and the passage of time had been erased considerably by some expert surgical work. She stood there now in the flood of lights from the generator as if she was in the prime of youth attending the world premiere of one her films. She smiled and slowly turned a full 180 degrees for the imaginary cameras while the crowds gasped. And gasp they did even in this remotest of corners of the Chambal valley, unable to apprehend that this was no vision but a real-life star amongst their midst. Maan

Singh's men pressed forward but refrained from getting too close lest the mirage disintegrate into the air.

'Sapna-ji, welcome, welcome,' ClickClick greeted the actress. 'We were expecting you and your assistant tomorrow.'

'I thought I would surprise all of you,' Sapna tittered while her companion got out of the car gingerly. 'You know what the Delhi fog's like in winter. The morning flights are always delayed for hours or are cancelled.'

'I've great news.' Eddie went over and embraced the actress. 'Our film's going to be a mega-hit.'

Either time had healed wounds, Ravan thought, or Eddie had a short memory. Hard to believe the latter though, considering that she had sent him to the hospital with VD. Three months back she had laid siege to Eddie's flat. Things were not going well for her and her husband; in truth, they were in desperate straits with a raft of cases against them. She was sorry, terribly sorry for what had happened all those years ago but it was not her fault. Men debauched and the women had to pay for it. Eddie was far too polite to remind her that in this case he was the one who had paid the price.

'You won't guess this in seven lifetimes. This is Maan Singh. The *real* Maan Singh. Dakoo Maan Singh.'

Sapna looked at the eunuch and sniggered. 'This? This is Maan Singh? The real Maan Singh?'

Ravan had been watching the bandit since the car had come to a halt in their midst. The presence of the woman, no ordinary woman but a silver-screen star, had an unsettling effect on Maan Singh. His eyes had turned murky and his mouth had twisted in a double helix of seething resentment and raw animal lust.

'I give you my word, Madam, you are in the presence of the genuine article,' Maan Singh spoke with repressed fury. 'You'll feel the fire of the real Maan Singh within a day or two at the most. But I have more urgent matters to attend to. Eddie-ji, you swore that no one would either leave or enter this place without my express permission.'

'Yes, I had but she was expected tomorrow and I was intending to clear the matter with you tonight. She is our second heroine, Maan Singh-ji. And the other lady is her assistant who will help with make-up and costumes and hair.'

'You've broken your word, Eddie-ji.'

'Unintentionally. I assure you.'

'We'll discuss this later. Understand that nobody leaves the premises now.'

'None of the men, of course,' Eddie intervened. 'But Sapna-ji and her companion can't possibly stay here. She's not used to such harsh living conditions.'

'Don't worry. She'll manage.'

'I certainly won't,' Sapna dismissed the possibility.

'I believe you will. Unless you want my second-in-command, Dilawar Singh, to shoot you dead accidentally right now.'

* * *

Someone had thrown a stone at the black glass of the sky and a lattice of fine cracks was spreading across it rapidly and now the sun had begun to seep out from the fissures. In the half-light the camera caught a cloud of dust on the horizon which kept growing till it turned into a rider galloping on a horse. A woman sat in front of the man, her mouth gagged and her hands tied behind her. Eddie in his Maan Singh avatar held her tightly lest she fall as they climbed a rocky mountainside. He reined in his horse, gathered Sapna in his arms and carried her into his hideout in a cave.

'Untie her hands and remove the gag,' Maan Singh ordered his deputy Samsher Singh who had followed him into the cave.

'So, this is Jwala Singh's sister, Mamta-ji?' Samsher Singh patted Sapna–Mamta's cheek and, while removing the gag, pulled down the pallu of her sari. 'Not exactly a spring chicken but what a dish.'

'Maan Singh, you are going to regret this,' Sapna–Mamta spat fire. 'My husband and brother will come after you and tear out every limb of yours.'

Samsher laughed theatrically and wiped off the vermillion from her forehead with the back of his hand. 'Well, that takes care of your husband. As for your brother, he's been looking for us for a decade now. We wish him luck.'

'You've had a hard ride.' Eddie Maan Singh's voice had a softer edge. 'Rest a bit and then we can talk. If you need anything, just ask Samsher and he'll help you. I am going round to the temple, Samsher, to thank Shiv-ji for a safe return from the lion's lair. Look after the lady. I mean that.'

* * *

'Cut,' ClickClick said abruptly. 'May I have a word with you in private, Sapna-ji, Ravan and Eddie?'

'If you must,' Sapna snorted.

'Please.'

'Have it your way.'

'I intend to.' ClickClick, Ravan and Eddie disappeared along with Sapna into the tent that served as the office.

Sapna switched on a blasé 'What now?' expression as she sat down. ClickClick had asked for nine retakes of the scene in the hideout and it had only got worse.

'Let me come clean with you. When I am the director, I make sure that I have the last word in casting decisions. I was dead set against casting you for the role of Jwala Singh's sister. Eddie, Ravan and I go back a long way and generally they listen to me. But this time Eddie was adamant for reasons not quite clear to me. I told him he was letting his emotional baggage get the better of him. I realized we weren't likely to see eye to eye on the matter and I gave in.'

'Where's this long spiel leading?' Sapna did a good imitation of being bored.

'I'm beginning to think that Eddie was right. You fit the part. But that's if you stop acting the diva and get under the skin of Jwala Singh's sister.'

'I might do that if I was treated like a human being instead of being herded with fifty men, twenty of them thugs.'

'I know how unhappy you are about having to stay here in the haveli in this godforsaken place. It is unfair and unacceptable, I accept that fully. We had booked you into the best hotel in Gwalior. But as you know we are no longer in charge here.'

'I can sue you and these two jokers, Ravan and Eddie. Don't forget it's in black and white in my contract that I will have a suite in a good hotel.'

'You could do that though you do know that there's always a clause specifying circumstances beyond our control. Even you will grant that we've bent over backwards to make you comfortable. We put you and your companion up in a separate room in a separate wing of the house. You are the only one to have two electric heaters and a toilet and a shower arrangement. Now, if you want this ordeal to be over as much as we do, we'll shoot at least two shifts a day from now. There's a lot riding for us on this film. And unless I'm mistaken, for you too.' ClickClick let that last sentence sink in. 'Asmaan has written a Bollywood movie which will appeal to the masses but is also a brilliant study of obsession and how it can pervert both the good and the bad. You are the one who's caught between your brother and Maan Singh. It's a critical role since it blurs the line between the villain and the hero. If you don't internalize the role, there's no depth to the character and her awful dilemma will never come through. And then you know what will happen on the editing table. There will be no trace of you left. The choice is yours.'

Sapna glared furiously at ClickClick and turned to Eddie and Ravan. 'Are you going to allow this ClickClick Nobody to talk to me like this?'

'He may be Mr Nobody to you but he's the director of the film,' Eddie told her. 'He has the last word in all matters relating to direction.'

Sapna might have fumed and raged but she knew the stakes. She was the closest thing to a heroine apart from the tawaif in this male-dominated film. If she didn't make good this time, she might as well call it a day. Besides, in fairness to her, she was a pro.

By the time the director and Sapna got back, the real Maan Singh, Dilawar and three of their inner group had joined the shooting.

'Let's do that shot in the cave again,' ClickClick said. 'Maan Singh has gone to the temple and left you in charge of Mamta, Samsher Singh. Clear?'

The actor playing Samsher nodded his head.

'Camera ready. Silence. Dilawar-ji, that includes you too. Every word you whisper will be on the soundtrack.'

'Action.' The camera started rolling and they were on to the second shot.

* * *

'Sure, I will take care of Mamta-ji, very, very good care. After all, she's our guest, a very special guest.'

'Stop there, Samsher Singh. If something should happen to me, my brother will hang every one of you.'

Samsher shook his head sadly. 'What ill-omened talk is that? There's nothing but love for you in our hearts.'

Samsher Singh kept advancing towards Mamta. She tried to slip out of the cave but he was faster and had her pinned on the mattress. Mamta fought back, scratching his cheeks but he had his forearm pressed on her throat and she began to subside and her hands fell to the sides. He undid the top two buttons of her blouse and lifted her sari up. She screamed. He slapped her hard and clapped his hand on her mouth.

'Why, my dear, is this any way to behave when someone professes his love for you?'

Eddie–Maan Singh had opened the curtain and was watching Samsher's antics. He stood over him now, grabbed him by the hair, turned him around, shoved his knee into his crotch and flung him violently to the ground.

'Son of a bitch. You are a blot on the Rajput race. How dare you touch one of our guests and that too in my house? No one has insulted Maan Singh the way you have.' Eddie–Maan Singh leaned over the cowering Mamta and covered her breasts with her pallu. He then dragged Samsher out of his cave. 'Dilawar, Shaan, Salamat, is anybody around or has everybody died on me?'

Dilawar rushed out from one of the other caves, half-dressed.

'What's the matter, sarkar?'

'Take him away, Dilawar. Lock him up. We will decide his fate later. You are my deputy from now on. It's an honour but also a big burden. Take one wrong step and you'll find yourself in worse straits than this vermin here.'

When Eddie got back, Sapna–Mamta looked up, terrified. It was Eddie–Maan Singh's turn to show his true colours. 'I'm so ashamed, can you ever forgive me?' Eddie–Maan Singh spoke to her quietly. 'I will never be able to hold my head up in front of you. I'm not afraid of your brother. But I am a Rajput and you are my guest, and one of my men has dishonoured you.' Maan Singh leaned over, ripped out a piece of string from a cushion cover on the mattress and handed it to Mamta.

'Tie it around my wrist. You're my sister now, Mamta-ji. My sister for life. If anyone should as much as touch you, I give you my word, he'll have to deal with me. If you are ever in any trouble or need me, I will be there to protect you.'

Maan Singh went over to a cupboard and took out a jewellery box from a chest at the back of the cave. He picked up a gold and meenakari necklace and tied it around Mamta's neck.

'It was my mother's. Now it's rightfully yours.'

Tears welled up in Mamta's eyes. 'I'll never forget what you've done for me, how you've saved my honour, Maan Singh-ji.'

'I've done nothing special, Mamta-ji. As our ancient books will tell you, there's never any obligation between brother and sister. This morning I kidnapped you as a bargaining chip to get back three of my men whom your brother had captured. Now I'll escort you back personally.'

Mamta spoke more to herself than to the dacoit. 'I've two brothers now.' She bent down, and picked up Maan Singh's hand and placed it on her head. 'Bless me, brother.'

19

The lights went off.

'What the hell's going on?' Eddie yelled.

'The generator motor's failed,' the electrician announced.

'In the middle of a shot?'

'This is not one of those trained generators which fails only after it's been given permission.'

'Smartarse,' Eddie swore under his breath.

'How long will it take to repair it?' ClickClick enquired.

'I need to identify the problem first.'

'Approximately?'

'Offhand at least two or three hours. Could be more.'

'Try and hurry up, will you? There are women here, we can't stay without lights.'

'Where's Sapna-ji?' Ravan asked.

'She was here a moment ago,' her make-up artist-cum-hairdresser said.

Eddie cast his eyes around. Sapna was nowhere to be seen. Then he hit every panic button he could. The memory of last evening would haunt him till he breathed his last. Correction, there was no element of memory in it. It was now, this very moment, more pressing and urgent than the present could ever be. It was and would always be page one, sentence one in his life.

They had gone to a distant location prepared to shoot late into the evening. A couple of tents had been pitched for the cast and for the director and producers. It was 8.30 but they still had to have dinner. Sapna was resting on a camp bed in Ravan, Eddie and ClickClick's tent. She had taken it into her head that she was in imminent danger, that Maan Singh's men were eyeing her, or to use her phrase, 'always snooping around, leching and lusting after her', and sneaking into her wing of the haveli at all hours. She was convinced that the dakoos were spying on her when she was taking a shower or changing her clothes and insisted that the make-up woman pace up and down outside her room at 5 in the morning and shout 'Anybody there?' at every second step. The poor woman kept guard wrapped in five or six blankets and bleated like a sheep every time the B-grade star yelled, 'I can't hear you. I bet you are snoozing. Move, did you hear me, move. Catch those Peeping Toms who are jerking off watching me take an innocent shower and let me know who they are. I'll kill them if they come within so much as ten metres of our room.'

Sapna was now the butt of much salacious humour amongst the cast but they took care to poke fun at her behind her back. Her helper was not so lucky. They mimicked the calls of wolves, tigers and hyenas. They covered themselves in the white or black sheets used for the shooting and floated past her like a procession of ghouls while chanting her name in a tremolo. They lay in wait for her and grabbed her from behind. The make-up woman would shut her eyes tight and burst into tears but held back her screams for fear that Sapna would discover that she never moved beyond the lit doorway.

Sapna's way of dealing with the threats to her person was to spend most of the time between shots and after the day's work in the company of the two male stars and the director. There were times when she got on their nerves but they had to admit that the dacoits didn't exactly inspire confidence; actually, many of them were living clichés of the villains in Hindi films. The only difference was there were no tricks of make-up here. The missing limbs or eyes were literally missing. The scars, gashes and bullet wounds were the real thing. But there was no denying either that Sapna was paranoid. Perhaps it was just her way of seeking attention. They had tried to tell her that Maan Singh had personally assured them that no harm would come to them while he was around. But of course that did not mollify her or calm her down.

Yesterday evening the three men were relieved that Sapna had dozed off, as was often the case, in the middle of a sentence and they did not have to make conversation or massage her ego to keep her in good humour. They didn't even notice when Maan Singh crept into their tent. After weeks of being with him they still could not understand how he could glide into their midst without making a sound despite the fact that like most villagers he wore sandals that crunched or squeaked at every step to warn off snakes and other animals. He had explained to them that a dacoit's survival depended not only in muting his footfall but in keeping his heartbeat and pulse on hold. That sounded rather dramatic but they were still clueless about how he could cut off the sound box of thick-soled leather sandals. His index finger was pressed against his lips as he looked at them and turned his face back to Sapna. Then they saw why his gaze was transfixed on the sleeping actress. A scorpion in burnt red and metallic blue was standing pensively on her belly, swivelling its head, trying to figure out which direction might prove the most productive to explore.

Sapna sighed and the gentle breeze from her breath seemed to give the creature pause. It shone like a priceless jewel from the Nizam's vaults on the actress's dark-green gauzy salwar-kameez. It had made up its mind now and lifted the first pair of its dainty legs like a lady picking up her skirt to step over a puddle, but the prong of the right leg got caught in the mesh of the cloth and the scorpion tensed. And along with him Maan Singh and the other three men had petrified into fossils. The creature's tail rose like the taut arm of a flamenco dancer, hung motionless above, ready to deliver its lethal sting. The little loop of the gauze let go of the trapped foot and the arachnid relaxed and its tail fell back. Oh, with what supreme elegance this armour-plated creature with eight stiletto heels moved on the catwalk. And each time it advanced, its heels seemed to pierce right through Sapna's flesh. Any moment now she would be irritated by the pronged legs and move or her hand would scratch irritably at her belly and that would be the end.

Maan Singh's knife was out from its leather sheath at his calf and resting lightly but firmly on the gradient of Sapna's right breast even as his left hand was poised to clamp down on her mouth in case she woke up and decided to scream. The scorpion hesitated for a moment at the sudden appearance of cold steel in its path. Its head swept slowly across the vista, assessed the situation for any danger lurking around those twin peaks, processed the information and stepped forward.

The scorpion extended its two front legs over the blade and started to bring the second pair over. Sapna opened her eyes, saw Maan Singh looming over her, and began to scream even as the dacoit rammed the palm of his hand over her mouth. She could see the scorpion as it retracted partially, its tail arched all over again to inject the poison, but the blade had scooped up the eight-legged creature and thrown it in the air. As it hit the ground, the bandit crushed it with his pathan sandals. By then the actress had already passed out.

When she came to, she spoke just once, 'I'm going home tomorrow, come what may.'

It was so much better, they felt, when she prattled on and on about nothing in particular and told them stories about her film triumphs and her dog who understood every word of English, especially if it was delivered in an Oxford accent, but not Hindi or any other Indian language and which proved conclusively that he was an Englishman, very likely Lord Curzon who had gifted the brass lamp shade which hung above the entrance gate to the Taj Mahal in Agra. Or it could be Lord Linlithgow or even Lord Dalhousie, who had annexed all the local principalities and kingdoms into the British Empire. He was so choosey about his own companions. Wouldn't even look at any low- or high-class Indian breed or pariah. You can't hide blue blood, it always shows. If only she would tell her mindless dog stories today. But she sat still as a stone, refusing to eat or acknowledge their presence, making them feel personally responsible for the evening's horrific events.

'Of course you're going home,' Eddie reassured her. 'Fortunately, the shooting for your role will be over by tomorrow anyway. We'll hire a car for you and your companion and it will take you straight to Delhi and you can catch the first flight out to Bombay.'

It was uncanny how Sapna was the only one to have blanked out the terrifying incident of the previous day and had been totally focused on her work today. ClickClick had not asked her for a single retake, not even for the long tracking shot where she's running frantically through the ravines to warn the dacoit leader against visiting the tawaif's kotha since it's a set-up arranged for by none other than her brother, Jwala Singh.

Then, at the climactic shot where she asks Maan Singh to bless her, the generator had decided to conk out and she was gone. They looked everywhere for her, they combed the ravines, they turned the camp upside down but she wasn't around. An Ambassador car was waiting at the mouth of the ravine where they had done most of the shooting that day. Eddie waved out to the driver as he walked past on his way to the police station to report that Sapna had gone missing. Something was not quite right, he retraced his steps. Sapna was sitting in the car, tears streaming down her eyes.

'I can't take it. I can't take it any more.' Eddie was not sure whether Sapna was talking to him or herself. 'I hate this place. I just want to go home, please. Please let me go home.' She kept saying the same thing over and over again as if it was a mantra that would transport her instantly to Bombay.

'The generator's failed but it will only take a couple of hours to repair.' Easy does it, easy does it, Eddie cautioned himself. He had to walk a thin line, he must be diplomatic, not overpromise, and yet be reassuring. 'All we need to do is finish the last shot and I give you my word you'll be on your way.'

Ravan, ClickClick and Maan Singh had joined Eddie by now.

'It might take two hours or it might take two days to get the generator working again,' Sapna said matter-of-factly. 'I can't spend another night here.'

She was right of course, there was no telling how much time it would take for the generator to be fixed. But how could they permit her to leave without completing that last bit? They would have to prevail upon her to stay by hook or crook.

'We've already been here for over a month and you can imagine how anxious we are to get back to Bombay,' ClickClick tried to reason with her.

'I'm sure you are. But my contract said seven days. Today is the eighth. I have more than fulfilled my end of the bargain. I just can't take it any more.'

'All of us, including you, have invested so much time and effort in this film and if you'll permit me to say it, it's been such a labour of love,' the director persisted, 'you'll agree that it's not worth abandoning the race when we are so close to the finishing line.'

'I'm going home.'

'She's right. Let her go home,' Maan Singh spoke quietly.

ClickClick and his two colleagues looked at the king of bandits in dismay. Who the hell had asked him to butt in at this critical moment? Did he have even a vague idea of the money involved? There was not the remotest possibility of their being able to come back for a reshoot. And even if for a moment they were to suppose, just suppose merely for academic purposes, that their financiers opened their anus-tight purses and gave them a free hand, how were they going to get Sapna to come back to the very place which had nearly killed her? Oh, how could last night's saviour turn into today's destroyer?

Sapna smiled at the dakoo gratefully. Her attitude to him had undergone a radical makeover. Like the character she was portraying, she would have been happy if Maan Singh had declared himself her rakhi-brother.

'That's settled then.' Maan Singh ignored the shocked faces of his three male companions and spoke as if a deadlock had been resolved after much back and forth and a consensus that pleased all parties had been reached. 'Do you give me your word that come what may, she will catch the flight to Delhi tonight?' He did not wait for an answer. 'In that case, Sapna-ji will go halfway to accommodate you. If the generator is repaired within an hour or two, she will do the last shot. If the generator is still not working, too bad. Time and Sapna-ji will wait for no one.'

Sapna was not sure exactly how the coordinates of the discussion had altered. She had the feeling that there had been a certain amount of quick-fingered use of words but she couldn't vouch for it. The dacoit, however, did not give her or anyone else time to dwell on his verbal moves.

'Do you know what we are going to do now? I'll give you three guesses though you would not get the answer right even if you had three thousand shots at it.' They were getting used to Maan Singh's methodology now. He might raise a query but made certain that you didn't get a chance to answer. 'We are going to play chhuppa-chhuppi.'

'Here?' Sapna asked incredulously.

'Can you imagine a better place to play hide-and-seek than the ravines? You might be hiding right next to me and I would never find you. We'll all become children again and have a grand time.'

The king of bandits had taken full charge now. He gathered the cast, crew and his own men together. Maan Singh's enthusiasm and excitement were infectious. The crisis was past, or at least postponed, and even Sapna's companion, Sushma, joined in with gusto and schemed and planned where to hide.

'Where's that newspaper guy?' Maan Singh queried Eddie.

'Must be around somewhere. I'm sure he's already hiding.'

'He's been absconding since this morning. The last anyone saw him was at eleven o'clock.'

'Are we going to play or not?' Sapna asked impatiently.

Maan Singh smiled good-humouredly. 'Shall I count to ten?'

'But let's first do "*Akkad bakkad*" to find out who will be "it". *Akkad bakkad bomay bo, assi nabbe purey sau, sau ka lata titter mota, chal madari paisa khota.*'

'No, don't waste time. I'll be "it". Shall I count till ten?'

'No, no way. I need time to hide so you won't find me.'

'Up to fifteen?'

'Till twenty-five. And no cheating. You'll count slowly. You will not see me but I'll be watching you count.'

'Done. Is everybody ready? Good. One, two, three, four, five...'

Maan Singh was right. They had all regressed to childhood. Everybody ran helter-skelter and the ravines echoed with screams, protests, disagreements and frolic. Every time one of the players was discovered, there was pandemonium, hoots of derision, objections and outcries of 'Unfair, unfair', laughter and sudden silences. As is almost always the case, the initial euphoria which had been so palpable when they had started shooting the film on location had vanished at least a fortnight ago. But now all the travails and hardships, the cold winter mornings, the boring food, the boredom, the silly tiffs and fights and the awful claustrophobia of being forced to live in such close proximity were forgotten. It was such a change from their daily routine, they wondered why they had not played the game before.

The light had begun to change. It had turned golden, not jaundiced yellow but an enchanted warm glow that suffused the sky and the ravines and the very air in between. It was so pure and forgiving, it cleansed the heart and healed the soul. It was impossible not to be affected by it. The actors and the cast and the crew felt a kinship not merely to their fellow-men but to all things animate and inanimate. It was the time of godhuli when the cows kicked up soft clouds of dust and their bells tinkled in celebration of their homecoming. The sun mellowed and the sky was kitsch; roses, roses, roses all the way to the South Pole. There was so much activity and sound and noise and yet the earth seemed to be saturated with an uncanny sense of peace. After the fourth game, Maan Singh announced a prize of five thousand rupees to be shared amongst those who managed to escape being caught. The money would get whittled down to a trivial sum by the time it was distributed but Eddie was taken aback by how competitive this children's game had made him. It revived memories of the time he had spent as a six- or seven-year-old in that Hindu organization called the Sabha. He wanted to win in every category and he made sure that he did. They even instituted a new award called the Star of Hindustan to honour his achievements. He was damned if he was going to get caught today.

Eddie was squatting down behind a ravine wall, inching forward, trying to be as silent as the big dakoo himself. Every now and then he raised his head and peeped out to check if anyone was around or following him. Two ravines to the right, Ravan too was creeping forward surreptitiously. Both of them were dripping with sweat and streaked with dust. They would have to bathe before shooting resumed. And then Eddie turned to ice and his breathing ceased. The wind zigzagged and whistled through the ravines and not too far away you could hear the shouts and shrieks of the players. Slowly, very slowly Eddie raised his head. At the end of the ravine next to his, Sapna was lying spread-eagled on the ground. One of the last rays of the sun lit up her face and her naked breasts. Even in the dimming light, Eddie could see a dead pain in her eyes. She was past crying, past moaning or protesting. Her sari and petticoat had been yanked up, her hands forcibly stretched back above her head and as Maan Singh's exposed buttocks and the bumpy line of his spine rose and fell in rapid thrusts, her body twitched convulsively. Standing watch and watching them avidly was Maan Singh's deputy, Dilawar Singh.

'Take her,' Maan Singh told his deputy as he stood up. 'She's yours.'

Dilawar unbuttoned his trousers. Ravan leapt down, soft-landed behind Eddie and whispered, 'Gotcha'. He was puzzled that Eddie did not react to being caught and followed his friend's gaze. Sapna was trying to pull her sari down but Dilawar was lying prone on her, leaning his weight on one hand and hiking the sari up again with the other.

'Oh Dilawar, I almost forgot to tell you what Aminabai said to me,' Maan Singh spoke a shade too casually to his assistant but Dilawar stopped fiddling with the string of Sapna's petticoat and looked back at his boss in growing terror. 'But what's the point of telling you what you already know?'

The generator began to throb and the lights came on. Maan Singh held the gun against Dilawar's head while raising him up by his long hair with his left hand.

'I just want to look into your eyes. I've spent the last seven months trying to figure out who squealed on me.'

Maan Singh pulled the trigger. Dilawar's head exploded and his brains and fragments of his skull flew in all directions and splattered over Sapna as he toppled on her. Ravan and Eddie shuddered and shook and held each other tightly, hoping they would both disappear without a trace just as they had wished all those years ago when they were children and had found one of their neighbours, Shobhan Sarang, hanging from a hook one early morning in CWD Chawl Number 17. Maan Singh's men and the whole unit were racing towards the sound of the shot but came to an abrupt halt at the sight of the corpse and the bandit. Ravan walked up to where Sapna was lying on the ground. He picked up Dilawar's deadweight off the actress and laid him down a few metres away.

Eddie ran blindly and rammed into Maan Singh. 'What have you done? What have you done to poor Sapna-ji?'

Maan Singh regained his balance and smashed the butt of his gun in Eddie's face. 'What any real man would.'

Eddie's right eye was already swelling into a balloon. 'You know tae kwan do and kung fu, Ravan,' he yelled as he tried to stanch the flow of blood from his face. 'Do something. Teach this bastard a lesson.'

Maan Singh ignored Eddie's wild ravings. 'Paperwaley, I thought I had told you no one was to leave the camp.'

'But I was right here.'

Maan Singh stood beside Patel and looked him in the eye. 'You are lying.'

'I ... I ... I was writing your story in my tent,' the journalist stammered.

'Lying again. I wonder why I've a feeling you're never going to write any more stories.'

'Why? What have I done?'

'You took me for a fool.' Maan Singh raised his gun and shot Patel at point-blank range. Just then a voice on at least four or five loudspeakers broke the congealed silence of the dead.

'Maan Singh, this is Jwala Singh. I have a hundred policemen with me. And more are on the way. Put your hands up quietly and surrender. Otherwise, there will be a bloodbath and not one of you will escape alive.'

'Welcome, Commissioner.' Maan Singh scoured the environs to check the source of the voice but the multiple speakers foxed him.

He ducked, aimed his gun skyward and fired a welcoming volley while his men crept on their knees and slipped into the maze of ravines. 'I have been expecting you. I don't like to be kept waiting. I must warn you that I have at least thirty-five people from Bombay here, all of them shooting a film. Two of them are women, a famous actress called Sapna and her helper. I can't imagine that the highest-ranking police officer in Madhya Pradesh would want the deaths of these innocents on his head.'

A shot rang out and Maan Singh was hit in his arm. 'I've got you in the crosshairs of my automatic, Maan Singh. Next time it won't be your arm.'

A shell went off and dense clouds of smoke rose in the air just as one of the dacoit's men dragged Sapna away. Things got a little confused after that. Someone was using the big floods, the spotlights, and the gas lanterns as target practice and soon, while the generator continued to thrum and vibrate angrily, an oppressive airless darkness descended. There were volleys of gunfire though no one seemed to know who was firing at whom. In a matter of moments the treacherous ravines, the banks of the Chhoti Ganga and the clumps of trees on its banks had turned into a battlefield. People were running helter-skelter, terrified, screaming and bleeding.

What followed was a random show of firepower as if a momentary silence was a sign of weakness and you needed to prove to the enemy that you could outblast him. The body count kept going up slowly but inexorably. AK47s, Uzis, hand grenades, rifles and pistols, it was obvious that both the dacoits and the police saw this as the final confrontation and were staking everything they had on it. It was impossible to gauge whether the deaths were from friendly fire or the accuracy of the enemy's guns.

Neither Maan Singh nor Jwala Singh could consider a temporary ceasefire till daybreak. They both knew that the ravines were congenial as hideouts, but not for a battle to the finish. Yet being rational was never an option, they would continue like this till they had either no ammunition left or everybody was dead. There was no way of telling whether the reinforcements that the commissioner had talked about had arrived and Maan Singh and his men were surrounded on all sides. Or whether it was just a ploy to scare the dacoit. A tent caught fire and the blaze crackled and swirled dangerously in the wind. Within seconds, all the flammable chairs, tables and props were up in flames.

'We can't leave Sapna-ji there.' Ravan and Eddie were lying flat against the wall of a gully, almost hugging it to make themselves invisible. 'She can't be all that far away. Let's make a run for it and get her over to a safe place?'

'Is there such a thing?' Ravan asked.

'What thing?'

'A safe place?'

'Hey, we haven't been hit so far.'

'But we might.'

'Are you coming? Or shall I go on my own?'

'All right.'

Ravan zigzagged as he sprinted across. The first bullet caught him in the thigh and the second lodged below his shoulder blade. 'Stay where you are, Eddie,' Ravan croaked as he went down. But Eddie was already halfway when he too got hit in his ribcage and stomach and fell.

Hours passed. It was the longest night of their lives and, any moment now, it could also be their last. Ravan felt a strange sense of peace. It had taken him a long time to realize that if you really loved someone you'd lost, you would treasure the person, not the grief. Piya would always be with him. But he was not going to place her on an altar and start a cult of worship around her. For better or worse he was still alive and there were pressing matters to attend to.

He had to get back to Bombay without delay. Asmaan was waiting for him though maybe this time he was far more impatient to be with her than the other way round. There was so much to tell her. As far as he was concerned she was not second-best but number one, two, three and every other number in the world. She was the sum total of all the numbers, odd, even, plus, minus, decimal point, everything. Asmaan had tried every trick to point him towards life after Piya's death. She would have made a packet had she sold *Jaan Se Pyara Dushman* to one of the major production houses instead of Ravan and Eddie. He had been loath to admit it but he knew that she had written the film as a desperate mouth-to-mouth resuscitation measure to revive his interest in life.

He had taken her for granted because she was so undemanding. She would come over, clean up his place, cook for him, take him to a film or coax him to go out for a walk with her and all the while he would resent her and persuade himself that she was intruding on his life. Sometimes, Asmaan would ask him if he would prefer it if she left him alone and he would say, yes, I would like that. Most of the time she would reply, 'Too bad. I'm staying.' But once in a while she would leave and he would go berserk and call her up to ask her how she could abandon him. There was no end to his contrariness. She moved in with him after waiting months for him to ask her. He never did, he suspected now, because he was banking on her to take the initiative. Oh, what an arsehole he was. What was he trying to prove? His grief, his loss, his memory of a precious love? Did he want to build a Taj Mahal for Piya who loved him unconditionally but had moved on to another world, a world he knew nothing about? He dared not ponder the prospect of what he would have done if Asmaan had decided to let him stew in his own obsessive grief. Or what would have happened if someone else had walked into her life and walked away with her.

Ravan tried to raise his head to look for his friend but the pain in the shoulder overpowered him and he lay back in a stupor. This wouldn't do at all. Eddie, ClickClick and he were supposed to finish shooting, wrap up everything and take the train along with everybody else out of Gwalior the day after tomorrow. Their tickets had already been booked. Asmaan and Belle would be waiting for them.

He had no idea how badly Eddie was hurt. Damn, was he all right? Ravan was not very good at it but he tried his hand at praying for Eddie to some universal God though he couldn't sustain it. And what about Sapna-ji, ClickClick and the other members of the film crew and cast? Were they alive, injured or dead? He said his goodbyes to them and wished them well wherever they were.

The rim of the horizon was faintly visible now. Ravan drifted in and out of consciousness. He had turned into an icicle but it didn't bother him. Everything had receded into the distance, his heartbeat, the excruciating shooting pain radiating towards his neck, the awful stink emanating from the blood that had stained his costume, the rigor-mortis stiffness of his body, the sound of the bullets and hand grenades zinging around, the occasional whimper and cuss word, the breathtaking beauty of the dawn, the low ghostly mist flowing imperceptibly and filling the ravines, the grass bending with the weight of the frost, the thought that his mother would hear of his death and hurt like an internal wound that would never heal.

Dawn was flooding the east and the darkness on the edges of the earth was in disarray and dire retreat. Ravan could see Maan Singh pulling the trigger of his gun several times but apart from empty clicks nothing issued from it. The dacoit chieftain undid his bullet belt and checked if there were any cartridges left, then threw his weapon and belt down in frustration and rage. Jwala Singh walked towards him unhurriedly, his gun pointed at the bandit merely to emphasize the futility of any last-minute desperate measures. 'Your knife, the one at your calf, throw it down quietly and raise your hand.'

Maan Singh ground his teeth and swore as he bent down to do his mortal enemy's bidding and as he straightened up, the tip of the knife-blade was between his index finger and thumb. It happened so fast it was impossible to see that he had leaned back just a fraction to get leverage and fling the knife when a bullet from the policeman's gun knocked it out of the bandit's hand. 'Another stunt, and you will breathe your last. Raise your hands.'

Jwala Singh unlocked the handcuffs at his belt and clicked them around the dacoit's wrists.

'Sorry, Commissioner, I don't think he's safe in your hands.' There was a new man on the scene. He had appeared, as the cliché went, from out of nowhere. That flamboyant fireball was up and about now, taking long jaunty leaps into the sky. The high drama in the Chambal valley meant nothing to the sun as it carried on its business as usual as did the birds on the ground, tapping and pecking at invisible seeds, tiny worms and God alone knew what else with their rapid beaks, and the chameleons who flung their tongues like lassos on their prey and withdrew them just as swiftly. It was odd, to say the least, to see someone in a three-piece suit first thing in the morning and that too in the Chambal ravines. The sun was in Ravan's eyes and he couldn't make out the new visitor's features. But he couldn't get rid of the feeling that the man seemed familiar, someone he had seen or heard before.

'Let Maan Singh go.'

'I knew it!' The dacoit chieftain beamed. 'I knew you would come to my rescue.'

Jwala Singh stood undecided for a few moments. He had finally got his man and now he was being asked to hand him over. You could see the terrible dilemma on the policeman's face. He took off the handcuffs reluctantly as Ravan watched in amazement and hung them on the loop at the waist of his trousers.

'I owe you one, Three Point One.' Maan Singh couldn't contain his gratitude. 'You're the only true friend I've ever had.'

'You don't owe me anything. You gave me shelter for all those years when I was in trouble.' Three Point One smiled warmly. 'But you should know that two people can't be in the driver's seat at the same time.' Three Point One fired. It was a good shot. It went through the vermilion tilak on the dacoit's forehead.

'I'd told you, Commissioner Sahab, to finish the matter right then and there when I informed you that you would find the dacoit in Aminabai's place on that fateful Tuesday. Prearranged encounter deaths are an old tradition amongst the police force in our country but you had a problem with your conscience at the last minute and decided to take him alive. I can't afford that kind of sentimental foolishness again. Besides, as you know, I never leave behind witnesses.' The pistol went off again. The 'twin images from opposite sides of the mirror' still did not coincide but at least they lay side by side.

Three Point One a.k.a. Bashir Akhtar went over to where Dilawar lay with his skull smashed. 'Did you really think I would appoint you as Maan Singh's successor, Dilawar, after you betrayed him, so you could do the same to me?' He shook his head in disgust. 'Poor Maan Singh, he couldn't make the transition from being a bandit chieftain to being the kingpin of the mafia in the north.' He gazed at the ravines thoughtfully for a long time and was about to tuck his gun in his shoulder holster when he saw someone in a police uniform lying on the ground and was instantly alert. Three Point One walked over to the policeman, his gun cocked again. The celluloid Jwala Singh had turned an ashen blue and there was no sign of life.

'Oh, it's you, Pawar.' Three Point One felt his pulse. There was hardly any. 'So we meet again after all these years.' He slipped his foot under Ravan's back and flipped him over, examined his wounds and turned him over again. 'You should know your limits. Music is your forte. Why didn't you stick to it instead of going into acting and producing films? The first time I heard the music from *Hulla Gulla*, I couldn't believe that it was the same Pawar whom I had known since his taxi-driving days. You and your friend Eddie have given the world so much pleasure.' He paused. 'But *Hulla Gulla* will always be my all-time favourite.' And then and there he started to sing. It was absurd, the birds were chirping, the flies were feeding ravenously at the bloodied bodies and the vultures were wheeling overhead, and here was Three Point One singing lustily to the dead. There was nobody around and he had no reason to be self-conscious. The ravines resounded with his voice.

Big fish eat small fish.
Small fish eat smaller fish.
Smaller fish eat even smaller.
And what about the smallest?
They turn into sacrifish.

But small fish'll become big fish
And forget they too were li'll fish
And could easily have been sacrifish.

Old money can't recall it was
At one time nouveau riche
And just as boorish.

So make a wish.
Dear little fish
That you don't turn
Into sacrifish.

It was not a bad voice. It had a faintly gravelly timbre to it. With a bit of training and practice, it could be developed into a fairly mellifluous instrument. He had been a big fish swallowing medium-sized and li'l fish for so long, he was totally unaware of the irony of that song on his lips. Three Point One cocked his gun and aimed it at Ravan's head. 'The only people you can trust are the dead.' The gun was still pointed at Ravan but Three Point One seemed to have second thoughts. 'Why waste a bullet when you'll be dead any minute now. I don't want my lucky talisman's death on my hand. Bye, Pawar, I'm sure the police will be here soon and cremate you with the rest of your people. May you find peace in the next world.'

Part Three

20

It was late at night. Eddie and Ravan sat on the stoop of CWD Chawl No. 17 in jeans and faded t-shirts. Ravan was discovering that when you have nothing to do, one way of occupying yourself was to scratch the stubble on your face or move south and give the goods there a good jiggle, rub and scratch. He wondered if Eddie's and his mother had looked into the future and realized that it was not a good idea to move into those swanky apartments with their sons. Indeed, had they done so, they and their children would have found themselves on the pavement like more than half of Bombay

If the Maharashtra government had had any sense they would have applied to UNESCO to make the CWD Chawls a world heritage site. The chawls were very likely older than the pyramids in Egypt and unlike those tombs, they housed the living. It has to be admitted that some of the buildings had a dislocated hip and stood askew now, undecided whether they wanted to stand upright or lie down, others tilted precariously forward or sideways, and a few of them had been propped and re-propped, and two years ago the Municipal Repairs Board had worked extensively on them, which incidentally had put them at even greater risk than before but hey, they were still standing, weren't they? These chawls survived on sheer hope, the willpower of the residents, and the insupportable but monumental corruption of the bureaucracy, the local municipal corporators and the government. Nothing had changed unless, like Eddie and Ravan, you were returning after a long interval. Then, for a brief while, things looked a little more run-down and seedy and there was an even greater shortage of water than when they were children. But soon these things would slip out of their consciousness.

Ravan could see that Eddie and he were a textbook case of that phrase 'reversal of fortune'. Oh, what a rise and fall it was. They had climbed up all the way from CWD Chawl Number 17 in Mazagaon to the eleventh floor of Dharti and Akaash on Pali Hill. And now they were back where they had started. It was hard to comprehend that they had not even been able to go back to their apartments after the fiasco in the Chambal ravines. Maybe it was a good thing that it had been a clean break. It would have been sheer torture watching every single item in all the rooms being noted down by the auctioneer and his team, then being sold for a pittance, and grieving over their loss. Unless it's a much sought-after painting or a rare Persian carpet, the value of most articles lies in the memories they evoke. The way things had worked out, it was no mean mercy that neither Eddie nor he could remember half the things they had had to part with.

After the crazy shootout in the Chambal ravines, Eddie, Ravan and many others in the crew had been saved when the police had finally arrived and transported them by ambulance to the hospital in Gwalior. Two days later, Asmaan had flown to Gwalior and accompanied Ravan and Eddie on the Punjab Mail along with a doctor who kept them drugged till they were admitted to St. George's Hospital. Belle had arrived from New York by the end of the week and the two women had taken turns to look after them and fend off the reporters for the three-and-a-half months before they were given permission to go home. There was, however, no stopping the police dropping in at all hours and waking up the two patients and conducting lengthy interrogations. Since Eddie no longer had his apartment, Belle had had to go back to her parents in the Railway Quarters at Byculla.

Mrs McIntyre had put up stiff resistance to the idea of Eddie moving in with them but Belle had been adamant and had her way. Well, for a fortnight anyway. After that, Eddie would rather have jumped out of the window than suffer Daphne McIntyre's malevolent sarcasm. She hated him. Who else but he was responsible for dear Veer leaving Belle? So Eddie went back to his mother's place. Asmaan's family on the other hand was not about to allow her friend

Ravan Pawar to share her room merely because she wanted him to have a roof over his head. She had always been a woman with questionable morals but imagine wanting to live in sin with a Hindu man who didn't even have his own place. Sorry, they were not about to sit quietly and permit such scandalous debauchery to take place while they were still alive. She might not have any sense of shame but they did and that was the only reason why they refused to allow him to move in.

Back in the CWD Chawls, the grey streaks in Parvatibai's hair had multiplied but Violet still dyed hers black although she was a little careless these days and the white roots at the central parting emphasized the black even more. In truth, she had good reason to continue to wear black. She had not merely lost her husband, God had seen it fit to take her young daughter away too. She occasionally wondered in her heart of hearts whether Pieta was the victim of the same man who had killed her husband and now, it transpired, had destroyed her son's highly successful threefold career by enticing him to start on the most foolish venture of his life: producing a film. She had known from the beginning that no good would come of it and her words had come true. Eddie was back in the chawl with his mother and Granna – and without a job or a rupee to his name.

It was, however, not all downhill for the CWD Chawls. The grocer and the haircutting salon on the ground floor had lined all their shelves, drawers and cupboards in purple laminate and their premises were lit with bright neon tube lights. A couple of the tenants had sold their rooms to a burgeoning new service industry which hired out security guards, and had moved to the distant suburbs. For an under-the-table price of course, enough to buy a slightly bigger place in the ever-expanding outer perimeter of Bombay and, with any luck, have a little bit left over as a nest egg. Some of the homes had a fresh coat of paint. One tenant's son had become an allopath and opened his clinic next to the hairdresser's while another room on the ground floor had been rented by an optician. The excitement in Chawl Number 17 had risen to fever pitch when the young doctor installed a second-hand air-conditioner in his clinic. There were even rumours that he might be getting a brand-new bride and car and who knows even a flat in a pukka high-rise, all three being supplied by his in-laws-to-be.

'Shall we start a band?' Ravan asked Eddie.

'Whose? Your Cum September Brass Band or my Bandra Bombshells?' Eddie laughed. 'You have to admit, it must have taken sheer genius to have come up with those names.'

'Do you think the Beatles, the Doors or the Who sound better or make sense? If you succeed, any name's just fine. If you don't, the most memorable names in the world won't get you anywhere. How about trying out a new name?'

'Sure. You get the money to buy the instruments and the clothes, just a couple of hundred thousand and we'll be in business. I need hardly add that not a single group in Bombay does well these days, it's all those new-fangled DJs now at parties and weddings. But that I am sure is no cause for worry for you. And pray who's going to join our band? Belle? Asmaan? Or the great Asha Bhosle?'

'Okay, wise guy, you've made your point. But you haven't come up with any ideas either about how we're going to survive without hand-outs from Belle or Asmaan, not to mention free housing and meals.'

From across Chawl Number 23 they heard the sound of weeping and wailing.

'It's Mr Tamhane's wife, isn't it?' Eddie asked Ravan. 'Can you believe it, he died last afternoon and his body's still here? If they were Catholics, the body would have been sent for embalming, but they are Hindus. Why the hell are they delaying the cremation?'

'Crying's not going to help her. Nobody, no Hindu, Catholic or Neo-Buddhist, has agreed to help carry the body of the court clerk to the crematorium.'

'Isn't the son, Anant, going to move his butt? The body will have begun to smell horribly by now.'

'Not much to choose between the father and the son. Stingy as hell and always willing to pick a fight. Never did either of them lift a finger to help a neighbour. You watch, not a soul will come to their aid.'

Ravan remembered the time long, long ago when Anant had got married. His father, the court clerk, had sweet-talked Ravan and hired the Cum September Band. They had played the whole day and late into the evening but at midnight Tamhane Senior claimed that the band should pay him and his family for having suffered their 'atrocious, farting spastic din' and refused to give Ravan even a quarter of the promised amount for their work. He didn't even give the members of the band the meal that was their due for having played on such a happy occasion.

'Clam up,' Eddie whispered. 'Anant's coming here.'

'Quick, let's go home before he asks us to help him.'

Too bad, Anant had cornered them. 'Eddie, Ravan, my father passed away last evening.'

'Do offer our heartfelt condolences to your mother,' Eddie said in a lugubrious tone.

'Will you help me carry the body to Chandanwadi?'

'Why don't you ask your own neighbours?' Ravan countered.

'They are not decent people. My parents have known some of them for forty or fifty years but they won't lift a finger to help a neighbour. They don't even respect the dead. I know you are not like them. Please help me.'

'Sorry, but we have a prior business engagement.'

Anant cackled. He had his father's fractured laugh that left you in no doubt about how contemptible you were. 'Business engagement? Like what? You guys have been jobless since God knows how long. You're failures. Nobody wants to take you on even as extras any more.'

'Piss off.' Eddie had to admit that Anant had a wonderful talent for hitting the raw nerve. 'Find someone else to carry the bier.'

Anant Tamhane looked sourly at them as he gathered the spittle in his mouth. For a moment Ravan thought he was going to spit on him as he had done on Pieta's head from a floor above when they were children, but he spat on the ground and walked away.

'Tamhane, oh Tamhane Junior,' Ravan called out after him.

Anant stopped but kept his distance, watching them suspiciously. 'What?'

'What will you give us?'

'Give?' Anant asked irritably. 'Give you what?'

'What will you pay us if we help you carry your father?'

Anant looked at him disgustedly. 'You are despicable. How can you be so unfeeling? The shastras tell us that doing a good deed is its own reward.'

'Good, you do the good deed and keep the reward all to yourself. How about that?' Ravan told him sanctimoniously.

'And you can keep your beloved father too,' Eddie added his two bits. 'Right next to you for the rest of your life.'

* * *

It was early in the morning when Eddie hollered from his kitchen window, 'Let's work out at the Sabha gym, Ravan, and then have a cup of tea at the Irani's.'

Parvatibai was on the verge of asking, 'Why don't you have tea at home?' but thought the better of it. Her son was a grown-up man and would resent his mother controlling his every move starting from such trivial matters as to where he should have his first cup of tea in the morning. Not that she would advise him on the major issues either. She had been awkward when she visited him at that place in Bandra where he lived, or rather had lived. She felt uneasy though Ravan always sent the car for her. It was Pieta she missed terribly. She had not been merely good-hearted, she was genuinely interested in Parvatibai and what she thought about things. She bought her saris and knick-knacks, an onion slicer, an electric mixer and a masala-maker. They talked about any and every subject, the falling standards in the city and national politics. Pieta asked for her views on the disappearance of the queue system in Bombay, the rise of chain-snatching incidents on the road and on local trains, and whether dynastic rule was a good idea.

Ravan, on the other hand, hardly spoke to her. Parvatibai did not for a moment doubt his affection for her but he had always been a quiet child. He kept his thoughts to himself. His way of life had altered so much, she found it hard to relate to him and sometimes even to recognize him. He used to fly abroad with Eddie to perform for audiences in London, New York, the Middle East, Africa and in countries whose names she had never heard of. He wore three-piece suits, held vast crowds spellbound and they kept shouting once more, once more. Was this the boy who would make a face when she attempted to hum along when he sang '*Dil deke dekho*'? 'Don't you want to finish cooking?' he would ask when what he meant was, 'Can you spare us this torture?' Now he had come back home and she did not know what to say to him.

Ravan got into his jeans, pulled an old t-shirt over his head, said, 'I'll be back soon' and left. The sky was dreary with black clouds grumbling as they rolled past. For the past month there had been no sign of the sun but the monsoons had been playing truant and there was talk of serious water shortage if it continued like this for the next ten days. Eddie and Ravan were halfway to the Irani's when they saw Anant running towards them.

'Oh no, not again,' Ravan muttered.

'How much do you want?' Anant asked.

'One hundred. Fifty for Eddie and fifty for me.'

'Come on.'

* * *

When you were a child you got to know a few of the other CWD Chawls because some of your friends lived in them, while most others remained closed books. Chances were things wouldn't change much when you grew up; you went to your grave, that's if you were a Catholic, or were cremated if you belonged to the majority community, without having a clue about what was transpiring in the neighbouring building. CWD Chawl Number 23 was diagonally opposite Chawl Number 17, yet Ravan and Eddie had never visited it. Ravan wondered whether each individual chawl had a different body odour. Even from a distance of fifteen metres, the Tamhanes' chawl exuded a sickly sour smell.

It was not yet seven but as usual the women had already had their bucket baths and were preparing breakfast for the children and packing lunch boxes for their husbands. The menfolk were just getting up. Some were making their way to the toilets, Postman Groundnut Oil or Dalda Hydrogenated Oil tin cans filled with water held by their oddly dainty thin handles. Some were standing in the balcony, brushing their teeth, while you heard a few cleaning their tongues and making the most revolting sounds as they first shoved their middle fingers down their throats and then their entire arm till it disappeared into the pit of their bellies. By the time Eddie and Ravan climbed up to the third floor, they were ready to throw up whatever they had eaten in the last year, maybe two. It was an overpowering smell that penetrated into their lungs, slipped into their bloodstream, and crept into the lining and folds of their brains. They had covered their noses with their kerchiefs but it was no use. Their knees were wobbly and all they wanted to do was to run. Anything, anything to get away from that slow, rotting, putrid smell of death.

Oh, how Eddie cursed Ravan in his mind. What had that idiot-friend of his got them into? They were on the fourth floor now. At the end of the corridor they could see two men with wet face towels pressed against their noses striding up to Anant. One lifted him up by the scruff of his neck while the other punched him in his solar plexus.

'Get rid of that body, you bastard. We'll go to the health authorities, we'll call the police, we'll go to the papers and splash the news across the country. We'll throw your father over the balcony. The dead body's a plague and all of us will die of it.'

Anant was in tears and stammering. 'I'm t-t-taking it away. I mean t-t-the the body, my father. Just wait. Please don't call the police. I have got two friends with me now. We'll be gone in a few minutes, I promise.'

'You've got all of five minutes. After that your father goes crashing down to hell.'

The court clerk was lying on the bed, shrunken and desiccated as a dried Bombay Duck. The soft, semi-transparent jelly-like fish was a local delicacy and one of Ravan's favourite dishes when it was fresh and fried in a shallow pan with either salt and chilli powder or covered with rice-flour batter. Ravan had no idea how the British masters of India had turned the Marathi word *bombil* into Bombay Duck, but one thing was certain: he would never be able to eat or even touch that fish again.

Mrs Tamhane stood, her nostrils flaring, and glowered at Ravan and Eddie. What's with you? Ravan was struck by her hostility. We didn't kill your husband nor did we threaten to throw him down.

'I know all about you. You are insolvent and you've got dozens of cases filed against you. Murderers, that's what you are. Nobody knows how many innocent people you killed in the Chambal valley. If my husband had been alive and still working in the court, he would have sent you straight to the gallows. And now you want money for carrying the body of this noble, upright man of the law. Shameless blackguards.'

She was thin and translucent but her hands were like crabs and Ravan had implicit faith in her murderous pronouncements. Those pincer claws would have no problem strangling both Eddie and him.

'Have it your way. We'll take your leave then.'

Anant panicked. 'Aai, you keep out of this and let me handle the arrangements.' Mrs Tamhane gave the outsiders a look which turned them to instant ash and disappeared into the kitchen. 'Don't take it to heart. She's just overwrought because of Father's death.'

'Where are the other two?'

'Which other two?'

'You need at least four men to carry a dead body.'

'What do you think I'm paying you for?'

'Fine. You pick up the front of the bier and we'll lift the back-end.'

'I can't. I'll be carrying the clay pot and the ghee.'

'In that case our charges are double.'

'You said one hundred. You gave me your word.'

'Forget it. Come on, Ravan. Let's go.'

Poor Anant, if only his father were here to advise him. He was caught on the horns of a dilemma but this was no ordinary bull, it was a barasingha and he was being tossed and gored on its multiple antlers. He looked around desperately for a clue, anything to hold on to the two men, but couldn't bear the thought of having to pay more.

'My father's very light. He had TB, you know.'

'You don't say.' Eddie went in for dramatic overkill. 'Oh no, Ravan, now we'll get TB and die of it. Our families will be infected and the next thing we know everybody in our chawl will be dying of it. And then the whole of Bombay, all ten million of its residents, are bound to catch it. And then we really will be mass murderers. Sorry, Anant, we can't help you.'

'Don't go. Please don't go.'

'The money?' Eddie was deadpan. 'Please understand if it's TB, it's three hundred rupees.'

'It was two hundred a minute ago.'

'Think about it, your father may be dead but he could still kill us both.'

'I'll give you half just now and half when the job is done.'

Eddie was about to acquiesce but Ravan blocked him. 'No deal. Your father and you taught me not to trust you, remember? At your wedding.'

'How do I know you won't cheat me?'

'You can't. But I don't think you have much of a choice.'

It seemed to cause Anant intense distress to part with the money, especially now that Ravan had told him they could not be trusted and simultaneously reminded him that he had little choice in the matter. Anant gave each of them a hundred-rupee note and a fifty-rupee one. Ravan and Eddie smirked jubilantly at making Anant triple their fees but, when they got close to the corpse, they discovered what a blunder they had made. They grabbed every cotton sheet and bedcover they could lay their hands on in the Tamahne household and wrapped the dead man tightly from head to foot so that he looked like an Egyptian mummy.

'How can you cover my father's face?'

'Your father's rotting, Anant, and stinking worse than a dead rat,' Ravan told him.

'You watch your tongue. Speak of my father with some respect.'

'If you had any respect you wouldn't have kept a dead man for over thirty-six hours in the Bombay heat.'

'Those sheets and bedcovers, we use them every day. You can't take them.'

'We just did.'

They were on their way. The court clerk was stiff and not as light as Anant had made him out to be. From the fourth to the third floor was difficult but from the third-floor landing it was an ordeal which no nightmare could match. Nobody had pointed out to Eddie and Ravan that there is a science to bamboo bier-making; perhaps it's even an art form. Since Anant had not tied the four cross-bars of the bier tightly to the longer poles, the bamboos kept shifting and along with them the court clerk too slid back and forth. One of the poles came undone and now Tamhane Senior lurched from side to side and, every few steps, leapt right out as if he was in a desperate hurry to meet his maker. It had dawned on both the pallbearers by now that it was essential to tie the boisterous old man up.

'We need some rope, Anant,' Eddie called out to the son who had gone ahead with the clay pot and the ghee, 'to tie your father.'

'Sorry, but the two metres I bought have already been used. I don't think my father would like being trussed up.'

'What are you talking about?' Ravan was convinced that Anant was going wacko. 'He won't feel a thing, he's dead, Anant.'

'But his soul's still hovering above. It will depart only after the thirteenth day when we've done the shradh.'

Eddie realized it was pointless arguing with the man. Men, women, children, grandparents and mothers with babes-in-arms of CWD Chawl Number 23 stood with their noses covered with kerchiefs or sari palloos, watching the funeral procession pass by. Nobody, however, offered to lend a helping hand. Quite the contrary, the Tamhanes were persona non grata and there was a palpable hostility towards the two outsiders who had come to help them.

'Hold it, Ravan,' Eddie called to his friend. 'Stop.'

'What now?' Ravan asked tetchily. He knew it sounded absurd but he was willing to wager that the deceased court clerk had gained weight and was getting heavier by the minute.

'We'll slide the old man down.'

'Are you crazy?' Ravan protested but he was more than willing to try anything just so long as he did not have to carry Tamhane down three more flights of stairs.

Eddie balanced the bier carefully on the banister and ran alongside, clutching the bamboo frame and the makeshift shroud with his right hand. They were doing pretty well and some bystanders whistled their approval till Eddie missed the third-last step and stumbled, and the court clerk flew into the air, grazed the rust-stained ceiling and dropped into Ravan's outstretched arms. There was a roar of applause and clapping from all those around. The impact of the falling body was so great, Ravan nearly dropped Anant's father. It occurred to him at that moment that if Eddie's father, Victor Coutinho, had had butter fingers, make that butter arms, or had lost his concentration for a moment, baby Ravan would have turned to purée and instead of Violet, his mother would have accused Victor Coutinho of murdering her son.

'What are you doing?' Anant went ballistic. 'He's my father.'

'I know. He is like a father to Ravan and me too.'

Ravan couldn't believe the humbug Eddie was capable of. But as was his wont, he instantly went overboard and made a big show of carrying the corpse with exaggerated care.

'Don't, don't worry, Anant. We'll treat him like a dew-drenched petal. Like the peacock feather in Krishna's headband. Like a half-boiled egg.' Eddie was on a roll now. 'Like, like a newborn babe. Like he was as insubstantial as mist.'

'Okay, okay,' Anant interjected. 'I get the point. He's in good hands.'

They were at the bottom of Byculla bridge when the two pallbearers laid the bier on the pavement and sat down.

'Bastard, it was your bright idea,' Eddie swore at Ravan.

'As if you didn't pocket half the money.'

Tamhane Junior looked back and was alarmed that he couldn't

see Eddie and Ravan. Then he spotted them and was furious. He retraced his steps.

'Why are you wasting time?'

'Sit down for a minute.'

'Hurry up. I haven't got all day. Besides it might rain any minute.'

'Fine, carry the old man yourself.'

'I paid you even though you blackmailed me. Charged me thrice the agreed-upon price. Now do your job.'

'You mention the money again, and we'll leave your father in your care. Why don't you try and carry your old man?'

Ravan got up and walked over to Anant, snatched the clay pot and tin of ghee and placed them on top of the body.

'What are you doing? This is a gross violation of the rituals prescribed in the Puranas.'

'Come on. Give us a hand. You take over the front. About time you found out how heavy a corpse is.'

'Sorry, I can't. That's your job.'

'Have it your way.'

There was rumbling in the sky but no one seemed to be bothered. It had been like this for weeks. Anant watched the two pallbearers disappearing into the crowds and ran after them. 'Please, don't leave me alone.'

They had gone barely fifty metres but Anant was already panting like a dog, ninety-two or maybe a hundred-and-fifty times a minute. The bridge over the Central Railway tracks was not a very long one but a 45-degree gradient with your father on your shoulders was not exactly a joyride.

It began to pour. The cannons in the skies boomed ceaselessly and lightning cracked the sky. Ravan had underestimated the rate at which the dead put on weight. With the rain pelting down, Tamahne seemed to gain a kilo every thirty seconds. From bantamweight, the court clerk had graduated to heavyweight and was still gaining.

Anant stopped without notice and plonked himself down on the ground. The court clerk lay on the pavement. Runnels of water came racing down the bridge and the dead man was soaked to the bone and maybe all the way to his soul but Anant was oblivious of his father's condition. Five minutes passed and then ten, yet Anant showed no sign of getting up. The wind was blowing and both Ravan and Eddie had begun to shiver.

'Another forty metres,' Eddie stuttered, 'and we'll be at the top of the bridge. After that it will be all downhill.'

No response. 'Come on, Anant,' Ravan begged him. 'Eddie and I must go home soon.'

Tamhane Junior was immune to Ravan's pleas. He no longer cared whether the two pallbearers stayed or left. It didn't matter to him if his father was whisked away by the floods of water rushing down in torrents. He had given up. Ravan and Eddie hefted up Tamhane Senior and put him down instantly. The winding sheets had absorbed such vast quantities of water, the court clerk weighed as much as a whale now.

'Help me,' Ravan said as he bent down.

'Forget it.' Eddie was adamant. 'There's no way we'll be able to take him to the Chandanwadi crematorium.'

'I know. Listen to me. Five steps, that's all.'

'Not one more, I'm warning you.'

'Scout's honour.'

Eddie was about to point out that neither of them had ever been a scout but the words stuck in his craw as he watched his friend in horror. The lunatic waited till the rain eased up. When he saw an empty truck approaching, he laid the bier in front of it. The brakes squealed and screeched and the truck came to a halt. The vehicles behind honked furiously, braked hard and took a detour around the truck while calling the driver names. The lorry driver opened the door, leaned his head out and let loose a string of abuses, all of them centred on copulation with family members.

'We came all the way from Sholapur to get our father admitted to J.J. Hospital.' No sooner had he spoken than Ravan realized his blunder; the hospital was a mile ahead, but it was too late to retrieve the situation. People were starting to gather around the corpse and there was only one way to win them over to his side. It was now or never. He burst into tears. 'We came all the way from Nagpur to get our father operated,' Sholapur was not distant enough to milk every drop of sympathy, 'but the poor soul passed away on the operating table. Oh God, how are we going to face our mother? What will we tell her?'

Eddie pointed his finger at Anant as he quietly tucked the cross hanging around his neck inside his shirt. 'It's been such a shock for our brother, he's lost his powers of speech.'

'*Bhainchod, to main kya karun*?' the truck driver began, then realized that he had to be careful about his choice of words. 'I mean, may your father's soul rest in peace, but what am I supposed to do?'

'All we want is a lift to the crematorium at Chandanwadi.'

'Bhadwe, is that why you stopped my truck? My boss wanted me to pick up cargo at Masjid Bunder an hour ago. I got delayed because of the rain and now you want me to carry your father's corpse? Don't you know it's bloody bad luck to carry a dead body? Move out of the way.'

Eddie lay down by the side of the corpse. 'Go right ahead. But you'll have to run over me first. May my beloved mother's curse be upon you,' he intoned in his deepest voice. 'May your sons turn out to be pimps, murderers and criminals. May your wife cuckold you and take on lover after lover while you travel all over the country.' The imprecations rolled off Eddie's tongue with such celerity the truck driver shrivelled with terror. 'May your truck have a fatal accident. May the whores you sleep with on your journeys give you terminal syphilis. May your daughters give birth...' Eddie could have gone on for at least another five minutes but the driver had got the drift.

'Shut the fuck up. Shut the fuck up. Get in with your accursed old man.'

The truck took off. Ravan and Eddie crouched next to the court clerk while Anant sat in a corner, staring at the traffic. There was a full kitsch-rainbow in the sky and the sun peered out shyly from behind the dark clouds like an auspicious omen. But Ravan and Eddie knew by now that the gods, the sun and the moon have their own agendas and they don't run in tandem with the yearnings and wishes of humankind.

21

Shankar-rao, Ravan's father, did not like it but he had little say in the matter. Between 10 a.m., when Parvatibai finished the morning's cooking and sent off the tiffin carriers to her clients, and 12 noon, he had to vacate the one place in the house which had been his and his alone for nearly four decades. No dog or property developer had guarded his turf as watchfully and truculently as the elder Pawar. He had resisted the idea, actually he had fought and thrown a tantrum, but Parvatibai had put her foot down. The bullet which had got lodged in Ravan's shoulder in the shootout in the Chambal ravines had been removed but it had severely impaired the flexibility and movement of the muscles and nerves in the area and the doctors had advised physiotherapy and daily massages with oil. The Pawars couldn't afford a physiotherapist and, anyway, Parvatibai was certain she could do a far better job.

There was a time when she would have been happy to sit on the floor and gently but firmly rub the Ayurvedic herbal oil into her son's neck, shoulder and shoulder blades, but the arthritis in her knees had got to a point where it was impossible to do so. Today, Ravan was in much worse shape than he had been for the last two months. He was moaning and grunting like a pig in rut and calling upon various deities. 'Haré Ram, Narayana, Parameshwara, Krishna.'

'What's happened, Ravan? Why are you again in such pain? What are these red welts on your shoulder? Where were you yesterday morning and half of the afternoon?'

Ravan was not about to tell his mother about his and Eddie's adventures with Anant's father. If she found out, she would worry that her son had suffered a relapse after such a long and difficult recovery.

He had the impression that after the removal of the bullet, his head had been tamped down like a cork in a wine bottle, and prayed that some kindly soul would do him the favour of pulling it out with a corkscrew. The doctors had pronounced that the nerves had been severely damaged and they did not think there was much chance of his being able to turn his neck even fifty degrees, but of course there was no arguing with a mother who was primitive enough to believe in the curative powers of a herbal oil that her grandmother had used to bring life back into the paralysed half of her husband's body.

Ravan himself was willing to try any Ayurvedic or Unani medicines, poultices and steam baths or other alternative treatments just so long as the pain and the compression in his shoulder eased. But the oil his mother swore by had such a strong odour, Ravan nearly gagged on it. He was convinced that it was made from animal faeces, rotting eggs, kerosene, and God alone knew what else and the awful aroma was added only to camouflage the nature of the contents.

Parvatibai said matter-of-factly that the strong smell would vanish after the first couple of minutes. It took Ravan a while to understand what his mother was trying to tell him. It was like the toilets in the chawls. In the first minute, your breathing apparatus revolted and you almost ran out, but then the olfactory nerves switched off and you were no longer aware of the smell.

For once, he and his father had ganged up against Parvatibai but for very different reasons. Shankar-rao didn't give a damn about the smell of the oil; all he wanted was his bed back. He had threatened to leave home for good and Parvatibai had said he was more than welcome to do so. He chose the middle path. He went out for two hours every day and returned only when he could repossess his bed.

Two months of the massage had not altered Ravan's condition but his mother had been perversely obstinate. He had tried arguing with her but to no avail. What he couldn't deny though was that after the first ten minutes, he slipped into a bhang-like trance. The pain levels went down and he was dead to the world. Then, in the previous week, he had discovered that the muscles in his neck were less taut and the lock that had been put on them seemed to have unloosened just a wee bit.

Ravan had had plenty of time to reflect on the debacle in the Chambal ravines. Nine members of the cast and crew, not to mention Ramchander and the hawaldar, hadn't made it back. ClickClick was alive but had still not recovered. Sapna had survived but only on hefty doses of tranquillizers; she no longer went out or met anybody, and a cousin of hers had taken her with him to Delhi. Poor Harish Patel. If the journalist had not been so keen to file his 'big' story, he would not only have survived but lived to cover the far bigger story of that last night in Chambal.

Jaan Se Pyara Dushman was dead long before it could reach the editing table. All the footage that had been shot had been taken over by the banks and financiers. As had been all the music. Not a single producer, director or superstar had lined up outside CWD Chawl Number 17 after R&E got out of hospital. And no one had asked them to compose the music for their films or at least choreograph the fight sequences. They were bad luck and there's nothing worse in the Hindi film world than to be in the vicinity of losers. Didn't you know that, call it what you will – a panwati, hex or a jinx – bad luck was a zillion times more infectious than any plague, even that new one called AIDS.

'I'll never be first. Second best is the best I can do.' The lines from Asmaan's song had haunted Ravan on the location shoot. Once they got back from Chambal, he would tell Asmaan that she would have to rewrite the song. She was never going to be second best ever again. Yes, he had planned to ask her to move in with him, bag and baggage. A bit late for that now since the banks had taken possession of his apartment in Akaash. Now, once again, Ravan found himself in the same quandary he had faced when Pieta and he were courting. There was no place where Asmaan and he could have some privacy.

* * *

Falling ... falling ... falling...

Eddie couldn't fathom what had got into him that he could have behaved like such a dickhead with Belle. It had upset his mother no end that the Anglo woman had come back into his life although Violet might have even reconciled herself to Belle if only he would get married to her. But Belle was in no hurry. It didn't make a difference to him either whether the two of them lived in sin or got married.

After the hospital stint was over, Eddie had finally caved in and gone to stay with Belle at her mother's home. But the outcome, as he knew from the start, was a foregone one. According to Mrs Daphne McIntyre, the young Malaviya heir-apparent was a real aristocrat. So good-looking and well-mannered and he looked after Belle's every wish even before she herself knew what she wished for. He was Belle's ticket to luxury yachts, a villa in Monte Carlo and the good life. Not that it had played any role in Mamma McIntyre's fondness for Veer, what a preposterous idea, but you had to admit that he was pure gold, no symbolism there. And Eddie, he was not even dross, just plain trash.

It was quite a feat on Daphne's part not to say a word and yet make silence such an asphyxiating instrument of ill-will. Which by itself wouldn't have affected Eddie so much. The trouble was Belle could see the terrible effect her mother was having on her relationship with Eddie, and was determined to make amends for all the years she had neglected him. She couldn't bear the thought of him going back to his mother's place. She had discovered a mantra called 'think positive' and she preached it round the clock. This had rather unfortunate consequences. All this while, Eddie had dreamt of poisoning Daphne and her long-suffering martyr act. Now his focus had shifted to Daphne's daughter. He was willing to strangle her merely to scotch that ineffable and relentless fount of optimism.

* * *

'Ravan. Ravan Pawar.' Someone woke Ravan up from his musings but he was too far gone to respond.

'Ravan Pawar,' the man called again. Ravan would have continued to ignore him but his mother wouldn't let him be.

'Don't be rude, Ravan. At least find out what the man wants.'

'What is it?' Ravan went to the kitchen window and yelled.

'Come down and I will tell you.'

Ravan pulled a t-shirt over his head and went down. For a minute as he walked down the stairs his hopes had been raised. Maybe it was a producer who wished to hire Eddie and him. But one look at the man from close quarters and he realized how mistaken he was. This was the guy who had been selling chikki and peanuts to the children outside the municipal school since the time he himself was a student. He had gone grey but obviously business had not improved much. He was still wearing cotton paijamas and nylon kurtas.

'Where's your partner?'

'Why call me if you want to talk to him?'

'I have business with both of you.'

'What business?'

'Do you remember Shinde, the plumber opposite the school?'

'Yes. What about him?'

'His grandmother died this morning. We need to take her to the crematorium.'

'You think we've started an undertaker's business?'

'I'll pay you both.'

'Why would you need us? I'm sure Shinde's got enough neighbours who will help him.'

'I won't lie to you. We're Dalits. But there's something else. Shinde's grandmother got leprosy last year. She was being treated and was on the mend. But in our society once a leper, always a leper. That makes Shinde an untouchable twice over. Shinde's a proud man. He doesn't want any favours from our neighbours. Even his son was reluctant to help.'

'Who else will help carry the body?'

'Shinde and I.'

'How much?'

'Hundred for the two of you.'

'Sorry. Carry her yourself. Last time we got three hundred.'

'Last time there were three of you.'

'The third guy was the dead man's son.'

'Is it because we are Dalits?'

'What's it to me whether you are an untouchable or Raj Kapoor? It's very, very hard work. That's all.'

'That's a lot of money for us.'

'I'm sorry. You can always go to somebody else.'

The vendor stood irresolutely clenching and unclenching his fist. Ravan wouldn't look at the man for fear he would go soft and settle for one-fifty or even one-thirty.

'Call your friend.'

Ravan remembered someone telling him that you didn't need to spit if you did something loathsome, all you needed to do was swallow. His Adam's apple had been working overtime in the past few weeks but today he had reached the nadir. Just a few months ago, Eddie and he were making thousands every month. Now he was willing to haggle with this man over a dead woman for the princely sum of two hundred rupees. All the saints told you that you couldn't take money to your grave, but what they forgot to mention was that you couldn't make it to the next day without money either.

Ravan looked even unhappier than his would-be customer. What had he got himself into? One day as a corpse-bearer was enough for a lifetime. The only other funeral he intended to attend was his own. He should have put his foot down instead of being polite and finding himself in an awful predicament all over again. Do you know what your problem is, Ravan? he asked himself fatuously, you just don't know how to say no. He was an ace at wisdom-after-the-event. He stopped at the landing on the first floor. Why bother to climb up all the way to the fifth floor when he knew that Eddie would flay him alive if he so much as mentioned the words pallbearer or bier. All he had to do was linger on the staircase for a few minutes and then go down and tell this man that he was sorry but his friend had said no and that would get him off the hook.

'Eddie.' Ravan preferred not to venture inside. Since Pieta's death, Violet had reverted to her earlier loathing of Ravan. The door was open and Ravan could see inside. Mrs Coutinho was doing exactly what his mother had done a few minutes ago except that she was massaging Eddie's back with Tiger Balm. She looked up with distaste bordering on antipathy.

'Eddie's sick.' She got up as if to stress the next three words. 'Because of you.' She gave him one last disgusted look before disappearing into the kitchen.

'Come on out, Eddie.'

'What for?'

'I need to talk to you.'

'It's over a week since we carried old man Tamhane and I still can't turn my head and my back is suffering from rigor mortis.'

'Please.'

'Whatever it is had better be good.' Eddie took his time getting out of bed and to the corridor.

'Promise me you won't fly off the handle.'

'I already know it's going to be something I can't stomach.'

Ravan took a deep breath. 'Now remember I didn't initiate this.'

'Cut to the chase, Ravan.'

'Okay, here's the deal. Do you remember Shinde, the plumber opposite the municipal school who had that lovely daughter Rajnigandha? He wants us to help him and a friend of his to take his grandmother to Chandanwadi.'

'It was nice knowing you, Ravan, but goodbye. Don't bother to come back.'

'Just this once, Eddie. Four pallbearers and three hundred rupees for the two of us.'

'Read my lips, Ravan. No.'

'You take two hundred and I'll take one hundred.'

'What's with you, Ravan? Why not just come clean and admit that you are doing this not for Papa Shinde but to impress his magnificently endowed daughter, Lady Rajnigandha?'

'They are Dalits and nobody wants to touch the corpse.'

'I'm sorry about that, but no. Go home, Ravan.'

'Bastard.'

The vendor was sitting on the steps of the stoop. He looked at Ravan's face and got up to leave. 'Your friend refused to come?'

'I'm sorry but the answer's...'

'Let's get on with it.' Eddie was already walking ahead.

* * *

They were lucky. They had an extra hand, one of Shinde's cousins had joined the group.

'Ram, Ram, Jai Ram. Ram, Ram, Jai Ram, Ram Ram...' Shinde mumbled the name of the god monotonously till, halfway to the crematorium, Ravan started to sing '*Thumak chalata Ramchandra, bajat painjaniya*'.

It was a clear, powerful voice and Ravan himself had no idea why he had broken into song. Perhaps he couldn't bear the dismal droning from Shinde, perhaps he hadn't sung for so long he needed to find out whether he still had a voice. Perhaps he merely wanted to reassure the grandmother that she would go to meet her maker with a song accompanying her. Or perhaps he wished to tell her that no one could deprive her of the dignity and respect that she deserved. On the third line, Eddie docked in and then they were all singing a grand farewell to the old lady.

Shinde had none of the miserliness or the mocking bitterness of the two Tamhanes and he was grateful to Ravan and Eddie for the warm send-off they gave his grandmother. On the way back he treated all of them to chicken biryani and phirnee at Star of India. It was evening by the time the two former extras got home and flopped down on the steps of their chawl. Ravan handed over two hundred rupees to Eddie. The trip had not been as painful or exhausting as the one last week but neither had it been a leisurely saunter in Simla. Eddie had been sensible and padded his shoulders with four pillowcases before coming down but Ravan had not had the foresight to prepare for the final sojourn of the old woman and groaned that he was willing to lie down and die right there in front of Chawl Number 17.

Eddie started walking up the stairs.

'Eddie.'

'What now?'

'One favour, please. The last one.'

'No, no and no. I told you never again.'

'Give me the money you got from Shinde today.'

'What?' Eddie burst an artery.

'I'll return it in thirty days. Twice, if not thrice the amount.'

'Oh boy, I didn't realize that we were that serious about young Ms Shinde.'

Ravan blushed a deep red. 'No longer so young.'

'Careful, guru. Scout the territory first. She may be crazy about somebody else. Don't forget you and I are no longer the most desirable bachelors in town.' Eddie took out his wallet and gave Ravan the two hundred rupees he had just got. 'All the best. Ravish the lady with your charm.'

22

The full implications of what he had just said to Ravan dawned on Eddie as he climbed the stairs. 'All the best. Ravish the lady with your charm.' He had got carried away but he was no longer so certain that he wanted his brother-in-law, albeit in a technical sense the relationship was valid only in the past tense, to make out with another woman. Admittedly Pieta was no more but it still smacked of infidelity. He had no idea what had gone on between Asmaan and Ravan but that was only because she was trying to yank him out of the dumps. But for her, Eddie too would never have recovered after Belle had shut down all channels of communication with him. His mother had never looked at another man, at least he thought so, even though it was clear that his father had not lived up to her expectations and she was a much-disappointed woman. He would have liked to discuss the rights and wrongs of the situation with Pieta herself but that, of course, was no longer tenable. But honestly it would be edifying to know what she thought about her husband's new love-interest.

There was something else that occurred to him. What did Ravan have in mind when he said, 'I'll return it in thirty days. Twice, if not thrice the amount?' Rajnigandha was indeed fulsomely endowed in all the right places but it was doubtful that she was a cash cow. For a moment, Eddie wondered if Ravan had hatched some devious plan to win over Shinde's daughter and then be her pimp. After all, his and Ravan's predicament was beyond desperate. Ravan had even gone back to the owner of the fleet of taxis for whom he had worked so many years ago and had asked for his old job as a taxi driver. The man had thought Ravan was joking and laughed it off.

The prospects didn't look any better at Eddie's place either. He had caught his mother glancing at him when she thought he was reading the paper or staring aimlessly at the ceiling. How could he forget that look? All her old fears had come back to haunt her. He was a failure. She had always known he would never amount to anything. His stint in the movies and the music business was nothing but a scam, something that he had fabricated, and as usual she had fallen for it. Or at best, it was an aberration, a fluke, and now reality had taken over.

* * *

'Ravan, you don't have to tiptoe around Pieta's name for fear that I might get hurt. She and I were friends, remember? Not the closest, but friends nevertheless. She would make some quirky remark that would just crack me up. When she was relaxed and on a roll she could keep it going for minutes on end. Though I have to confess sometimes I found her far too earnest and intense.'

So did I, Ravan thought, so did I. Everything Piya-Pieta did was done with such fierce passion. He remembered their lovemaking. It was almost like an ecstatic religious experience for her. Every time it felt as if it was the last time and all life would cease after that. Maybe she had a premonition of what the future held.

'I told you it was fine to mention Pieta but I didn't say you could get lost in her.' Asmaan pinched Ravan back to the present. She called any time she had a day off, which was not very often, and they would spend a weekend away. But Ravan felt uneasy that he was not footing the bill and it was she who had to fork out the cash.

'I'm still earning, you're not.' She obviously had read his mind. 'As things stand we don't meet too often. I like your company, I like the sex, I enjoy watching movies with you and telling you about my work and the stories I'm writing. Do you mind?'

'You don't know how much I want to be with you but I don't want to be a burden on you.'

'You are not. Now can we skip the subject?'

More often than not, Ravan would oblige but sometimes his

conscience got the better of him. 'How long can I keep living off you? It's just not right.'

'I've a suggestion to make,' Asmaan said in a matter-of-fact voice. 'If it bothers you, as it should, that you aren't paying when the two of us spend the night together in a hotel, and that you're being a drain on my resources, you must jot down the amount in your diary; charges plus taxes of course. And bear in mind the food bills and the tips which over a period of time would amount to quite a bit. And don't forget the price of ice cream or whatever else that we have on the spur of the moment. And if we're going out of town, you should make it a point to note the petrol bills.

'You do know that I would go to any lengths not to make you feel obliged to me. One of these days when you're flush with money, I expect you to pay me for every expense I have incurred on your account with compound interest. Now if you're through, I would like to take this opportunity to share some trivial things with you.

'You see, unlike you Hindus, I have only one life. So I would like to make the most of it. Actually, even if I had seven hundred thousand lives, I would still like to make the most of each one of them and keep asking for more after the seven hundred thousand were over. Now here's something I can't quite explain: for some absurd reason I have the feeling that I love you. And have loved you for a long time. I have no sense of guilt about feeling randy and having a good time with you. But if your accounting obsession is more important to you, I can certainly make the ultimate sacrifice for you and give you up.'

At some point of this cosy, friendly, low-key soliloquy, Ravan stoppered his ears and started yelling that he had got the message and he would never again mention the subject.

* * *

'Where the hell have you been? Even your mother didn't know your whereabouts.'

Ravan had parked himself in the porch of the squat Sabha gymnasium. He was stripped to the waist but even so his jeans were soaked with sweat. It was past noon and there was no one around. The CWD Chawls drooped listlessly, exhausted in the humid heat. The gulmohar and mango trees and the two banyans were dusty and as becalmed as a sepia print. A BEST bus braked, squealing agonizingly like a dog that's been kicked in its behind. Ravan was oblivious of his surroundings and the ambient sounds and noises and didn't look up from his work. 'I've been around. A bit busy.'

'Doing what?'

'Oh, this and that,' Ravan said absent-mindedly as he continued to paint a four-wheeled cart similar to the one used by vegetable vendors or the guys who sold grated ice-lollies stuck on sticks and doused with virulent-looking red, green or yellow syrup to children outside every school in Bombay. But the cart had some unusual features. On either side of the flat bed, Ravan had attached metre-long poles and bridged each end with a couple of cross-bars.

'That's very enlightening. What's that four-wheeler you're working on supposed to be?'

'That, my friend, is the start of our new business venture.'

'Ours?'

'Yep, yours and mine. You contributed two hundred rupees. And I put in a hundred plus my labour not to mention the fact that the idea is mine.'

'You spent the money I gave you,' Eddie's decibel level had risen by two octaves and was still climbing, 'on this wooden junk?'

'That's right,' Ravan said smugly.

'You told me you were chasing that oomph bomb, Shinde's daughter, and that's why you wanted the cash.'

Ravan smiled. 'I didn't. You assumed that. I thought it safer not to mention why I wanted the money.'

'Oh, you devious creep.' The vein in the extreme left of Eddie's forehead was juddering like the needle of a radiation detection device that had run into a nuclear explosion site. He tried to get his voice under control but not too successfully. 'You intend to sell vegetables?' Eddie's voice was heavy with sarcasm. 'Or are you planning to start a bhelpuri stall on Chowpatty?'

'Of course not.' Ravan dismissed the suggestion that he would be involved in something so banal. 'This is the official vehicle of Om Shanti, Shanti, Shanti Antim Yatra Services. We are going to offer something no one has ever offered Hindus. Final journey services.' The three shantis were chanted like in a Sanskrit shloka.

This was more than Eddie could handle. He turned beetroot-scarlet and became apoplectic. 'You, you, you, you,' his tongue kept tripping on the 'you' but finally managed to graduate to the next word, 'you bastard.' He pushed Ravan till he was wedged between him and the wall. 'Give me back my money. Now. Right now. I'm through with you, Ravan. I just want my money back. And I don't want to see your face ever again after that.'

'What's your problem, Eddie? Why are you getting so upset? This is not a cart. It's going to be a money machine; nothing less than the god Kuber's vehicle. You watch. It's going to make money hand over fist for us. We're going to be rich, Eddie.'

'Just shut up.' Eddie was squeezing Ravan's throat. 'I want my dough back, that's all.'

'I can't breathe.' Ravan's voice was squeaking through a sugarcane press. 'Take your hands off. Please. You want to know about the money, right?'

Eddie let go of Ravan. 'Oh, go to hell.' Eddie kicked the cart so hard it keeled over. 'I'll give you till tomorrow. I don't care how you get it, just get it.'

* * *

They were bickering far too often since they had got out of the hospital but mostly they had been just picking at each other like dogs who have nothing better to do than gnash their canines and bark at each other as a 'time-pass'. That last encounter, however, Ravan had to admit, was far more serious. It was evident he had completely miscalculated Eddie's reaction. He had presumed that Eddie would be impressed by the ingenuity of the idea of setting up a Hindu funeral service, one that no one had thought of providing before and which catered to a genuine need, and was thus bound to be a money spinner.

How could Eddie not see that they needed to make money, lots of it and very, very fast? It was three months since the *Indian Express* had broken the story that the authorities had nearly completed negotiations for the redevelopment of the entire complex of sixty-three CWD Chawls plus the premises of the municipal school, the office building of the Life Insurance Corporation of India, the large playground where the Ganesh festival was held and the Sabha had its premises, and the all-marble Neo-Buddhist temple which was built just three years ago. The developer was not named but was described as one of the biggest players in the field. As a major concession, the unnamed real-estate developer would enlarge the old Ganesh shrine into a magnificent temple dedicated to several gods and goddesses and would rebuild the Neo-Buddhist one and donate a larger-than-life statue of Dr Ambedkar.

The enterprising mole who had dredged out the original contract dating from the earlier part of the twentieth century had obviously been richly rewarded. The document stipulated that if the buildings were in a parlous state such that the lives of the tenants were endangered, the authorities were within their rights to demolish all the structures on the condition that the tenants were allotted equivalent housing anywhere within the far-flung Bombay metropolitan area.

Ravan looked at his mother and realized perhaps for the first time that Parvatibai was not a force of nature or earth mother as her clients often referred to her. She was vulnerable and though she put up a brave front and a good show of not being daunted, Ravan could see defeat in her eyes. She had no idea how she was going to survive this tidal wave which would wipe out all traces of her past. Her son was back with her and her worst fears had come true. He was unemployed like her husband and sitting at home. How was she going to earn a living after relocating to some place of which she had not heard? Ulhasnagar, Mira Road or whatever. There was a whole new Bombay that she did not even know existed. How was she going to get clients and even if she did get a few, how was the food going to be delivered?

How foolish Eddie and he had been. They should have bought the flats in their mothers' names. That way at least those would not have been repossessed by the court receiver, and their families, not to mention they themselves, would have had their own place to stay without fear of being shifted to Vashi or Virar. Was there anything more futile and barren than the wisdom of hindsight?

One thing was certain. No, it was anything but certain. He could not, he would not see his mother going down. Ravan laughed at the thought that there was anything altruistic in his motives. He had never been good at maths but even he could manage this simple bit of arithmetic: if Parvatibai went under, so would he. It was no different, he was sure, for Eddie. It was always the women who kept them afloat, Parvatibai, Eddie's mother Violet, Granna and Pieta, Belle and Asmaan. Sure, men could be macho but only because of their womenfolk.

He had to admit that he was desperate and desperate people do foolish things but starting a funeral service seemed like a good idea. Good times, bad times, there's just one constant. It was there thousands of years ago and it would be there into the future as long as there were human beings left on the planet: people die. Wasn't that one of the preconditions of a successful business? That your client base will always be secure and will always require your goods and services? He had done his homework carefully and all the conditions were right. The only problem was three weeks had gone by but there was no sign of any business. It was as if the people of Bombay had decided not to die since the time he had set up the Om Shanti, Shanti, Shanti Antim Yatra Services. But that of course wasn't the case. In the CWD Chawls alone there had been two deaths in the last twenty days.

Ravan was returning home towards midnight when someone grabbed him by his collar near the Irani cafe and dragged him several metres. He knew who it was. Eddie had been looking for him for the past two weeks but he had managed to evade him by staying out of the house till 11 at night and sometimes even later and getting out early in the morning.

'Okay, start-up whizkid, you think you can avoid paying what you owe me just because you come home late and leave early?' Eddie was jostling him, provoking him to fight.

'I was planning to see you tomorrow morning.'

'Sure, you've been so busy, you asked your secretary to make a note of it in your appointment diary.' Eddie was shadow-boxing with him now, deliberately making contact with his face and punching him on the arms. 'But let me be naive and take you at your word. The only reason you would come to see me is because you've got my money, right? Good, let me have it.'

'That's exactly why I was going to see you tomorrow. To talk about money.'

'What's to talk? Give it to me and I don't care if I never set my eyes on you again.'

'I'll return it in thirty days. Threefold.'

'Famous last words. Perhaps I'd misheard when you told me that you had invested all my money in some half-arsed scheme to transport the Hindu dead to the other world. Maybe you said you would return it in three years? Or was it thirty?'

'I know, I know I said a month. So many people die every day, I thought if we provided a useful service, we would earn a lot of money. That way, both our mothers needn't worry that we were jobless. And they could also relax about the future.'

'Seven days. If I don't have the money by then, I'm going to the police and have you put behind bars.'

'Be reasonable, Eddie. If we don't have any clients, how am I going to get the money?'

'Did you ask my advice before you started this business or bought that useless contraption? Tell you what, you can shove it up your…' Eddie's mood changed without warning. The truculence was gone and replaced by a self-loathing that was so out of character, it was far more disturbing than the repressed violence in him.

'Oh, what's the point? Who am I fooling? Even if you return the money, how far will it go?' Eddie straightened Ravan's shirt collar and turned to leave. 'Go home, Ravan. Your mother is worried about your coming back so late every night. Forget the money. I'll go back to Randhir Baweja or Resham Singhania and take whatever work either of them gives me.'

* * *

How had he allowed things to come to such a pass, Ravan wondered, that Eddie could contemplate going back to see those two conmen who were known as the New-Generation music-makers? After they had recovered from the trauma of *Jaan Se Pyara Dushman*, at least the physical aspect of it, Eddie and he had thought that if they swallowed their pride and went to see the younger music directors about working for them, they would jump at the opportunity of having such experienced people to do the donkey-work and take the full responsibility of the orchestra. Plus they could arrange the music, something not too many Indian composers even today could handle.

The first, Randhir Baweja, had made the two of them wait outside his office for five consecutive days and then had asked whether they had had any experience in the business. 'Now I get it, you are those two panwati bandwallas who wanted to become actors and went to the Chambal valley to shoot a dacoit movie and killed everybody from the cast and crew.' He smiled, delighted with his own wit. 'Are you any good with electronic music? Computers are the engines of progress in music these days. I record at least two songs a day, sometimes three. Producers and directors today want fast music with an international sound. What I am looking for is researchers in global music.'

'Researchers?' Eddie had asked. 'You mean if the film is set against a Turkish backdrop, you want to have information about various Turkish musical traditions and instruments? Or if the hero is visiting Spain, you want the dope on Spanish music and flamenco dancing?'

'Something like that, but for the Indian market. You listen to the latest in African, Middle Eastern, Hungarian, or Mexican music and pick the liveliest or the most seductive numbers and build up a library with different categories. Rock 'n' roll, blues, sad, upbeat, joyous, rap, end of the world, tense, violent, chilling, emotional, tear-jerking, romantic, tragic, love, first love, and so on. Then, all we have to do is refer to our library, select a song or an instrumental track, something that's not known here; or if it is, we add some masala, change a few things, sex it up and we are in business. Actually what I like to do is to borrow not from just one source but two or three, so that we come up with something like a collage but one where nobody can detect the originals. It's exactly along the lines of what Bollywood does routinely, borrowing the storyline from two or three different Hollywood films or sometimes even stirring the cocktail with a French or Italian movie plot.'

Ravan and Eddie had never had problems basing their songs on Indian ragas when the occasion demanded it and sometimes even quoting Mozart, Beethoven, or Debussy to add a Western touch but Randhir Baweja was talking about a rather loftier pursuit: outright plagiarism, the new genre of 'cut and paste' music.

Their next stop had proven to be even more humiliating. Resham Singhania was a twenty-seven-year-old composer and singer. He claimed he composed at least three songs a day and had built up a bank with four thousand three hundred tunes and was adding to them every day.

'You guys are not merely old school, you are finished, obsolete. But out of respect for your age, I will give you a chance. Compose two tunes for me, one tragic and one for an item number and leave them with my secretary this evening. Let's see if you are any good. Remember, I'll call you, not the other way round.' All these years, Ravan and Eddie had not cared to compose in a vacuum. Poetry and music, they had believed, came from the same umbilical cord. But that was when they were E&R. Times had changed. Resham Singhania did not call back. It was clear he had not liked their work. Two months later, their songs were on the radio. The music was by Resham Singhania.

Right now, Ravan's first priority, however, was to prevent Eddie from further humiliation by trying to see either Randhir Baweja or Resham Singhania again. Ravan remembered the necklace Maan

Singh had forced Ramchander to return. Someone had stolen it when he was lying wounded and semiconscious in the ravines. Ravan looked at the ring on his finger. He had not removed it since the day he had got married. He had to pull and tug at it to wrench it off. The skin under the precious metal was bleached white. 'Forever,' it said on the inside of the chunky gold band. 'In this life. And in the afterlife.' It would be the last of Piya once he had sold it. What use was a dead woman to him? How come you couldn't understand I wanted you, Piya, not the child? Let go of me. Don't hang around my neck like a faithful albatross and underline my failures and my sins and forgive the trespasses I didn't commit. Leave me in peace.

He was sure it was worth far more than what the jeweller in Thakurdwar gave him, and he should have scouted around before selling it, but it fetched enough to return Eddie's money and there was still a little left over to print two thousand handbills.

'When you lose your nearest and dearest,' the leaflet asked, 'should you be spending the time grieving for your loved one or should you be running hither and thither getting death certificates, dealing with endless red tape, warming the hands of grasping clerks and bureaucrats, buying flowers, wood, ghee, in short, making exhausting funeral arrangements? Now for the first time in India. Om Shanti, Shanti, Shanti Antim Yatra Services. We will lift the entire burden off your shoulders. All you need to do is to give us the doctor's certificate and light the pyre. The rest is our responsibility.'

Girgaon, Byculla, Lalbaug, Dockyard Road, Sewree, Reay Road, Wadala, Masjid Bandar, Dadar – every morning Ravan would set out at 7 and return at 9 or 10 at night, slipping the handbills under the doors of chawl dwellers and affluent flats, shoving them into the morning newspapers, and distributing them in offices. He waited, if not for business, at least for enquiries to pour in. There had never been such an offer made in the history of Hinduism, maybe in the history of India itself. Wasn't anybody even curious about this entirely new business venture? Apparently not. It was clear that they had done exactly what Parvatibai or he himself did with handbills when they got them: crumple them into a ball and toss them into the waste-paper basket. No, no one bothered to hire Om Shanti, Shanti, Shanti.

Then the monsoons broke and broke all records and Ravan and Eddie's luck broke too.

23

'Name?' Eddie asked the questions and Ravan jotted down the answers on a printed form.

'Ravindra Shetye,' the man sitting in front of them at a table answered.

'Height?'

'Whose?'

'Whose do you think? Are you the one who has to be cremated?' Ravan snapped at the man. 'The dear departed's.'

'Sorry, what did you say?'

'The height of the deceased,' Eddie said, trying to soothe nerves.

'Can't you people speak in simpler language?'

'The one who has gone to his heavenly abode.'

'Who's going to let him enter heaven? The old man was such a crook he would corrupt both God and heaven.'

'Please speak respectfully of the dead. We don't want to know his life history. Only his height.'

'Must have been five-feet-seven or eight.'

'Name?'

'Ravindra Shetye is my name.'

Ravan looked at the man exasperatedly. 'In that case we should light the pyre under you. What's the name of the one who has been "offed"?

'Dhondoba Sudama Shetye.'

'Weight?'

'How would I know?'

'If he weighs more than sixty-five kilos, the charge is fifteen rupees extra per kilo.'

'Oh no, he must have been twenty or twenty-five kilos at the most.'

'Wow. He must either be a five foot ten dwarf or he's been on a fast unto death. We'll weigh him when we come to your place to pick up the body.'

'Sandalwood, eucalyptus or ordinary wood?' Eddie asked as if there had been no interruption.

'Ordinary wood.'

'Ghee or vanaspati to light the pyre?'

'He's not even worth kerosene.'

'We can offer ghee from cow's milk, buffalo's milk or goat milk,' Eddie continued in a monotonous voice.

'Dalda.'

'Three varieties of red shawls are available,' Ravan said. 'Which one would you like?'

'I think a white sheet will do.' Eddie had got the measure of the man and didn't wish to waste any more time. 'I'm sure Shri Ravindra Shetye doesn't want anything fancy.'

'Quite right. If it was I who was lying there, I assure you, my father would have abandoned me on the footpath and let the municipality take care of me.'

* * *

At the Shetye home, Eddie and Ravan picked up the mat with Dhondoba Sudama Shetye lying on his back and put it on a second-hand, or maybe it was a third-hand, portable Avery weighing machine.

'Seventy-eight kilos. That means you have to pay extra for the thirteen kilos over and above the stipulated sixty-five.'

'Maybe we should chop off both his legs and he'll be sixty-five kilos. Won't make a difference.' Ravindra Shetye, it was evident, was the epitome of the ideal son. 'The bastard's dead anyway. Beat me black and blue every day when I was a child.'

'Sure, go ahead.' Ravan shut the order book and made as if to leave. 'Let's go back, Eddie.'

Eddie wondered if Ravan was acting up to get a point across or was in earnest. Ravan wasn't sure either. Did he really not mind losing this client's business?

'Sorry, why are you getting so het up?' The man apologized. 'Just ... just kidding.'

If there was one simple truth this business had taught Ravan, it was this: never ask whose grief was fake and who was really devastated. Perhaps even in the most stricken of people, an element of performance must creep in. Besides, who could tell whether the chicanery of the performers did not conceal a grain of real grief and repentance? Was Ravindra Shetye making his father out to be a scoundrel only because he wanted to cover his own impecunious state or was he genuinely a victim of a hateful father?

'With a band or without?'

'No band-fand.'

'What about bhajans to accompany your father on his way to the other world?' Ravan asked.

'Just Ram, Haré Ram, Jai Ram. Haré Ram.'

'That Joshi from your building asked for Meera bhajans.' Eddie tried to do some marketing.

'Damned show-off. Carrying on with his neighbour's wife while pretending to grieve for his own.' Shetye looked sourly at Eddie and Ravan. 'All right. We'll have bhajans.'

'Spiritual songs from films or bhajans of the great saints like Tukaram, Kabir, Dnyaneshwar, Tulsidas, Meerabai?'

'Sai Baba's. When will you take away the body?'

'The auspicious time today for the atma to be wafted into the next life is at eleven minutes past four.'

* * *

A bit difficult to believe, Ravan thought, that just three months ago Om Shanti Shanti Shanti Antim Yatra Services itself was about to breathe its last and ready to go on its final heavenly sojourn.

Neither the funeral cart nor the fliers had had any effect. The barren spell in his personal fortunes, however, had been completely eclipsed by the fate of his city which was in the grip of the worst drought in living memory. It had last rained on the day Eddie and he had taken the court clerk, Tamhane, to the Shankarseth Hindu non-electric crematorium. A month-and-a-half had gone by and then another fortnight. The water levels in the reservoirs had sunk so badly, there was talk that just eleven days' water supply was left.

Midnight, 12 September. Ravan had just taken the decision to put Om Shanti Shanti Shanti to rest when he heard a strange sound that he couldn't place. It went on and on till Ravan was forced to get up and look out of the kitchen window. It was the wind wailing and sobbing, recalling ancient wrongs and grievances, licking old wounds and reopening them and vowing vengeance. It ran wildly from one corner of the planet to the other and then it changed into a Rottweiler snapping at your heels and suddenly leaping up, sinking its canines and full set of teeth into your neck.

It started to rain. Nothing out of the ordinary, just the normal business-like, round-the-clock pummelling of the Bombay monsoons as if they had not played hard-to-get for so long and there had never been the terrifying spectre of drought. The people of the city looked up at the dark rumbling skies in amazement and kept saying, 'The rains, oh my God, the rains. Can you believe it, it's a miracle.' They ran out to the streets, the terraces, the sea-face. They laughed dementedly and cried for no reason at all, they sang and danced and hugged each other. The church carillons rang joyously and temple bells tolled all night long and the azan the next morning was recited with such clarity and fervour, it moved even the non-believers.

By the night of 15 September, the exuberant largesse from heaven had turned into an act of God, a rain from hell. It was a mindless thing, a cosmic machine dumping a thousand Niagaras on the western littoral of the subcontinent. Indeed, the vengeance of God was as enigmatic as the Creator's largesse.

The thunder and the bludgeoning rains drowned all else, the church bells, the azan, the frantic prayers, speech, even horns. Everything, but everything came to a standstill. Trains, buses, planes, taxis were marooned on every track, road, highway and airport. Hundreds of thousands of people were stranded at every railway station on the Central, Harbour and Western Railway lines from Victoria Terminus, Churchgate and Bombay Central stations to Dadar, Bandra, Andheri, Thane and beyond. Torrents of water raced down Peddar Road, Malabar Hill, Tilak Bridge, Antop Hill and every other gradient. Cataracts, rapids and whirlpools sprung up at every corner and washed away entire slums, pavements and the meagre belongings of those who lived on them. The banks of the Mithi collapsed, taking huts perched precariously on them, and mudslides killed many of the residents. The waters kept rising at an alarming pace. The ground floors of numerous buildings were flooded and the tenants had to move up to the next storey. The city was awash and the city was going under.

Dead cattle with bloated stomachs had begun to float on the flooded roads. And every once in a while a dead man or child joined the flotilla. Chawl Number 17 experienced the first intimations of mortality. Its south-western corner sank a full six centimetres. The building now had the look of a corpse with a collapsed shoulder. For the first time in its life a picture of CWD Number 17 had made it to the national media and you could also see it on page one of the *International Herald Tribune*. An editorial in a leading newspaper from the capital went so far as to wonder aloud whether the building was symbolic of the state of the polity itself. And yet the rains showed no sign of letting up even after three days.

Ravan was sitting on the landing of the stairway, fed up of being cooped up in the house, when a man passed him by. He was drenched, panting and shivering.

'Would you know where Ravan Pawar stays?'

A bailiff from the court, Ravan was certain. Only someone representing the law would venture out on such a foul day.

'Why would you want to see him?'

'If he's not there, could I see Eddie Coutinho?' The man shoved his hand in his shirt pocket and took out a piece of paper that had turned to pulp. With trembling hands he unpeeled the folds of the sheet. 'Om Shanti Shanti Shanti Antim Yatra Services.'

From that point there was no stopping the people who came looking for Ravan (Eddie too, but you got to the Pawar home first) at any time of the day or night from near and distant parts of Bombay. The rains may have started out as prayers answered and then turned into an end-of-the-world deluge but either way people kept dying as is their wont. Even more so if you were old or sick because it was close to impossible to get a doctor or to make it to a hospital. But what changed Eddie's and Ravan's fortunes was not the dead. It was the fact that the living were loath to help carry the dead body to the nearest crematorium, which could be anywhere between two to five kilometres away or even accompany the departed through foul waist-high water. The word spread and soon the two new entrepreneurs could not keep up with the demand.

However, there were problems. Ravan knew that his mother was not one to complain or speak up and yet he understood what was passing through her mind. He could see how relieved Parvatibai was that after nearly a year of sitting around doing nothing he had finally found work, and yet there was no getting away from the fact that she seemed just as unhappy as before. There was no storm brewing, that much he knew. When it came to his mother there was never any possibility of a confrontation or a sudden eruption. If there was a problem, she sorted it out in her mind first and if she thought it deserved to be aired, she spoke about it and made her stance clear.

'May I have a word with you, Ravan? I hope I'm not disturbing you.'

Here it comes, Ravan thought, though the formality of the tone took him by surprise. It was 11 at night, way past Parvatibai's bedtime. Ravan was doing the daily Om Shanti Shanti Shanti accounts at a tiny table he had set up in the corridor outside his home.

'How's business, son?'

'It's okay. But it will take a lot more work before we are known in the market.'

'I'm glad to see that you are working so diligently.'

Small talk from his mother? The night was full of surprises. What next, Ravan wondered. 'What is it, Aai?' Ravan's dimples deepened in a suppressed smile. 'Something bothering you?'

'I've never commented on the different jobs that you've done over the years. And it would be ridiculous to opine on the new one especially since you are employed after such a long time.' Parvatibai stopped not knowing how to proceed. She took a deep breath. 'What I'm trying to say, Ravan, is that though I believe in the dignity of any kind of useful labour and though I've had to work all my life, something about the work you are doing now makes me uneasy ... I don't know why. Maybe that's only because it's unfamiliar. My clients have been complaining about it. They don't want food from a funeral home. They joke about finding a pinkie or a toe in the food.'

'But the dead bodies are never brought here. Nor do you serve non-vegetarian food.'

'They are customers. They feel good when they can complain. Most of them just want to tease me for having a son who has an unusual business. I pay no heed to them.'

Ravan could understand his mother's predicament and even sympathize with her. The dead were 'impure', at least as far as Hindus were concerned. Maybe there was even some good science behind it. Anything and everything organic rotted much faster in the heat and the humidity of the tropics. Cremation was as much a safeguard against myriad plagues as it was a sacred practice to liberate the soul. Perhaps the latter was just an afterthought meant to give spiritual sanction to the former. You got rid of the body as quickly as possible: you performed the rituals, lit the pyre, came home and cleansed yourself by taking a dip in the river ... or a bucket bath.

Ravan's neighbours were less forgiving of his new profession than his mother. They took care to look disapproving or worse, disgusted, if they ran into him on the road, and crossed over to the other pavement and spat noisily. Children were warned to stay away from him and if he tried to talk or play cricket with them or win them over by offering toffees, they were to refuse. If he persisted, they were to scream for their parents or, in an emergency, tell the nearest adult that Ravan Pawar was molesting them. Anybody who spent the better part of his day with the dead could bring nothing but ill-luck and misfortune. He was no better than those untouchables really, who lived on the ground floor. His very shadow would pollute you.

'But it's obviously bothering you.'

'You'll agree that it's not amongst the professions that come to mind easily when one thinks of a job or a career.'

'Would you prefer that I gave up the funeral business?'

Parvatibai mulled over the question. 'I think I can live with it.'

She didn't have to, at least not in such close proximity. Business was good and Om Shanti Shanti Shanti had its own premises now. Eddie had found a room for rent on the ground floor of Chawl Number 63 at the other end of the CWD housing complex, and within a few months they were able to get a telephone connection. It was hard work, very hard work even when it was not raining. Like doctors you were on call at all hours of the day and night. It was amazing how often customers treated you like servants and even expected you to clean up the mess that the dead might have made before they breathed their last. Since they were going to pay, they would not lift a finger to help you carry the body six or seven storeys down narrow staircases.

Whatever Eddie and he had learnt was through trial and error. Cash payment only and that too, the full sum in advance. No doctor's certificate, no go. If they had to negotiate even a single storey, Eddie and Ravan would not move till there were at least four others to help carry the body down. Om Shanti Shanti Shanti was more than willing to pick up the ashes at whatever time the crematorium staff asked them to but for a fee. Weight was one of the major bones of contention. The relatives of the deceased were convinced that the dead were dead and hence weightless. The professional weighing machine should have laid all arguments to rest. It did not. The most common charge was that they had fixed the scale. They were called despicable mercenaries making money from other people's grief. Ravan and Eddie never, never forgot that the client was always right ... so long as he coughed up the full sum.

While the money would not buy a Rolls Royce, if they kept at it, in a few years both Eddie and Ravan would make enough to buy two one-bedroom apartments. Besides, Om Shanti Shanti Shanti was nothing but a stop-gap arrangement, a stepping stone, a halfway house to getting back to their vocation. Or two vocations. Acting and music.

You could hear Eddie and Ravan coming back late at night after sending an elderly woman into the furnace at the electric crematorium at Chandanwadi, may her soul rest in peace. They had had to wait to collect the ashes and take them over to the Sofia College lane. The dead woman's son who had flown down from Sydney wished to fly back the next morning and wanted the ashes to be handed over that very night. He appeared to be cheesed off with his mother. She had always been demanding, he said. Always complaining that she missed him and could he and his family not visit a little more often. The two grandchildren must have grown up so much. The last time they had been home was five years ago. She couldn't seem to understand that Sydney was home and not Bombay. Parents can be so thoughtless, he said. What he hated most was her telling him that at her age there was no saying when she would be gone. And then just to make a point and make him feel guilty, she had flown the coop. Trust her to die at such a critical time in his career. It was the time of year when performance reports were filed and it would be decided whether he would jump two grades and be eligible for the post of deputy general manager of his division. His boss was a slippery customer and he wanted to be present when such a crucial review was in the offing.

Ravan and Eddie turned left at Opera House. No opera had been performed there for decades and it had been converted into a cinema even before the British had left the country. The cinema theatre too had long since been closed down and Bombay seemed to be taking a snooze at the only time it could, long past midnight. Ravan and Eddie pushed the Om Shanti Shanti Shanti cart up the bridge leading to the seafront at Chowpatty. As they reached the top, Eddie jumped up and sat on the cart in a padmasan, holding the woman's ashes in his hands. '*Badan pe sitare lapete huey, o jaan-e-tamanna*', he burst into a Shammi Kapoor song from the film *Prince*, as Ravan, leaning heavily forward, lifted his feet off the ground. The cart gathered speed, careening down crazily and as it turned right towards Hughes Road. Ravan joined his friend, their voices clear, rich and resonant. The wind blew their hair back and they closed their eyes and projected their voices all the way to the moon and the stars. Oh, this was pure joy and exhilaration ... singing liberated them as nothing else could.

* * *

Falling ... falling ... falling...

Life played such weird tricks on you, Ravan thought, it left a hole inside you that could never be healed. Every Hollywood and Hindi-film courtroom drama told you that in the eyes of the law you were innocent till proven guilty. What they didn't tell you was that there were times when you were guilty till proven innocent. And here was the catch: there was no way to prove that the criminal, or let's just say the guilty party, was someone else and not you.

How many times had Eddie and Asmaan asked him what had gone wrong between the three of them and Meenakshi Venkatraman and he had merely shrugged his shoulders and said he was as much at sea as they were. The only one apart from him who knew what had happened was Piya-Pieta. But she too had got it only half-right. He was not really interested in the rights and wrongs of things. Like Piya, Meenakshi Venkatraman also had left a perpetual gaping hole inside him. He had worked so hard to break into her impenetrable silence. It was as if he had made her his life's mission for a couple of years. He had finally slipped through her reserve and circumvented or demolished the various walls she had built around herself. She had become his music guru and finally she had agreed to sing for Asmaan, Eddie and him. And then all that effort had come to naught. She wouldn't record for the trio any more. She was no longer Ravan's teacher. And she refused to talk to him or the others.

He marvelled at how the young could so casually destroy people and relationships built over years. Why was he blaming only the young?

Grown-ups did the same without a flicker of conscience either. Years would pass and the hole would remain whole. What a shame that a little bit of third-rate wordplay would not cure him. Perhaps it would have helped if he could have kept the flame of pure animus that he had felt against Sukanya alive after he realized that she had been true to her word and had spoken to Piya. But he felt no bitterness against her. In truth, that was the problem. He felt nothing, just a numbness in that empty hole.

24

'I've been consulting Prajapati-ji's lawyer,' Asmaan said.

'What about?' Eddie asked. Asmaan, Ravan and he were sitting in the dingy Irani cafe outside the CWD Chawls compound, sipping tea that had been boiled with milk and heaps of sugar for several hours.

'We're figuring out how strong a case you have for repossessing the rights and the print of *Jaan Se Pyara*.'

'Who's we?' Eddie wanted to know.

'Belle and I.'

'You've been in touch with Belle behind my back?'

'Well, now it's in front of your back. Incidentally, I don't have to take your permission to talk to a friend. Whom, as it happens, you seem to have done your best to alienate.'

'I deserved that.'

'Now shut up and listen, both of you. Prajapati-ji's lawyer thinks we have a damn good chance of winning the case and is going to put us in touch with the best copyright lawyer in the country.'

'Where's the money going to come from?' Ravan piped up.

'Hey you small-time accountant, Belle and I are going to invest our money and hire this top gun of a lawyer. The two of you are the legal producers and it will be our contention that the banks did you out of, not just all your property but of all else that is rightfully yours. I am talking about the film footage, the music, etc. Then, with your express permission, Belle and I are going to become partner producers. We're not doing you any favours. We're going to be partners in the profits. We are going to retrieve every single centimetre of the film that you guys shot.'

'But the film is not finished yet.'

'I know. I'm in touch not only with Belle but Sapna-ji also. The film is complete except for her last shot. She's not terribly enthusiastic but I don't give up that easy. Take my word for it. We're cranking up the publicity machine and getting ClickClick on board; he's almost completely recovered but will always have to use a walking stick.'

'You're not serious.'

'I've never been as serious as I am about *Jaan Se Pyara*. Yes, as the name suggests it's at least as dear to me as my life. Don't forget it's my story, one of the best I have written.'

Ravan called out to the waiter. 'One more round of that horrid chai and a full plate of those awful pastries, the sight of which will make even the dead puke.'

'Ravan Pawar,' Eddie jabbed his finger into his friend's chest, 'maybe, just maybe we're going to be in business after all and make a name for ourselves finally as actors.'

'I've got even better news,' Asmaan said coyly.

'Are you going to tell us,' Ravan asked, 'or are you going to keep it all to yourself?'

'Okay smarty-pants, you don't deserve it but here it is. I am writing the sequel to *Jaan Se Pyara* where the two of you, as well as the director and the cast, are in the Chambal ravines and your bizarre parallel story unfolds just as it actually happened. It will make an amazing film. Bollywood's so obsessed with dacoits and hero-worshipping the mafia, we're going to show them just what unscrupulous, evil bastards and murderers they are.'

* * *

'You've got to give this up.' Violet caught Eddie as he was going out of the door.

'Give up what?' Eddie was disconcerted by the overwrought edge in his mother's voice.

'Don't pretend you don't know what I'm talking about. This ghastly cremation business. It's contrary to everything in our Christian faith.'

'For heaven's sake, Mamma, no one's forcing you on to the pyre.'

'Aren't you ashamed to talk to me like that? I'm a Catholic. Even on pain of death I will not follow these ungodly customs. Don't you fool yourself, Eddie Coutinho, you are bound straight for hell with that awful man who…'

Eddie shook his head slowly in warning. 'Don't, Mamma, please don't.'

'When I read the name of the shop, I'm mortified. My own son running that business. I'm so ashamed I can't raise my head when I go to church or meet any of our neighbours.'

'That shop's giving us our bread and butter and putting money in the bank for a flat, hopefully before this building crashes or is demolished.'

'We can live off the money I earn. Or we'll starve. Anything is better than what you're doing.'

Eddie turned to Granna. 'Can you make sense of this? Mamma can't stand it when I'm unemployed. And now when I finally get a break, she doesn't want me to work.'

'Don't you dare interfere,' Violet warned her mother. 'This is between my son and me.'

Granna smiled. 'I hope you don't want me to take your permission to hug my grandson.' She kissed Eddie. 'I love you, Eddie. Don't you ever forget that.'

'You've got to give up this Hindu business right now.' Violet was back on the case.

'Ravan says that as soon as we've saved some money, we can start a Christian funeral parlour. He has big plans. He wants us to go public and invest in a chain of Om Shanti Shanti Shanti ventures. In a few years he expects us to go national.'

'Ravan this and Ravan that. I hear nothing but Ravan. From the day he came into our lives, he's brought us nothing but grief. Promise me you'll stop seeing that Satan from today.'

'Stop seeing Ravan?'

'Yes. Get rid of that man and this despicable business venture. Now. Even amongst Catholics in Goa, only the untouchables would sully their hands with death.'

'This whole business is Ravan's idea. I was against it and fought with him. But he stuck to his guns and made a success of it. Imagine, despite the way I behaved he made me an equal partner.'

'That man has done black magic on you and you are such a fool you can't even see that he's leading you straight to hell.'

Eddie had forgotten how he hated and dreaded these fights that did not go anywhere and left both parties bruised and bitter. He had taken it for granted that all this was behind him. He recalled how pragmatic and wise his mother had been when Pieta had announced that she was getting married to Ravan. Now suddenly he was discovering that they were back to square one. The impasse left him exhausted. He was furious with his mother for meddling in his life and for being so obtuse, but he had to hand it to her. She was no mean adversary; she was obdurate and she wore him down. It was maddening that she expected him to choose between Ravan and her. The trick was not to fight her. Leave the arena. Get the hell out. The problem was how. The only place he had was his mother's. At least for now.

* * *

Death happened to other people. For all practical purposes, Ravan, Eddie, or anyone below forty-five or fifty was immortal. But the constant exposure and proximity to death in the past few months had begun to affect Ravan in curious ways and made him even more introspective than he already was. Naturally, the physical deterioration and the peculiar smell were the most obvious aspects. But it was the faces of the dead that stayed in his mind and intrigued him. Sometimes, especially if it was an accident case, the victim arrived with his or her eyes open. Surprise, disbelief, pain, the horror of grasping that this was the end, remembering things unfinished; you could read what you wanted into them.

Those who died in their sleep usually, though not always, had a peaceful look on their faces. Were they dreaming when they made the transition to another world or was it because they had led such exemplary lives that they had no regrets and were eager to finally get together with their maker? The terminally sick grimaced – perhaps the pain caused by the disease and the accompanying failure of vital organs was unbearable or perhaps breathing their last had entailed unendurable effort. But they were not the only ones who frowned. The mouths of the deceased were frequently distorted in a rictus of such anger, sourness, or distaste, who was to say whether they felt life had cheated them or they still had scores to settle?

The dead were said to be dead because they had nothing, absolutely nothing in common with the living. The dead didn't give a damn. They didn't have a care in the world. Pain, rancour, attachment, anger, greed, jealousy, sex, meant nothing to them. When he was in school, Ravan had to study the life of the Buddha, the principle of the golden mean and his noble eightfold path which would free a human being from all attachment to this life. The Buddha, or rather, Gautam as he was known before he became the Enlightened One, had gone to several gurus, meditated in the forest for years, starved himself almost to death. What for? There was no beating the wisdom of death. Death was the golden rule. In one fell stroke death put an end to attachment of any sort. Whether you wanted to put the golden mean into practice or not did not make a difference. Like it or not, you were detached from life like the engine of a train which takes off without its bogies.

And then there were the ones left behind. The sandalwood, the embroidered shawls, the ghee, the roses, the spiritual songs: Ravan was not about to dissuade anybody from buying them for the deceased. He was only too happy to pocket the high margins on these items. But he could not fathom why anyone would spend that kind of money on the dead when the whole abracadabra meant nothing to them. Shah Jehan built the Taj Mahal in Agra in memory of his wife Noor Jehan; Christians spent thousands on buying plots of land and caskets to bury their dead; and Hindus who couldn't bear to part with money for any philanthropic cause, bribed Lord Venkateshwara in the Tirupati temple, Sai Baba at Shirdi or their favourite local deity with a diamond-studded crown to assure the dead passage to swarg, the Hindu version of heaven. Why was this largesse and generosity almost never directed at the living? Perhaps everything we did to enshrine and remember the dead was because we did not want to be forgotten when our time was up.

* * *

My dear Eddie,

I'll dispense with the preliminaries and pleasantries and come straight to the point. We've had our ups and downs, mostly down after I left for England that first time. I was the main culprit then, though I could quibble and remind you that it was I who was rash enough to want to marry you but I could see you had doubts about how I would adjust to living in a slum, though you were far too polite to express them. I may have been hurt but you were wiser than I was. In fairness to myself, I had also warned you that distance plays havoc with a relationship. That's no excuse for ditching you but loneliness is a desperate business and warps the mind alarmingly.

Then I met you-know-who and it suddenly seemed as if I could have anything, absolutely anything without even having to ask for it. That was a heady feeling and I now realize that it turned my head, not necessarily for the better.

I had no idea that I would meet you so soon after I got back to India. But I can't deny that I knew that sooner or later I would run into you. The one thing I was absolutely certain about was that you hated me and could never forgive me. I had let you down and had not even had the courtesy to write you a 'Dear John' letter. I deserved your wrath. I could have handled your fury. But it was your turn now to let me down. You didn't blow up, you didn't ignore me, you didn't throw a tantrum. No sign of animus, no recriminations. You were friendly, almost ferociously so. I couldn't make out what you were up to or if there was a well-thought-out strategy behind your unfailing amiability. Imagine asking us out to dinner the first time you met me with my snooty new boyfriend. Were you being devious? Or had I missed something crucial about you in all the years we were together?

My new companion behaved as obnoxiously with you as only the over-indulged and spoilt-rotten children of the nouveau riche can. I thought that would provoke you to retaliate and vent your long-bottled-up ire against me. I misread you once again. You were unrelentingly good-natured and I hated you for it. I was convinced it was an act and waited to catch you out. If it really was an act, you were a far better actor than I had given you credit for. My guilt made me more and more hostile and my silence only encouraged my companion to be even more crass and uncouth. And all the while I kept hoping that your mask would slip and you would show yourself for the hypocrite that I thought you were. By the time the break-up with Veer finally occurred, I had had my fill of my playboy companion.

The trouble with golden ages, as we all know, is that we recognize them only after they are over. If I sound nostalgic and sentimental, it's because that's exactly how I feel, and no apologies for that. I like to think that you owe your career as a music director in Hindi films at least partly to me. Do you remember there was a time, Eddie, and that time lasted for a long time, when you detested Hindi cinema and everything it stood for? You were right and wrong. The stories were generally execrable and they did go on forever but consciously or unconsciously, you were drawn to the most remarkable elements in these movies. Truth to tell, I knew early on that the music and the lyrics often had a touch of genius to them. Nothing surprising about it. After all, some of the finest poets and the most committed idealists in the country were working in the film industry at that time.

Did you ever imagine, Eddie, that you, Asmaan and Ravan would inherit the mantle of those wonderful writers and composers? Almost all Western-educated Indians and foreigners are uneasy and apologetic when it comes to Hindi film songs. What would they know about how much happiness artists like you have disbursed over the years to the poorest of the poor and the richest and everybody in between? It's almost impossible to understand how the finest lyricists and music directors can imbue a three-minute song with immortality. One of these days, someone will get around to studying the film lyrics from the forties, fifties, sixties, seventies and realize how much they share with the likes of Cole Porter, the two Gershwins, Kurt Weill and Irwin Berlin. How can one not marvel at the seemingly effortless turns of phrase and idiom, the humour, the biting and at times corrosive irony and the delightful and unorthodox rhyming, the effervescence, the lightness of touch and the sheer audacity and philosophical insights in throwaway lines. Take a bow, Sahir Ludhianvi, Majrooh, Kaifi Azmi, Indiwar, Javed Akhtar, Gulzar, Asmaan and so many others. As to the music directors, there are far too many to name just now but you did them proud. I liked, no, I loved every moment I spent with the three of you even though at times I hated your guts and your nitpicking ways.

This might sound like an afterthought but our living together ran parallel to our musical careers in Bollywood: those were the best times we had. Both of us were a little more mature and the fact that we were not perpetually tight for money also helped. We actually enjoyed each other's company, in bed and out of it. I sang wonderful songs for R&E. You worked at three professions. We made love, we laughed and took it for granted that the good times would last forever. It did not occur to us that we too would get around to singing '*Those were the days*'. Ravan told me that you had actually taken him with you to buy a wedding ring. I never did see it and suspect that it too was picked up by the banks.

Jaan Se Pyara Dushman happened despite all the odds and, within weeks, it was all over. I might sound really unfeeling and offend you but I am glad Piya was not there to see everything wiped out by something the insurance companies call force majeure. How can it be, I ask myself, that we are nothing without our work, without our vocations? When I was much younger, I used to resent my mother pushing me all the time to make something of myself. You were like my mother in this respect. Maybe you were not all that clear about whether you wanted to be an actor or the lead singer in a pop group. But you wanted, boy did you want to get out of the chawls and make a name for yourself. And you had ambitions for me when I had none for myself. That's what our angry scraps were about in those days.

I went to London under duress and learnt that I was as transparent as air. People walked through me. If nobody notices you, you cease to exist. I was so lonely, I would have done anything to attract attention. There were times when I seriously considered becoming a tart just so I would have company. I lay awake at night and planned and schemed about getting myself a pimp who would set me up in business. I was lucky. I went to a bar one evening after work and out of a desperation that teetered between now or never, grabbed the mike from the male singer and sang eleven songs without a break. Maybe I didn't sing, I cried and wept and poured everything I had learnt over that year in solitary confinement into that evening.

It was shameless exhibitionism, an embarrassing baring of the soul. It was crude, it was true, and it was an impromptu performance, but a performance nevertheless. Would you believe it if I told you that it came straight from the heart and yet I was also acting? I didn't care whether the guitarist, the saxophonist and the drummer caught up with me or not. I wanted all eyes on me and I was damned if I was going to allow the lead musician or the owner of the pub to interfere till I had got just that. It helped that I was a woman. The legit male singer was naturally furious with me and fought to whisk the mike back but the audience wouldn't have any of it. A fortnight later I replaced him. I did it consciously and without scruple. Sometimes I wonder if only the comfortable and cosy can afford to have a conscience. I had caught the bug and I wasn't going to let go of it. I had a soul-destroying job in the daytime and the only time I came alive was when I stood on the raised platform, closed my eyes and set out to conquer and annihilate the customers in a pub or at a gig.

I am told we are the lucky ones, we have something we enjoy doing. But how do people who retire manage to carry on? Is it a living death? Why do I ask, I saw you and Ravan die daily in front of my eyes. And take my word for it, the dead are the most bitter and unforgiving people on the planet. There's only one thing worse than those who have been deprived of their calling and of the purpose and meaning of their lives: friends and lovers who reassure them that they'll turn the corner any moment now. Something or the other is bound to turn up. Oh, the platitudes pile up into Himalayan heaps but the good, well-meaning souls can't or won't shut up. I have seen a look of sheer loathing in your eyes when I have said something encouraging and disgusting like when one door closes, another opens. 'No, it doesn't,' you spat out the words at me. 'It's a coffin. When that door shuts and the nails are hammered in, you are dead.'

If someone had told me a few years ago that I was my mother's daughter, I would have carved out the person's innards. I still might but on the rare occasion when I may be in a mellow mood, I might confess that yes, there are times when I exhibit her worst tendencies. I tried again and again to inspire you (the Lord save the world from that putrid *Readers' Digest* instant therapy) with tales of the great role models, those who never gave up when they had lost everything. Yes, including the stories of men and women who had lost their limbs or voices but were not deterred and certainly not vanquished, and how they always managed to make a fantastic comeback. My love for you was strong and steady and I would stand by you, come what may. I tried to get you to live with me at my mother's after the disaster in the Chambal ravines. You tried it for a fortnight and went back to your mother's place. Oh, Eddie, there was no insult, injury, outrage or humiliation greater than that. And yet I forgave you. I was so selfless, noble, and full of the milk of human kindness, I was bent on supporting you for the rest of my life just so long as you echoed my gospel of hope, the brighter side of life, the light at the end of the tunnel, and everything that happens, happens for the best.

By the third month, you couldn't take it any more. You told me, 'Do me a favour. Leave. Go to London. Go to America. And don't bother to come back.' Not your exact words but I got the message. What is that phrase about nothing as dangerous as a woman spurned? I was more than willing and ready to take a knife and shove it straight into your rotten heart. I was so hurt, I was on the verge of going back to my former boyfriend and asking him to get one of his goons to bump you off. Once again luck was with me. I got an offer from a London agent and I left. I was through with you once and for all.

So what is this endless short history of our relationship leading to? I got up late one morning six weeks ago and came upon an article in *The Guardian* about Ravan and you. It said that the two of you had segued into a new career. In your latest incarnation, the two of you are supposed to be pioneering a whole new field and perhaps starting a brand-new industry from scratch: an all-in-one Hindu funeral service. I wasn't quite sure whether to believe the story, considering that it's a drastic disconnect from your previous forays in the Hindi film industry which does take a very big leap of imagination to comprehend. I called up the *Guardian* office and they sounded offended. 'We don't print figments of the imagination as news,' the senior editor told me haughtily. Om Shanti Shanti Shanti Antim Yatra Services, that's quite a mouthful. But just yesterday a reader's letter in *The Guardian* noted that a famous American poet runs a funeral parlour, albeit a Christian one. That should make everything kosher since 'America' is father, mother and role model for not only our country but for two-thirds of the world. I must, however, confess it takes some getting used to, this unusual way of earning a living. *The Guardian* article had an unexpected side-effect. It brought back memories of your monumental ingratitude and to my horror I realized that you were exceptionally wise when you asked me to get the hell out of your life. We were not doing each other any good then.

This is what I am about to propose. I have done seven albums so far. The second and the fifth earned gold status and nearly went on to become platinum hits. As to the rest, many of them received good and sometimes excellent critical notices, they sold well but never figured in the top ten or even the top fifty. I am now recording my eighth. That makes for a not insubstantial body of work but I fear I may have plateaued out. I have no idea what the future holds for me. Or to phrase it baldly, whether I have any more hits in me. I have stayed long enough in the States to have made some good friends, a couple of them very dear ones. But the fact is I am homesick.

Why don't I say it point blank, I am sick for you. And I miss our musical sessions and recordings. R.D. Burman, Madan Mohan,

Roshan and several other Hindi film music directors went through lean patches but they came back even more popular. I know Ravan and you have been biding your time along with Asmaan. I know what you are going to tell me: I'm daydreaming, that I am an incurable optimist. And then you are going to fling Sehgal Sahab's line at me. All of us come with an expiry date. And yours is long past. Luckily, Sehgal Sahab proved his own axiom wrong. He came back with a bang and kept on banging till he got a call from his maker. Besides, if I know anything about you and Ravan, you don't know how to give up.

But all that is beside the point. I am coming back anyway. If you will have me back, not like a cross you have to bear but as an inseparable partner in whatever life is left to us, it would be marvellous. On the other hand, you are at liberty to tell me to stay clear of you. And while that would not exactly be welcome, hell, I would still have my freedom. Besides, don't forget, as the Urdu poet said, *tu nahin, aur sahi.* I owe you this much, Eddie.

In case you feel you are willing to suffer my company again, I would love to give it another shot. No conditions attached and altogether devoid of any expectations. One last thing, I am still pissed off with you for going back to your mother though I left you with no other option. Still, you could have borne a little more unhappiness for my sake.

Say hello to Ravan. And as Asmaan must have told you, we are resurrecting *Jaan Se Pyara.* Keep your fingers, toes, ears and eyes crossed that we succeed and you will be back in business.

Love,

Belle

25

'Make sure that the top quarter of the pyre is sandalwood.'

It was 3 in the afternoon and Eddie and Ravan had just finished a late lunch when the new customer turned up. He was in expensive white clothes and seemed tense and brittle with grief.

'With due respect that will be rather expensive, sir.'

The man dipped into his briefcase and counted out seventy-five thousand-rupee notes. 'Will that be enough?'

Ravan didn't dare speak but Eddie's blasé expression suggested that he and his partner only dealt in these denominations.

'More?'

'Sixty-five more. Sandalwood prices have gone through the roof,' Eddie chipped in. They had not seen that kind of money since the time they'd been in the film business.

'What about bhajans?' Ravan had found his voice again. 'They induce an atmosphere of such calm and tranquillity, they are a bridge between the here and the hereafter. We think of our mission as Om Shanti Shanti Shanti just as our name says.'

'Sing them loud and with feeling and fervour.'

'That will be extra.' Eddie wasn't going to let Ravan's otherworldly outburst get in the way of business.

'Don't worry about the money. Here's ten thousand more as an advance towards incidental expenses.'

'Anything else you would like us to do for you?'

'The family has been through a very trying time for the past few weeks. I'm afraid all of us are too overcome with grief to think of anything else.'

'We understand how stressful all this must be for you.' Eddie's voice had a deep, solemn timbre as befitted the occasion. 'Please don't fret about a thing. We'll take care of every single detail. We'll make sure that the departed soul finds heavenly peace.'

'When should we come to pick up the deceased?' Ravan asked. Couldn't afford to make a mistake with such an important client.

'Eight-thirty p.m., tonight. We are sticklers for time. Nine to nine-fifteen is the most auspicious time to send the soul on its last journey.'

'Who will light the pyre?' Ravan was still filling in the blanks in the Om Shanti Shanti Shanti 'Deceased' form.

'Here's a baksheesh of a little something.' The wallet was out again and his hand clasped Eddie's.

'Like we said, leave everything to us.'

'Eight-thirty p.m.' The man pushed his dark glasses up and dabbed his eyes with a silk kerchief.

He was stepping into his Maruti Esteem when Ravan ran after him. 'You forgot to give us your name and address, sir.'

'Shagun Building, Flat number 2701. Ridge Road, Malabar Hill. It's the penthouse.'

'And the name?'

The car was already out of sight.

* * *

It was uncanny the effect that the articles in *The Indian Express* and *The Guardian* had had on the Om Shanti Shanti Shanti business. Action Bank had already financed the purchase of a wide-bodied, second-hand van. What a shame the van wasn't ready. It was still in the workshop, being fitted with a platform for a bier and plush sombre black upholstered seats for the closest mourners. It was clear that with this new client, they were entering a new era. Soon, hopefully very soon, Ravan and Eddie would invest in another office in a tonier part of town. Belle would do the interior but they had already decided two things. The colour scheme would be shades of subdued off-white and a top-of-the-the-line sound system would play bhajans by none other than R&E round the clock. And of course the CDs would be on sale, but again everything would be low-key and the atmosphere would be Om Shanti Shanti Shanti.

Eddie rang the bell of apartment 2701 of Shagun while Ravan waited by his side, a trifle uncertain of what lay ahead. They had been moving steadily upmarket but the twenty-seventh storey of a building on Malabar Hill was as close to the abode of the gods that you could get. Eddie and Ravan had mastered the etiquette of death and grief by this time and could at a moment's notice pull down a shutter of impassive efficiency over their faces while being solemn and solicitous. But would that be enough in these loftier realms or was something else called for? Should they be full of an unobtrusive sympathy that would bring a sense of inner peace to those who were grieving on the twenty-seventh storey? Should they offer condolences and recite verses from the Bhagwad Gita?

It would have helped if they had been able to find out a little more about these people to get a grip on the caste and community traditions they would be likely to follow but they didn't even know their name. They had scanned the list of the apartment owners in the spacious but unostentatious lobby but there was a blank for the twenty-seventh storey. Were they industrialists like the Birlas, Tatas and Ambanis? Were they royalty? The Scindias of Gwalior, the Maharani of Jaipur who was always on the list of the ten most beautiful women in the world in *Vogue* magazine, the Holkars of Indore and the princes of Baroda, all had at least one residence in the city. Were these the beautiful people with whom Jackie Onassis had dinner when she visited Bombay and stayed at the Taj Mahal Hotel?

Ravan and Eddie were both in their new all-white uniform, white kurtas and white cotton trousers that narrowed from the thighs down and were starched and ironed to papadam crispness. Shagun must have been one of the earliest high-rise apartment blocks built in the city. The construction was solid unlike the cardboard residential skyscrapers on Cuffe Parade. The apartments looked palatial even from the outside.

'What's taking them so long to open the door?' Eddie sounded peeved. 'I hope we didn't get the apartment number wrong.' He rang the bell again.

Ravan was sure that they were being watched from the peephole. The door opened just enough for them to see the left eye of the man inside. You could hear Sanskrit shlokas being recited solemnly. It was obvious this was an orthodox Hindu household bidding goodbye to the dead person.

'What do you want?'

'We are from Om Shanti Shanti Shanti Antim Yatra Services. We were asked to report here.'

The two-inch gap in the door closed. Five minutes passed. The man who had hired their services appeared, accompanied by another person.

'Can't you keep an appointment?' The man was in an all-white, three-piece suit with a white tie and a white silk kerchief tucked carefully in the jacket pocket. Eddie wondered how he hadn't noticed the man's pockmark-ravaged face when he had turned up at the Om Shanti Shanti Shanti office that afternoon. Was it a bad case of teenage acne or smallpox?

'Eight-thirty p.m., that's when I had asked you to come. I had stressed eight-thirty p.m. exactly. You've come a bloody forty-five minutes too early.'

'We didn't want to be late. Especially for such an important engagement.'

'We're conducting the final ceremonies. You were given an appointment for a precise time. The least you can do is to stick to it. Come back at the right time.'

* * *

'Raise your hands high,' an assistant to the man who had hired them instructed Eddie when they returned three-quarters of an hour later.

'What for?' Eddie asked.

The man gave him a dead stare. Eddie raised his hands while the man checked his limbs, joints and crotch as if he was a horse for sale and then shifted to Ravan with the same lack of emotion.

'They're okay,' the man said to his boss and led them to an anteroom.

'Give these people tea,' three-piece white suit instructed his assistant, 'and make sure they don't wander around.' He looked at the two visitors. 'Let me give you a piece of advice. Do exactly as I tell you and everything will be okay. Sit down. And don't move. I'll call you two when the time's right. Have you got that?'

'Yes.'

'I hope so for your own sake.'

The anteroom was at an angle, separated from the rest of the apartment which was effectively invisible. A frosted-glass door on either side seemed to lead to two different parts of the house; the left to a private wing from where Sanskrit shlokas and prayers could be heard, and the other to the drawing room where the man in the white suit had disappeared.

Ravan looked out towards Marine Drive. Legions of threatening monsoon clouds were tearing across the Arabian Sea towards the landmass, piling over each other, balancing drunkenly and tumbling down, leaving behind gashes and rents through which the full moon spilled over the Chowpatty sands and the city skyline in a crystalline light that illuminated every minute detail in the landscape. The only way one could fall in love with the city these days was to see it from a height. The traffic, the noise, the smells, the gobs of spit and snot on the streets, the dog and human shit on the pavements fortunately did not levitate all the way to the twenty-seventh storey.

The sea was as frisky as a peacock in heat and flaring its plumage three metres high as it collided against the rocks and the tetrapods and cascaded down on to the pavement. A security guard barged into the anteroom every now and then and surveyed the outside scene with a pair of binoculars. Imagine, having someone round the clock to guard you on the twenty-seventh floor, Eddie thought. Only ministers and politicians like the Sena bosses had protection 24/7. The people who owned the terrace apartment must either be fabulously rich or they were in constant danger. It was spooky to think that they could be a target not only for sharpshooters from the buildings around but perhaps from the air and the sea. The lives of the super-rich, Eddie realized, would always be a mystery.

A little later, the minion appeared with a loaded trolley of tangdi kebabs, cheese balls, fish tikkas, papads and other savouries and wheeled it out of the door on the right. Simultaneously, as some kind of fair exchange, a draught of cold air wafted into the anteroom. Eddie was instantly up and peeping through the circle of clear glass in the swinging door.

'Come and sit down, Eddie,' Ravan said. 'The man told us "don't move". Let's not get into trouble.'

'Don't you want to know who these people are?' Eddie kept the door just a little ajar and watched mesmerized. Ravan could no longer hold back his curiosity and joined his Peeping Tom friend. A meeting of some sort was in progress. Eddie and Ravan had learnt by now that grief didn't intrude when it was a question of business, especially if the deceased had been suffering from a long-drawn-out chronic illness. Most of the men, including the man who had visited them at the Om Shanti Shanti Shanti office, were sitting on an exquisite carpet with luscious clusters of red and light-green grapes hanging from the tendrils of curling, delicate vines. Only two men sat on the leather sofa with the back of their heads to Ravan and Eddie. The one on the left must have been younger because his hair was jet black while the other's was a flaming hennaed autumnal rust. Eddie couldn't see their faces but there was no mistaking the weight of the authority they exercised. They had the kind of voices which made you pause for orders. It was clear to both Eddie and Ravan that the man they had thought was the boss was at best an assistant.

The official part of the negotiations seemed to have ended for the mood was relaxed and the Scotch was making everybody loquacious. Anytime one of the bosses spoke, everyone shut up and listened attentively.

'May I take the liberty, sahab, to tell you something that comes straight from my heart?' the man with the tar-black hair asked the older one by his side. He was obviously high, very high.

'*Arre huzoor, hamein sharminda mat kijiye.*' The older man patted the younger one on his back. '*Khullam khulla dil ki baat bataiye.* After all, that's why we're together today. Speak your heart out.'

'Not even in my wildest fantasy had I imagined that that our bitter rivalry would ever be transformed into such deep friendship. Who would have believed, least of all my mother, that you would, of your own free will, hand over the master key of your empire at a time when you are not merely at your peak but are just about to climb to ever greater heights?'

'My friend, as President Reagan said, "You ain't seen nothing yet." If mortal enemies like Egypt's Sadat and Israel's Begin could embrace each other, why not the likes of us? I have been entirely open with you. Your accountants have been through both the official and the other set of accounts. And you have seen that there's no hanky-panky. All I asked for was that some assets should be in my name so that I don't have to be dependent on you or anybody else in my declining years. Now that that has been done, I can relax and will have no reason to interfere in how you conduct the affairs of the new combined operations.'

'You are truly a man of vision and wisdom, sahab,' the younger man said. 'As the Urdu poets have told us time and again, no sacrifice is great enough for a friend, least of all the sacrifice of one's life.' The words had begun to turn into banana peels and he was slithering on them.

'Do you know what the problem with our country is? The elderly don't know when to retire gracefully. I decided that I would not hang on to power well into my dotage but bow out while the going is good. Who better to take over the reins than you, my friend?'

'Janab, this is indeed the highest praise I have ever received. I will honour you all my life and seek your sage guidance in all matters.'

'You flatter us.' The older gentleman smiled benignly. 'But let me remind you, you can't clap with one hand. I may have extended the hand of friendship but I will always be beholden to you for your generosity of heart in grasping it so firmly.'

'Let us seal this friendship with a warm embrace.' The embrace didn't quite materialize for the speaker's heavy eyelids closed, his head drooped to one side and he was instantly snoring with a blissful smile on his face.

'Oh!' The older man sitting next to him patted him. 'Our friend's fallen asleep. Let him rest.'

The door to the anteroom was pushed open suddenly and Eddie and Ravan were flung back. 'I thought I had told you to sit down and not move.' The second-in-command was not pleased. It was clear he was not used to being disobeyed and there was a scary menace in his voice that teetered on the brink of violence. He was about to strike Eddie but lowered his hand. 'Sit down. If you don't follow my orders, I will personally throw you over the parapet. Do you understand me? As I had informed you both earlier, we've taken care of the bier. Ten more minutes and we'll hand over the departed and you can take the body to the crematorium. Now go and wait outside in the passage till I call you back.'

When they were finally allowed into the private quarters of the house, what they saw were a dozen or more mourners, all in white, standing around a bridal bier. An elaborate bamboo canopy was covered with such a dense mesh of vines and leaves that no light could penetrate it. Both exotic and familiar flowers like orchids, daisies, forget-me-nots, glaxonias, roses, marigolds, wax flowers, chrysanthemums, lilies and rajnigandhas were tucked in artfully. The dead person's face, no telling whether it was a woman's or man's, was covered with a veil fine as mist. As if that was not enough the two side openings of the canopy itself were also screened off with the same exquisite netting.

A couple of the men were weeping quietly while others stood silently with their heads bowed. One by one they bent down and touched the rim of the bier and did a namaskar. It was unusual amongst Hindus for the face of the corpse to be so completely covered, albeit with flowers, but Ravan had discovered that funeral customs differed not merely from community to community and caste to caste but also from sub-caste to sub-caste. But there was one other reason why on rare occasions the face of the dear departed was concealed. Sometimes, surgery or an accident damaged the face so badly, the family wanted to remember it from happier days. What impressed both the outsiders was how dignified this funeral was. There was no breast-beating, loud crying or imprecations addressed to the sky about the unfairness of the loss of a loved one. Perhaps that was because there were no women around. The two friends were not unfamiliar with the widow of a dead man insisting on accompanying him to the other world.

'Here's the death certificate duly signed by the doctor and the other necessary papers.' White suit, white tie handed them the certificates. 'Please check them.'

Eddie and Ravan went over the papers. 'Yes, everything seems to be in order.'

'Seems to be?' The man was incensed.

'You misunderstand us, sir,' Ravan said soothingly. 'Just a figure of speech. Everything's in perfect order.'

'Good. Here's twenty thousand extra just in case...' He handed over an envelope to Ravan. 'Count it. We don't want any trouble afterwards.'

'We trust you, sir,' Eddie said ingratiatingly.

'But I don't trust you. Count.'

Ravan flipped through the notes one by one and nodded. 'It's okay. Thank you.'

'Goodnight.'

'Will anybody be accompanying us?'

The deputy broke down and his voice was barely audible. 'The son of the deceased and all of us relatives would of course have accompanied you, but his mother suffered a heart attack last night and he's with her at the ICCU at Breach Candy Hospital. Our guruji, Sant Maharaj-ji, told us God looks after the dead but we must look after the living. We are all rushing to the hospital because the doctors feel that she too may not...' He left the sentence unfinished. When he had recovered he added, 'So I'm afraid you will have to perform the last rites.'

'Oh, how very sad,' Eddie said with a catch in his voice. He was a past master at that sort of thing. 'Do please give the lady our heartfelt condolences. We also wish her a speedy recovery. Rest assured we will do all that is necessary.'

* * *

It was ten to nine. Both Eddie and Ravan were silent and strangely subdued as they emerged from the Shagun compound. The traffic had thinned out and they stood undecided about which direction to take, Hanging Gardens on the left or the road that led to Teen Batti, and after the U-turn down to Marine Drive.

'Let's take the departed soul down by the sea one last time,' Eddie said. 'And then turn left over the bridge leading to Opera House.'

'I don't know about you,' Ravan said when they were at the U-turn at Teen Batti, 'but I'm relieved to be out of there.'

'So am I though I must say the money feels good and within a fortnight Om Shanti Shanti Shanti will be on wheels.'

'I can't wait to dump the cart.'

'I used to hate it for the longest time but I think I'm going to miss it. We should have a branch on Malabar Hill as soon as possible. Maybe this is where we should have our head office.'

'I don't know,' Ravan said, 'I don't know…'

'Know what?'

'Isn't it strange that no one, not a single person from that family is coming with us to light the pyre?'

'It's odd but the same thought's been on my mind, though I've tried to reason with myself. As the guru of these people told them, God looks after the dead but we must look after the living.'

'I guess you're right.'

Eddie stopped the cart abruptly. 'Ravan, we forgot the bhajans.' He took a deep breath, closed his eyes and slowly slipped into the bhajan that the blind saint–poet Surdas had composed so many centuries ago. Like most mystic poems, it was non-denominational. '*Nainheen ko raaha dikha Prabhu / Pag pag par thokar khau main*'. Show the way to this blind one, oh Lord / Every step I take, I stumble.

The first time Ravan and Eddie had heard the words, they had taken them literally till Asmaan had pointed out that those with

20/20 vision were often more blind than the sightless and so needed to hold God's hand if they wanted to navigate the calamities that life sprang on them. E&R had tripped and fallen so often, the poem had taken on a personal meaning. Its significance had only grown over the years and Surdas's words had given them succour at the most difficult of times. Ravan joined the singing and then Malabar Hill was resounding with their voices.

They didn't shout or bellow, they had grown up without mikes and had learnt that if you want to be heard, raising your voice didn't help, you had to project it. That way, maybe the good Lord Himself might hear you. They didn't know the dead person but were buoyed up by the feeling that the bhajan would give him hope and heart. In the quiet of the night there was something deeply moving about the purity of their voices. People on the road stood still to hear the song, and cars stopped honking and made way for them. What matter if the passers-by didn't understand a word of the mystic poetry, it was the magic of the melody and voices that mesmerized them and allowed them to enjoy a moment of stillness in this frenzied city. The road started descending steeply at the governor's bungalow and they had to dig in their feet and lean as far back as possible to prevent the cart from flying off on its own.

They were going faster down the slope. The lights at Nariman Point and Marine Drive shone brilliantly. Any moment now the neon Centaur above the Air India building would let fly the arrow from its stretched bow as it revolved a full 360 degrees. They shot past the house and garages of the reclusive man who owned more vintage cars than the former maharajas and then they were at sea level and turning towards Chowpatty. Ravan and Eddie stopped the cart in front of Wilson College for a minute to let the deceased take a good long look at the Arabian Sea.

Twenty days, Eddie thought as he watched the waves sweeping the sands like a dog licking its wounds, just twenty days and Belle will be back in Bombay. How often had he been told that failure was the best schooling you could get if you wanted to change your life for the better. What bull, all it did was to make you intolerant and insufferable. Had Belle and he grown any wiser with time and all that they had been through? Would it work out this time? Or would they discover that human beings don't learn a damn thing or change: change for the better, that is. Why was he beating about the bush and avoiding the one subject that was at the top of his mind. Should he ask Belle when she was in Bombay this time or not? What if she said no, she didn't care whether he slipped a gold ring on her finger or not?

'Hey, Eddie. What's up?' Ravan interrupted Eddie's reverie. 'Time to head forward. We don't want our client to wake up because of hyper-oxygenation from the sea air.'

They turned left towards the bridge to Opera House. They were nearly past Pancharatna, the commercial and residential multi-storeyed building whose first five or six floors were the closest thing to a diamond bourse in India, when they got stuck in a traffic jam. This was an extreme understatement. Pancharatna and the lane almost adjoining it had the highest density of population per square centimetre in the whole world. But that was only between 10 a.m. and 7.30 p.m. After that it was dead. It was 9.30 at night now. What was going on, where had these hundreds of people come from? And why were they milling around and holding up cars, cycles, buses and taxis heading south downtown or on the other side all the way to the suburbs?

How could he have missed it, Eddie wondered. They were at Roxy cinema, it was Thursday night and *The Return of Bharat* was being premiered. It was house full, and the tout on the pavement was muttering the magic formula, *Paanch ka pachaas, dus ka pachhattar. Paanch ka pachaas, dus ka pachhattar*. A five-rupee ticket for fifty bucks and a ten-rupee one for seventy-five. The original *Bharat* was the movie for which Ravan and Eddie had choreographed the final fight sequence and for which the director had not paid them a paisa, nor mentioned them in the credits. It had turned out to be one of the biggest money-grossers in Hindi cinema. Expectations for the sequel were even greater.

'What are you doing, stupid?' Ravan yelled at Eddie. 'Push the cart straight ahead and let's get out of here.'

Ravan tracked Eddie's eyes as they scanned the hoardings above Roxy cinema. He knew instantly what was going on in Eddie's mind. Well, Eddie was welcome to fantasize about seeing the movie tonight as much as he wanted but it was just not going to happen. Eddie could beg, plead, grovel but Ravan would put his foot down. And that was that. Ram, Ram, Haré Ram, he chanted the name of the righteous god like a mantra. Ram, Ram, Haré Ram. Ram, Ram, Haré Ram. Ram, Ram, Haré Ram. Indeed those four words would have parted not only the cinema crowd but the very sea. A dead body deserves respect and don't forget, it's best kept at a distance. Ravan made it through to the other side of the road. He looked around, no sign of Eddie. Was this any time to loiter and linger? Eddie was standing beside him, waving two tickets.

'No. We are not, I repeat, we are not seeing the movie tonight,' Ravan said truculently, defying Eddie to contradict him even as he snatched the tickets from his friend's hand. 'Tomorrow yes, but not today.'

Eddie was crestfallen but wouldn't look Ravan in the eye.

'What's your problem? Is the movie going to run for just one day? Or do you think the government will ban the film tomorrow?'

'First day, first show. That was our credo, remember? We haven't seen a movie for over a year now. We can afford to indulge ourselves for two-and-a-half hours today.'

'Are you crazy? Who's going to cremate the body? We gave them our word.'

'So we did. And I've no intention of breaking it. All I'm saying is that we watch the film first and then light the pyre. The dead are not in the habit of running away.'

'And what do we do with him?'

'Leave that to me.' Eddie took the cart into the narrow lane next to the theatre and parked it comfortably in a quieter part of the road.

'Here? For two-and-a-half hours?'

'Who's going to take him away?'

Ravan gave Eddie a look of incandescent hostility. 'No.'

Why was Ravan kidding himself? Few people knew the mystique

of the phrase 'First day, first show' on premiere night better than Eddie and him. It was pure hypnosis. You could reason with it, argue and quarrel with it, tell it to piss off, resist it tooth and nail, slug it out man to man, but you knew the end result from the word go, you had no say in the matter. Even if you were drugged unconscious, you would sleepwalk to the cinema house. When you gotta go, you gotta go.

'The movie's about to start. Are you coming or not?'

Ravan was still shaking his head as he entered the theatre.

During the intermission, Ravan rushed out to check whether the cart was still there. He was surprised to find that it was raining heavily. He was drenched by the time he got to the cart. It was an eerie feeling to be in that lane late at night. The place was deserted now. The vendors who sold tea, sugarcane juice, chutney sandwiches, vada pau, bhel puri, pau bhaji, chhole, ragda and other savouries to hundreds of workers and clerks in the diamond trade during the day had closed shop. Normally they would have been sleeping on their handcarts or flattened-out cardboard boxes on the pavement. But thanks to the rain they had had to find some other shelter. The Om Shanti Shanti Shanti cart was parked where they had left it. The heaps of garlands on the corpse were soggy and the scent of the flowers, especially the lilies, had turned shrill and asphyxiating. Ravan was suddenly seized by the thought that there was no body under that huge floral mass. He checked, poking and clutching at it at different points. The dead body was still there, dead as ever.

'What took you so long?' Eddie whispered in the darkness when Ravan got back.

'Just making sure.'

'Making sure of what?'

'Nothing really. Just making sure that everything was okay.'

Eddie made a face in the dark. 'You're dripping like a leaky pipe.'

* * *

Ravan was up and edging towards the exit even as the hero, Bharat, spun, bounced and somersaulted, dodging the missiles that the villain

Dr Doom fired at him from his electronic console at lightning speed. Now, Bharat was lying face down on the floor. As he slowly turned around to breathe his last, you could see the blood from the wound in his chest turning his white commando tunic scarlet. 'Yippee, gotchya,' Dr Doom yelled jubilantly as he flung the console away and waved his hands triumphantly. The camera closed in on the dead hero. One of his eyes opened and looked stealthily at Dr Doom. He ripped off his shirt with the fake blood and the bulletproof vest under it to reveal his superbly contoured, muscular body. He leapt up in the air in slow motion, almost touching the high ceiling of the castle as he grabbed a long sword hanging on one of the walls.

'Wrong.' Bharat's voice reverberated in the vast room. 'I gotchya.'

Dr Doom was flummoxed. 'What happened to the blood?' he asked as he looked frantically for the console that he had so gleefully thrown away.

'Just tomato ketchup from the special effects department,' Bharat answered, whirling around his own axis. The sword flashed by at a thousand rpm, slicing through Dr Doom's body from the head down. Astonishingly, Dr Doom had not suffered a single nick or cut. Bharat landed on the floor and wiped his sword with the silk scarf tied like a sash around his waist. He looked at Dr Doom a little puzzled, went close to him and whistled the theme song. That draught of air was enough to make the villain fly apart in wafer-thin discs. The crowds in the cinema house whooped and screamed with delight.

Ravan was sure he would hate the sequel to a film that had given Eddie and him such heartburn but it was fun to watch so long as you anaesthetized your brains and got into the spirit of things. Damn. It was past midnight and still pouring. They were hungry and tired and it would be a long time before they got back home. Neither of them was in the mood to talk or sing. Instead of the fifteen-minute walk on a normal day, today it was a twenty-five minute slog through flooded streets to the crematorium opposite Marine Lines Station. But it was not all bad news. The heavy rains ensured that they were the only customers at the crematorium and would not have to wait in a queue. The sandalwood had been soaked with rainwater and its subtle, delicate fragrance clashed with the strident scent of the lilies and was almost immediately vanquished.

Eddie and Ravan were on friendly terms with the staff of the place and the pyre was quickly prepared. They lifted the bier and placed it on the wooden platform. Ravan sang '*Amhi jato amuchya gava*' and Eddie followed it up with a '*Kabira khada bazaar mein*'. After the songs, the two of them stood quietly for a minute and Ravan did something he had never done before.

'I'm sorry that your son and the other members of your family are not here to perform the last rites and to see you off on your last journey. According to the Puranas and tradition, it is the eldest son's duty to light the pyre and thus to release the soul of his father.' He spoke in a quiet, measured voice. Eddie looked at him quizzically but didn't interrupt his friend. 'We can well imagine how you must feel not to have them with you when you are about to set off on a journey from which you are not going to return. It's unusual, to say the least, to have strangers perform the last rites for you. But as the saints tell us, we come into this world alone and we leave on our own. The only one who will hold your hand is God. We hope you've had a full life and have no regrets about this segment of your cycle of life being over. You don't know us but we would like to assure you that we will be your two sons and will perform the necessary rites and rituals. We wish you well. Who knows what your next life will bring. Perhaps we may be reborn as your sons in the next life. Goodbye and have a safe journey. May your soul rest in peace.'

It was such a simple goodbye and so unexpected, Eddie was strangely moved. Trust Ravan to think about the terrible fate of a man having to depart without his folks being around. Eddie poured the ghee on the wood and they got down to lighting the fire. This was always a tricky business. There was a science to it and some art too and over the last year they had become adept at it. One of the things you learnt quickly in the Hindu funeral business was that if you were not careful, you could get badly burnt. The sparks sputtered and scattered like small Diwali fireworks. Which meant that you wore nylon or polyester shirts only if you were suicidal. Sometimes little red-hot cinders flew out and singed you and could even blind you. Today, however, the wet wood would not catch fire. Ravan and Eddie gathered old newspapers from the crematorium office along with a half-filled bottle of kerosene. They soaked the papers with the crude oil, placed them under the logs of wood, and lit them. Some of the sandalwood showed signs of feebly coming to life but Eddie knew that it would not last. They would have to try something more effective. He went back to the office, collected two steel tubes which were kept for such emergencies, and both Ravan and he began to blow air into the spaces between the logs of wood. The whole place filled with a heavy acrid smoke that burnt the eyes and stayed lethargically close to the ground. It was hard work and they had to keep at it for over fifteen minutes before the wood began to glow from within.

Ravan performed the last and most important duty of an eldest son. He picked up the pot of clay and gently knocked a hole in it. He went around the pyre once, leaving behind a trail of water. That done, he smashed the clay pot. It was a symbolic act but with the most profound significance. The fire would crack the skull just as Ravan had broken the pot and the soul would be liberated from the confines of the flesh.

The sandalwood was soon crackling in earnest and Eddie handed over the ornate urn in which the ashes of the departed would be gathered to the member of the staff on duty. Ravan and he would collect the urn in the morning and would go over to Shagun and offer it to the family. The man in the white suit had insisted that the ashes had to be returned to them as early as possible. Nothing special about that, Eddie thought. Hindus were always in a rush, first to cremate the body and then to immerse the ashes in the waters of the holy Ganga if they were rich. And if they were not and lived in Maharashtra, they settled for the poor man's Ganga, the Godavari in Nasik.

To bed, to bed. It had been an exhausting day and they couldn't wait to go home. They packed up and were ready to leave when they heard an eerie, unearthly sound. It was so high-pitched and thin, it had to be a transmission from an astral body millions of light years away. 'Ayyyyyyyyyaaaaaaaaiiiiiiiiggggggaaaaaaaaaaaa.' Ravan wondered if it was a cry from some malicious spirit that had reanimated the corpse when it had been left unattended for so long while they watched the movie. Wasn't that the reason Hindus were so keen on finishing the cremation in a hurry? The two friends tried to trace the source of the noise. How dumb of them, it was the pyre emitting that weird signal. It was too early for the skull to crack open and the brain to sizzle but burning wood always made peculiar sounds as the moisture within it evaporated and the logs creaked, moved, adjusted and crumbled, but it was nothing like this freak ululating that appeared to be above the range that the human ear was capable of registering. 'Vachawaaaaaaa, bachhaaaaaaaoo, bachhaaaaaaaaaoo.' The mountain of flowers exploded with volcanic ferocity and Ravan and Eddie were showered with crushed buds and petals. A solitary hand shot up and the two friends began to speak in tongues. 'Dha, dha, dha pa, pa, pa gha, gha, bha, bha. Mamamamama.' And then even the octave of pure terror was gone, their tongues retracted and all they could manage was the primal silence of the unborn.

26

They stood transfixed to the ground. They would never move again. The government coroner would declare them dead and note in his report, cause of death: cardiac arrest of unknown aetiology. Anthills would grow over them as they did over Valmiki, the highway robber-turned-poet who wrote the Ramayana, and the sandpaper of time would grind them to dust. Now the other hand rose and a disembodied voice pleaded in Hindi, '*Bachao, arre koi bachao mujhe.* Save me, someone please save me. Where am I? These must surely be the flames of hell. I deserve it, oh God, I deserve it. Anybody there? Call the fire-brigade. All those innocent people I killed, the people I blackmailed, the money I made on the black market, the prostitution rings I ran, I'm paying for my sins. Oh God, are you deaf? Save me.'

What followed though was so execrably phoney, even the House of Ramsay, which had a near monopoly of the most dreadfully rickety horror films in the Hindi film industry, would have cringed. The sandalwood logs tumbled and rolled down and the ghost of the dead man leapt up, and was doing the tandav of Shiva. He was leaping, hopping and bouncing up and down, not letting his feet rest even for a second on the burning logs. 'Where am I?' he was screaming at the heavens. 'Save me, dear God. *Bhagwan ki kasam*, I'll never kill again. Shankar Bhagwan, if you save me, I'll build a temple for you, and buy you a crown of the finest diamonds.' The ghost looked down and saw two men staring spellbound at him. '*Abey bhosdike*, are you deaf? Can't you see I'm going to burn to death? Get me down.'

Ravan and Eddie were already past Charni Road Station and still running with the Om Shanti Shanti Shanti handcart.

* * *

Falling … falling … falling…

Ah the past, how it preyed upon the present. It made it plain that it was more urgent and pressing than the here and now and elbowed out all current thoughts and concerns. How often had Ravan teased open old wounds and asked himself where had he gone wrong: if he loved Piya-Pieta so much, how come he did not know what was going on in her mind till it was too late? Why had he let her down when she had begged and pleaded with him to hold on to her and not to let go of her as she lay dying?

A recorded loop had run in his head since the time she had left him. How could she have got pregnant when all the doctors she had seen, starting from the one who had brought her back from the dead after that butcher-woman from Falkland Road had performed the abortion on her, had warned her that it would be extremely dangerous if she conceived again because her scarred uterus might rupture. Surely she knew that the word 'dangerous' in her case was nothing less or more than death? Pieta and he had talked things over before they had got married and she had decided to be on the pill. When do husbands and wives begin to conceal and deceive and start keeping things from each other? Pieta and he were so close; more than husband and wife, they were lovers.

By the time he found out about the pregnancy, it was too late. 'Why, Piya, why?' he had asked her when he discovered her deceit.

'Because I love you. Because I want to make up for lost time. Because you did not give up on me. Because you are so good to me. Because I want to have your child and make you happy.'

'But I am happy with you. Isn't that obvious?'

'Yes, it is. But I wanted to make you happier.'

'You are all I want. I don't need anyone else.' Why was he arguing? She was not going to listen to him or to reason. 'Piya, please listen to me. I beg of you. Let's abort the baby.'

'I would rather die. Once was enough. Never again. Besides, it's too late for that.'

'We'll go to the finest doctors, we'll do it under anaesthesia and the most hygienic conditions. I promise you, it will be absolutely safe and painless.'

'Sssshhh…' She put her index finger on his lips. 'We'll soon find out whether it's a boy or a girl.'

She was right. They would find out. For better or worse. And it was far sooner than he had expected. She was in a great deal of pain and flitting between consciousness and a coma as they rushed her to the operating theatre. She had bled so much, she could barely whisper. 'It's going to be a girl.' She smiled wanly but she looked so happy. 'I know you wanted a girl. Next time around, we'll have a son.'

She was such a sensible woman normally, she thought things through, weighed the pros and cons and only then did whatever she thought was the right thing. But what had happened to her now? What utter drivel was she talking? Didn't she know how far beyond serious her condition was?

She was on her first bottle of blood when they brought her back some hours later. 'How's the baby doing?'

'Doing fine.'

'When do I get to see her?'

'They are just cleaning her up. And checking if everything's in order.'

'Why shouldn't it be?'

'It's just a precaution. They do it for all newborns.'

'Is she as good-looking as you are? What shall we call her?'

And then she was gone, telling him, 'Don't let me go, Ravan, don't let go of me.'

'Are you happy now,' he wanted to ask her, 'you stupid, stupid, stupid, stupid, stupid woman.' Oh, how he hated her for leaving him. And it wasn't a girl but a boy, a still-born boy. Ravan could never forgive himself. How could he have trusted Piya-Pieta, he should have got a vasectomy done a long, long time ago if he had really wanted her to live. He had killed her as surely as if he had put a bullet through her head.

* * *

Parvatibai woke Ravan up at 11 in the morning to say that three customers were waiting for him on the landing. They had been to the Om Shanti Shanti Shanti office and someone had directed them to CWD Chawl Number 17. Ravan hurriedly washed his face and went to meet the visitors. The younger sister of one of the men had been murdered the day before she was supposed to get married and then thrown into the sea, and the body had been recovered the previous day.

'The coroner's office says we won't get the body for two more days. We were told that you know people there and can get it back much faster. Will you help us?'

No, he would not. He was sorry about the sister who would have been a bride by now but he wanted out of the funeral business. Where had Eddie and he gone wrong? How could they have made such a terrible mistake? The doctor who had signed the death certificate had stated in the most unambiguous terms that Shri Haridas Pandey had died of a brain haemorrhage leading to a coma followed by death. Was one to conclude that Dr R.P. Raheja, the senior cardiologist at Happy Health Hospital, could not tell the difference between a person who was dead and one who was still breathing?

The peculiar thing was that while the previous night had proved to be the scariest experience of their lives, there had been moments which were as insanely comic as anything he had seen in the silent Keystone cop movies. Even now he couldn't excise from his mind the image of the dead man hopping like a firecracker on the burning logs. The high pile of sandalwood had come tumbling down while he nearly got buried under it. And yet, if Haridas Pandey was alive, it was not impossible that Om Shanti Shanti Shanti had packed others off to their eternal resting place when they had not given up the ghost.

'I'm no longer in this business.'

'My parents are devastated, especially my mother. We want to cremate the body as soon as possible without letting my mother see it. Please don't say no.'

Ravan wasn't sure whether he had meant it when he had told the man he was through with the business. How was he planning to get by if he closed Om Shanti Shanti Shanti? Eddie and he got possession of the body at 1 a.m. and it was cremated immediately.

* * *

The sun flashed blindingly into Ravan's eyes and he looked up to trace its source. A Maruti Esteem came to a halt in front of the Om Shanti Shanti Shanti office-cum-storeroom and one of its windows was beaming the sunlight like a floodlight into his face. The glare was so strong, Ravan had to duck to avoid it. The front and rear doors of the car opened and two men in dark glasses and AK-47s in their hands fired in naughts and crosses, infinity-loops, parallelograms and pentagrams at the stacked bamboos, earthen pots, shawls, strings and ropes, biers, tins of Amul ghee, white sheets, and the bottles of the purifying waters of the sacred Ganga. Ravan rolled under the wooden table where Eddie was crouching. Three minutes of sheer mayhem and the car doors banged shut and they were gone. Ravan stared blankly at the destruction. The spray of bullets had ripped through the plaster and brick of the walls, and split the bamboo poles and sent splinters flying. Ghee from blasted Amul cans dripped on Eddie's face. Shattered glass lay all over the floor and the water from the Ganga was snaking towards the open door. The shards of the broken clay pots caught Ravan's eye. It was not a good omen. The symbolism of death was all around him. The pots were smashed for the dead, not for the living.

Eddie and he were trying to comprehend the devastation when Ravan noticed the oversize postcard lying on the floor. It showed men and women in a graduated series of torture chambers. He flipped it over. There was no mistaking the exquisite calligraphy. It was Urdu written in Devnagari script.

> I've asked my men to leave two calling cards. This one and the one that shattered your shop and peace of mind a moment ago. Just a foretaste of what is to come.
>
> I was wrong but one lives and learns. I know now that a talisman too can go bad when it is perverted by the devil. The only option is to scotch it before it can do any more harm.
>
> You were asked to perform one simple task with more than adequate compensation attached to it. But you made a mess of the job. In a day or two, I will know for certain whether you

betrayed me and joined hands with the enemy or whether you are just a fool.

You should know better, Ravan. When you play with fire, the fire will consume you. You are going to discover that the seven jehannums shown on the flip-side of the card are like jannats compared to what lies in wait for you.

Next time we will meet face to face.

'What the hell is this?' Eddie asked as he peered over Ravan's shoulder and read the card.

'Exactly what it looks like, a postcard from hell,' Ravan whispered.

There were about fifteen curious people gingerly edging towards Om Shanti Shanti Shanti and peering inside.

'What's that supposed to mean? Who's this guy who's written to you?' Eddie asked as he wiped the ghee from his face with a ripped white sheet from one of the shelves on the wall.

'Bashir Akhtar, the mafia king of Bombay.'

'Sure, the two of you are on a first-name basis, right? Actually you are brothers. Twins is even better.' But within seconds Eddie's flippant incredulousness had turned to panic. 'You mean the mafia don attacked our two-bit shop?'

'We'd better report this to the police.'

'Why?'

'Because whether we like it or not, they are going to be here. We might as well get some protection from whoever these killers are.' Ravan hurriedly cleared a path through the rubble with a broom. There was a crowd of at least forty to fifty people outside now.

'They couldn't even shoot straight. They missed us. It can't be all that serious.'

'You think they were playing at cops and robbers? They missed us because they were instructed to.'

'Why would they do that?'

'I think we've got mixed up with the wrong people.'

'How do you mean?'

'Like you said a couple of days ago, there was something very fishy about that man waking up on his funeral pyre. Are you coming or shall I go to the police on my own?'

'I thought you hated having to do anything with the police.'

'I do, but do you see any way out?'

Eddie switched off the lights, got the keys and locked the doors of the shop.

The tenants from the CWD Chawls, pedestrians, layabouts, children returning from school were all clamouring around Eddie and Ravan and jostling them.

'What happened?'

'Was anybody killed?'

'How come you are alive?'

'Is a film being shot here?'

'Yes. I heard Dharmendra and Amitabh Bachchan were shooting for their latest movie. Who are the two heroines?'

'What's the name of the movie?'

Ravan was impatient and hostile as he elbowed his way out but Eddie was smarter.

'Chawl Number 43. That's where Hema Malini and Rekha are doing a dance sequence with Dharmendra and Amitabh.'

* * *

'We'd just opened our shop.'

'You mean today was the opening ceremony of your shop?' Inspector Jamkhede asked.

'No, no.' Eddie couldn't believe the policeman was so obtuse. 'The shop is more than a year old. We were opening it this morning when a beige Maruti Esteem glided to a halt in front of our shop.'

Ravan took over. 'The doors opened and there was a shower of bullets from AK-47s.'

'Please stop, please stop. I beg you.' Someone in the lockup at the back was either being thrashed or tortured.

'Stop faking it, you bastard.' There was a dull cracking sound followed by an excruciating scream. 'Throw water on the swine. We need a confession from him today.'

Ravan looked around. No one seemed to notice that the prisoner was in distress and could be crippled for life. How could Ravan forget being taken into custody by the police when he was still a very young man? They had humiliated and beaten him without even bothering to cover his naked body. But why go so far back? How could he forget the sanctimonious rapacity of the lone policeman, Shyamlal, who had turned up with that limping harbinger of misfortune while they were shooting in the ravines and had brought the cast, crew, ClickClick and R&E to their knees?

The sight of a policeman even in the distance made Ravan nervous and completely irrational and yet not for a second did he think that his fear of the man or his tribe was anything but rational. In their eyes you were guilty before and after you were proven innocent. Why was he quibbling, they were not interested in such irrelevant matters as guilt or innocence.

There was nothing truer than pain, not even love, God or death. It stripped you bare to the soul. Something struck him then. It unnerved him and undermined his deepest assumptions about himself. Was it possible that his discomfiture and distress were not so much about the man in the lock-up, or the very idea of torture, as they were about himself and his own well-being? If he could get away from that piercing noise, it would not matter what happened to the man. Perhaps he himself, Ravan thought, was as violent and willing to inflict pain as anybody else. The prisoner had regained consciousness and was yelling in agony again. Ravan had a hard time preventing himself from rushing to the back of the police chowki and strangling the man if only to stop his screaming.

There were framed pictures of Bapu and Jawaharlal Nehru on the wall. The colour had been leached out of them and, at some time in the past, water had seeped into the frames and fluted both the leaders. The Father of the Nation had such a warm, kindly smile but what was he doing here? Ravan could not think of anyone more unsuited to these vile surroundings than Gandhi-ji. Were the powers-that-be even vaguely aware of the irony of mandating that every police station in the country put up his portrait? Perhaps they were. They were happiest when they were double-talking. Or was the right word hypocritical? The policemen seemed immune to the toothless Mahatma's presence. Why were police stations always so depressing, Ravan wondered. Their walls never got a fresh coat of paint. But that was not the problem. Policemen's wages were execrably low, but that too was not the issue. Even the pettiness of their minds and their boundless greed could be forgiven but it was impossible to understand why they exuded such a dislike, no, much more than that, an animus for the very people they were supposed to protect.

'Sir, shouldn't we file an FIR for these people?' the constable assisting the inspector asked.

Inspector Jamkhede raised his hand imperiously. 'Don't teach me my job, Hawaldar Dahake. This story is like a Hollywood thriller. I want to hear it in full first, then we'll see.'

'They blew up the entire shop.'

'How long did the firing last?'

'At least three minutes. Everything in the shop was destroyed.'

'Three minutes of shooting and you got away without even a nick.'

'Yes, but we had hidden under a wooden table.'

'Fantastic, you must be supermen. *Abé bhosdiké, hamein chutiya bana rahé ho kya?* This is Bombay, not Chicago.'

Ravan thought Jamkhede was right. He wouldn't have believed the story if someone had narrated it to him. Eddie was almost on the verge of telling the man that the 'ch' in Chicago was pronounced as 'sh' as in ship and not 'ch' as in chip off the old block.

'Next thing you'll tell me is that Al Capone was here. You want to file this cock-and-bull story as an FIR, Dahake?'

'No, sir, you're right,' Hawaldar Dahake said sheepishly. 'We should keep them in the lockup to teach them not to waste our time.'

'I intend to. All this drama is for just one purpose. They want publicity and will do anything to grab a headline.' He took out a fifty-rupee note and gave it to the constable. 'Get me a pack of 555s. And don't take your time pissing against every lamp-post you see.'

Eddie was incensed. 'Why don't you come and check our story?'

'You think I've nothing better to do?'

A sub-inspector hurriedly walked in from the wireless room. 'We just got a message from the central office telling us that they are expecting the worst gangland wars that the city has witnessed. The rumour's that two men from our area tried to burn Jagannath Jadhav alive on a cremation pyre but he escaped and has gone underground. The whole city is to be put on high alert.'

'Tell the CID branch to round up all the squealers and stool pigeons and pump them for information about who could have conceived and executed such a devious plan.'

'Yes, sir.'

Inspector Jamkhede turned to Eddie. 'So you think we should check your story? What does your shop sell?'

Eddie felt Ravan suddenly go tense. 'What else?' he asked rhetorically. 'Groceries. That's where the money is. You should try our Basmati rice. We don't get it from just one particular village, we get it from one specific farm. You've never tasted anything as delicious and perfumed.'

Eddie was enjoying himself far too much and Ravan feared he was bound to slip up.

'What did you say your name was?'

The question was directed at Eddie but Ravan butted in.

'I'm Sadanand Puranik and he's Ramchandra Mishra.'

'What's the cross doing on Ramchandra Mishra's neck?'

'The fool's fallen for a Catholic girl. He thinks wearing a cross will impress her.'

'Shame on you, Mishra. And you, why do you always speak for him? Doesn't he have a tongue?'

The sub-inspector rushed back in. 'I think you'll want to take a look at the new message, sir.'

'Now what? Can't I get some work done here without constant interruptions?'

'I'm sorry, sir, but Kareem Sultan's body was found in the canal of the Worli Pumping Station.'

'Kareem Sultan? Bashir Akhtar's second-in-command?' Inspector Jamkhede was out of his seat and halfway to the wireless room. 'You two wait here.'

Constable Dahake was back with the pack of 555s. He had taken his time and was relieved to see that Inspector Jamkhede was not around.

Ravan pointed to the wireless room and said, 'He wants you in the wireless room. Double quick.'

The constable hurried to meet his boss. Eddie and Ravan slipped out of the room. 'So that man whom we nearly burnt on the pyre is Jagannath Jadhav and not Haridas Pandey as the death certificate said,' Ravan whispered to Eddie. 'We were meant to eliminate the competition.' They must have walked barely ten metres when they took off for the thousand-metre Olympic race. They were convinced that any moment now they would hear the sirens from the police cars coming after them. First turn to the left and then the third one to the left again and only then did they ease off. They stood, bending doubled up and breathing rapidly. It was Eddie with his head between his knees who noticed the white Jaguar creeping up on them from behind.

'I think we're being followed,' he whispered.

Ravan bent down farther.

'Is it the police?'

'It's Three Point One.'

'Who?

There was no time to answer. The front window of the Jaguar sank down and the man at the wheel spoke softly.

'How are you, Ravan? Who would have thought we would meet again. Good Lord, are you all right?' Three Point One asked with an excessive show of concern. 'You look quite shaken, as if you had seen a ghost. No ghost, I assure you. You've just reported a crime to the police, haven't you? I'm told some hooligans with AK-47s gutted your shop. Now that the Shanti Shanti Shanti from your shop has vanished, what will you call it? Om Vinash, Vinash, Vinash?' He made the three words sound as if it was the magic formula for invoking Yama, the god of death. 'That might be more apt now. A foretaste of what is to come. Get in.'

'Who the hell does this guy think he is?' Eddie murmured.

'Just do as he says,' Ravan whispered as he got into the backseat.

'A few preliminary questions to clear the air and then we'll get down to the serious business of what to do with you. If you are reasonable and give honest answers, we'll be done in no time. But if you aren't, you are going to make me angry, very angry. You should know by now that's not such a good idea.' He let that sink in. 'So what will it be? Are you willing to cooperate? Or…'

'Depends.'

'Really? Depends on what, smartarse?'

'On whether I know the answers and whether you believe me.'

'We'll find out soon enough. Question number one, were you acquainted with Jagannath Jadhav before we handed him over to you?'

'No, I'd seen his name in the papers but that's all.'

'How much did he pay you?'

'Pay me? For what?'

'Good try, Pawar, but don't try my patience. For not cremating him but waiting till he woke up?'

'How would we have known the man on the bier was Jagannath Jadhav? The name on the death certificate said Haridas Pandey. Besides, he was declared dead by the cardiologist at the Happy Health Hospital.'

'So how did he wake up?'

'You tell me. It was the most terrifying experience of our lives.'

'You think I'm some newborn babe still suckling at his mother's breast to buy your crappy story. He had ingested enough sleeping pills to put an elephant to sleep for hours.'

'Maybe you gave him the wrong dose. Or the stuff you gave him was fake or diluted.'

Ravan was a pretty good actor, Eddie had to admit. He hadn't let on that thanks to his best friend, one Eddie Coutinho's perverse insistence, they had gone to see a movie while the putative corpse of Jagannath Jadhav was lying outside Roxy Cinema.

'Don't get smart with me, Pawar. You knew exactly who it was, don't ask me how, but you waited till he was up and made a deal with him.'

'If that was the case, how did he receive so many burns all over his body?'

'You don't expect me to buy that sob story, do you? It was just something put out by Jadhav to gull the police. How much did he pay you?'

'For trying to kill him while he was drugged? You've got to be joking. I'm sure he's looking for us at this very moment.'

'Do you have any idea how much planning went into this project? I had considered every angle. I could have bumped him off, but I wanted to avoid the usual gangland wars which garner so much bad publicity. What I had in mind was to achieve my purpose without drawing any media attention. The whole job would be done on the quiet and in a way that would make it impossible to detect that I had any connection with the end result. All you had to do was your bit, that's all. Once you had lit the pyre and collected the ashes, not a trace of Jagannath would be left. The competition would have been wiped out and no blood would have been spilt. You got a whole lot of money from me to cremate the guy. But you were so greedy you cut a deal with Jadhav.'

'We were just doing our job, we had no idea it was for you.'

'The fact is you did not do your job. And now thanks to your failure I am paying through my nose to persuade the media and the police to keep a lid on the story till I find out where Jagannath is holed up. Soon after we got acquainted, when you were starting out as a taxi driver, I had given you a bit of advice. But you forgot it. "I had no idea", "I was ignorant", "I didn't know", all these may very occasionally be valid reasons, though mostly they are pathetic excuses, but they have no place in law. And the reason is clear, because whatever your bullshit story, it does not alter the fact that immeasurable and irreparable damage has been done and you are responsible for it. Get this straight, Pawar, you and your stupid friend here are going to pay for it. For all the planning gone waste, the colossal harm done to my reputation, the police feeling the heat and turning up the heat on me and threatening to put me behind bars even though I am their godfather and patron-saint. I've lost my deputy, Kareem Sultan, and most important of all, my empire is in greater danger than ever before. A gang war will play out when I had gone to such lengths to eliminate the competition.'

A distant siren was blaring. Bashir Akhtar's forehead crinkled as he looked into the rear-view mirror. Ravan turned around and saw a police jeep cutting through red lights.

'Get out, both of you. Right. You will be hearing from me.'

The Jaguar slowed down a trifle and the passengers nearly got run over as it took off even before they had alighted.

'Oh, one little suggestion.' Three Point One reversed the Jaguar. 'If I were you, and Allah be praised that I'm not, I wouldn't try anything smart like attempting to leave the city or the country. Remember, you're being watched. Constantly. Try anything funny and you will regret it.'

'Who was that?' Eddie asked.

'Bashir Akhtar. Alias Three Point One. The mafia boss.'

27

On any other day, Eddie and Ravan would have gone for a walk near the docks or to Marine Drive if they had wanted some privacy to talk about business matters or anything else that was on their minds, though in fact they hardly ever did since their line of work now involved so much trudging on busy roads. Or they could have sat in their shop and had a serious conversation. Both those options, however, were not viable today. That left them with little choice but to go to the terrace. What next, that was the question, the only question. They were both conscious that they had reached a watershed event in their lives. The choices they made now, the decisions they took tonight would mean life or death for them.

'How do you know this guy, this mafia boss Bashir Akhtar? You've never mentioned him in all these years. He was on such familiar terms with you, I'm beginning to wonder if you were a member of his gang. He called you by your first name.'

'Believe it or not, we go back a long way, Bashir Akhtar and I,' Ravan told Eddie. 'I had just started driving a taxi and he was one of my first passengers. He left a package under the front seat of my taxi without telling me and disappeared since the police were chasing him. When I discovered the stash the next morning, let's just say, I borrowed a little of that money. That's how I made the two suits that would, purely by chance, bring you and me together when we were extras. Well, I have spent the rest of my life repaying that minuscule loan that must have by now been cleared a thousand times over. Bashir Akhtar has no qualms getting rid of even those who gave him shelter and protected him for years when he has no more use for them. You saw how he killed Maan Singh and Jwala Singh, didn't you? Take my word for it, all talk of a code of honour amongst the mafia is hogwash. They have no sense of loyalty, no nothing. They'll go back on their word any time. They'll use you and then stab you in the back. That's one thing Three Point One taught me and I'm grateful for that.'

'Is he really dangerous or is it mostly hot air?'

'No idle threats, Bashirbhai's as good as his word. You should never underestimate him.'

'So what do you suggest?

'We pick up the money from the safe in our office, catch a bus since Bashir Akhtar's men hopefully will not attempt to bump us off in front of so many people, and go to Mohammed Ali Road.'

'Why Mohammed Ali Road?'

'Maybe some clothing shops will be open and we can buy burkhas, old-fashioned ones that cover the face and have a lacy grill in front of the eyes.'

Eddie smiled. 'I know where to get them.'

'How's that?'

'Because in a previous life as the helper in a speakeasy, I used to pick up moonshine from Danda and Versova and head back in a burkha.'

'If we get them, we head for VT station and take the first train out.'

'I thought you just said your Bashir Akhtar doesn't make idle threats.'

'He doesn't and I don't doubt that someone's keeping an eye on us. But I'm hoping he's counting on our being paralysed with fear. And God knows I am. But maybe, maybe he'll be just a shade less vigilant at the moment since he went to such lengths to psych us. Anyway, this is our only chance to make a getaway.'

'Where would we go?'

'If we're lucky we disappear to some tiny place. We lie low till it's safe. That's if there's any place in the country safe from Bashirbhai.'

'For how long?'

'I don't know. We'll have to play it by ear.'

'I'll have to be back within a fortnight. You know that Belle's coming back to India.'

Ravan smiled for the first time. 'Let's see if we make it to the shop first.'

* * *

Ravan peered out of the entrance to the chawl. He looked to the left and then to the right and pulled back immediately. Eddie rolled his eyes and smirked; Pawar was acting as if he was in a James Bond flick. 'Looks okay,' Ravan whispered and sprinted all the way to the municipal garbage van which was parked close to their shop these days since the truck depot was being concretized. He stopped and crouched behind a car. Eddie was getting a little tired of Ravan's cloak-and-dagger act. There was nothing happening here, the place was dead. The garbage dumper truck bursting with the refuse of the last two days stood as usual in the corner. Three cars were parked in the vicinity, an Ambassador and two Premier Padminis in front of Om Shanti Shanti Shanti. Amazing, how much the CWD Chawls had changed. Till a few years ago, a car driving into these premises would have created a minor sensation. Today many of the residents had refrigerators, some had graduated to air-conditioners and Bajaj two-wheelers, and some of the shop owners even owned cars. But there was no one around at this hour and if Ravan was banking on a melodramatic denouement with the mafia men appearing suddenly on the terraces with hand grenades and bombs and holding the chawl dwellers to ransom, or a sudden air attack strafing the two of them, Eddie would have been happy to point out to his friend that *The Guns of Navarone, The Dirty Dozen* and *Where Eagles Dare* had long since been taken off the local screens. The only option left to Ravan was to wake up the seven men sleeping on the pavement and ask them to strip just in case they were hiding who knows, bazookas or nuclear weapons on their persons. Eddie ran over to where Ravan was and squatted next to him.

'You stay here. I'll open the place. And if everything's okay I'll call you.'

'I'm coming with you.'

'No. You cover me just in case...'

'Sure, but where's my gun.'

First, Ravan conjures up the bogey of an impending Armageddon, Eddie smiled to himself, and then wants to take the enemy on single-handedly. Go ahead, Eddie thought, you want to be a hero, be my guest. Ravan had trouble finding the keyhole in the darkness and fitting the key in but now the lock clicked open. Eddie stood up to join his friend as Ravan pulled the horizontal bolt back and threw the doors open. He stepped in and the lights came on. Three men carrying automatic weapons and looking as phoney as Hindi film extras pretending to be international thugs were sitting on chairs in the shop.

Ravan had half expected that his precautions would come to naught. There was good reason why Bashir Akhtar was called Three Point One. He was always one up. During the years when he had been away from Bombay and was writing his unsigned missives to Ravan, he had often articulated his own beliefs and principles about what it took to be a leader, in his case, to be a mafia don, albeit one who was biding his time in the wilderness. Fear, he stressed, was of primary importance. And to that end, firepower and brute force were absolutely essential, but never enough. It was the element of surprise that was the key factor. Tonight was a classic example of his strategy, both were available in equal measure. But something was amiss. All three men were speaking Marathi and one of them looked oddly familiar.

'Suswagatam. Welcome, welcome. You sure made us wait a long time.' One of the men spoke in Marathi and the coin dropped. Jagannath Jadhav. Ravan realized that he had been so obsessed with Three Point One that he had overlooked the one man who had the most pressing reason to come looking for Eddie and him.

'How did you get in?' Ravan's voice was an unsteady croak. He was surprised he could ask such an asinine question. Jagannath Jadhav was sitting in their shop; did it matter how he got in?

'We went to your home pretending to be customers. Your mother was very kind and told us that you would be going over to your shop. But since you weren't there, we decided to wait for you. One of my men, Arjun, was a professional lock-picker before he joined me. Then I had the brilliant idea of giving you a surprise. He locked us in and left. I see from your reaction that it was better than that, a real shocker. Waiting in the dark could have been a little difficult but there was enough light from the ventilators to play teen patti and the time just flew. But enough chatter. You really should take better care of your shop. Not that it will matter any more. I just want to return the favour you did me.'

The CWD Chawls were gradually switching off lights and going to bed and Eddie could hear every inflection in the man's voice. Damn, he was still standing in the glow of the light from the shop. Eddie quickly moved behind the municipal garbage van, trying to figure out who that man was and what those black tar-like packets wired to each other were doing on the walls, on the main loadbearing column of the building and the iron beam in the ceiling of the shop. And then it hit him. That voice belonged to that man who had done the dance of death on the pyre. How could Eddie ever forget him? If only he had not been so smart-arsed, if only he had taken Ravan seriously, he might have been more vigilant and perhaps detected that something very suspicious was going on.

'I'm afraid I don't quite understand.'

'Oh, I think you do, Shri Ravan Pawar. But I'm more than willing to explain. I'm delighted to invite you to your own funeral. It's going to be the most expensive funeral the country has seen. You'll be proud of it. We'll bathe you with the finest foreign perfumes. Channel-Flannel, Black Satin, White Satin, everything imported we'll pour on you. We'll call Lata-ji and Anup Jalota-ji to sing bhajans in your memory. It will cost a packet-and-a-half but cost is no consideration since you are so fond of music.'

Ravan shook his head in despair. 'What are you talking about, Jadhav Saheb? You owe your life to us.' Ravan too switched to Marathi, hoping that their common mother tongue might help establish a bond between them and perhaps even give his words some credibility.

Jesus Christ, those wired black packets must be explosives. This Jadhav was planning to blow up the whole building. The wire connecting the black stuff had to lead out of the shop, Eddie figured, if Jadhav and gang who had planted the device were not to be blown up with it. Where the hell was it?

'*Abey maderchod*, do you think you can make an ass of me twice over?' The suave if rather overdone sarcasm had been replaced by something far more uncouth, a vivid and violent street idiom. 'There I was being roasted on top of a pyre of sandalwood, screaming and begging you and your friend to save me, and what did you two do? You kept looking as if you were watching a Charlie Chaplin comedy. Now it's my turn. I'm going to watch a Laurel and Hardy film of a double funeral right up to the end and laugh my head off.' He looked at his companions with a conspiratorial air. 'That's what we're going to do, aren't we? We're going to have a rollifucking funny time.'

There it was, Eddie heaved a sigh of relief, the wire had been covered unevenly with earth but showed up behind the garbage dumper truck. Good work, he thought, and utterly pointless. How was he going to neutralize the trigger device?

'We had nothing to do with what happened to you. We are as much victims as you are. Even more so because we were innocents caught in the crossfire between two enemies. Om Shanti Shanti Shanti, our funeral service, was merely told to make arrangements for someone who had passed away. When we reached Shagun, we were handed a death certificate with the name of Haridas Pandey and a dead body with the head covered. How could we have possibly known you weren't Pandey but Jagannath Jadhav.'

Eddie opened the door of the garbage truck softly and looked for the keys. The driver Tawade always kept them under the foot mat but they weren't there tonight. Damn, if he didn't start the truck in the next minute or two, Ravan would be no more and neither would the building. His eyes wandered frantically all over the inside of the driver's cabin. The van should have been sent to the junkyard at least twenty years ago. The seat was torn, the floor had a gaping hole, the door at the other end opened any time it felt like it, the rear-view mirror was broken and even the plastic altar housing the small Ganesh image was cracked and held together with a piece of green wire. As to the engine, it was more temperamental than any superstar. It only worked on odd dates or maybe it was the other way round.

'A likely story. Bhai must have planned the whole operation down to the last detail since the time he started to make overtures to me at least half a year ago. He wouldn't have left the most crucial aspect of his plans to the last minute. I bet you didn't know that Bhai and I go a long way back.'

All the way back to your umbilical cord, Ravan thought. You are his son but will not acknowledge it. That's why you joined the enemy and became the boss. I know your history since there was a time when your father used to write confessional letters to me.

'Don't look so surprised, friends fall out and enemies make up. That happens all the time.'

'Look around, Jadhav Saheb. If we were part of his team, why would Bhai's men pay us a visit and wreck everything in our shop?'

'I must ask your forgiveness, Ganesh-ji,' Eddie told the elephant-headed god on the dashboard, 'but I need to hotwire the van.'

'Maybe you are innocent and maybe you are guilty as the devil himself,' Jagannath Jadhav said. 'What difference does it make? All I know is that you tried to burn me alive and made a laughing stock of me. I've done my best to suppress the story but word gets around. In my line of work that is the greatest taboo. No one, not even a babe in the crib, will take you seriously after that. There's only one remedy for it. The rule is simple. The punishment has to be totally out of proportion to the provocation. See that black clay-like stuff on the loadbearing beams. Doesn't it remind you of the plasticene we used to play with as children? It's called RDX these days and it's the hottest explosive in the international conflict zones. The results are absolutely spectacular. I thought we should try it out. My men have wired the whole place. I promised you disproportionate retribution. Payback time raised by a factor of ten. You are going to get just that. We are going to blow up not only your shop, but the whole building. All those who had lost faith and stopped trembling when the name of Jagannath Jadhav was uttered will regain it in a hurry along with the rigor. But first we need to know where your business partner is.'

'Oh him, he was so shaken by what happened to our shop this afternoon, he couldn't take it,' Ravan explained patiently. 'Between you and me, he has a nervous temperament. Some would call him a coward. I think it was just nerves. He's gone to stay with his aunt in Borivali. Her son is in Dubai and Eddie's going to join him there.'

One of Jadhav's assistants slammed his gun into Ravan's jaw. Eddie could see Ravan going down and the man kicking him before he crumpled on the floor.

'No, no, no. Look what you've gone and done. The poor chap's bleeding.' Jadhav seemed genuinely upset. 'Don't you know there are other ways to elicit information? Just tie his hands and feet and we'll run the car over his legs. He won't stop talking then.'

'Shall I tell you the truth, Jadhav Saheb? We've been waiting to meet you.'

'Because you are in such a fucking hurry to die?' Jadhav laughed melodramatically. 'You must take me for a real greenhorn to believe your bullshit stories.'

Ravan looked Jagannath Jadhav in the eye. It was a cold, hard look unamused by Jadhav's outburst.

'We're going to eliminate Bhai. You are welcome to join hands with us or we will go it alone.'

'*Abey chutiye*, do you have any idea who or what Bhai is? He'll wipe out a hundred or more like you before you can bat an eyelid.

Besides, Bhai is mine and mine alone. I'll take care of him. So stop wasting my time. Now where's your friend, Eddie Coutinho?'

'Bless me, auspicious god, help me rescue Ravan.' The lights of the garbage van came on blindingly and pinned the gangsters in the Om Shanti, Shanti, Shanti premises. The van drove into the shop. Jagannath and his men ran out, screaming, to one of the Padminis parked outside.

Ravan was running around the shop, yanking at the wires, disconnecting them from the RDX or whatever this fancy new explosive was called. Eddie reversed and rammed into the Premier Padmini, raised one end of the dumper and threw the other end open. The fermenting garbage came sliding down over the bonnet and windscreen of Jagannath Jadhav's car just as it was about to take off and piled up a little knoll atop the roof.

Ravan pulled hard one last time and the trigger device came undone. He placed it carefully under the front wheel of the garbage truck. Eddie flung the door open and hissed, 'Get in. Now. Did you hear what I said? Now. I'm off, Ravan. Bye.' Ravan ran back into the shop and opened the cupboard. There was no time to unlock the safe, instead Ravan pulled it right out and clambered in as the van crunched the trigger device and took off.

* * *

Falling … falling … falling…

Dear Eddie,

Good news. Asmaan and I've found a law firm in L.A. here who are copyright experts. Since they are planning to open an office in India, they have been in touch with someone who worked in their office many years ago and will now be a partner in their firm. He will cost an arm and a leg but his charges will not be paid from our pockets. They are keen to take on a high-profile case that will give their firm instant visibility in India. Don't forget they will not touch anything that they are not sure of winning. They will be registering two cases. One, to get back every centimetre of Jaan Se Pyara Dushman *that the banks and financiers took possession of. Simultaneously, they will demand a humongous sum for the damage done to your reputation when you were at the top of your profession by claiming that you were responsible for the mayhem created by the encounter between the police and the dacoits. Their fees will be deducted from the damages that will be due to you from the other party since our case is that they unlawfully took over what was your and your property alone.*

One last thing. Asmaan will not forgive me if she learns that I have told you this. Both she and I are buying new apartments on an instalment plan. You threw us out of your homes the last time. Never again. Next time we'll kick you out whenever Ravan and you misbehave with us. Nari Zindabad. Victory to all women.

Can't wait to be in your arms.

Love,

Belle

* * *

'So you think I'm a coward?' Eddie enquired as he struggled to change from second to third gear.

'What? What are you talking about?'

'You told Jadhav I was a bundle of nerves and a rat who had abandoned you.'

'I was stalling for time.' Ravan unlocked the safe and stuffed as much money as possible into his pockets and the rest into Eddie's.

'I'm the one who rescues you while they think you are the hero.'

'I don't believe this, you are worried about what those thugs think of you?'

'Sure, I don't want them to think that I'm a pushover.'

'So why are we running for our lives, hero?'

'I'm not. I'm just saving your arse.'

Eddie would have liked to pursue the subject but the truck demanded all his attention and skill. It was becoming increasingly clear that he had failed to grasp the nature of the beast. It was an earthquake on wheels. Its sole purpose was to dismantle and dismember itself as much as to unhinge anyone who had the gall to drive it or ride in it. The different parts inside it were at war. They jarred and juddered and ground into each other. How had the driver, Tawade, kept the dumper afloat and running when it was straining at the seams to fall apart? It was a miracle that he himself had survived the contraption. By all the laws of shake, rattle and roll or the science of vibrations, every cell in his body should have self-destructed along with the garbage truck a long time ago.

The truck thundered along, chased by hordes of stray dogs, and woke up thousands of birds, sending them flying from the safety of their nests into the night sky. By now it was evident that their current vehicle was all clamour and fracas but hardly had any speed even though the accelerator was all the way down. Eddie and Ravan were too tense to discuss their next move but in any case communication at this point was redundant. Their options were less than limited. Mohammed Ali Road and the burkhas were out now. If they were lucky they would abandon the truck at Victoria Terminus and board any, but any train leaving for wherever before those goons caught up with them. Men and women from the lean-tos and mats on the pavements blinked open their eyes to check if the juggernaut would run them over and went to sleep again.

The road was clear and the dyspeptic engine seemed to be settling down. Eddie was watching the road at the back as much as the road ahead. The smog was bad, it always was, especially in the dockyard area because of the exhaust from all those trucks and the dust, but you could still make out who was following you in the cracked rear-view mirror. So far so good. They were on P. D'Mello Road. Who the hell was this D'Mello, Eddie wondered. Not too many roads were named after Catholics in Bombay. They had left the Bombay Port Trust Quarters behind and then Wadi Bundar and were close to the Princess Docks when a dog ran across and Eddie swerved sharply to miss him. The dumper leaned heavily to the left as if wanting to lie down, but Eddie brought it back to a more stable centre of gravity and then swore. 'Oh shit, I can see the Padmini.'

'How far is it?' Ravan queried.

'It's closing in fast. They are driving without lights. That's why I must have missed them.'

'Take a left at the next lane and another to the right and park. We'll try and get a cab.'

Eddie swerved sharply left, then right. 'And then what?'

But 'And then what' had already come to pass. The engine made loud obscene sounds, as if it was trying to throw up while simultaneously farting, and gave up the ghost. Eddie slipped the wires with which he had started the engine in and out, desperately trying to stab the ignition into action.

'There's no petrol in the tank.' Ravan pointed to the dashboard and jumped out. They were running as if their tails were on fire. They must have covered at least five hundred metres when Ravan fell behind.

'What's the problem?'

'I think you should stop while I keep running.'

'Why?' Eddie looked bemused and not a little irritated. 'Why would I want to stop?'

'Because like you said you don't want Jagannath to think that you are a wimp.'

'Ravan, you fuckface, I didn't kill you when you bumped my father off but I'll get you yet.'

They ran, switching from one dingy lane to another. Eddie looked back and saw the ghost of a Padmini moving swiftly in the darkness. It was covered with what looked like surreal floral decorations and ribbons, and on its radio antenna hung the top half of a watermelon. A gun went off. Suddenly it was dead quiet and the two friends heard the car accelerate. They were in good shape but they couldn't possibly outrun Jagannath Jadhav's car. That's it, it was the end of the road for them. They were in front of the Mandvi Fire Station. The two friends looked at each other and had the same thought. They ran into the fire station and climbed up to the third floor.

All hell broke loose then. Every alarm in the world seemed to go off at the same time and the firemen were running hither and thither, slipping into their uniforms, shoes and helmets, and sliding down the polished brass pole that reached all the way down to the ground floor.

'What luck,' Eddie sighed and sank into one of the empty beds. 'Sometimes God actually hears us mortals, and what's more important, answers even a poor sinner's prayers. Good night, Ravan.'

Ravan went to the head of the stairs and peered down. 'Jadhav and his men are on their way up.'

'You're kidding. I was sure we gave them the slip.'

You could hear the footsteps on the stairs. Ravan yanked a fireman's suit off its hanger, threw it at Eddie and got into one himself. They were about to pole down when Eddie rushed back, picked up two helmets, plonked one on Ravan's head, slapped the other on his own and slithered behind Ravan.

'What took you so long?' the driver of the last fire engine waiting to leave the station screamed at them.

'Where's the fire, man?' Eddie asked.

But his attempt at humour was lost on the driver. 'The Taj Mahal Hotel. Seven engines are already there and they are asking for more. This is the big one. Where the hell are the others?'

Eddie shrugged his shoulders.

'I can't wait any longer.'

The fire engine shot out and turned left in a sweeping arc. Three firemen darted out of the station, and caught the behemoth on the run. Ravan and Eddie gave them a hand and pulled them up on to the vehicle. No point hanging around with these guys though and getting spotted. Ravan signalled to Eddie and they clambered to the top where the telescoped ladder lay flat on its back.

The roads were almost empty but the driver had switched on the siren at full volume. There was something desperately urgent Ravan wanted to remember but the siren kept drilling into his brain cells and was blanking out everything else. What was it? His mind had jammed up. Damn. And then it came to him. In one of his missives, Three Point One had written that the only reason he had outlasted the competition was because he never made a move till he had Plan B in place. Not just that, Plan B had to be at least as good as Plan A.

Actually, it had to be better, since something unexpected had to have occurred for him to dump the first plan. But there were times when, the mafia don had added, everything was working like clockwork and yet he switched to Plan B. That was because the only thing you can trust in this life is your instinct, what they call gut feeling. Bhai had a maxim from which he never strayed: There's only one way you can trust anybody in this life. Betray him before he betrays you. Better still, eliminate him before he eliminated you.

Nobody was asking Ravan his opinion on the subject, certainly not the two mafia bosses who were out to get Eddie and him, but there was one piece of advice in that litany of hate which he should have followed through on the night Jagannath Jadhav had risen from the dead. Instead of just Plan A and B, Eddie and he should have worked out the whole alphabet of plans. Even now, as they faced almost certain death, they still had no plan whatsoever.

'Whose bright idea was this?' Eddie asked Ravan. 'I can't believe we actually chose to jump from the frying pan into the fire. What now?'

They were already at the Prince of Wales Museum. Ravan would have to do some quick thinking if they were to escape from Jadhav and Bhai. He was not sure if Eddie had grasped who they were up against. 'There's bound to be chaos at the Taj. Let's jump off the fire engine as it's about to pull in at the hotel and vanish into the crowds who will be watching this real-life *Towering Inferno*.'

'What if we lose each other?'

'We meet at the booking office for long-distance trains at VT.'

The southern skies were ablaze with a wondrously changing son et lumière tableau. The colour of the night was the sacred saffron of the Hindus. Chinese dragons with long dancing tails and even longer tongues greedily licked the sky. Ravan could not fathom how a heedlessly ravenous conflagration could look so bewitching.

'Eddie.' The fire engine took a turn to the right at the Gateway of India.

'Yes?' Eddie waited for an answer. 'What?'

'Just in case we miss each other, or something should happen to me, all the best. Say bye to Asmaan, my mother and Belle from me.'

'What crap! Why will we miss each other?'

'Too many unknowns, that's all.'

The fire engine was already at the Taj Mahal Hotel. Ravan crouched to jump out and was about to slip into the thousands of people gathered to watch the fireworks but Eddie pulled him back. 'Look to ten o'clock.' Ravan glanced surreptitiously from under the visor of his helmet and saw Jagannath Jadhav and his men giving the firemen a once-over and then another. The snorkel ladder from their fire engine was going up and Eddie joined the other firemen waiting to climb it with Ravan behind him. Smoke was billowing out from the top of the six-storeyed Taj Mahal Hotel like some monstrous exotic black flower from the nether world. Ten-foot-by-ten-foot glass panes came crashing down and the flames leapt and lashed out wildly from the vacant windows.

Down below, the drama in the sky rocked ominously in the oily tar of the ocean. The owners of dozens of motorboats parked in the gooey black around the Gateway must have sensed the commercial opportunity in the fire and were offering the growing crowds late-night tours to view the spectacle from the sea. In the distance, ocean liners blinked and semaphored to each other and a couple of oil tankers blew their fog horns. More fire engines were converging on the hotel every minute and spilling out firemen. Sparks from the fireworks stung every nook and corner of Eddie's face and the taste of the acrid smoke raked his throat. It was a wonder that anybody would be fool enough to volunteer for this job. Eddie certainly wasn't going to. He was already climbing down.

'I'm going home.'

'Look down.' The three men who had dropped by at the Om Shanti Shanti Shanti shop and blasted it with their AK-47s were scanning the faces of the firemen while police contingents at the other end were trying to push the crowds back.

'I can't. I get vertigo on free-floating heights. I don't give a damn who's waiting down there for us. Move.'

'Don't do this, Eddie. We'll figure something out.'

'Who the hell are you to tell me what I can or can't do?' Eddie's foot was resting on Ravan's shoulder. 'Move or I'm going to kick you down three floors.'

'Go ahead.'

'Don't try your luck, Ravan. Get out of my way.'

Ravan didn't budge and anyway Eddie couldn't possibly go down now. The three men who had boarded the fire engine after them were egging Ravan to move his butt.

'You can't get in on the third floor,' the fireman ahead of Eddie yelled at him. 'The fourth is out since the fire might already have spread to it. We've been told to go to the top floor where the suites are and work our way down.'

Eddie swore at Ravan and gave him a dirty look as if he was responsible for the fire. He closed his eyes and began reciting desperate Hail Marys as he climbed up and stretched his right leg out from the ladder and stepped off the window into a dark room. Ravan spotted him just as he disappeared into the bathroom, shouting, 'Just pissing. Go ahead, I'll join you in a minute.' The other firemen rushed out while Ravan pretended to tie his shoelaces. The bathroom door opened a chink and Eddie peered out. 'Anybody around?'

'Nope. Let's go.'

Eddie was out of the room with Ravan at his heels. They were running blindly across the long corridors of the Taj. The smoke had become so dense, they couldn't figure out whether they were running towards the staircase or away from it. One moment the fire flew and attacked the ceiling, the next it was racing across the floor and in between it was devouring the antique wooden balustrade in the corridors.

'I don't understand it, how the hell did the fire jump from the third to the fifth floor? That's completely illogical.'

'Stop, Eddie, stop. We need to get our bearings right. Otherwise we'll never get out alive.'

Time was running out. If they didn't find a way out in the next couple of minutes, Jagannath Jadhav's wish was going to come true, they were going to be burnt alive. They had to do some quick thinking. The Taj faces the east – that much Ravan was sure about.

That is, if you didn't buy that apocryphal story about the architect, or maybe it was the contractor-cum-builder, having made a blunder and switched what was meant to be the harbour-facing front to the back, and the nondescript back to the sea. The problem was there was no way of telling which was the east or any of the other directions in this impenetrable smoke storm. A few metres away a door was flung open and through a rent in the smoke screen they could hear a woman screaming.

'*Mon bébé, mon bébé*. Someone 'elp me, please.'

Ravan and Eddie watched her silently. She was babbling non-stop and running around distractedly, tears streaming down her cheeks. 'Somebody 'elp me. Please, I beg you. *S'il vous plaît, aidez-moi, je vous en prie*.'

What was she doing here? The fire brigade people had said that the whole hotel had been vacated.

'French,' Eddie whispered.

'How would you know?'

'Because I studied French in school under Mr Lobo.'

'*Merde, merde, merde*,' she said.

'What's she saying?'

'I think she said Oh God, oh God, oh God.'

'Don't show your face or she might think we've been sent to rescue her.'

'Mon Dieu, *je vous en prie. Ayez pitié de moi*.'

'What's she saying now?'

'How would I know?' Eddie sounded peeved.

'You just said that you studied French.'

'Give me a break. That was twenty, maybe thirty years ago.' Suddenly he smiled disarmingly, throwing Ravan off-guard. 'I failed in French every year. Mr Lobo called me his only failure in life.'

There was a huge blast as if a bomb had exploded next door and Ravan and Eddie dove for the floor. A ball of fire the size of a baby elephant whooshed past, scorching their faces.

'Where the hell is she?' Ravan asked as the ball of fire receded.

'The stairs. She must be headed for them.'

They could hear someone sobbing loudly and then the woman, who Eddie claimed spoke French, materialized out of the swirling smoke. She saw the two of them and started howling. What had they done, why was she blubbering and bawling? '*Merci, mon Dieu, merci beaucoup.*' Her next move was even more puzzling. She flung herself at Eddie and embraced him and then it was Ravan's turn. Her hair was dishevelled and tears had left black smudges on her face. 'God is great. 'E answered my prayers and sent you.'

English had never sounded so strange and beautiful to Ravan. He wished he could mimic her accent not out of meanness or because he wanted to make fun of her but because it sounded so delicate and enchanting. She was tiptoeing on the words like a ballet dancer. And now she was dragging the two of them inside the Seventh Heaven suite.

It was a miniature palace made of exquisite mahogany, sheesham and cedar. It was also a paradise for fires. The place was full of antique furniture, some of it collectors' items, from the time that Jamsetji Tata built the hotel at the turn of the twentieth century. There were carved cupboards, a floor-to-ceiling wardrobe, a sideboard, an ebony dining table for eight, a roll-top desk, a secretaire, a mahjong table inlaid with rare woods of various hues, antique chairs, a chaise longue, a white jade chess set, a love seat, not to mention an intricately patterned and polished parquet floor. As if this was not a prescription for a holocaust, there were swathes and swathes of lavish drapes of silk at the windows, flouncing and swirling around various doors to the inner rooms and cascading down walls for no better reason than that the interior decorator had money to throw around. A portrait of the Emperor Shah Jehan inhaling the perfume of a rose fell from the wall and began to curl up as a flame licked it.

Eddie said, 'Non. Non.'

'*Parlez vous Francais? Quelle aubaine.*' That was it, the floodgates had been thrown open and wave after wave of foaming, frothing, breakneck French engulfed them.

Eddie realized he had put his foot into it and tried hurriedly to interrupt the gush but there was no stopping the lady. Finally he managed to get in a few words.

'Staircase. We are looking for the staircase.'

'I show you but first you save my Roland.'

'Who's Roland?'

'*Mon bébé.*'

'That's the firemen's job.'

'But you are firemen.'

'Sorry. We're fakes.' Ravan smiled sweetly at her. She looked bemused. 'We're just actors. On the wrong set. And in the wrong movie.'

'What you mean no firemen? How you wear uniform?'

'Just show us the staircase and we'll send the real fire brigade. I mean it.'

'Save my bébé, please. I beg you. He's sleeping in his room behind that door.'

'Then why don't you save your little angel?'

'I can't open the door. I try and try. 'Is nanny don't answer. I can't find the ADC either. Please, please, before something happen to my baby.'

Poor Emperor Shah Jehan, the only relic left from his portrait was the rose in his hand. Ravan's eyes were streaming from the stinging smoke and the heat was unbearable. All three of them should have been charred and turned to ashes by now but the room was huge and somewhere in that engorged smoke there must have been a vent which let in night breezes from the sea. It brought a breath of fresh air into the place for a minute and then fanned the fires even brighter. The glass in the windows went ping and crashed down in multiple shards on the floor.

'Let's go, Eddie. It's too late to do anything for the boy,' he whispered. 'The child must have been suffocated with the fumes a long time back.'

'Non. Non. Don't say that. Mon petit Roland is alive. I give you big reward.'

Shoot, the blaze was making such a racket, how the hell could she have heard him? Who was this woman, anyway? Her French and her accent were getting on his nerves now. I'll give you a reward. Sure, after we are all dead. Did she really think that they were going to fall for that oldest of gags?

'He's long dead,' Ravan said brusquely. No point mincing words now. 'Come on Eddie, let's go.'

As if on cue just then there came a childish, plaintive call. 'Maman. Maman.' The brat had a superb sense of timing.

'Roland, *mon bébé, mon cheri,* Maman will be with you in a minute. *Ou est ta nounou,* Therese?'

'Elle dort par terre.'

'Elle dort? Mais pour quoi?' The mother looked puzzled. ''E says the nanny is sleeping on the floor. 'Ow can that be?'

This time she didn't bother to plead with the two men to come to her help but kept banging against the door, trying to force it open. Ravan shook his head. So be it, he would rather die here than at the hands of Jagannath Jadhav or Three Point One.

'Stand aside,' Eddie told her peremptorily. The two men pushed hard at the solid mahogany door. No luck. They ran back some distance to get a good start and slammed into it full speed. It did not budge.

'This is not going to work,' Eddie muttered. 'We've got to try something else.'

'Is there another door leading to your son's bedroom?' Ravan asked the weeping mother. For the first time she seemed to grasp that she had lost her child.

'Non, there was one in the bathroom but eet's totalement blocked off and covered with a mirror.'

'Show me,' Eddie said.

She was right. There was a bathroom the size of the Coutinho home in CWD Chawl Number 17. A repressed hiss was coming from behind the mirror, and smoke kept escaping and clouding the glass. Eddie touched the glass surface and leapt back as if he had been electrocuted.

The silvery aluminium at the back of the mirror had begun to melt rapidly. Eddie was holding his hand under the cold water tap when the mirror exploded and spattered on the floor like fine crystal sugar. The plywood on which the mirror had been hung was now ash.

The fire from the adjoining bedroom lunged forward as if to torch them.

'This doesn't look good,' Eddie said.

'Not good at all.' Ravan took a deep breath and was already across the rectangular hole in the wall and on the other side. Eddie wrapped a wet towel around his hand and closed his eyes: he had to get this right or he was done for. He was into the next room, rubbing his arm where the sleeve of his fireman's jacket had been torn.

The bedroom was a war zone. A beam from the ceiling had collapsed and had felled a man dressed in a naval uniform at the door. The wiring leading to the fridge had short-circuited. The machine had blown apart, sundering the steel casing and everything in it, and a shard from a Coca-Cola bottle had pierced the throat of the nanny who was lying doubled up on the floor. Ravan looked at the bed. It was empty, just a blanket lying crumpled on it. He was flat on the floor now, peering under. No sign of the boy. Time was no longer running out. It was over and out.

The fire was flitting all over the place and blocking the view. Eddie hop-step-and-jumped around the room, looking for Roland.

'He's not here,' he yelled out. Ravan was staring absent-mindedly at his smoking right shoe as if it was someone else's.

'What do you mean he's not here?' Ravan queried. 'You heard him just as clearly as I did.'

'Maybe he jumped out of the window.'

A sliver of fiery wood dislodged itself from the ceiling and plummeted down. Eddie tried to quickly move out of its path but it balanced on his shoulder and back for a second before he shook it off.

'Let's go, let's go, let's go.' He helped Ravan up. 'Let's get the hell out of here.'

Suddenly he was screaming in horror and pain. The burning block of wood had done its job well. A spark had slipped through the rent and now the fire was roaming freely inside the thick sleeve of the fireman's woollen jacket. Ravan whipped off the blanket from the bed and wrapped it tightly around Eddie.

'What the fuck you think you're doing, Ravan?' Ravan wouldn't let go of his friend till the blanket had blocked any oxygen reaching the fire in Eddie's jacket. Eddie's eyes were wide open, as if he was witnessing the act of creation itself, and as bright as the fire. 'Jesus,' he said softly. 'Bless the Lord and bless the Virgin Mother and the fire that tried to burn me. I love you, Ravan.'

Poor Eddie, Ravan shook his head, he had no idea that fire unhinged people. His friend was obviously having a vision of some sort. Ravan turned around. Roland was lying on the bed, his tiny hands balled up into little fists and his eyes shut tight.

28

The helicopter woke Ravan up. He wondered why it was wheeling around all over the place. Were they looking for Eddie and him? Fortunately, both of them were lying on the ground next to the water fountain under the last arch of the Marine Drive flyover.

Going back to CWD Chawl Number 17 the previous night had not been an option since their homes were under surveillance. Ravan's right foot was swollen and hurting badly and Eddie's arm was red and raw and just right to eat if you were into a rather unorthodox variety of roast meat. They had been completely dehydrated and there was not a single restaurant open. The only place they would find water at that time of the night was the pyau built under the Marine Drive flyover by a charitable organization. They thought they would drink for at least an hour and empty half the tank and then head for either VT or Bombay Central, but four draughts and Eddie was prostrate on the ground.

'No, Eddie, no. We decided come what may, we are taking the first train available. If we're lucky, both Jadhav and Bhai will think we didn't survive the fire.'

'Two minutes, just two minutes and I will have recharged my batteries and be as good as new. Promise.'

'Two minutes. Not a minute more.' Ravan had every intention of waking Eddie up and catching that train. All he wanted to do was rest his injured foot for a minute, that's all.

When Ravan had finally opened his eyes, he realized that there was some mistake. The sun was in the wrong place. It couldn't possibly be that late. It wasn't even five minutes since he had laid down. He got up and sat upright. It was all Eddie's fault. 'Wake up, Eddie, wake up,' he called out frantically. 'Do you know what time it is? How could you go to sleep when I told you not to?'

Eddie refused to open his eyes. 'Leave me alone, Ravan. I don't give a damn if Seven Point Three or Jagannath bumps us off. I'm not getting up.'

That was the end of the conversation. Ravan took the stainless steel tumbler chained to a pipe next to the fountain, filled it to the brim and flung it over Eddie's head. Eddie turned on his side. Ravan was emptying the fourth mug when a taxi slowed down and the driver got out.

'Hey, does that fountain belong to your father-in-law that you are wasting water like it was…' The man didn't finish the sentence. 'Oh my God.' He stared first at Ravan and then at Eddie. 'It's you two. I don't believe it. I just saw your pictures in the papers.' A black Mercedes went past silently like an eerie shadow. 'They are looking for you.'

Eddie opened his eyes, looked at Ravan a long moment, shook the water off like a dog and said, 'I'm going to kill you, Ravan.'

'Who's looking for us?' Ravan grabbed the man by the collar, pushing him against the concrete wall.

'The police, the President's wife, everybody. It's in all the papers. You're hurting me.'

'Yeah, sure.' Ravan let go of him. 'She wants to get into bed with me, whoever she is.'

'You don't believe me? You are heroes. I'm taking you with me to the Oberoi Hotel. I want my reward for locating you.'

'*Abey, kisko chutiya bana rahé ho*?' Eddie's voice was even more threatening than Ravan's. 'Piss off. Go tell your fantastic tales to some other suckers.'

'The French President wants to meet the two heroes who saved his wife and son. Later on you both will get big medals, best they have in France. But just now anybody who's got news of you or your whereabouts will get a reward. That's me. My photograph will be in the papers too.' The man went over to his taxi, and brought back a newspaper with him.

'Look, look at these pictures.'

There they were on the front page with a thirty-six-point bold headline HEROES below the masthead of *Bittambatmi* and a photograph of the two of them on either side of the French woman they had met last night. She was carrying Roland, covered in a towel, while Eddie carried the nanny in his arms and Ravan, the naval officer. That paper was Ravan's father's mandatory daily reading. It had abandoned its inflexible format and splashed six of the eight pages with the pictures of the rescue of the French President's wife and their son, Roland. There were also photographs of the nanny, one Miss Delarue, and the dead ADC, Captain Gilbert Montand.

The copy told of the heroic deeds of Ravan and Eddie who had saved baby Roland, removed the glass shard from the nanny's neck, revived her and carried Captain Montand down instead of letting him burn in the fire. There were interviews with Mrs Coutinho and Mrs Pawar and here was the biggest surprise, page-long interviews with Eddie and Ravan, describing every second of 'Operation Saviours'. It was an absolutely marvellous cliff-hanger of a fabrication and they should have been delighted. From being the angels of death at Om Shanti Shanti Shanti, they had been transformed into the angels of deliverance and salvation. But the paper had as good as issued immediate death warrants for them.

Ravan looked at the firemen's uniform both Eddie and he were still wearing and whispered urgently to Eddie, 'The uniform. Get rid of it.' He was already ripping off his own jacket and slipping out of the trousers. The black Mercedes had taken a U-turn. Fortunately, it was going along the various Gymkhana grounds towards Nariman Point on the other side of the road.

'Good idea. No point wearing that uniform now. Come on, get in.' The taxi driver couldn't contain his excitement. 'It will be an honour to take you to the Oberoi in my cab. That's where the President and his family have shifted.'

'We'll find our way, don't worry,' Ravan told him brusquely.

'Please. I won't charge you for the ride.'

'No, thank you,' Eddie snapped at him. 'Please leave us alone.'

The taxi driver was crestfallen. 'I'll give you a cut from my reward. I want my picture in the papers with you.'

'Who's going to allow us to enter the Oberoi in these torn clothes?' Eddie asked. 'We haven't even had a shower yet.'

'You leave that to me.'

'Sure, you're such a big shot, you know Mr Oberoi personally.'

Eddie was about to start walking up the Marine Drive flyover when Ravan pushed him into the taxi. 'We've got company,' he muttered. Eddie looked back. The black Mercedes had once again turned round at the first traffic light and was heading in their direction. There was no mistaking who was sitting inside: Jagannath Jadhav and his three henchmen.

'You forgot your uniform.' The taxi driver picked up the firemen's clothes, dumped them in the seat next to him and shot out into the light afternoon traffic. He turned around at Wilson College and headed for the five-star hotel. Eddie was surprised to find that the French seemed to have invaded the city overnight. There were banners and hoardings in French everywhere. Even the Air India Maharaja was bowing and mouthing French on the huge hoarding.

The driver parked the cab by the sea.

'My name's Arbab. It means one who takes care of others. Just sit tight till I come back with someone who will take us inside.'

There were enough policemen at the Oberoi to repel a full-scale Pakistani naval attack on Nariman Point. But what was comic was the number of plainclothes CID men pretending to be tourists, loafers and vagrants in safari suits or crumpled kurta-paijamas. Arbab went over to the most disreputable-looking of the lot and produced his copy of *Bittambatmi*. He was back in a few minutes with the agent who could easily have passed off for a pimp at Foras Road. His mouth was full of tobacco and spittle.

'This is Premnath-ji. He's the chief CID inspector for South Bombay and head of the security operations today. We know each other since primary school. He wants to take a good look at you.'

Premnath. Just the right name, Eddie felt, for a plainclothes cop who would spread the gospel of love and nail you to the cross.

Eddie and Ravan got out of the cab and stood uncomfortably while Premnath-ji grabbed the newspaper from Arbab and kept going back and forth between the pictures and the original models. It was clear that he was not happy with what he saw but he was damned if he was going to either swallow or spit out the tobacco juice in his mouth to ask for some clarifications. He stabbed at the pictures of the two and kept shaking his upturned right hand in their faces. The two friends gathered that the CID man was querying them about something but hadn't a clue about what he was trying to get at.

Arbab had no problem following his schoolfriend's train of thought and immediately pulled out the firemen's jackets and trousers from the front seat of the taxi. That settled matters and the four of them crossed over to the Oberoi, Ravan limping badly but in an even greater hurry than the other three. Well, at least now they were away from the road. Premnath flashed his identity card, slung around his neck but hidden under his shirt, and was let in. The others would have to wait with the security guards at the glass doors.

'Where are they, our two heroes?' the manager, Mr Rodrigues, asked as he walked out of the glass doors with the CID officer. It was obvious that Premnath was still nursing the tobacco in his mouth. It would always remain a mystery how he had communicated with the manager of the hotel without opening his mouth. He raised his hand to bid the two men he had escorted goodbye. He had seen far too much in life to be impressed with good deeds or bad.

'Mother of God, the two of you stink to high heaven. Don't you read the papers? The President's going to leave for the airport after the skywalk demonstration. Couldn't you have changed into something more respectable?'

'Bye, Mr Rodrigues,' Eddie said sweetly. 'We don't wish to stink up your pricey hotel.'

'Do *you* read the papers, Manager Sahab?' the taxi driver went on the offensive on behalf of his two passengers. 'These people have been to hell and back to rescue the President's wife and son and the son's nurse. They were so exhausted, they haven't even been home but collapsed on the roadside.'

'I apologize for what I said. It's been a hectic time what with the President and his family and staff moving to our hotel so unexpectedly. Let's go to my office and I'll talk to the President's PA.'

* * *

'You're in luck. The President's wife insists that they will leave only after thanking you,' the manager informed the two visitors as he put the phone down. 'We are to meet them in the conference room in thirty minutes.'

'What about me?' Arbab refused to be left out. 'I was the one who brought them over.'

'Don't worry. You will get your reward.' He turned to Ravan. 'What size shirts and trousers do you wear?'

'Collar size 42 cm and 87 cm at the waist. For both of us.' Eddie thought it best to wind up this technical conversation. 'Medium size for the briefs.'

'In the meantime, you will go to the swimming pool stalls and take a quick shower. Your clothes will be delivered to you there.'

'We need to see a doctor. Ravan's foot is swollen and he can hardly walk because of the pain. And I've severe burns on my left arm.'

'I'll have the hotel doctor look at both of you.'

* * *

'We seem to have given the slip to Jagannath and Three Point One for the moment,' Ravan said to Eddie as they both showered in adjoining stalls, 'but while we may not see them, they're bound to be watching us. Where do we go once this French interlude is over?'

'How about asking our new guardian angel, Arbab, to drop us at VT as soon as the ceremony is through? I was thinking of taking the train to Goa. I could ask Belle to join us there. That way we'll avoid Bombay till things quieten down.'

Ravan would have liked to disabuse his friend by telling him that no place on the subcontinent, actually on the planet itself, was going to be safe for either of them but what was the point of adding to Eddie's woes.

'Let's get on any train we can. We'll take it from there. Maybe we'll be lucky and land up in Goa in a couple of days.'

The shower had revived them and the painkillers the doctor had given were beginning to work. They looked at themselves in the mirror. It was a long time since they had worn such fancy clothes. They looked good but there was no getting away from the fact that they had aged considerably in the last few days. They had been on a rollercoaster and now they were no longer sure whether they were part of a tragedy or a comedy, where reality ended and fantasy began. Just think of it. Were they really about to meet the President of France and his wife? Had Mrs President, or whatever her name was, forgotten that they had tried their best not to help her but to ditch her and run for their lives? If they had come through, it was not because they were selfless men of honour, nothing of the sort. They had been trapped between the standard 'devil and the deep' issue, it was as simple as that. And even at the last minute, when they had looked for the child, can you believe it, they had completely missed him and it was sheer chance that Eddie's arm was on fire and Ravan had pulled the blanket off the bed.

And here they were in the Regal Room in the basement of the hotel in front of a whole battalion of cameramen and press folk just as the President's wife was kissing them on their cheeks. She had tears in her eyes as she spoke with the help of a translator. 'In medieval times there used to be a test called ordeal by fire. The rule was that if you were innocent you would come out of the fire unharmed and whole. If, on the other hand, you were guilty, as witches and so-called apostates were, God made certain that the fire consumed you. My two friends here went through an ordeal by fire not for themselves but for me and my son. They fought against all odds: falling beams, pole-vaulting hydra-headed blazes, billowing smoke and suffocation. As you can see they both suffered severe burns and injuries but they rescued my son, Roland, his nurse who is in hospital, and me. Not just that, they brought back the body of the President's ADC. How can I ever thank them? If only there were a few more people like my new friends, the world would be a far better place.'

And now the President was telling Roland to shake hands with them and then he himself hugged them and invited them to Paris to receive the Legion d'honneur. The taxi driver, Arbab, too got a vote of thanks for escorting the two heroes to the Oberoi and the reward of ten thousand rupees. How in God's name, Eddie wondered, does one address the topmost honcho of France? Your Excellency? Your Honour? Couldn't possibly be Your Highness or Majesty. France, after all, was the mother of all democracies. Luckily, there was no time to thank the President and his wife since they were already late for an appointment before they left for the airport.

As the French entourage left by the rear door, Ravan saw someone familiar sitting at the end of the long room. Three Point One. The don gave Ravan a thumbs-up. It seemed the most natural thing in the world to find Bashir Akhtar sitting there quietly. Hadn't Ravan known all these years that the mafia boss and he were conjoined for life?

The journalists, TV reporters and cameramen were closing in around the new celebrities, waiting to interview them. 'Give us just two minutes to say our farewell to the President,' Eddie switched on his best fake smile, 'and we'll be right back.' Ravan tried to get Arbab's attention but the taxi driver was enjoying himself far too much being photographed and interviewed about where and how he happened to pick up the two heroes. The two celebrities slipped out and went up to the lobby. They ran across the road towards the Indian Express Towers and it was then they saw the black Mercedes making an illegal U-turn. All the cars on that no-entry road were honking furiously and blocking the progress of the offending vehicle to show their displeasure.

'Not the Express Towers,' Eddie cautioned Ravan. 'That's where Jagannath will think we're headed if he has seen us. The Air India building next door seems a better bet.'

The passage between the two buildings was closed to pedestrian traffic. The high-rise owned by the airline was under renovation and chunks of concrete and marble debris were hurtling down its sheer flank on to a net stretched like a trampoline between the fourth floors of the two buildings. They took a short detour and entered the Air India building. The security guard stationed in the lobby asked them to jot down the name of the party they wished to see and sign the visitors' register. Eddie signed Noel Menezes to see (there was bound to be a Pereira somewhere in that high-rise) Errol Pereira. Ravan's signature, Sagar Parmanand, had an even more elaborate flourish than Noel's.

They would have liked to take the elevator which went directly to the directors' floor at the very top and onto the terrace with the helicopter pad but that was out of the question since you needed to know a secret code to enter that lift. The doors of one of the other elevators opened and a dozen passengers stepped out. Eddie and Ravan got in quickly and hit the button for the top. Four well-dressed men who had just turned up waved frantically, hoping that one of the two passengers would push the 'stop' button and let them in. Eddie and Ravan waved them goodbye. Neither of them wanted company. They could breathe easy now. Ping, they had arrived at the very top, barring the directors' floor. A couple of workers were carting cement sacks up to the terrace and Eddie and Ravan followed them, picking their way alongside stacks of marble slabs which left hardly any space to walk. They stepped over the threshold and settled down in a corner on the Express Towers side. That way no one on the other side could spot them. A short, lean, wiry man in tight-fitting ballet-dancer's white clothes at the Arabian Sea-end of the Express Towers was yelling over the high parapet in an accent that was unmistakably French.

'Non, non. I'll cancel my walk if they don't remove the net. Il est simple. If there's no risk to life, there's no walk. Comprenez-vous?'

Debris from various floors kept crashing down. Eddie and Ravan had no idea what the Frenchman on the Express Towers was talking about but, whatever it was, all they wanted was a little quiet. They must have been very tired for they could barely keep their eyes open.

'Ravan. I thought you had given me the slip and I would never see you again.' Three Point One was standing at the other end of the terrace, surrounded by his henchmen who were armed with

Uzis while he himself was carrying a gun. As always, his voice was hypnotically soft and he spoke in bewitching Urdu. 'But I saw you and your friend from my helicopter as you hurried towards the Indian Express building. You were smart and entered the Air India building. Naturally I wanted to be here to welcome you and did an emergency landing on the terrace. Don't fret about the gun. It's merely a precautionary measure.' He pointed the blind eye of the gun at Eddie. 'It's going to blow your friend's brains out in a few minutes but you, Ravan, you merit special treatment. Oh, lest I forget, I checked on your story just in case. Good try. But now we know that the quantum of sleeping pills administered was more than adequate. We also know exactly what time you reached the electric crematorium. There's a gap of three hours that can't be accounted for. Ah Ravan, I trusted you. I sent business your way and what did you do? You betrayed your oldest friend.'

Ravan shook his head. 'You used me, that's all you did from the beginning. You conned us into thinking that someone was dead and we were to cremate the body. Imagine if we hadn't gone to the film at Roxy, we would have cremated your own son, Jagannath Jadhav, while he was still alive, and committed a murder.'

'Well, well, well. Signs of rebellion. At the risk of repeating myself, actions have consequences. And one of the consequences is your parents. It's a shame that they will have to pay for your misdeeds but it's a jungle out there, Ravan.'

'Leave my family out of this.'

'I'm afraid that's not possible. Someone's got to pay the price. Rest assured I won't do anything behind your back. I hate being long-winded. Just one comment and I will be done.'

Why was he listening to this man, Ravan asked himself. Why had he listened to him almost all his adult life? Why had he allowed Three Point One to terrorize him when he was not even thinking of him? The man was a constant static in his life that no Dolby system could eliminate. Yes, it was true that Bhai had disappeared from the scene for nearly a decade but Ravan had never been able to get rid of the noise. The concept of a father-confessor did not exist in either

Islam or Hinduism and yet Three Point One had appointed Ravan lifetime confessor. It went without saying that he had not bothered to consult Ravan in the matter.

There was something terribly malevolent about the handwritten missives. They came unsolicited and without a signature or an address. And no reply was possible or expected. Frankly, the notion of a reply would have horrified Bhai. His universe had room for only one person: himself. It was an order of self-absorption that considered his own son life-threatening. Misanthropy was the air he breathed. Everything and everybody, including his family, was not merely suspect and conspiring against Three Point One, but guilty without the remotest possibility of being proven innocent. The only way you could survive the depravity and insecurity of the man was to die before he murdered you in the most vicious and prolonged manner imaginable.

'I did some digging around and discovered that you have a Muslim lady friend. Quite a dish really though past her prime and a little overused. It appears she was more than obliging in the good old days when she, not to mention you both, were extras and needed work. Sleeping around with the union bosses is a hallowed tradition but when I proposed a little intimate tryst, the bitch suddenly acted coy and refused on the pretext that she was your woman. I had more urgent matters on my mind then but I will certainly visit her when all this is over. She's bound to come around. They always do.'

Ravan closed his eyes. He had let his parents down and he had let down the woman who had stood by him through his worst hours. He had taken his own time to discover that he loved her. But what use was that now? Try fighting two gangs of hardened criminals and murderers armed to the teeth when all you had was a eunuch's pride and the certain knowledge that both the mafia bosses would keep their word.

'Well, I've brought you up to speed. Now get into the copter.'

He aimed the gun at Eddie as two of his men walked towards Ravan to escort him. 'Time up, Coutinho. Say your last prayers.'

The man in white leotards was bending over the terrace wall of the Express Tower and screaming to someone down below once again. '*Non, non, non. Imbecile.*' He threw his hands up in the air and started shouting again. '*Comprenez vous, no net. No net.*'

The door of the Express Towers terrace burst open and Jagannath Jadhav and his men came out with their AK-47s blazing.

'Oh God, no.' Eddie dived for the floor, pulling Ravan down with him.

The crossfire was so intense it felt as if the bullets were not merely criss-crossing but meeting each other halfway and exploding. The goons sent to fetch Ravan crawled towards the door and locked it. A couple of bodies were lying inert and bleeding but there was no way to tell whether the men were wounded or dead. Bashir Akhtar and his remaining gang members were hiding behind the water tanks and occasionally venturing out for an instant and firing wildly.

Suddenly all was quiet. A police helicopter flew low overhead from over the sea. Above the racket of the blades, you could occasionally hear the pilot reporting to the head office about the flow of the traffic and the situation on the ground, making sure there were no untoward surprises in store for the French President, the first lady and their entourage as they left the hotel. Ravan waved out to the man in the cockpit and shouted that the danger was on the terraces and that he and his friend were about to be killed but the copter was already retreating over the sea.

The moment the whirring became distant, the two mafia bosses with their henchmen opened fire on each other again. This time there was no stopping them. If only they would wipe each other out totally, Ravan thought, Eddie and he would be able to make their escape. In all that noise and tension, Eddie and he had forgotten the Frenchman. He was bending over again and looking down the terrace wall at a rope stretched horizontally across to the Air India building and tied to a post a few floors below them. The Frenchman was shaking his head and banging his right hand against his forehead. '*Merde, merde, merde*. No luck, it's still there. Okay, I'll do a blind walk.'

Ravan craned his neck and peered out over the parapet. He couldn't believe his eyes. There were thousands of people gathered below, all of them looking up. And the oddest thing was that the French President, his wife and son were now on the terrace of the Oberoi. What were they doing there? For some unfathomable reason, the waif of a man in white leotards had climbed on to the parapet wall of the Express Towers. He picked up a long fibreglass pole leaning against the parapet and stood still with his eyes closed as if to internalize its feel and weight. What was he planning to do standing at that precarious height and that too on the ledge? Had the world gone completely insane?

'*Mon ami*, Jacques.' The President was now waving out to the Frenchman and talking to him on a bull horn from the Oberoi terrace. *'Bon courage. Vive la France. Vive l'amitié Franco-Indienne!'*

The man waved back to the President, made the sign of the cross and then, Virgin Mother of God, he tied a black cotton band around his eyes and stepped out on the wire, balancing himself delicately. And now he started walking very slowly, totally focused, one step at a time towards the Air India building. Believe it or not he was whistling. The gangsters had stopped firing. You could hear the crowd gasp. The man should have lost his balance and gone straight down but he seemed to be as surefooted as a man sleepwalking.

'Time to go, Eddie.'

'Go where?'

'We can't stay here and we can't take the stairs. Bashir Akhtar's going to open fire and kill us.'

'How do you know?

'The copter's coming back. Neither Three Point One nor Jagannath will fire at each other while the French President is on the Oberoi terrace and this man is doing his insane skywalk blindfolded. The moment the French President leaves, Jagannath and Bashir Akhtar will be at it again.'

'So what do you plan to do?'

'We'll just have to go over. That's our only chance.'

'Go over?'

'Over the edge.'

Sometimes Ravan spoke such crap, absolute and utter drivel.

'You've got to be joking.'

Instead of Ravan answering, Three Point One ordered the two men at the door, 'Get those two bastards. Now. Before the helicopter comes back.'

The two men started walking towards Eddie and Ravan but Ravan was already climbing on to the parapet.

'No time to hesitate, Eddie. Come on, let's leap into the unknown. It's exhilarating. You'll feel like a bird in the skies.'

Here he was, Eddie Coutinho, s/o Violet and the late – it had been a lifetime of 'late' – Victor Coutinho, suffering from such a bad panic attack, he couldn't breathe, he couldn't swallow his own spittle, he couldn't move. He was paralysed but that didn't prevent Ravan from dishing out dollops of Eastern or maybe it was just Hindu wisdom.

There was a violent draught of air as the copter began to do a U-turn out to the sea. There was no mistaking the sharp intake of breath from the crowd below as the taut rope swung wildly and the Frenchman struggled to keep his balance. Bashir Akhtar's men stood still halfway between the door and Ravan and Eddie, unable to breathe or move as they watched the man swaying in the middle of the tightrope. There was not a sound from the crowd below now.

What the hell was Ravan talking about standing there on the ledge? 'It's like nothing you've experienced before. Don't think about it. Just close your eyes and let go. It's the purest form of freedom. It's the closest you'll ever get to Nirvana.' How would he know what that is, you have to be dead to experience it. Besides, wasn't it meant only for Hindus? Would someone please shut Ravan up? Even better, strangle him. Ravan had stretched his arm to help Eddie up.

You could barely see the fibreglass pole as the Frenchman jiggled it left to right and right to left in an attempt to counterbalance the currents of air generated by the helicopter. The tension was unbearable as the rope kept swinging crazily. The tightrope walker lifted his foot to take the next step. He was bound to keel over all the way down. But now he was taking one more step and he had regained his rhythm and was making for the other end of the rope in the Air India building. Another couple of minutes and the helicopter would be overhead again.

'Climb up, Eddie, climb.'

'You crazy? I don't want to die.'

'You won't.'

'How would you know?' The 'man on the wire' was just ten paces away now.

'I've done it before.' Ravan smiled. He took Eddie's hand in his. 'Ask your father. He'll vouch for it.' Now they were both standing up there while Three Point One snatched a semi-automatic and fired at them.

Falling … falling … falling…

THE END

(You've got to be kidding.)

Acknowledgements

Forgive me but I am about to name the usual suspects once again. These are the villains who have constantly curbed my prolific creativity in spellings and grammar, in truth, the magical reinvention of the English tongue itself. They've turned the tsunamis and tornadoes of my words into piddling trickles. Yes, indeed the sourpusses and spoilsports have had the gall to derail, abridge, and butcher my magnificent flights of fancy and imagination. They see red everywhere, which is how an epic that was 2,597 pages now stands at a mere 362. Just think about it, after ruining my beautiful prose, my magnificent flourishes, my twirls and swirls, I am expected to thank these very same blackguards. Woe is me.

Enough horsing around. I am well aware of how much these good people have suffered at my hands and yet never lost their patience, meticulous concentration and critical judgment. First and foremost let me thank my supreme deity, V.K. Karthika, who never loses her sense of humour and yet will not stray from her belief in what comprises fine literature. Following close on her heels is the wonderfully patient, insightful and conscientious editor, Shantanu Ray Chaudhuri. Deepa Menon has often stepped in at the last minute and checked the text and my excesses. How can I forget Pervin Mahoney who has done a close reading of almost all my works and made invaluable suggestions. My first and last reader before each of my novels has been published is Tulsi Vatsal. She questions every word, has a razor-sharp scalpel and ruthlessly slashes flab and pretentious hokum. That leaves my friend, Prashant Godbole, the exceptionally multi-talented creative director who despite his 24/7 schedule has been helping me design the covers of my books.

God bless them all.

Authors are a strange lot. Like Hollywood actors and actresses who win Oscars, they will thank their mothers-in-law, their forty-seven second cousins, their spouses, dogs, children, grandparents but hardly ever the characters they create. I am no different. In all these years, nearly forty to be precise, I have not thanked Ravan and Eddie and told them how much I owe them. I have no idea how or why these two turned up in my life along with Violet, Parvatibai, Granna, Pieta, Belle, Asmaan, Three Point One and Tamhane Senior and Junior. How I have loathed the last three and loved the rest.

Time to say goodbye to them. Who knows where they will turn up next, in novels, serials or in movies? God willing, we'll meet again.